To Jan & Colchester
M/s Society

24. 4. 07.

Best wishes from   Jimmy Watson (Swainston)

BEYOND ALL LIMITS

THE PHOENICIAN

TONY J. SWAINSTON

Bloomington, IN  Milton Keynes, UK

authorHOUSE®

AuthorHouse™
1663 Liberty Drive, Suite 200
Bloomington, IN 47403
www.authorhouse.com
Phone: 1-800-839-8640

AuthorHouse™ UK Ltd.
500 Avebury Boulevard
Central Milton Keynes, MK9 2BE
www.authorhouse.co.uk
Phone: 08001974150

First published by AuthorHouse   2/21/2007

ISBN: 978-1-4259-9158-6 (sc)

Printed in the United States of America
Bloomington, Indiana

This book is printed on acid-free paper.

The author would lie to thank Mrs. Jacki Barber for her contribution, enthusiasm, and continued patience in assisting with the completion of this fictional novel.

CHAPTER 1

Tom Forster manoeuvred his wheelchair over to the window and looked out at the cold river estuary; inwardly cursing the continued numbness in his legs. His eyes gazed inattentively as the sun broke through a small gap in the purple grey East Anglia sky; highlighting a small fishing boat as it made its way out of the estuary into the murky North Sea. Tom's eyes followed the boat as it grew smaller and smaller until finally disappearing over the horizon. He sat gazing out over the water worrying as always about his wife and his two younger daughters so far away in Lebanon. They had been apart far too long.

The news this morning had not been good. Fighting had broken out again between Israel and the radical Hezbollah on the southern border of Lebanon, and although his family lived in the East of Lebanon, geographically it was only a few miles from down town Beirut. And he knew that the Israeli shells were beginning to get ever closer to the Eastern ports.

Tom drew a deep breath angrily rubbing his left leg, he tried not to feel bitter or angry, most times he could cope; but there were times when the world seemed bleak. He sat absently watching the point on the horizon where the little fishing boat had now vanished, and his mind drifted back as it so often did these days to that cold dreary damp January morning so many years ago, which had changed his life forever.

- - - - - - - - - - - - - - - - - -

Tom sat in his kitchen drinking coffee. He was deep in thought, preparing himself for a whistle stop ten-day business trip to Turkey, Lebanon, Egypt, and Italy. The small portable television in the corner suddenly caught his eye; the pictures being shown were horrific. He leaned across the breakfast table and turned up the volume. It was a live coverage report from Beirut, a massive explosion had just occurred at the airport; bodies were strewn across the tarmac, with burning aircraft in the background while the BBC reporter was relaying sheer panic.

"You must need your head examined, if you are going there," his wife said showing a slight concern in her tone, as she wandered into the kitchen and glanced at the television screen

"I am well insured," he joked sarcastically, although after watching the news bulletin; he was feeling more than just a little apprehensive. He took comfort in the thought that as he was travelling with one of his elder but junior company partners John Clarke, who had made many similar journeys.

1

Tom had married Jane at the age of twenty, she was a year younger, and now they had two daughters Danielle and Charlotte. For most of their marriage they had lived a comfortable and happy life.

Almost six feet tall, Tom was slim and athletic, with short light brown neatly styled hair. Not an out going character, but at the same time he never lacked confidence in his own ability. He had worked as the financial director for the family run business with his father for thirteen years.

In the past he had kept himself fit by playing soccer, but was now involved with one of the local cricket teams.

Jane was of average height and weight, short bobbed fair hair with additional blonde streaks that suited her fresh looking face, .she had never been sport minded, preferring to work in the home, cooking, sowing, decorating, and caring for her daughters.

Due to the success of the business and working longer hours, life for Tom and Jane had become very strained. They were starting to drift apart and beginning to see life from different perspectives. Over the last couple of years they had grown further and further apart.

Meanwhile the family business was starting to thrive and expand in different directions. Consequently Tom needed to make many overseas visits on behalf of the company to establish new contacts; this he was happy to do as it enabled him to obtain breathing space away from his home life. He had been preparing a long time before Christmas for this trip, and was really looking forward to it now that the time had come.

He glanced at his watch; the car should be arriving any moment now. Wiping away the condensation, he peered out of the window just in time to see it turn into the driveway driven by his friend Alec who had offered to take them to the airport.

Jane could see Carol was sitting in the front passenger seat, and could not resist commenting teasingly with a grin.

"I see your girl friend has come to see you off."

Although Tom smiled to himself, he ignored her, and kissed her automatically on the cheek, said his goodbyes to the children, and walked along the garden pathway leading from his house to the waiting vehicle.

As he got into the backseat of the car, Carol asked him if he preferred to ride up front with her husband, he just smiled, thinking of the remark Jane had just made.

"Thanks all the same, but I need to discuss some details with John when he gets here. Alec spoke over his shoulder as they drove away, keeping one eye on the road.

"Anyway Tom, where are you meeting your pal?"

"At north station, if that's Ok. He is coming in from Ipswich and hopefully on time. You know the problems with the damn trains these days."

By the time they arrived at the station the rain had become extremely intense, the road conditions looked as if they could cause a delay, especially on the M25 motorway if it turned to sleet or snow as had been forecast.

They had given themselves plenty of time prior to the flight departure at London Heathrow, just in case of any hold-ups

When John Clarke arrived Tom made the introductions, and they set off for what was expected to be a hazardous journey. Unexpectedly the rain eased, and they arrived at Heathrow for their scheduled flight to Turkey with considerable time to spare.

Alec and Carol voiced their concerns about their friend's visit to Lebanon and Egypt, and kept telling him to be careful; they too had seen the news bulletin. Tom thought as they checked in their bags *'On this occasion they are not the only ones concerned.'* He glanced at John for some reassurance; John looked totally unconcerned. *'At least he knows all the angles concerning the selling procedures.'*

They said goodbye to Alec and Carol and made their way through to the departure lounge.

"I am glad you're making this trip after what I saw on the news this morning, I wouldn't fancy it alone" Tom confessed as he picked up his briefcase as their flight was being called.

"No problem son, there's not much I don't know about that area" he replied with a grin.

John was an astute businessman, in his mid forties, slightly balding, about five feet eight, and had all the patter and charm that seemed to impress the ladies, most men saw him as a very likeable considerate person. He had a lot of respect for his young boss, and for Tom's father, which was mutual.

The board of the directors had decided a short courtesy visit to the major clients in certain countries would enhance business relations for the future, and although Tom was strong and focused in the comfort zone of his office he had no experience concerning the Middle East.

Customers in places like Lebanon appreciated the fact that not all westerners had given up on them. In spite of the conflict, generator sales were proving exceptionally good in both Lebanon and Egypt.

The flight to Turkey took four and a half hours. They were met by one of John's former contacts, a Mr Taki. They socialized for a couple of days, discussed contracts, and then flew on to Lebanon arriving the following lunchtime. As they disembarked from the aircraft at Beirut airport, Tom looked around at his surroundings

"Christ John, I never expected it to be as bad as this"

The scene was horrendous, there were burnt out aircraft and smouldering buildings, and a distinct smell of burning rubber and jet fumes hung heavy in the air. As they made their way across the tarmac to the waiting bus armed soldiers and police greeted them, some in dishevelled uniforms others in plain clothes. Clearly the authorities were on high alert, acting in a very excited manner, shouting and screaming at each other. The clouds of smoke surrounding the airport did nothing for Tom's first opinion of the country.

The bus trip from the aircraft was yet another unwelcome experience; more armed guards were waiting as they climbed aboard, making their way along the bus,

"Don't worry Sir, this is for your protection" one of the stewards reassured them. "We have had a spate of hostage taking in this area, so we have to take extra precautions"

They both sat down on the nearest seats and looked anxiously through the dirty windows of the battered bus; Tom noticed the rear doors were missing. His hand unconsciously gripped the side of his seat. *'Bloody hell, this bus has obviously seen some sort of action; judging by the state of it'* They seemed to go in a complete circle around the airport, until finally arriving at the dilapidated immigration area, where they were hustled off to join a long slow queue through passport control. Tom turned to John as they were leaving the baggage hall,

"I've seen something similar to this before, maybe not so bad, but close. That was in 1975 when I was in Nicosia during the fighting. I went on the green line with the UN where aircraft were still smouldering on the Tarmac. There had been some sort of major incident just before we arrived"

Raising his eyebrows clearly impressed and surprised on how Tom got special clearance to make such a dangerous journey, John asked in his strong northern accent,

"How the hell did you manage that? Is there something I should know before travelling with you young man?"

Realising he may have been a little loose tongued; he tried to cover up the indiscretion.

"Well, I had a friend in the UN, and his commanding officer invited me up there for a drink at the officers' mess". He had in fact been given security clearance; but had been told to keep it secret.

Knowing the area well, John looked slightly shocked at his friend's revelation:

"He must have been bloody nuts then. It's a wonder you got through the lines in one piece, I take it you had a fully armed escort?"

Tom realising he may be digging a bigger hole for himself, said:

"No, we only had two Gunners as escort, kept it simple. The more protection you had around you, just attracted more attention from the Turkish side.

Thankfully their short drive through Beirut distracted John, and no more was said on the subject. They looked in horror at the scene unfolding before their eyes as they passed through several checkpoints; building after building had been heavily shelled and destroyed. It looked as though nothing had escaped the bombardment.

"Bloody hell would you just look at that." John said in a hushed voice. "We are still in the West of Beirut, and the Muslim factor dominates this area. Just look at that mess"

The streets were littered with rubbish, blocks of concrete; burst water and sewage pipes appeared to have leaked in every street. It seemed impossible that people were still living in the bombed out buildings.

Tom could see washing hanging on made up lines stretching from one corner of a room to the other. Families were clearly visible in their homes from street level; as most of the facing walls were missing, it flashed though his mind the comparison to a child's dolls house with the front open.

In every side street there were the remains of burnt out vehicles or ones that had been crushed from falling masonry, which remained where it fell. The strong smell of burnt rubber and petrol fumes were still evident in the air seeping in through the broken air vents of the car. Tom was shocked, *'If this is Lebanon, how the hell can they afford generators in places so devastated as this?'* They passed through yet another checkpoint, and the atmosphere changed, they arrived at an area that appeared to be calmer. In fact, it was so quiet it made him feel a bit uneasy.

They were driving down a desolate duel carriageway; with high brick retaining walls on either side, they could see nothing. The car lurched as they both made a grab for something to hold on to as they started to sway from side to side. Tom looked wildly about him; he didn't realize that they were now in what the locals call 'no mans land' between East and West Beirut, between the Muslim and Christian sectors. John remarked rather too casually.

"They call this area suicide strip, many snipers are on the roofs, so hold your breath and keep your head down, and we will soon be into what is considered the safe area."

Tom didn't comment, but he could feel the hair on the back of his neck stand up. John looked at his young friend and half smiled to himself, having experienced all this before. He sighed, although he had made the trip many times, but even to him; things had clearly deteriorated over the past year since he had last visited this sorry, but once beautiful country,

"You know, Tom," John said wearily, "This bloody war has been going for more than three years, and as you know in all civil wars, there can be no winners, only losers."

Tom said nothing; he was still shocked from what he had seen. They sat back in their seats deep in thought, and continued the rest of the journey in silence.

+ + +

Maria Khoury a former novice Nun took a drastic step that changed her whole life when she joined the Lebanese Christian Phalangist army. Many ordinary people had been drafted into the army as part time soldiers, and were dedicated to the freedom of their country, none more so, than Maria, her dedication to duty had recently lead to her promotion to the rank of Captain.

The Phalangist army had recently been incorporated together with all the other Christian factions and was now known as 'The Lebanese Forces' or the 'LF' for short, foundered and lead by Bashir Gemayel, a robust leader of all Christians, who one day would become president. The LF was in direct conflict with all the religious armies and political parties that were controlled by Sunni Muslims and Palestinian sympathizers who were opposed to the minority Christian element in Lebanon.

Maria had lived most of her twenty-two years in Lebanon, westernised in both mind and fashion, and very noticeable with her olive skin and long dark hair. She lived at home with her parents, her twin sister Celine, and her two brothers, George, a year older, and Joseph, eight years younger. The twins were highly intelligent, and apart from their native Arabic, were fluent in French and German, plus Maria had some basic knowledge of Chinese and Japanese and had recently been studying English. Both girls had been part time fashion models in their spare time, which accounted for their fashionable dress sense.

Maria was a little more politically minded than Celine and had been president at her college. She had often been invited to speak on a platform to her fellow students for long periods. This gave her the confidence now as an officer, to address any Phalangist military meeting at short notice without script or concern.

The twins had joined along side many other young girls and women in making up the military shortfall on the Christian side of the conflict, during the early days of this bloody Civil war. Lebanese women were proud to be seen as equal by their male counterparts.

Maria had also been an airhostess for a short while which she had enjoyed, but felt that now her time should be devoted to the Lebanese survival cause within her country, a country that was now becoming more than ever under constant threat.

She was a popular confident young woman with a strong personality, which she constantly displayed wherever she went. Celine however was quieter and less confident; she had been working in France and Belgium with her elder brother, but had recently returned to Lebanon, and was now employed with a company that assembled household generators as the owner's personal secretary. This suited her quieter nature.

Maria's contrast to her sister was quite striking at times, although even she had her quieter moments since the war began. But, she was determined never to allow her military responsibilities and the horrors she had witnessed affect her focused outlook on her duty.

For some considerable time Maria had been working on an idea to flush out the handful of traitors who were working or living amongst them in their sector, causing suspicion and considerable unrest amongst her fellow Officers.

One morning while on LF duty, she decided to take her radical idea to her commanding officer. She saluted him as she entered the room:

"Good morning Sir,"

"Good day, Captain."

"Sir, with your permission I would like to offer a suggestion for detecting the traitors who are infiltrating our ranks and travelling abroad from within our community."

For a brief moment there was silence, as the C.O. continued reading. Without raising his head, he replied.

"At ease Captain, I'm listening."

Maria breathed a sigh of relief, and began to put forward her idea.

"As you know Sir; from my background I have some airline hostess experience, and I believe most people are willing to chat openly on an aircraft. Maybe through nerves, or just boredom, I really don't know,"

He glanced at his watch and relaxed back in the chair; he had known Maria since she was a child, and knew of her keenness and commitment to their cause. His hand stroked his chin as he faced her,

"And your point is?" She knew now she had his full attention.

"What if we train, say about half a dozen girls and place them with the Middle East Airline. We could then arrange for them to be seated beside a suspect to chat, gain their confidence, and get any information possible, such as why they travelling at this time? We all know, not many people can resist chatting to a friendly pretty girl"

Maria could see the glint of interest in his eyes as he queried,

"What happens when our aircraft are not flying out of Beirut?" she had expected that question and answered confidently,

"Then we get permission to operate from Cyprus, no problem,"

A noticeable smile crept across his weather beaten face

"Seems like a good idea, I take it you feel capable to being one of these 'pretty girls'?"

Maria recognised his intended compliment.

"If so considered, and ordered, Sir" He stood and looked directly into her eyes, before replying

"Right, we will give it a trial, well done captain, you have three weeks to choose and train your girls" He indicated her dismissal and added,

"I would like a full report of your plans across my desk as soon as possible"

"Thank you Sir!" She saluted smartly, turned and left the room.

As soon as she had time Maria sat down to ponder the task she had set for herself, she didn't know exactly whom she wanted for the job, it would be dangerous work. *'They need to be mature twenty to twenty-five year olds and of a university standard'*, she thought, *'and before I can start the training I must get high-level permission from the head of M.E.A, and from Cyprus Airways'* She leaned back in her chair chewing on the end of the pencil in her hand. *'It should be easy enough with the MEA, but can I trust the Cypriots?'* Frantically she leaned forward to scribble her thoughts into her notebook as they raced through her head. At last, she stood and stretched satisfied with her plan, deciding it was too risky to make her intentions known to the Cypriots, at least for the time being.

Forty-eight hours later Maria called the most likely women recruits to assemble at 1800 hrs that evening. For some it was very brief, after Maria opened the meeting with,

"Will all those who are married, or cannot speak fluent English, and who are not prepared to travel, please leave now."

A few minutes later she had less than twenty percent of the original total remaining. She looked at the small group standing before her, now she had to sort out the final six. Lining them up, she walked up and down several times, looking for at least a dozen girls that she considered would be most suitable for the job.

Fourteen candidates were finally short-listed for the assignment, as she took their names she chatted to each girl casually, noting each response.

"Right ladies, we will meet again in the morning at Ten a.m. after I have had time to study your files. I will announce my decision then."

As she watched them slowly walk away she looked thoughtful, *'This is not going to be easy,'* she had to get it right, *'A quick brain is almost more important than looks for this assignment'*

She sat working until late in the evening, finally making her decision, she had narrowed it down to seven. Rubbing her eyes, she yawned, now at last she could sleep.

The next morning she called the girls to her office, they all looked at her expectantly,

"OK ladies, it was a hard decision, but I have decided on, Vivian, Laura, Valerie, Alia and Nadia." And after a pause she added, "Violette and Nadine, you two will also be trained as substitutes. The rest of you, thank you, but will you now please leave the room."

Surveying the seven women left in front of her; Maria then started her brief.

"Right ladies, please take a seat and listen carefully. The assignment is this; you will be operating undercover aboard any transportation entering or leaving Lebanon, aircraft mainly, but ferry if required. Therefore you will be given brief basic training as hostesses, and will be positioned beside any suspect to obtain as much personal detail as possible. For example: why are they travelling, where are they going, what ever you can think of, as long as you get them talking. We will need you to report anything remotely suspicious. The training will take two weeks and you will be ready in less than three, any question?"

There was silence from her captive audience, so she continued

"From now on, you will be known only by your Christian name, no rank, no family name" she paused for a few seconds, "Is that understood ladies?"

The women immediately acknowledged her, she continued,

"If you are travelling as a passenger, and you are asked what you do as work, you can say that you are a stewardess, this will avoid any problem if anyone slips up and identifies you by name. And believe me this will happen".

The women listened intensely to their C.O. as she outlined her plan of intended action.

"I will take the first assignment as soon as we are all ready. You will work in pairs to start with, followed by individual operations. At no time are you to allow yourselves to be in a one on one situation with a suspect without prior permission from me. Is that clear?"

There was total silence. Maria raised her voice,

"Is that clear?

"Yes, Captain" came the joint response from all seven women.

"If you find that an additional meeting with your suspect is necessary, then you will request back up to avoid any problems. If you do not adhere to these rules, you will be dismissed from the team. There is always a replacement, even for me, so keep this in mind." She looked at their earnest faces and smiled,

"No heroes are required for these missions, so don't put yourself on the line."

Alia interrupted,

"Are we going to be armed, Captain?"

"You will receive a detailed contact under three coded variation, code red is for a priority suspect." Maria turned to Alia,

"However to answer your question, no, you cannot be armed on the aircraft, we would never get universal clearance for that" She continued with her instruction.

"Code yellow is for anyone that may be a suspect. Code green will simply be very low key, routine and basic surveillance. Once you receive your orders, you will be passed a colour coded document, to make it seem more natural we will not tell you their names, we don't want to make life too easy for you, do we ladies? "

The women laughed at the first sign of humour from their Captain.

Three weeks later, after the intensive and physical training was completed Maria took the first assignment, which was a code yellow. The seven trainees were positioned on board in various observation positions, two as hostesses and the rest as passengers. Although there had been no first class compartment on MEA since the war began, Maria knew from past experience that she had to work as a passenger in the forward section of the aircraft, money was no option in the espionage business, and very few wealthy people rarely opted to fly in the rear section.

She had pre-arranged an isle seat beside the male suspect already sitting by the window, she sat down and smiled at him fumbling with the cushion until it fell on the floor, allowing him to pick it up and make the first introduction. He smiled as he handed the cushion back to her,

"There you are, we should be taking off shortly." He continued smiling at her as she adjusted the cushion behind her back.

"Are you staying in Italy Miss?"

Pretending to show little interest she replied,

"Yes, and you?"

The man was in his thirties, well built and sporting a reddish blond moustache. He hesitated before replying.

"Just twenty four hours and flying back tomorrow."

Once the aircraft levelled and the seat belt sign was switched off, Maria got up to help the stewardess serve the drinks to the passengers in the business class cabin. She had often done this on flights when she was bored, but this time she thought it might impress her target. The reaction from him was just as she had expected, smiling, he called her over,

"I have been admiring the way you work, when you get a moment come and sit down have a chat."

'That didn't take long' she thought smiling at him "I will soon. Its just that I promised to help with these drinks, we are a bit short staffed at the moment"

Thirty minutes later she down in her seat, the film was about to start and the lights were dimmed, window shutters closed. Maria smiled at him as she settled herself in her seat.

He leaned towards her stroking his moustache,

"You are a very attractive girl you know. How would you like to meet me for a drink tonight?"

"Sorry," she smiled "when overseas we have to stay in our hotel. And by six o'-clock tonight I will be officially on duty for the return flight tomorrow, so, no alcohol." He looked disappointed,

"What about tomorrow night when we get back?"

"Maybe," Maria replied coyly. "Are you visiting friends in Rome?"

Then, as she had expected, he started to talk about the great time he hoped to have in Rome, and what a bonus it was as that all he had to do was deliver some confidential papers, adding with a wink,

"But I mustn't be late to bed, as I have to travel back tomorrow morning"

"Are you very important then?" she said trying to look impressed. He leaned towards her whispering confidentially,

"Well between you and me, they are just media news reports on what's going on in Lebanon."

"What is going on in Lebanon?" she asked innocently.

"Well I could tell you over dinner tonight" He smiled "How about if I come to your hotel?"

Maria deliberately hesitated,

"I am not really sure about that, we are not suppose to give our hotel location out to strangers, apart from that, I'm on flight duty tomorrow" She hesitated again, pretending to think about it.

"Well, Ok if it's only dinner I don't see a problem" She wagged her finger at him playfully," but no alcohol." Adding with a smile, "give me your contact number and I will call you later to arrange things"

Once the aircraft had landed and the passengers had disembarked, Maria and the girls left with the crew to be taken to their hotel for their one-night stopover.

Having contacted the target a few hours later, Maria made her way down to the restaurant; although she was aware that she was not showing the girls a very good example, having already broken her first rule of being side tracked on the very first assignment like this, but she had a suspicion that this contact could develop into a code red. She glanced across the room at the other girls who were already seated on a table tucked into a corner so they could observe their Captains technique, *'At least I will not be alone.'* However the evening came and went without undue incident.

It was clear that their suspect was a womaniser, and judging by his designer suit, and the amount of gold on his wrists and fingers, he was or had become extremely wealthy. She deduced from their conversation that he could be working for the Syrian foreign propaganda machine, and was getting even wealthier on the proceeds. It wasn't quite the code red that she was hoping for, and she knew that there was little point in having him arrested on his return leg, as the papers had already been delivered; also she had no absolute proof of what they contained. The next time he travelled, the LF authorities would search and most likely arrest him; once she had alerted them. His name and details would officially be posted on their computer database by that time.

After a few weeks, the system Maria had devised was beginning to reap the rewards of all her hard work, and was running smoothly, so she decided it was time to take a break and visit her sister Celine, and to catch up on a few

old friends.

CHAPTER 2

Although it was only a short drive from the airport, Tom was more disturbed than he thought he would be, by the devastating scenery before him as they drove from the sorry and demoralizing West Beirut into the Christian controlled East Beirut. They very soon arrived in the large town of Achrafieh, which was situated on the green line between the warring Palestinians and local Muslims against Christians. The stark difference between East and West was very obvious, especially when viewed for the first time. The West; could only be described as filthy, and the East although heavily bombed, appeared to be much cleaner, and the chaos that pervaded on both sides, seemed to be a bit more organized here in the East. Even the air was a lot fresher, and instead of the smell of burning rubber, a distinct smell of fresh baked bread penetrated the car making them feel extremely hungry. Tom began to realize, that he had been completely oblivious of Lebanon's problem prior to this trip. In fact, he had been, like many westerners not even sure of its geographical position.

Eventually the car arrived at the offices of Jean Bitar, a vibrant and energetic buyer who had previously purchased equipment from John's former employer. Tom slowly got out of the car, he was still feeling quite shocked at what he had just seen.

"How come the reports we get on our news back home are so muted?" he commented in disbelief. John responded irritably,

"Because most of the world's media are ignorant to the fact that a Christian country is being ripped apart without anyone really caring. There is no oil here, so why should they worry? But believe me, when the penny drops it will be far too late for many of the poor buggers here".

Tom looked at him in surprise; he had never heard him express such a strong opinion on anything before. As they were about to enter the office, John reverted back to his usual jovial manner:

"Now young man, keep your mind on the job"

Tom laughed as he noticed the female staff through the glass.

"Contrary to public belief I am not a womaniser, well not all the time" he grinned

"Well the fella you are about to meet most definitely is, and he isn't very fussy, any woman with a pulse would do."

There were three girls in the office, two typists busily working in one corner of the room, and a third girl at the larger desk in front, Tom couldn't help noticing she was extremely attractive. He gazed idly around the office, taking in the shabby furniture highlighted by the wintry afternoon sun that streamed through the dirty bare windows. His observation was interrupted a few minutes later when the door to street squeaked open, admitting another visitor to the office. At first he thought he was seeing double, the woman who entered was almost identical to the girl he had just been admiring. She was an absolute stunner; it took his breath away. As she removed her coat, she revealed a very fashionable knee length pencil cut skirt, white cotton blouse, with a black waistcoat, fine black stockings and very high-heeled black shoes. She wore her long dark hair neatly clipped back at the sides showing an interesting oval shaped face, although rather pensive expression.

She knew that she had caught the attention of the foreign guests, and acknowledged them with a brief smile before slowly crossing the room to sit on a chair in front of the girl who mirrored her.

Tom took time to survey her more closely; trying not to be too obvious as the two girls chatted quietly in Arabic. It came as a shock to him when he realized; that for the first time in his life he was instantly attracted to a woman. He felt totally mesmerised unable to tear his eyes away.

She felt him watching and gave him a knowing glance, which he was not quite sure how to interpret. *'She is unbelievable'* Tom thought, *'absolutely perfect.'* He could feel his pulse racing, *'If only she knew what I am thinking'*. At that moment her large brown eyes glanced at him over the paper she was reading, as if she knew exactly what he was thinking. A little embarrassed he looked away.

Maria knew she had made an impression, which was exactly what she intended and once he had turned away she smiled to herself. This last little scene did not go un-noticed by Jean Bitar who had just entered the room, or by John who glanced towards his partner; Tom's facial expression said it all.

Tom took another quick look at her, he would have liked to speak to her; but he could only hear Arabic spoken between the girls, and he couldn't understand a word. He strained to listen, just in case he heard any recognisable English words in their conversation.

Jean Bitar was in his mid forties, a very confident formidable figure; dressed in a matching shirt, necktie, and jacket. He stood five feet six tall, slightly balding with well-worn features, not a particularly handsome man but quite a womaniser according to John. In a deprived country such as Lebanon had recently become, money certainly talked, and Jean used this only too well.

Tom was suddenly aware that John was introducing him to Jean; he quickly bought his attention back and leaned across the desk to shake his hand.

"Very pleased to meet you at last,"

"And I am pleased to meet you young man," Jean shook his hand vigorously.

After the introductions had been made, they settled down to discuss business. Jean made several verbal references in Arabic to the girls, John remarked casually,

"The young lady that just came in Jean, is she new? I didn't see her last time I was here." He smiled, "you sure kept this one secret. Is she involved with the business?"

Jean replied in a rather hostile tone, without raising his head from the brochures that he was reading. "If she is not involved then she shouldn't be here, should she?"

There was a long pause as he slowly lifted his head, and added quietly,

"She is involved as you say, with me,"

John felt uncomfortable; wishing he hadn't mentioned it, he assumed she must be Jean's latest girlfriend.

"I didn't realize, sorry,"

There was an awkward silence for a moment or two, Tom glanced at the young woman, but once again got absolutely no reaction or expression. He had been well and truly blanked.

The big surprise was to come a few minutes later, when from behind him he heard a quiet voice speaking in English but with a strong local accent,

"Mr Forster, would you like to take coffee?"

Tom swung round in his chair; it was the young lady in question. The surprise on his face brought a smothered chuckle from the other girls. He immediately accepted her offer with a stuttering

"Please" and a weak smile.

But once again she ignored his smile, looking past him at John,

"Mr. Clark, you also would like?"

A broad grin broke out on John's face as he too accepted. Tom started laughing as the penny dropped. Jean looked up enquiring coldly, as the girl made her way back to her seat.

"What was the big joke, did I miss something?"

Quickly smothering his laughter Tom replied,

"It's nothing really; we were remembering John's earlier questions about the young lady. We have just realised; that she understood everything he was saying. What's her name?"

Clearly annoyed at their interest, Jean snapped,

"Ask her yourself."

Making the most of the break for coffee Tom took up the challenge, even though she may have been his client's partner for all he knew. He moved his battered chair along the threadbare carpet towards her, and was now directly facing the young woman. She looked him directly in the eye anticipating his question.

"Maria Khoury and this is my sister Celine, as you can see we are twins"

Tom could see they were very much alike, he nodded and smiled to Celine, then turned his attention back to Maria thinking, '*They certainly are like two peas in a pod, but, this one; Maria, she's different she's- - -* His thoughts were interrupted when Maria spoke,

"You have been here to Lebanon before, Mr Forster?

Tom smiled,

"No, this is the first time," He frantically tried to think of something intelligent to say, "It's a shame about the situation here; but I hope it finishes soon for everyone's sake"

She looked at him coldly.

"It will only finish when the big powers stop interfering and when they want it to finish, not before. Both the East and your West are using us as pawns. Who do you think is supplying arms and supporting Israel? Who do you think is supplying and supporting Syria?" '*Careful Tom*, he thought, '*that's obviously a touchy subject*'

"I guess you have a valid point"

He changed the subject quickly; the last thing he wanted was to upset her. He nodded his head in the direction of Jean, with an expression of disbelief on his face

"Is he really your boyfriend?" '*Oh God*' he could have bitten his tongue off, '*why did I say that*'

"Do you work here?" He added quickly, hoping he hadn't insulted her, but judging by the look on her face, he had.

"Why would anyone think such a thing?" she responded indignantly, and then she recalled Jean's comment earlier,

"Oh I see. That was his little joke for the day. I am not that sad, or desperate." She looked around the office in disgust, "And I would not want to work here either!" adding proudly,

"When I am in Lebanon, I am employed part-time for what is left of our police department" She sighed, "At what is left of our damaged airport."

Tom looked into her eyes, smiled and stirred his coffee, trying to analyse her feelings, and decided it was time to talk about something else. Maria's mood softened, she gave mischievous grin,

"Is it Ok? I am sorry but I just assumed you would prefer Nescafe, being English"

He grinned back at her; relieved that she seemed relaxed again.

"Oh, yes thank you it's just right,"

Tom drank his coffee, watching as the girls packed up their work for the day. Usually the employees left the office around six in the evening except for Celine, who usually arrived later than the others, and left around seven to avoid the traffic congestion. Maria regularly came to see her sister when she was in that area to drive her home. As long as the work got finished Jean didn't care, time was no longer important to the Lebanese people, but life was.

Tom sat for another hour and listened intently; while John and Jean continued their discussions about generator purchases, Jean was smart in business hoping that John would be tired after the long day; and agree a special deal more suitable for him. But Tom knew that John had been around the block many times in business, and was not likely to agree to anything, especially on any first day.

Eventually the meeting finished, and they all retired quite exhausted back to Jean's apartment, where it was assumed would be a safer area than any restaurant or hotel.

John commented to Tom as he sat drinking whisky in Jean's lounge.

"This is not bad boy, bit more comfy than a hotel. Most of available hotels around here appear to be in more need of maintenance, rather than bomb damage." He stood to refresh the remainder of his drink with ice, "However, it is not recommended to be out on these streets after dark, there are too many 'no go areas', you have to be a local to know exactly where they are".

John grinned as he topped his glass up with more whisky,

"Jean is well known as a very hospitable host, expense has never been an object."

The next day started warm and sunny, even though it was mid winter and still only nine o'clock in the morning. It was intended to be a full day for the two Englishmen, visiting workshops and detailing specification for certain local projects.

The down side for Tom was when he realised, this particular Friday was Celine's day off, which meant her sister had no reason to be at the office. Jean, mocked him,

"Don't look so disappointed young man, she will be in the office tomorrow, and we have a party arranged in your honour at my home tomorrow evening. I will insist she is there"

Tom looked at John in surprise,

"Bloody hell John, am I that obvious?" John nodded his head, grinning.

Tom continued thoughtfully,

"I wonder why Jean is being so pleasant now regarding my interest in Maria. I got the distinct impression he didn't approve." Then he grinned, "I might even get a chance to chat with her on her own."

John gave a wry smile,

"Maybe, but I don't fancy your chances."

He knew that this attractive girl was having quite an effect on Tom, and it did concern him slightly, and he wondered if he should warn him off or not, especially where Jean was involved, 'Oh what the hell' he thought, 'It's none of my business, Tom's quite capable of taking care of himself'

Saturday morning was another early start at the office. For Tom it was a day worth looking forward to. They arrived at nine o'clock, and he was a little disappointment to see that Celine was not at her desk, but to his relief she arrived a few minutes later. And just as he hoped, later during the morning Maria appeared with a package for her sister. She looked absolutely stunning again, which was well appreciated by both her English admirers. John nudged Tom and whispered,

"Bloody hell my friend I do believe you may have made a hit with her, she really has put on her Sunday best."

Maria wore a deep red jacket, matching waistcoat, and black silk blouse. Her black knee length skirt had a long high split at the side, set off by very high heel shoes. A heavy gold cross and chain, hung from her slender neck, complemented with gold dangling earrings.

"Close your mouth Tom," John hissed at his friend.

Tom was soon to learn, that Lebanese woman, especially Christian women of Maria's class, were highly influenced by French fashion.

Maria acknowledged the visitors; making sure to treat them both equally, although the only reason she was there was to see Tom. She chatted to her sister in Arabic while she once again organized the coffees, and then sat down to wait for the kettle to boil, without another glance in Tom's direction. He couldn't take his eyes off of her, as he fantasized, 'I wouldn't mind seeing her in her policewoman's uniform'. When the kettle had boiled she made and handed him a coffee, 'Here goes. It's now or never.' He took a deep breath.

"Are you going to the party tonight?"

Her whole body stiffened, she was clearly taken aback by the direct question, almost hostile in a way, although it was difficult to calculate, 'Christ you would think I had just proposed marriage,' Tom thought. Maria collected her thoughts quickly; it had taken her by surprise; but she was really rather pleased. But no way under any circumstances would she show her true feelings, especially in front of Jean, or indeed in front of her sister.

"Sorry" she said, "I am on duty tonight."

That really was a body blow for Tom, but he wasn't going to leave it there. He smiled,

"That's a shame; I would have liked to have had the chance to talk to you, before we leave for Egypt tomorrow"

Maria was still trying to keep her feelings hidden from all the watchful eyes in the office, and was not quite sure how to deal with this situation. Although she realised that she was attracted to him and flattered by his attention, she had also noticed the wedding ring on his finger. 'At least he didn't try to hide it,' she thought, 'I wonder how he has the nerve to ask me to come to Jean's party, if he is married,' she felt very confused.

Maria knew that he was watching her every movement, and felt a quiver of excitement run through her body. Her mouth felt dry and she ran her tongue around her lips to moisten them, not realizing the effect that it had on Tom. Speaking briefly to her sister she prepared to leave the office, but as she passed by Tom she lent towards him and whispered,

"I will try to make it, but I am unsure right now." Adding in a much louder voice and a slight teasing grin aimed towards her admirers.

"Goodbye gentlemen, have a safe trip."

Now Tom was confused, he wondered if he had pushed her too hard. But he thought, 'what the hell, if you don't ask you'll never know, I haven't got time to mess about' His eyes followed her as she opened the door and left the office. The door creaked loudly as it slowly began to close. Tom in a rush of blood leapt out of his chair to catch the door before it shut. He went outside; she was about four to five yards away, it was he thought his final opportunity.

"Maria, try your best to make it." She stopped abruptly in her tracks on hearing his voice, and a little smile crept across her face. Then she slowly turned her face now expressionless. Tom, seeing her blank expression; nervously shouted above the noise of the traffic,

"See you later hopefully, Ok?"

She acknowledged him raising her eyebrows slightly, and one corner of her mouth lifted in a faint smile. Then she turned away, once again the smile spread across her face, as she calmly walked away with a very confident slightly exaggerated wiggle, carrying her jacket over one shoulder, Tom noticed, and not for the first time, she had a very cute bottom.

He watched as she crossed the dusty road, as several car horns sounded their appreciation; accompanied by the shrill wolf whistles from a couple of scooter riders. Tom muttered to himself 'If she gives even a slight glance then she is interested' convincing himself as he waited, 'Come on girl, turn' then finally as she sauntered into the car park she gave the briefest of glances over her right shoulder towards him before disappearing out of sight, cleverly done in order to show that she had not totally ignored his interest. Tom had waited for some indication from her, and was satisfied by this small but significant gesture.

When he returned to the office, Jean gave him a look that told him instantly that he was not a happy man, but nothing was said. John tried to defuse the atmosphere, with a joke.

"You stand no chance young man, that's a cold shoulder if I ever saw one, I must have a word with your father about you when we get back"

Tom ignored John's remark, but his face took on a slightly defiant expression, which Jean was quick to notice.

Later, back at Jean's apartment, they showered, changed and joined Jean in the lounge ready for the party. The doorbell rang two or three times in quick succession, several young women arrived, some with partners, some like Celine came alone. Tom watched anxiously, as people continued to slowly arrive, but still no Maria. He had almost given up on her coming, when the doorbell rang once again. Tom's pulse raced, as the figure he had been hoping and praying to see again before he left Lebanon; was standing in the entrance.

Maria, who loved to tease her admirers, certainly had not missed this opportunity to impress. She wore a striking short black dress, which appeared to cling to every part of her shapely body. Once again she wore gold accessories, including a six-inch gold-chain belt that hung loosely around her narrow waist. As she walked past Tom towards Jean, she said to him quietly,

"I can stay for just an hour, at the very most."

Jean stepped forward to greet her with a kiss on either cheek, he had overheard Maria's comment, and remarked possessively,

"You will stay until I say you can go."

Tom glanced at Maria to see how she would take a remark like that, because from his short analysis of this young lady, he guessed she would not take kindly to that type of instruction, especially in front of guests. Maria smiled, but he noticed for a brief second, a flash of anger in her eyes, '*That's not done him a lot of good*' he thought smugly, '*now at last the party can begin*'.

The beer and spirits flowed freely, and the drinking was heavy, no one bothered about drinking and driving laws anymore, as there was no one to enforce the law anyway. Tom was sitting with John enjoying the conversation with some other guests, when they were interrupted by the sound of drumming; combined with loud Arabic music that blasted out without prior warning. The atmosphere became electric, the whole party joined in with clapping; supporting the beat of the music as the lounge floor vibrated, and there was a feeling of expectation in the air. It was something that Tom had never ever experienced in his life before.

Then dramatically framed in the doorway Maria appeared, her chain belt extended so that it rested very loosely on her swivelling hips. The floor cleared instantly as she swayed hypnotically to the rhythm of the music '*Now I have to be very careful*' she thought. Tom couldn't believe his eyes; his face was a picture. Nadia one of the other office girls went over and sat beside him, cupping her hand over her mouth as she spoke very loudly, trying to make herself heard over the extreme noise.

"Hi Tom, I am Nadia, Maria is my best friend, and one of the very best amateur Arabic dancers around here. Mr Bitar takes advantage and likes to show her off, she is well aware of this." She scrambled in her bag and took out a lighter for a cigarette. "He thinks he can control what we all do. That is why she did not want to come tonight"

Nadia drew heavily on her cigarette, puffing the smoke away from Tom as she continued to explain.

"Maria thought about you leaving tomorrow, and wanted you to be left with a good impression of the Lebanese people. She wanted to show you that we do have fun as well as all the fighting."

Tom looked at the earnest face in front of him, and at Maria dancing especially for him. He knew he would never forget this moment as long as he lived.

Maria danced for almost twenty minutes, and she was trying to leave the floor, but her audience didn't want her to go with shouts of 'more! More!' She refused; smiling and protesting that she was too tired to continue. After one hour; true to her promise; she got up to leave with her sister, walking across the room she spoke to Tom.

"Please don't say anything about us leaving to Mr Bitar until after we have gone. If you want to you can send me a telex to Nadia's office, it will safe there. She will give you the number." She smiled shyly at him, "Please do when you get back to the UK"

Not wanting to give Tom the impression that she was too interested, she added almost as an after thought,

"If only, to say that you both arrived safely."

Then taking the opportunity while Jean was preparing food in the kitchen, the two young women said goodbye to their friends and started to leave, as Maria went to pass Tom, she stopped again and said in a quite voice.

"Have a good trip and give my warmest regards to your wife and children."

She felt she needed to let him know that she knew he was married, and she wasn't going to get involved with a married man, even though she was very attracted to him. It was the first time he had been so close to Maria, her perfume was strong, obviously expensive; although he was no expert, and the fragrance lingered with him for the rest of that evening, but one thing was certain, he understood the hidden message in that last remark.

Tom and John left the next morning for Egypt, driving back more or less the way they had come; along suicide strip, and then into the more intensely war damaged area around the airport. Both men were tired after the heavy night before, and Jeans generosity with alcohol; added to the effect. They had a long boring wait in the very primitive departure area before walking to the plane. As they settled down in their seats for a short flight to Cairo, John queried,

"So old son, what did you think of Lebanon, or need I not ask?"

He continued without waiting for a response,

"You know, this city was the most fantastic place to visit in the past. Many labelled it, as the Monte Carlo of the Middle East, and that clearly didn't suit their neighbours. Although I may add; they all used it as a playground for their own ends."

Tom remarked thoughtfully,

"I wondered what it was like before they ruined it, the people here seem to be living for each day now, I suppose it's because they don't know what the next day will bring, and it's a damn shame."

John glanced at Tom saying rather cautiously,

"Jean told me Maria has a boyfriend, an accountant, and very possessive. He said her sister also told him that they argue a lot because she is very strong minded."

Tom shrugged,

"Yes I know, she told me about him." He didn't know, but he wouldn't admit that to John *'There was no reason why she should have mentioned it'* he thought. *'Anyway, I never told her I was married, but it seems she knew from that last remark.'*

Knowing how much an effect Maria had had on Tom, John tried to be tactful,

"She is an extremely smart young lady by all accounts, but I got the impression that Jean has an interest too."

Tom shook his head in disagreement,

"And I got from you the distinct impression he has an interest in any female. However I can tell you she doesn't feel anything in that way for him. From what I understand talking to Nadia, none of them think much of his manner sometimes; they say he is a control freak,"

Then, after thinking for a moment he said,

"What do you know about Jean, is he for real?"

"In what way do you mean?"

"He seems to have it too comfortable. The war appears to be of benefit to him, I am sure without it he would struggle."

John had to agree, Tom was making sense.

"You could be right, but isn't it the case in all wars, some win, most loose."

Tom shrugged again,

"I suppose that's true, he certainly appears to be able to make things work to his advantage. Do you know about his background?"

"Not a lot, but I think you will have an opportunity to find out for yourself if you're really that interested"

Tom laughed

"You mean, via Maria? Maybe I will do that, but as she doesn't actually work for him, I don't suppose she will know much, other than from her sister."

At that moment the stewardess bought round the tea and coffee, and they settled back to relax for the short trip ahead, nothing more as said on the subject of Jean or Maria.

Egypt was a very short stay, which was just as well, with President Sadat and Premier Begin holding their summit in Cairo. The more up-market hotels were fully booked, the only one left was the Hollis Hotel in down town Cairo; which was cheap in all respects, costing equivalent to three pounds sterling a night, Tom laughing about the state of their abode joked,

"You would have thought for this money, we would have received a full English breakfast"

"Not to mention the luxury bathroom and room service," John retorted

They laughed, not being too concerned, as their stay was only for one night.

Checking out of the hotel early the next morning, they met with another of John's previous buyers, who invited them to take tea on his rooftop garden. Through the early morning haze they could see a gold painted mosque, and heard the prayers being transmitted by microphone and loudspeaker, echoing all around them. For Tom it was another magical experience that he would remember, long after the trip was over. It didn't take long to conclude their business in Egypt, and then they flew on to Rome for another brief meeting. Both trips were short, and had been considered as mainly courtesy calls. Then after a couple of days stop over in Italy to unwind, they had completed their agenda, and took the flight back to the UK.

CHAPTER 3

They arrived back in the UK feeling tired but content, and as they emerged through customs pushing their trolleys; they found Alec patiently waiting in the busy arrivals hall. He acknowledged them with a pleasing smile,

"Let's grab a coffee; you both look as if you could do with one"

"Good idea" Tom replied. They made their way to the small coffee shop situated close to the arrivals gate

"How did your trip go, anything interesting happen"

John looked at Tom grinning,

"Answer the man Tom," He said putting his arm on Tom's shoulder trying to put him on the spot.

Tom; knowing exactly what his partner was trying to do, was unperturbed,

"Well Lebanon was very interesting; it had so much more to offer than the other three countries." He returned John's broad grin, "It certainly needs a follow up soon, don't you agree John?"

Alec looked from one face to the other,

"Don't tell me, I know. There is a woman involved"

Replacing his hand on Tom's shoulder, John tried to look serious,

"Jesus, Tom you are so predictable"

Tom shook his head sadly,

"Unfortunately Alec, I have as you know a reputation that goes before me, which I can assure you is not warranted,"

Before Alec could reply, John interrupted,

"You may get one that will catch up with you one of these days young man, and believe me I should know"

Alec laughed,

"It seems to me John, you have been teaching our friend a lot in a short time"

Emphasizing his deep northern accent, John growled,

"I think he could teach me a thing or two, the young bugger"

Still joking they made their way out of the airport to the car park, and towards Alec's car.

John shivered,

"Christ, its cold here, you really feel it after where we have been"

"You are not wrong there," Tom said, rubbing his hands together in an effort to keep them warm.

The traffic was heavy as usual on the motorway, and eventually they arrived back home after more than three hours on the road, longer than it took to fly from Italy.

Alec dropped Tom off first, but he was still very curious about the trip, he knew something had happened, judging from all the innuendos.

"Three hours Tom, and I am still awaiting all the gossip on Lebanon"

Tom ignored the remark; laughed and thanked him for the lift quickly closing the car door behind him. Alec started the engine; he still had to take John to the station,

"I will find out sooner or later," he yelled out of the car window as he drove away.

Tom still smiling went into the house, there was no sign of Jane waiting to greet him, but at least his daughters were very happy he was back home.

During the next few days he constantly monitored the news for anything concerning Lebanon, he thought about Maria, wondering where she was, and what she was doing, and above all, was she safe. He just couldn't get her out of his head.

His obsession with Lebanon didn't go un-noticed by Jane; she knew that he had something on his mind since returning home.

"You've changed since you got back from that place. I suppose you spent half the time chatting up the women, especially as you were with that womaniser for ten days"

Tom didn't answer, this time he wasn't going to take the bait. He made up his mind to ignore her comments, but all the same he thought, 'this time she is a bit closer to the truth than she may ever know.'

As the days went past, he resigned himself to the thought that there was no chance of anything further developing with Maria, especially not at the moment. He knew his marriage was all but over. But he like Jane was deeply concerned for the welfare of their two young daughters, if Tom finally made any move to leave.

Tom buried himself in his work, doing everything he could to forget Maria; he had to accept that she could be married by now, or dead; given the life she lead. He had sent her a telex as soon as he had arrived home; but so far had received no reply. That fact alone worried him, but he was hesitant about sending another message knowing her difficult situation, not to mention his own. He tormented himself day and night thinking of what to do, until one Saturday morning when he was alone in the office; he finally made up his mind. Sitting down at the telex machine he quickly typed out a brief message and sent it, but as it went through he panicked, 'Oh hell, I hope she won't mind, I wish to God I knew where the damn telex was situated,'

Maria received Tom's message the same day; and although she was quite pleased she didn't respond immediately, it was not a priority for the moment plus she was still wrestling with her conscience. Her strict moral upbringing told her that any relationship with a married man was wrong, and would certainly be doomed from the start. Apart from that, she didn't want to be the 'other woman.' But it was not that simple, every day she thought about him; even when on duty, and she really did not want this distraction in her life.

Many weeks after his visit, and ten days after he had sent his brief message, he received her telex response,

'DEAR MR FORSTER, I THANK YOU FOR YOUR CONCERN IT WAS WELCOMED.

HOW ARE YOUR GIRLS? I EXPECT THEY MISS YOU WHEN YOU TRAVEL.

WE ARE UNDER A LOT OF BOMBING, ESPECIALLY IN THIS AREA, BUT AS YOU SEE WE ARE SURVIVING. PLEASE TELEX ME ANYTIME OR WRITE.

YOU HAVE THIS ADDRESS, BEST REGARDS FROM YOUR FRIEND MARIA'

'Very formal' he thought as he read it, 'still, anything is better than nothing.' Feeling rather elated, Tom immediately sat down and wrote her a letter, keeping the details very friendly, asking basic news concerning herself and her family, knowing very well that the slightest suggestive remark would almost certainly put her off.

Meanwhile East Beirut, and in particular the Lebanese Forces were coming under very heavy bombardment. Late one afternoon, Maria was on her way back home from the Airport where she had been on duty, when another attack started; she pulled over quickly abandoning her military jeep, and ran across the St George Hotel car park hoping to reach cover in the hotel. But before she could get to safety she came under sniper fire, out of the corner of her eye she spotted an old rusty water tank and threw herself behind it. She lay there for a moment panting for breath, as missiles came in over her head. 'Oh my God, that was a bit near' she thought keeping her head down low. Looking around she could see there was no way she could move from this spot, and no one could get to her. She settled down for a long wait; but she was extremely worried, she knew from the direction they were heading; that the missiles passing overhead; would be dropping very close to her home, and she had no means of knowing if her family was safe. 'Please, God, keep them safe' she prayed silently, 'please don't let anything happen to them'.

For more than twelve hours she was trapped behind the tank feeling totally helpless unable to move. Eventually darkness fell, and there was a lull in the fighting, Maria decided to take a risk. She calculated that the sniper would by now have given up on her, perhaps assuming that she had been hit, so she made a dash for the jeep. To her relief there was no fire, and she managed to start the engine. *'Thank you, Thank you dear God'* Maria put her foot down and headed back to Jounieh. After almost thirty-six hours in uniform she was ready for a very hot shower.

Thankfully when she arrived home, the family was safe and overjoyed to see her, there had been several near misses in the area, but the most important thing was they were safe.

Like most Lebanese people, Maria lived hour-by-hour, and day-by-day. But still she could not shake off these advancing feelings she had for the Englishman. In fact she was annoyed with herself that these feelings seemed to be growing stronger; the last thing she wanted was for this to cloud her practical judgment, especially given her position of responsibility. She needed to have all her wits about her for her own safety; and for those she was working with.

The following day Maria sat in her small office at the airport, drinking coffee and smoking a cigarette, she thought about Tom, and decided she must try to put him out of her mind and concentrate solely on her work. 'Right,' she thought, giving herself a little shake. *'The first thing I must do as soon as I get a chance is to check on how the girls are progressing with the airline project',*

Just at that moment a loud explosion rocked the building, *'Here we go again'* she grabbed her jacket and ran down the stairs to the dilapidated makeshift departure gates, outside she found an empty single deck bus on fire, it had been hit in the fuel tank by a stray rocket. The bombardment had begun once again.

Twenty-four frantic hours later, in the worsening situation of Lebanon, Maria took advantage of a lull in the fighting, to read the reports on the activities of the five young women that she had recruited earlier. The first detailed statement she read was from Alia, in which she gave details of one of her first encounters.

September 6th
During my first flight to Italy from Cyprus as a passenger on a code green assignment, I was sure I had seen one of the other passengers on an earlier flight. Having carefully considered that my original assignment was a low key 'green', but not wishing to miss a possible opportunity, I immediately got into conversation with him, and discovered that he travelled to Italy almost every fortnight.

He was a sales representative for an electrical company called J C D Corporation with offices in Italy, Cyprus and Lebanon.

The conversation was fairly brief; however I made a note of his seat number and investigated with airline security upon arrival in Rome concerning any background that they may hold on their database.

While making those enquiries, I found J C D did not in fact have an office in Lebanon, but they did have a very large warehouse there, which they leased out to smaller companies. I became very suspicious that he could not define an office from a warehouse; therefore I left a message with airline security in both Larnaca and Beirut once I had returned, recommending that if he booked another flight, I needed to be on that same flight.'

September 16th

Maria continued reading as Alia described how on her next flight she found out about the suspects life style and reasons for travelling, also she noted; his name was a Philippe Faucheaux. "Well done Alia" Maria said out loud to nobody in particular.

September 22nd

She skimmed down to the bottom of the report to see that Alia had passed the assignment over to Vivian when the suspect changed his destination.

Maria read the report, feeling very pleased that her idea appeared to be working, she checked through the rest of the papers to see if she had the follow up report from Vivian. Her report read as follows: -

September 23rd

This operation is now classed as a 'Code Red' Therefore I immediately applied for assistance to be on standby, I then went to the Hilton hotel to enquire if a Mr Faucheux was staying at the hotel. The receptionist confirmed that a Mr Faucheux was indeed registered, but was departing early the next morning.

September 24th

I arranged to be at the airport at 0600 hours, before the first departing flight took off, to see if I could identify him from the photograph Alia gave me. I spotted him at the check-in desk of the Hungarian Airline, and noted that the flight was scheduled to leave at 0810 hrs. I quickly booked a ticket and made a call to my commanding officer. He arranged for one of our agents Antoine Karem who was already in Hungary to meet me in Budapest airport upon my arrival.

Faucheux was pointed out to Antoine and he followed him to the ticket desk of Yugoslavian airlines. Faucheux purchased a ticket for a flight to Zagreb, which was due to depart in six hours. We then decided to hire a car and drive through the border to arrive in Zagreb before Faucheux.

We waited for him to clear customs and followed him to a small hotel on the edge of town where he booked a room for two nights.

Faucheux was overheard asking the receptionist if she knew of the company A.S.S., she told him it was two blocks down and within walking distance, but it was too late as they were closed.

September 25th

Early next morning I arranged for more photographs to be taken of our man both entering and leaving the premises of A.S.S. We noted that the briefcase he had with him on entry was not with him when he left the premises, this can clearly be seen on photograph numbered five and eleven attached.

Antoine and I were able to get a window seat in a café opposite the A.S.S building in order to observe the suspect. After more than an hour and fifteen minutes Faucheux left A.S.S and returned to the hotel.

I asked the waitress if she knew what business A.S.S operated. She said she believed that they sold surplus military equipment.'

At this point Maria's attention sharpened and she read on quickly, as Vivian continued with her report.

'Antoine decided to investigate by posing as a buyer. When he returned he confirmed our suspicions that behind the innocent frontage lurked a professional arms dealer who boasted of the fact that he could obtain anything in the military field that could not be seen on the shelf.

Antoine drew up his own short list of various conventional items, which included automatic firearms, pistols, ammunition and body armour in quantity every month. The assistant confirmed that there would be no problem with supply, asking him to call back that same afternoon, by then he would be able to give him an idea of costs, apologising that they were busy arranging another shipment for a previous customer.

Antoine asked if he could witness their method of packing and preservation as the last time he made a purchase, the goods were found to be rusty by the time they arrived by sea.

That afternoon at 1600 hrs Antoine returned to A.S.S. The man asked him to follow him to the back of the building where three of his staff were preserving and packing a massive range of guns, ammunition etc. A minimum of thirty cases was being prepared for shipment.

Then came the breakthrough we needed to confirm our suspicions Antoine noticed an address on several case lids already marked for shipping: -

MV "MONTA STAR"
Via TRIESTE SHIPPING LINES
TO THE ORDER OF: - J C D CORPORATION
(ELECTRICAL EQUIPMENT)
BEIRUT (WEST) LEBANON

Antoine thanked him for his quotation, (which is attached with this report) and advised him that he would return after consultation with his people,

No questions were asked regarding destination of the equipment, it should be noted security at ASS was extremely poor.

September 26th

Faucheux was due to leave the hotel for the airport mid morning for his return flight. Both Antoine and I returned to Budapest by road. - - - - -

Once again Maria skimmed the rest of the report; which was mainly just wrapping things up, only pausing to check the date and signature at the end.

VIVIAN 22-56-5-78.30th September.

She smiled to herself as she gathered up the papers, feeling content and quite proud; and very satisfied of the work her girls were doing. She left the office and went to see the C.O. He looked up with a smile as she entered the room.

"Good Morning Captain, success I hear"

She saluted smartly and returned the smile.

"Yes Sir, the girls have done very well"

He gestured for her to sit,

"Your idea Captain, they cannot take all the credit"

She acknowledged the complement with a small nod, but her face was serious,

"The question is Sir, in reference to Vivian's report, what can we do about the destination of the arms?"

"No problem captain, we can change direction of the vessel and guide it into Jounieh port, and once it is there, we will seize the equipment."

He leaned back in his chair

"By the way did you know that Faucheux is not his real name, we know him as one Stephen Matheson, and he is not French, but an American by birth?"

Maria looked up in surprise,

"No Sir, I did not. So the Americans will ask for his release then?"

He nodded his head confirming her statement,

"Yes I am afraid so. The Americans want him back; they say he is a diplomat. But we will not be in too much of a hurry to assist them, let him sweat for a while."

Unable to hide her irritation at the system she replied scathingly,

"I am sure you don't really believe that, Sir. He will be free within days of his return to the States"

The C.O didn't answer, but his eyes acknowledged her in agreement as he indicated the meeting was over. Maria rose to her feet saluted, turned on her heels and left the office.

Although she was very happy with the way that the operation was working, she was disappointed that the suspect may eventually get away with only a few weeks hard labour in a Lebanese prison.

CHAPTER 4

Oblivious to Maria's continued situation back in Beirut, Tom's life continued as normal. He had arranged to take a business trip to Mexico with another colleague Donald Clemence. Don was a well-liked mechanical engineer; and a bit of a joker, and had worked along side John Clark for many years in the past. He was also a seasoned traveller, and he was looking forward to this trip with Tom.

"Ok Tom" Don said with a twinkle in his eye; heading for the top shelf of Smith's bookstore at Heathrow,

"Let's see what we can find for the old boy." Bill Tate, the person they were planning to visit, had asked Don to bring some 'men's' magazines with him. So they picked out four copies that Don thought suitable.

"I can never understand why anyone wants to buy this crap." Tom remarked innocently, as he followed a few steps behind Don to the pay counter.

Don slapped the magazines onto the counter with a flourish, and announced loudly to the pretty young Asian girl behind the counter.

"These are for my young friend here but he is much too embarrassed to ask for them"

The assistant looked at Tom in some disbelief, or at least that's what he hoped. He laughed rather self-consciously, and nodded meaningfully to Don thinking, *'I owe you one mate.'* Don tucked the magazines into his flight bag; and didn't stop chuckling about his little joke until they boarded the aircraft.

The journey to Mexico was exhausting; it included two flight changes, and all in all took twenty-four hours. They were completely shattered; neither of them had managed any sleep. After they wearily made their way through the airport, Don phoned Bill,

"We have arrived old son, see you tomorrow" and with a grin at Tom he added, "Remind me to tell you, I've got a good joke about Tom and your magazines"

Tom grinned ruefully,

"You're never going to let me forget that are you?

Looking about him with interest as they drove to the hotel, his first impression of Mexico was not quite what he expected. The city was a very noisy bustling place, with high levels of air pollution. The people in general, he had been told, were very pleasant towards the English, *'but, I will wait and see on that one'* he thought is eyes darting in all directions trying to take in the busy scene.

Don relaxed back in his seat totally unconcerned at the chaos surrounding them; he was a very confident person and seemed to know his way around wherever he was.

"Thank God we are going out of town tomorrow to get away from all this. Bill's home is on the way to Acapulco, cleaner air and much calmer. Anyhow for tonight we will make our own entertainment"

"Fine by me" Tom replied.

They eventually arrived at the hotel, and after a couple of hours rest and a change of clothes, they were ready to go out. Don called a taxi.

"Take us to where the action is my good man" He confidently said to the driver.

"Yes Sir," the man grinned putting his foot on the accelerator, throwing them both back into the seat. The taxi took them to a sleazy looking club off one of the main streets. Tom eyed it up cautiously while Don paid the driver. They walked through the shabby doors into a dingy badly lit foyer. As their eyes accustomed themselves to the light, they saw several women in various states of dress, and in some cases undress; hurrying towards them.

The two men looked at each other,

"Are you thinking what I'm thinking?" Don said.

"Yep." Tom answered.

There was nothing discreet about the type of business being traded here. Simultaneously they both turned about and headed straight for the exit, so quickly in fact, the taxi driver had not had time to move.

"Not your scene Sir?"

"You could say that," Tom replied, with a broad grin at Don

The taxi driver drove off chuckling to himself.

"Where to now Sir?" "Oh find us somewhere reasonable to eat" Don muttered; feeling rather embarrassed, he had made a big mistake; and received a large dent in his ego.

Tom grinned feeling rather smug at his friend's discomfort,

"Seems to me we have another little joke to tell Bill"

They eventually settled for a nice little restaurant not far from their hotel, but without the action! Later that night Tom got ready for bed thinking about what he had seen so far of Mexico. '*What a contrast to the Middle East! I thought Lebanon was relaxed, but nothing like this*' He pulled back the bedclothes, '*I suppose it's a bit like some parts of the States, but with a lot more noise*' He yawned crawling tiredly into the bed.

The next morning they were up early and had arranged for a hired car at the hotel; ready for the long drive to Bill's house. The trip would take about six hours along the coastal route, and as it was a beautiful warm day, they decided not to rush, but to enjoy the journey.

Bill Tate welcomed them warmly. He was a typical ex-pat, who had originated from Newcastle in the north of England many years ago, and was now married to a Mexican woman. Since his marriage he had worked for his wife's father, buying and restoring English manufactured engines.

It didn't take long for them to complete the business they had come for, but it was far too late for them to return the same night. Bill, with true northern hospitality, offered to put them up, and they spent a very pleasant evening eating and drinking with him and his wife. Don took great pleasure in relaying the joke he had played on Tom at the airport, but wasn't quite so amused when Tom retaliated with his tale of the nightclub. They left for the airport early the next morning feeling content, but slightly the worst for wear.

As soon as he returned to the UK, Tom wrote to Maria, he tried not to get too intense, as he was still very aware this could easily frighten her off.

He wrote the same as before, every day things about his own children's welfare, and enquiring after her mother, sister and brothers. Basic ordinary interests nothing more, the letters were few and far between, sometimes three months apart. But slowly he knew that they were building a stronger relationship.

It was January again, and the opportunity came to go back to Lebanon. He thought very hard about the idea, especially now that he knew more about the risks in Beirut. He paced about the office, and then made a decision. *'To hell with it, I've just got to see her again. I must be totally insane, but this time I'm going alone.'*

Two weeks later he flew the near empty MEA plane into Beirut, no sooner had it landed, a single deck bus pulled up at the bottom of the steps. Tom descended with the thirty or so other passengers. Even though it was mid-winter he felt the warm spring like air on his face, *'Great, no need for my overcoat'* he thought slinging it over his arm.

The bus dropped them at the arrivals hall, and he looked around juggling with his overcoat, suitcase and briefcase. At the front of a small group of people had gathered to greet the few passengers, he spotted his name on a board being waved by an old man Jean Bitar had arranged to escort him through the airport. Once through customs and out of the building, he found Jean waiting outside by the barrier in his car. Tom had been told before he left home that nobody unauthorized was allowed inside the terminal building, or could leave a car unattended these days for obvious reasons. Jean greeted him warmly enough, but as they drove off; Tom got the impression that he had something he wanted to say. So he opened the conversation,

"How is everyone at the office?"

"Fine," Jean answered slowly, but then continued with a rush.

"And I guess you know that Maria is getting engaged to her boyfriend and they plan to marry soon?" Jean glanced at him to see his reaction.

Tom felt like he had received a kick in the stomach.

"She goes away at weekends with him and they stay in hotels together"

He struggled to keep his face passive and not show Jean what he was thinking. *'The bugger is getting a kick out of this, and I don't believe a word of it'* Then another thought struck him. *'I wonder if he has been reading our mail. But even if he has, there was nothing to suggest anything, no more than friends.'* He felt irritable *'Anyway, I'm here to take an order for generators for God's sake'*

It was becoming clear to him that the man was either jealous; or a control freak, *'Maybe he sees me as a threat.'* he thought. But all the same, Jean's attitude had annoyed him.

When they arrived at Jean's home where he would be staying, Tom tried to put the feelings behind him, as he was still looking forward to seeing Maria.

It had been arranged that on following Saturday, Maria, her mother, and Jean's English girlfriend Janet would take Tom shopping to Tripoli in the north of Lebanon The trip had been organised so that Tom could buy some cut price gold jewellery, which the area was well known for. He planned to buy presents for his family.

Maria arrived promptly outside Jean's house to pick up Janet and Tom. She got out of the car holding out her hands and kissed Tom warmly on both cheeks,

"Welcome once again Mr Forster; I am very pleased to see you"

She kept her greeting casual, but her heart was beating a lot faster than usual. Tom searched her face for some sign, but couldn't detect her feelings one way or another. He smiled a warm greeting to Maria's mother, and then they all settled themselves in the car and headed off to Tripoli.

The traffic was heavy because of the many checkpoints en-route, and it took most of the morning to get there. Although it didn't leave them a lot of time to shop, Tom managed to buy all the items he needed. They just had time for a drink before setting off for the return journey before dusk. In spite of the day spent together, they had very little time to talk, and there was definitely no mention of Maria's so called marriage. Tom felt a bit confused, *'Perhaps Jean has got it all wrong'* he thought, *'I'm sure something would have been said if it was true,'* His thoughts were interrupted when they came to yet another Syrian checkpoint. They were waved through with no problems, but a short way down the road as they approached the Christian area; they could see heavy smoke in the distance very close to where Maria and her family were living, it looked as though many buildings were ablaze.

There was deadly silence within the vehicle, not a word spoken for the next few miles. Tom looked out anxiously as they passed a building that had taken a direct hit. *'Bloody hell this looks serious, it must have started while we were in Tripoli.'*

Suddenly from out of nowhere, a very young; and in Tom's opinion; poor excuse for a soldier stepped into the road in front of their car waving a gun; and ordered them to stop. Walking around to the driver's side he leaned on the doorframe of the car and slowly looked at them all one by one, his eyes resting on Tom for a brief moment.

"Where are you going?" He demanded arrogantly in Arabic, grinning as he rested the AK47 rifle against the side of Maria's temple in an extremely provoking manner.

"Beirut" She replied without moving a muscle.

"Do you really want to arrive safely?" he said with a broad smirk on his face.

She turned her head very slowly towards him,

"Please yourself"

By this time there was direct eye-ball-to-eye-ball contact between the soldier and Maria. Tom although not understanding the language was beginning to feel extremely nervous, there was no mistaking what was going on. He felt a driblet of sweat trickle down his forehead as he detected the developing hostility in the soldier's attitude. *'Christ what's going to happen now'* he thought trying not to panic.

There was not a sound from the two women in the back seat, they had obviously experienced this sort of intimidation before, and Tom found himself holding his breath.

It seemed like an hour, although it was only minutes before the young soldier still grinning stood to one side and waved the gun in the direction of Jounieh. Maria drove off, swerving from side to side in the road, all the time looking in the rear mirror. It was not unknown for the soldiers to fire at departing vehicles.

Once out of bullet range she relaxed, and twisted around to smile to her mother and Janet, "Are you both Ok?" and then noticing Tom almost on the floor of the car said casually,

"Don't let this put you off coming again" adding with a grin, "They are all big boys when they have a gun in their hand, they could see you were a foreigner and wanted to show off, that's all. He most likely thought you were an American"

Tom slowly eased himself back into his seat wiping the sweat of his hands on his trousers,

"Why are the Americans more likely to be impressed?"

"No," Maria laughed. "But these rubbish Syrians are anti-American, due to the US support of Israel that's why." Maria looked straight ahead her face expressionless. "Don't worry we are used to it."

Tom could see that the conversation was closed. They drove on silently with just the odd word now and again, but the atmosphere in the car was still tense.

Maria was worried about the thick smoke blowing across the dual carriageway, but calmly continued to drive, although she was very alert. Tom didn't notice; he was deep in thought.

'I can't believe she stayed so calm. I wonder how many times it happens?' He glanced at her

set expression, 'I suppose she's trained to stay calm. Christ, I don't think I could live like this.'

Eventually they arrived home to find all was safe, there had been damage nearby, but for now all was well. Janet was taking Tom and the car back to Jean's, so Maria and her mother got out. She walked round to the passenger side and leaned in the car window,

"Tom, you know there is a party tonight at Jeans, well, this time I really cannot make it.

Nadia said she will keep you company, and Jean understands why I cannot go. But don't worry, Janet and I will take you to the airport on Monday, we can chat then."

Tom felt very disappointed about the party, but he noticed that Maria was at long last calling him by his Christian name; it was a minor break through as far as he was concerned.

Later that evening at the party Nadia arrived, and immediately came and sat beside him. He smiled to himself, 'I wonder if Maria has told her to keep an eye on me?'

"Hi Tom, are you Ok?"

"I'm fine thanks, and you?"

"Yes. I'm good" she replied hesitantly, clearly trying to think of what to say next. She put her hand on his arm, looking at him anxiously,

"Tom, Maria likes you a lot, and she really wanted to see you. But she does not like being used by Mr Bitar as his personal possession. And for some reason he is not that happy that Maria has shown friendship towards you. I don't know why, as he has no hold on her whatsoever, and she has never given him any reason to think so"

She continued earnestly,

"Maria is a very strong person, very focused, and nothing will change her, especially with her responsibilities involving her LF duties,

Tom agreed with that character assessment from what he knew of Maria, which thinking about; it was not a lot. He took her hand smiling, "Would you like to dance?" Nadia accepted with a shy smile. "Would you mind if I take my shoes off? I will never be able to dance in them" She was quite short, even with high heels she was still only a little over five feet, and when she removed her shoes to dance with Tom she barely came up to his chest.

He smothered a chuckle as he and caught himself thinking *It's a bit like dancing with my youngest'* He whispered in her ear "I think to be sure to whom I am online with, I will call you little barefoot." Nadia laughed delightedly at her new code name, but then she looked serious.

"Tom, Mr Bitar told Maria what he had said to you about her relationship with her boyfriend, and she was very angry, as she has never been away with him, ever! That is another reason why she isn't coming tonight"

When the music stopped they went back to their table, but Nadia had not finished defending her friend.

"You must not say I told you, Maria is very close to a very popular enforcer of 'Lebanon for the true Lebanese Muslims and Christian, not for Palestinian or Syrian' he is known only as 'The Phoenician.' It is said that she is the only one who knows his true identity. That is how much her work is regarded in our country. So please don't ask her to give more at this time, she doesn't have it to give"

From a corner of the room Jean was watching proceedings between Tom and Nadia, he had seen them dancing, and whispering. He could hardly hide his joy, *'That's good, our English friend appears interested in Nadia'* he thought, and decided to encourage this new relationship as much as he could. Towards the end of the evening he approached Nadia with a smile,

"Nadia my dear, you really must stay here tonight, it's far too late for you to be going back alone"

"No Jean I am sorry but I have to go, don't worry about me I have a Taxi friend arranged" She knew exactly what was in Jean's mind.

She liked Tom as a friend, but he was not her type, even if he was; she would not have stayed, and certainly not to please Jean Bitar.

The next morning Tom was feeling very unsettled, the faint distant bombing he had heard all through the night, was getting louder; and a lot closer. Local military sirens had been wailing outside his bedroom window most of the night and morning, and there was rather a lot of black smoke blowing in the breeze, "I really don't like this at all" he muttered to himself and went in search of Jean. He found him reading a paper in the kitchen, "What the hell is happening Jean, what are we supposed to do? Jean sighed testily; he was not interested in the Englishman's worries, and just shrugged his shoulders,

"It is no problem; don't worry about it"

This was no comfort to Tom; he was worried. *'How the hell do you not worry with all this going on around you'* He thought peering out of the window. *'They all seem so bloody complacent about it; it must be a way of life to them now'*

The bombardment in the distance continued through the rest of the day; and most of the night and Monday could not come quick enough for Tom. He was packed and ready to leave at five in the morning, even though his plane did not leave until twelve thirty. *'The sooner I get out of this bloody place; the better I will like it'* he thought pacing up and down the room.

Just after eight o'clock, Janet came into the lounge looking resigned. "Maria is obviously stuck in traffic, if she is not here in ten minutes we will have to leave without her" she wasn't happy about another trip to the airport on her own.

Tom's heart sank, that meant he would not see Maria before he left. He went back to his room to collect his suitcase feeling both concerned and depressed. He stood and looked around the room he was vacating; and he heard his name being called from the street. Leaning his head out of the window he was delighted to see Maria,

"Tom, there is no lift working, please tell Janet I am waiting in the car"

He excitedly grabbed the rest of his things, and ran to find Janet, and soon they were on their way to the airport. It wasn't far to go, usually it took forty-minutes on a good day, and anything up to two-hours on a bad one. Luckily this was a good day; and they arrived with time to spare. Tom booked in and then went back to the area where Maria and Janet stood; they were waiting behind the railings that separated the passengers and non-passengers. He laid his overcoat over the railings; wishing he could speak to Maria alone, but Janet showed no sign of leaving At last after several minutes of stilted conversation, she begrudgingly took the hint and made herself scarce.

His hand crept nearer to Maria along the top of the rail, but he hesitated, *'best not scare her off yet'* he thought, so he desperately reverted to a weak chat-up line,

"It was a pity you didn't make the party, it was a good evening, but it could have been a lot better of course,

"I heard you enjoyed yourself," she said with a grin, teasing him. It was just as well

'Miss Barefoot' didn't stay over, wasn't it?"

She had said it as a joke, but Tom had noticed the inquisitive expression. His heart lurched, *'Aha! She does have feelings after all'* He thought triumphantly. Looking directly into her eyes he smiled gently, "That was never an option"

"And Nadia told me that she had explained my position to you, even though I didn't feel it was up to anyone, to explain anything, to anyone on my behalf."

He had to laugh at her defensive statement,

"Correct. And the suggestion of her staying over night was Jeans, not mine. What he had in mind; I can only guess. If it was what we both were thinking

39

then it was always going to be a non- starter. Nadia is definitely not my type. A nice girl; who thinks a lot of you, but still not my type"

Maria's gave him a cheeky grin, "Oh, and what is your type?" but before he could reply she changed the subject.

"Anyway let us forget that, I have found you a couple of photographs. Not that recent, but I haven't changed much in two years I hope. Take care of your girls Tom. I know you are good father and they need you so much, especially at that age"

Tom was thrilled, as he had asked for photographs a few times in letters; but there was never any reference to his request.

"Thanks" He smiled; "I really appreciate that," He reluctantly glanced at his watch, "I have to go now, it's half past eleven" He was anxious not to miss his flight.

Maria put her hand on his arm smiling up at him,

"It is Ok, you can stay until noon, I have arranged with a friend of mine to come to collect you when it's time"

Tom had never known a half hour go so quickly; there was still so much he wanted to say. He nervously glanced at the bomb-damaged clock in the hall, it had almost reached noon. This airport and in particular certain foreign aircraft flying into here had been prime targets in the past; by the Arab extremist, and it was now an area that was mostly avoided by the Christian Lebanese if at all possible. He was torn between wanting to stay with Maria, and getting the hell out of this area as fast as he could.

A young man in smart police uniform appeared at his elbow,

"Hi Maria, all set?" He asked with a perfect English accent.

Maria nodded to him; and reached out for Tom's hand, she drew him towards her and kissed him on the each cheek very close to his lips. He held her tight for a brief moment, until she finally drew away very slowly. He felt her warm sweet breath on his face.

"Have a good trip home dear Tom; keep thinking of us here in this bloody hell"

Tom caught a glimpse of a tear as she turned swiftly away signalling to Janet, then she disappeared from his view. He picked up his coat and followed the officer through customs where a waiting armed police escort met him. From there he went straight to the aircraft; that had clearly been waiting just for him. '*Wow, now I know what its like to be royalty*' he thought, feeling rather elated.

One of the officers escorted him directly to his seat; Tom thanked him and settled down for take off, and began to reflect on his very brief trip. He felt something in his top pocket and pulled out what looked like a picture card, turning it over he read, THE PHOENICIAN and underneath was added, '*Will always protect you*' it had been hand written, presumably by Maria.

He remembered what Nadia had told him about this elusive person calling himself 'The Phoenician' so what with this, and from all the private attention at the airport; he concluded that Maria certainly had extremely high-level connections.

As the aircraft left the runway he thought about Maria. '*That girl sure is a mystery, and beautiful with it. I'd love to know exactly what it is she does, she has obviously got quite a lot of influence round here*' The more he thought of it, the more he liked the buzz it gave him; in spite of the apparent danger.

Looking around at his fellow passengers, he smiled politely at the pretty young lady sitting next to him, although separated by an empty seat. She smiled back at him,

"Hello, are you American or English?" She enquired.

"English" Tom replied with uncharacteristic patriotic pride.

"Good" She replied with a grin.

"Why good?"

"Because I, like my family are anti- American." She saw the expression on Tom's face. "I am sorry if that offends you"

Tom decided to take the middle ground on this issue.

"Why should it, everyone has the right to have their own opinion"

"And your opinion of America is?" she persisted.

"Mixed, to be honest, American people in general I like very much, but some of their foreign policies I do not"

"Exactly" she agreed nodding her head vigorously.

"What is your name?" Tom asked changing a subject; the last thing he wanted was to discuss American politics all the way home.

"Valerie, and yours?"

"Tom; nice to meet with you" He replied as he leant over the empty seat to shake her hand.

"What is so special about you; that we all had to wait for you?" she smiled teasingly.

He grinned back at her. "Extra protection from a loved one"

"A woman obviously" which was more of a statement, than a question.

"We English are so obvious, it seems," He laughed.

"Only when the woman is not your wife" she nodded her head in the direction of his wedding ring. '*Very clever, but cheeky*' he thought, '*this is going to be an interesting trip by the sound of it.*' It was clear that she was having a bit of fun with him, and he had always thrived on banter from his sporting days.

"True." He smiled, I have been hijacked by this beautiful Lebanese woman who is playing hard to get"

"And of course she will know you are married, another good reason to play hard to get, as you foreigners call it" Valerie smiled knowingly.

Tom grinned,

"One day she will change her mind, given time."

She laughed at his confidence,

"Don't wait too long my friend she may never do that. Then you will have wasted so much of your time"

Changing the subject, as her last words were not what he wanted to hear, Tom asked,

"What do you do for a living?"

"Hostess with this airline, but I am on holiday at the moment. I am going to London to visit my parents in Berkshire, do you know it?

"Vaguely" He replied pulling down the table ready for lunch which he could see coming down the isle. The meal was then served; and after they had eaten, they relaxed back in their seats, occasionally chatting amicably during the remainder of the five-hour journey to Heathrow. When the plane touched down they walked together from the aircraft; and eventually parted at the immigration desk.

"Good Luck, Tom, I hope Maria will wait for you." She said with a broad smile, and headed for the long queue of foreign passengers waiting to pass through customs.

Tom smiled back to her and waved goodbye; going straight through the British passport channel, and then just as he emerged through customs; a thought stopped him in his tracks. *'Did she just say Maria? I am sure I didn't mention her name'*

CHAPTER 5

The letters and faxes continued between Tom and Maria, and so far he had managed to keep his Lebanese interest a secret. Only Sally his secretary knew about the developing friendship, and he hoped she could be trusted. She was a pleasant woman in her mid forties, and recently divorced, plus she understood the problems he was having with his marriage, having been through a very similar situation herself. He had wondered if she would find it difficult to fit into a family controlled business, but after a few months it felt like she had been there forever.

Early in the New Year, he received a letter at the office from Maria telling him that the war in Beirut had intensified, and that living conditions had deteriorated even further. Middle Eastern airlines were no longer flying and the only route into Beirut was by sea from Larnaca in Cyprus. *'Oh shit, that's all I need'* he thought. *'I hate bloody boats at the best of times'*

It was an unsettled time all round for the Forster family, they were having a few problems with the business; which led to a joint decision to dispense with the services of both John Clark, and Don Clemence. Although they parted amicably, the decision had not been an easy one for any of them to make.

One morning in early April he sat in the office feeling totally fed up, he slammed shut the folder he was reading causing Sally to jump. "Right; that's it. I need a break, I'm going to Lebanon"

"Good idea Sally replied; without as much as a raised eyebrow. When and where?"

"Cyprus, and as soon as you can arrange it" he grinned as she picked up the telephone. The journey on the ferry between Cyprus and Jounieh was not something he was looking forward too, but he needed to see Maria.

The day before his departure he was finishing off some work in the office, still feeling very apprehensive when he turned to Sally,

"At least this time I know a bit more about where I'm going, and what I'm doing"

She smiled reassuringly,

"Don't worry Tom you'll be fine"

"I'm sure I will," he smiled, "What would I do without you?"

"How about a pay rise?" She laughed.

The following Thursday morning he flew to Cyprus and took the eleven o'clock overnight ferry to Jounieh. He found his tiny cabin and settled himself down for what he hoped would be a good night's sleep. The next thing he knew it was morning, *'I can't believe I was worried'* he thought as he climbed wearily out of the narrow bed. *"Nothing to it, except the stink of this bloody diesel,'* The smell of the diesel made him feel sick, there was no way he could face the thought of breakfast, giving the small dining room a miss, he went out on deck for some air to clear his head; and to settle his stomach as he patiently waited for the ferry to dock.

Glad to be back on dry land; he hailed one of the waiting taxis lined up at the dockside to take him to Jean's apartment. Jean seemed pleased to see him; and led him out to the roof top terraced garden where he had already opened a bottle of wine,

"Was it a good trip Tom?" he asked filling the two waiting glasses.

"Not bad, better than I thought, although I still hate the sea, can't trust it at all." He just had to ask. "Will we be seeing Maria tomorrow night?" he knew Jean always arranged a party on Saturday nights. Jean looked irritated.

"I don't think so, she is very busy with her work, and I don't think she is interested."

"This is getting ridiculous' he thought exasperated. *'I know that's not true, he obviously has no idea how close we have become. What the hell has he got against us seeing each other?'* From the look on his host's face he decided not to pursue the subject, he would wait until he saw either Nadia or better still Maria herself.

On Friday evening before the party, Jean took Tom to one side; in spite of his attitude; he quite liked the young man, so he decided to tackle things from a different angle, by taking a friendlier approach.

"Tom, about Maria, let me give you a word of advice. In my experience two cultures do not mix; I was married to an English woman some time ago, and as you know I still have an English girl friend. So I really know the problems that this brings." He gave a sad smile shaking his head slowly,

"I am concerned for both of you, and I don't want to see either of you get hurt"

He paused and took a deep breath wiping his face with a large white handkerchief.

"For instance you take Janet she is a very jealous woman, typically English. We Middle Eastern males do not accept this attitude. The women here accept that their men may haveother women on the side, it's almost considered to be our right"

Tom looked at the sweaty little man, surprised that he was so blatant with his chauvinistic confession; he tried to hide his annoyance,

"Thanks for the concern, but we shall just have to wait and see. I know Maria is too busy to get involved right now, but apart from that," he gave a short laugh, "I can't ever see her agreeing to share any man"

There was a lot more he could have said, but considering he was a guest, he just added,

"And besides that is your custom as a man, not ours"

Avoiding any discussion on that point Jean replied slightly exasperated,

"That's what I mean, she is totally unique and very special to us all Tom, don't forget that"

Tom suspecting Jean's real reason for trying to put him off was jealousy, although he couldn't imagine why, but he couldn't resist tormenting him.

"Oh I know that, and one day I hope to be in a position to appreciate how unique she is."

Jean was a little taken back,

"What about Jane and your kids, you plan to separate or divorce?"

'That's none of his bloody business' he thought, fighting back his annoyance, but he coldly answered him anyway,

"At the moment I am only there because of the children, I know that's not a good reason, but for now it is the best I can do." As far as Tom was concerned it was the end of this conversation, but Jean seemed genuinely concerned, he gave a deep sigh,

"That's very sad; maybe I can have a word with your wife when I come over. I plan to be there during the summer. I promised your secretary Sally I would take her out for dinner," he brightened considerably. "How old is she by the way? And what is she like?"

'Here we go, looking for a bit on the side as he calls it'

Tom was horrified at the thought of Jean interfering in his marriage, but said nothing; he didn't want him to get any more ideas. Smiling grimly to himself, knowing Sally would kill him if she knew what he was about to say,

"Sally, oh she is around your age, recently divorced and looking forward very much to meeting you, I think you would make a nice couple," Jean looked pleased at that. Tom quickly crossed his fingers behind his back as he thought. *'At least that's diverted him away from the subject of Maria'*

The Saturday evening party was all set, and Jean waited for his guests to arrive. Maria had tried to excuse herself from coming to the party, not that she didn't want to see Tom, but she was very much aware of Jean's obsessive and controlling nature, and she was trying to avoid him as much as possible. But, even though he didn't like him, Jean had contacted her boyfriend and invited him to come as well; he knew Alain would bring Maria with him.

Alain was also curious to find out what this 'Tom Forster' he had heard so much about, was really like. So he accepted; and insisted that Maria came as well, if only to see; that in spite of what he had heard, she at least; had no feelings to hide.

Tom stood quietly at the side of the room waiting for Maria, watching as Jean greeted his guests as they came in. When at last she arrived she looked stunning, she was dressed in a black satin stretch cat suit; over which she wore a gold lace jacket. She had left her hair long loose just how she knew he liked it. His pulse rate increased as he caught her eye across the room.

Maria looked away quickly and glanced around at the other guests assembled, she was acutely aware of the situation Jean had set up her for this evening. Tom followed her with his eyes as Alain took hold of her arm and together they walked over to join a small group of people on the opposite side of the room. After all the guests had arrived and were settled with their drinks, Jean loudly announced in Arabic to the room that Maria would now dance for them. Maria shook her head; angry that he had assumed she would dance without asking her first.

"Come Maria, you cannot refuse to dance for our guests"

"I am sorry, I am not prepared; and I am very tired" she replied looking over at Tom. Recognising the message in her eyes, he casually walked across the room to where she was sitting. It was very quiet, the musicians were still waiting for Maria's decision, and he could feel the atmosphere in the room as all eyes were upon him as he approached the group.

Most of the guests in the room had heard of his interest in Maria from the rumours circulating in the office, and now with Alain here, they were expecting a possible confrontation. At last he reached the table where they were sitting and he put out his hand towards Alain,

"How are you, I am Tom Forster. I'm a close friend of Maria." At this point he deliberately paused before adding, "Oh, and of course; a supplier of generators to Mr Bitar"

He knew he had confused them by mentioning Maria before Jean Bitar. But `What the hell' he thought. *'All's fair in love and war'* he smiled to himself as he saw the recognition in Maria's eyes before she quickly looked down. She knew exactly what he was doing.

Having now taken full control of the conversation Tom continued confidently.

"And you must be Maria's boyfriend; I am very pleased to meet you"

Alain was absolutely dumb struck; he had no idea how to handle this, it was not at all what he had expected. Tom glanced quickly in Jean's direction, he looked furious. *'I don't think he liked that'* he thought smugly.

There were one or two looks of admiration for Tom from the other guests, he had cleverly diffused what could have been a very awkward situation, and most of them realized what Jean had tried to do.

Alain was still struggling to regain his composure, but managed to mutter grudgingly,

"I am pleased to meet you also, as you know I am Alain Chaddad, please join us," adding after a quick look to Maria. "Although I am afraid we have to leave soon"

Jean butted in testily, "Not before Maria dances for us, you don't" He was still annoyed that his plan had failed.

Maria glanced quickly at Tom, who raised his eyebrows nodding in approval to Jean's request, proving to them all; that from now on, he was in control of the situation. Jean looked defeated, he knew from that moment; he had not only lost the battle, but also the war. For a brief moment Maria felt uneasy, followed swiftly by relief, 'Well; *now they all know he loves me.*'

She nodded to the musicians the drums and the music started, slowly she rose to her feet, and glided onto the dance floor closing in cleverly on both Tom and Alain, showing equal attention to them both. Her body moved exotically to the extremely sensual dance rhythm. And then kneeling on the floor in front of Tom, she swayed backwards almost putting her head on his lap. He slowly bent forward until he was only inches away from her lips, but she swiftly pulled away.

He was over the moon with the attention she was now showing towards him, 'Whew, she's good' He thought, '*in fact she's bloody marvellous*'

Alain's face was like thunder, and as soon as Maria had finished dancing he stood up and took her arm, "Come Maria, we're going now". There was no argument there; Tom was quite content with the way things had gone, and Maria was quite relieved to go, she had had enough tension for one evening.

Trying to gain some ground again, Jean sidled up to Tom,

"Of course you know why they had to leave early don't you?" Tom didn't answer, so Jean continued, "Oh yes, Alain is taking her away for the weekend to a lovely little hotel high in the mountains"

Tom laughed and walked away; he was no longer impressed with this silly man's pathetic tales.

The following day Jean behaved as though nothing had happened, so Tom decided to leave well alone, he was far too happy with all that had happened the previous night.

Later that afternoon to his delight Maria phoned him,

"Hi Tom, I have just got news that the airport is open again, and there will be no problem getting a ticket." She knew he hated the thought of returning home by the ferry. And then she added,

"You know Tom; I wouldn't have believed it, if someone had told me that you would speak with Alain like you did. I was very impressed. What made you do it?

Not one to miss an opportunity Tom replied swiftly,

"Because I fancy you like hell, and one day.......... Maria interrupted him,

"Please don't say any more, leave it for now Tom, try to let things take their course, Ok?

You have a good flight home tomorrow; and come again soon, big kiss"

With that she then closed the line. He stood there for a moment the receiver still in his hand. '*What did she mean,' leave it for now?'* He didn't know what to think.

When he arrived at the airport Monday morning he collected his ticket, a porter then greeted him; took his case; and checked it in for him at the first class counter. '*That's odd'* he thought. '*I didn't book first class; I didn't think they had first class now'*

The porter then escorted him to the First class lounge; where he sat on one of the more comfortable seats looking about him feeling a trifle confused, until he heard a very familiar voice from behind him,

"May I check that your papers are in order sir?"

He smiled and slowly turned; his heart leapt upon seeing Maria.

"Wow!" He exclaimed; she was dressed in her full police uniform, complete with revolver in its holster, with handcuffs dangling from her belt. Instinctively he put his arms around her and hugged her never wanting to let her go. She eased herself away, tenderly kissing him on each side of his face; he laughed delightedly pulling her back towards him,

"Will you arrest me if I refuse to let you go?"

"Man-handling a cop while on duty, I would say that's mandatory life,"

Tom liked her quick fire humour, Maria then looked across to her friend who was sitting at a makeshift desk only a few metres away from them. The young girl smiled and held up both her hands indicating that they had only ten minutes before boarding. Maria acknowledged her with a slight nod of her head.

"So you arranged all the preferential treatment did you? He inquired tenderly.

"Of course, special treatment for a special guy"

"That's nice" He wanted to say so much more.

"Tom, I must go now, I am on high alert security today, but I just wanted to see you, and say have a good trip. Please keep in touch. Tania over there will look after you until you board," adding

"Love to your girls"

"What about me?" He protested.

She just smiled and kissed him on the cheek again; then quickly left the room. Tom watched her leave then walked over to talk to Tania for the remaining minutes until it was departure time.

Once again he was escorted by one of Maria's police colleagues directly to the aircraft. '*I think I could get used to this special treatment'* he thought as he took his seat for the flight home.

Back in England the following day he watched the news about Beirut on the television, it was not good. He went to his office and sent a telex to Maria's office at the airport; using their password code,

'MARIA ARE YOU THERE?'
'YES TOM, WHAT NEWS YOU HAVE?'
'JUST CHECKING. WE HEARD ON TV OF HEAVY BOMBING IN YOUR AREA'

Maria's reaction came back instantly,

'SURPRISING. I THOUGHT ALL EUROPEANS THINK WE ARE SUNBATHING ON THE CHRISTIAN SIDE WHILE THE OTHER SIDE ARE DYING. THAT'S HOW IT'S NORMALLY PORTRAYED ISN'T IT?'

He replied.

'YOU SOUND HAPPY TODAY'
'WHAT'S YOUR PROBLEM SWEETHEART, ARE YOU MISSING ME ALREADY?'

The machine clattered again.

'NOTHING, I'M SORRY, JUST ON EDGE I SUPPOSE. IT HAS BEEN A VERY BAD DAY
HERE TODAY, MANY KILLED.'

Quickly he typed.

'THAT'S NOT GOOD. WHY NOT COME ACROSS TO CYPRUS FOR A FEW DAYS
FOR A BREAK. I CAN MEET YOU THERE AND WE CAN SPEND TIME TOGETHER.'

Instantly the answer came back

'SORRY THE SITUATION HERE DOES NOT ALLOW ME TO LEAVE. I HAVE WORK TO
DO, MAYBE ONE DAY.'

Before he could respond, another message came.

' HAVE TO CLOSE. SHELLS ARE STARTING AGAIN, HAVE TO LEAVE, BYE .X'

The line disconnected leaving Tom feeling very concerned. He could do nothing except to continue trying to get re-connected without success. The Lebanese telex service was out of order for almost six weeks; he was frantic with worry. Then very early one morning long before he arrived in the office, a short telex came through.

'MARIA IS OK. SHE SENDS HER REGARDS AND HER LOVE TO YOUR GIRLS BUT
NOT TO YOU. SHE SAID YOU WOULD GET THE JOKE'

Tom laughed to himself, and guessed correctly that the telex came from Nadia, but he was not bothered as long as Maria was Ok.

A few days later it was time for Jean Bitar's arrival in England. Tom had little option, other than to return his hospitality, by asking him to stay with them, although he knew it could be dangerous, especially after what Jean had said about speaking to Jane. But on giving it a second thought, he decided he really didn't care anymore.

The day after Jean arrived, bearing in mind the spot he had put Sally in, he had organised a dinner party. He thought it would not be quite so awkward for her to meet Jean, if she were invited together with some of his other friends. To his relief Sally and Jean got on fine, so there was no apologising or explaining to do at the end of the evening.

The following day Jean, as ever the troublemaker, decided to have a heart to heart with Jane, He walked with her into the garden.

"Do you mind if I ask you something?"

He never gave Jane chance to reply as he continued,

"Tom told me you are both very unhappy in your marriage. Can I help in any way?

Jane was angered by this intrusion into her private life; he couldn't have done or said a worse thing as far as she was concerned. She looked at him coldly.

"I am sorry I don't wish to discuss my marriage with you or anyone else. Please excuse me."

Absolutely furious; she spun round and walked back into the house, leaving Jean to continue his walk in the garden alone.

The next morning Jean returned to Beirut, and Tom was more than pleased to see him go, after the problem he could have unwittingly caused.

He thought that Jane would never leave the subject alone, but to his surprise as the weeks went by, and apart from a slight coolness between them, not a word was spoken on the subject, which at the moment suited them both.

The telex's and letters continued to flow to and from Lebanon for the rest of the summer. Maria continued to offer what he believed to be genuine excuses as to why she couldn't meet him outside of Lebanon, but he knew in his heart that they would be together one day when the timing was right, and he was content to bide his time

CHAPTER 6

Tom was alone in the office when the telex machine whirred, he walked over to find an urgent message from Jean Bitar requesting him come to Lebanon, and to bring one of the company's technical specialist with him. *'No problem Jean,'* he thought, *'but this time, there is no way that you are going to stop me from having some time alone with Maria'*

Jean had booked Tom and the technician Roger Long into a hotel in West Beirut this time, and Tom knew this area of Lebanon was considered by most people to be extremely dangerous.

'I bet the bugger stuck us here deliberately; to make it harder to see Maria' He thought grimly.

Most people nowadays; unless it was absolutely necessary; didn't venture out after dark, which Jean knew only to well. Tom gave himself a mental shake thinking, *'I'm getting as neurotic as he is'*

At the end of their first mornings work, Jean approached him with a big smile,

"Right young man I have arranged for Maria to meet you at the 'Ca'dora' fish restaurant for lunch, you had better go straight there, and she will be waiting"

That certainly surprised him, the last thing he had expected from Jean, and he didn't need telling twice.

When he got to the restaurant he found Maria already seated waiting for him, he kissed her warmly on both cheeks, and sat down opposite her at the table, but before they could speak Jean walked in accompanied by Roger, Janet and Nadia.

Jean smiled, "Hello you two, you don't mind if we join you do you?"

'The bastard' Tom thought, he had noticed the glint of triumph in Jean's eye, *'He's not going to get away with this'*

He hid his annoyance, as he knew that he couldn't make a fuss in front of everyone, especially Maria. So he waited until they had finished lunch, then stood up,

"Sorry folks, but you must excuse us, we have arranged to meet some old friends of mine for coffee; and we are late. We will see you all later"

Tom glanced over at Jean; he knew he would not be able to object under the circumstances, although if looks could kill he would have been dead on the spot. He put his hand out to Maria; who rose and smiled pleasantly to the others without batting an eyelid, and then together they left the restaurant.

Maria burst out laughing as they walked to her little yellow Fiat parked outside in the makeshift car park.

"You are cheeky, you know that? Did you see Jean's face?"

"He deserved it" Tom laughed.

"What now? Maria asked, "Would you like to go back to my home for a coffee, my mother is at the hairdressers so no one will be there"

"That would be great" He tried to look calm, but his heart was thumping, *'At last'.*

It didn't take long to cover the short distance from the restaurant to her home. Her apartment was on the top floor; and the only way up was by three flights of tiled stairs.

"That's quite a climb!" Tom said as they reached her apartment.

"You get used to it" Maria laughed, she opened the door and they stepped inside the cool apartment.

"Please make yourself comfortable. Would you like to take coffee or brandy? Or would you like something else?"

Tom hid a smile; he would prefer the *'something else.'*

"That would be nice, Brandy please"

She poured the drink and placed the bottle in front of Tom saying,

"Please excuse me for a minute Tom I won't be long" then she walked towards a doorway into what he assumed was a bedroom.

Tom couldn't believe his luck. His western mind was racing into overdrive; *'perhaps this is where she slips into something a little more comfortable'* he thought hopefully.

The settee he was sitting on was low and rather soft, and as he leaned back and crossed his legs he knocked the table, tipping both the bottle and the glass over onto a very expensive looking carpet. "Oh Shit!" he swore; panicking as he desperately started to mop up the sticky substance with his handkerchief. Just then Maria returned.

"What happened?"

He squirmed with embarrassment,

"I am so sorry; I sort of leaned back and.. ." His voice trailed off as he looked at the mess in dismay. Maria laughed at the expression on his face and darted off to the kitchen for something to clean up with.

"Don't worry, these things happen"

She took over the mopping up still trying to reassure him that it was not a problem. He could do nothing except sit there and watch feeling totally stupid. It was not an easy task; and it took considerable time before she finally cleaned it up. Then she glanced at her watch,

"Oh! I am so sorry Tom, but its four o'clock. I should have picked my mother up from thehairdressers by now. We really have to leave. I am so sorry,"

He got up from his seat, shaking his head in disbelief; *'I don't believe this'* he thought irritably, *'why the hell did I do that'*

Maria positioned herself in the doorway waiting to lock up, and as he put his coat on, he felt her lean towards him; he could smell her expensive perfume again. Misreading the signal he bent over to kiss her on the lips, but she twisted her head slightly, offering her left cheek towards him instead.

"Let us stay friends Tom, don't ruin what we have. Neither of us is in the position to takethis any further; just value what we have for now"

His heart sank, *'Oh sod it! I thought we had got past that stage by now'* he thought, feeling even more despondent.

Maria drove him back to Jean's office, she could see he was upset, but she still had some reservations about their relationship. He sat next to her not saying a word, feeling quite depressed. She tried to open a conversation, but chose an unfortunate subject,

"Mr Bitar told me he liked your wife, he said she was very pretty and intelligent"

Tom turned slowly to study her face,

"How am I expected to answer that?"

But before she could respond, he continued scathingly,

"He is just trying to put a wedge between you and me, She may be pretty because she is blonde in Jean's eyes, but to be fair I would say more like attractive rather than pretty.

"She told him that she has seen my photo. The one I gave you at the airport I expect"

She said quietly, focusing on the road ahead,

"Yes, I know, I think she went through my briefcase and destroyed them."

Maria was beginning to wish she had not brought the subject of Jane up. But then Tom laughed,

"And that reminds me, I need some more now."

She was so relieved to see him smile again,

"Ok don't worry I will post you some new ones soon"

Nothing more was said on the subject of Jane, but they both sat deep in thought for the rest of the journey.

After dropping him off at the hotel, she drove off to collect her mother. Tom went upstairs to his room and stretched out on the bed; thinking back over the afternoon. He was still feeling a bit annoyed at the missed opportunity, but the more he thought about what happened; the funnier it got. *'No one will believe this story even if I told them. Even 'Frank Spencer' couldn't have cocked it up any better.'* He lay there grinning. *'Perhaps I should send it to the TV people; it would make a good script.'*

The next few days passed quickly having concentrated on the work they had come to do. Tom didn't get another chance see Maria again before he left, but to his delight she telephoned him just as he was leaving the hotel,

"Hi Tom, I must be quick, but I just wanted to wish you a good flight. Keep in touch when you get back home, Take care" There was a click and the phone went silent. He would have dearly loved to talk to her, but there was no chance. He gave a deep sigh, *'One day!'*

The following week Maria was being driven to work by Elie Toubia, one of her male army friends, when their vehicle slowed down and ground to a halt just as they were passing a notorious Syrian army observation post. Maria was on instant alert; it was well known that woman and girls had been abducted in these areas never to be seen again. If any of them managed to survive, they had usually been gang-raped. Although her whole body was tense, she said calmly,

"Maybe you have run out of fuel"

He shook his head, "No, It can't be. I'm sure there's plenty" He frantically pumped on the accelerator panicking slightly, he knew the petrol gauge wasn't working; so he really couldn't be sure.

One by one, four scruffy looking soldiers appeared from a camouflaged tent, pitched about one hundred yards from the un-made road. They were pointing to the Jeep and started to walk towards them.

Keeping as calm as she could, Maria slid across the seat and grabbed the wheel.

"Quick, Get out and push. I will turn it around; we may be able to roll back down the hill"

Maria watched in the mirror as the soldiers got closer, she could now see they were armed. Careful not to make any sudden movement she reached gingerly into the glove compartment and took out a pistol, checking that it was fully loaded.

Elie whispered with some urgency in his voice, as they came closer,

"These bastards are armed Maria"

"I know. Take it easy, let them make the first move"

The soldiers were laughing and pointing at Maria, Elie defiantly called out to them.

"We don't need your help"

"You don't" one of the men shouted back, "but I think she could do with a little help, from all of us" he laughed and took his gun out of the holster.

Maria had to act quickly; she knew the consequences if she didn't. There was no chance of help and there would be no witnesses. She jumped out of the jeep and fired a single shot hitting one of the soldiers in the head; he fell to the ground and rolled down the slight embankment. The others crouched down and started firing back at them. From their limited shelter behind the jeep Maria and Elie returned fire knowing that they had only six rounds each. Two more soldiers were hit which left just one, who waved his hands high in the air screaming,

"Ok I give up, I don't have a weapon,"

Elie, stood and slowly walked around the rear of the jeep towards the soldier, the man now had both his hands behind his head; hiding the gun from Elie's sight. Maria strained to see what was happening,

"Elie watch out he has a gun"

She heard a single shot. Holding his stomach Elie dropped to the ground, Maria gasped, she had only one shot left and she knew she had to make it count, or she was dead. She waited. The Syrian soldier calculating that she had spent all her ammunition; stood up confidently; and came towards her. She felt every nerve in her body taut. He was now only three or four yards away, with Elie clutching his stomach in agony, lying at the soldiers' feet.

"I will finish him off, if you don't come out"

She didn't move, but then she heard his gun click as he prepared to exercise his threat, and without hesitation she stood and fired; hitting him in the temple, he was dead before he hit the ground. *Thank God* she thought as she knelt to comfort Elie.

"Let's get out of here before there are any more problems, can you get into the jeep"

"I think so. Are they all dead," he asked.

"I'm not going back to check, but at least two are for sure" she replied helping him to his feet,

"Better that we get you to hospital, as quick as we can. I just hope this bloody jeep will start,"

Bleeding heavily, he clambered across the back seat. Maria got into the driving seat and prayed. Luckily the jeep began to roll; and what petrol there was left in the tank started the spluttering engine, backfiring as she steered the vehicle back down the hill.

After a moments silence she started breathing normal again,

"That was as close as it gets,"

"Yeah! I am so sorry Maria; it was obviously out of petrol. I really thought we had enough"

Maria was shaking as she battled to control her emotions, offering up a small silent prayer for the dead soldiers, even though she was fully aware that if she had have been taken by them, she would not have survived the ordeal.

She felt a shudder run through her body as she thought about what had just happened, it was her first direct kill, and it was not a good feeling.

A few months passed without any serious incidents at the airport, which encouraged MEA to resume their scheduled flights between England and Lebanon.

Once again a telex came through for Tom from Jean for more assistance. He gazed at the paper in his hand thoughtfully, '*I don't really need to go, but I might with a bit of luck get to see Maria*' He smiled to himself, '*Anyway I don't suppose James will mind the company*' That decided; he picked up the phone to call James.

A retired army officer, James Hutchins, was freelancing with the Forster Company as an electrical engineer, and was proving to be a useful asset. They agreed on a date; and booked the trip for the following week.

The flight itself was not good as there were extremely strong winds and neither was the landing! Heavy rain greeted them as they alighted from the plane and boarded the dilapidated airport bus. Now he was familiar with the country's structural condition, Tom could see that little had improved at the airport; in fact it appeared to have become a lot worse, it was a total shambles now.

With all his previous experience, he was able to give James a verbal guided tour as they drove through West Beirut and down the now familiar suicide strip.

"It was about at this point in the road; where one of Jean Bitar's American associates was shot at last month. He was on the way to pick up his wife from the airport; but didn't tell her about it not wanting to alarm her. And then on their way back, a snipers bullet shattered their rear window; just missing her." Tom gave a rueful smile. "Needless to say, she is not exactly impressed with her new home right now"

James nervously looking up at the buildings around them muttered,

"Can't say I blame her, you must be off your bloody head coming over here. Know what I think? A good British battalion would have this lot sorted out in days"

'*That's a typical arrogant ex-British army officer remark, the locals won't like that*' he thought grimly. '*If only it was that simple!*'

Apart from work, James was a man of few words, and only spoke when he felt he had something worth saying, and Tom rather hoped that this would be one of those occasions.

For the three days they were in Lebanon, unfortunately Maria was on duty, and was unable to see Tom socially; much to his disappointment, as it was the main reason why he had come. It appeared there was something brewing in that area; and all leave had been cancelled.

As it turned out Tom and James were on the last flight out of Beirut airport before a serious hijack incident took place, after that; the airport was closed for some considerable time.

The telexes and letters between Maria and Tom had become more open in content during the remainder of the year. Maria mentioned in her letters that she was getting very tired and depressed with the situation in Lebanon. She also missed her sister Celine dreadfully

Celine had left Jean Bitar about a month ago, and taken up a lucrative job offer in Canada, it was a lot safer for her there and with the high wage she was getting, and she was able to send some money home. Also like a lot of other young people, their younger brother had been shipped out to the USA for his own safety, and to enable him to finish his education at University. It was a big financial burden on the family, but one that everyone agreed would be money well spent. The little extra that Celine was sending from Canada was certainly helping in that aspect.

After much soul searching, Maria decided to retire from her police duties at the airport, but to continue putting all her energy into the airline programme that she had set up with the LF, which to her satisfaction, was proving to be very successful. She reasoned that with her duties with the LF, she could still be doing a useful job, as well as travel to the USA.

CHAPTER 7

It was Ten days before Christmas, and England was in the grip of a very cold winter spell, when Tom arrived in the office early one morning; and noticed he had just missed an incoming telex on the machine that had been aborted for some reason without a message. The telex call sign printed out was unfamiliar to Tom, but he was able to recall the sender. He typed.

'THIS IS TOM FORSTER ARE YOU TRYING TO CONTACT ME?'

After a short pause the answer came back.

'TOM, THIS IS NADIA, MARIA IS TRAVELLING TOMORROW TO THE STATES, SHE IS STAYING THREE DAYS IN PARIS, BEFORE FLYING ON TO NEW YORK, SHE WILL TRY TO CALL YOU FROM THERE.'

He replied instantly.

'I NEED TO CHECK SOMETHING, CAN YOU TELL ME THE NAME I GAVE YOU?'

The answer came back almost immediately.

'YOU MEAN BAREFOOT?'

Tom smiled to himself,

'YES. THANKS FOR THE INFORMATION NADIA. WHERE IS SHE STAYING IN PARIS'?

'THE 'MEURICE HOTEL NEAR THE 'RITZ'

'WHY?

'IF SHE HASN'T LEFT ALREADY, TELL HER I WILL TRY TO GET THERE. THE WEATHER IN UK IS AGAINST IT, BUT I'LL TRY MY BEST'

She replied,

'OK, NO PROBLEM, I AM SURE SHE WON'T OBJECT, BYE NOW'

With that he closed the line, and immediately booked a flight with the travel agent for Heathrow to Paris to coincide with Maria's expected arrival.

The journey to the airport was horrendous; with heavy snowstorms and force nine gales, he thought he would never get there. When he eventually arrived; almost everything had been shut down because of the weather. Most of the incoming aircraft were being diverted to other airports around the country. Tom looked about him in dismay. '*Now what?*' he sat down on the nearest seat feeling very despondent.

"You too buddy? Hi I'm Carl Johansson; you look as though you need to travel as much as I do." Tom turned to see a cheerful looking man with an unmistakable American baseball cap; offering his hand.

"Hi, I'm Tom Forster. I guess you're an American?"

"No you guess wrong, Canadian" he grinned, "I really need to be in Paris, I've an appointment I can't miss. Do you think we would have better luck at the ferry port?"

"It's worth a try," Tom said a bit dubiously. But Carl having spotted the ideal travel partner in Tom was already on his feet.

"We need to get across to Victoria station quickly, to get the train to Folkestone. What do you think?"

He smiled at the Canadian, he was thinking, *'I've also got an appointment I can't afford to miss, but not quite in the same way,'* and he readily agreed to give it a go.

They managed to get one of the few taxis still working in spite of the weather, and arrived at Victoria station in time to board the last train to Folkestone. When they arrived at the Port, there was just time to purchase their tickets before quickly boarding the ferry. Tom noticed it was already rocking about in the harbour under the strong winds. This didn't bode well for him, being no lover of the sea. *'I must be totally off my head to do this journey for the love of a woman,'* he mused. *'But what a woman,'* the thought of Maria brought a smile to his face.

The Ferry was crowded, "I think everyone else had the same idea" Carl grinned as the made their way down to the seating area only to find there was no sitting room left. They looked about them, all the bars were battened down and locked as rough seas were expected, and the only place to sit for the night was on the footrest of one of the empty bars.

The weather worsened with the gales becoming even stronger, resulting in people throwing up all around them. Tom averted his eyes as a young boy emptied his stomach a bit too close for comfort. *'At least this time'* he thought grimly in an effort to console himself. *'I will get the chance to see Maria without any interference from Jean Bitar.'* He swallowed hard. *'That's if I arrive in one piece!'*

As they sat hunched up leaning on the bar trying to take their minds off the rocking boat and the scene all around them, Tom was surprised to find himself telling Carl about his travels and Maria. He didn't normally confide in strangers but the Canadian had a natural ease that made him feel relaxed.

"Have you ever had any type of military training in the past?" Carl queried suddenly.

"No, not exactly, why do you ask?" Tom answered a bit taken a back. It seemed a strange question coming completely out of the blue.

"Well, from what I can gather, you travel quite a bit, and seem very confident. I just wondered if you have ever considered a little light activity for your Queen and country. "

That captured Tom's attention,

"Sounds intriguing, what does that entail?"

"Keeping your eyes open to a certain degree" Carl replied "Or should I say being aware of what is around you at all times and report every so often to your own people in London"

Tom's mind raced,

"Become a Spook you mean, doesn't one need training?"

"Are you interested or not?" Carl eyed him keenly trying to gauge his reactions. He saw the spark of excitement in Tom's eyes, and his effort to appear casual.

"Yeah possibly"

"Ok," Carl said, keeping his tone equally as casual.

"You will be contacted sometime during the first few weeks after Christmas" He stood up and stretched, "Fancy a walk to get some air? We should be coming in shortly"

"Is that all? Don't you want my contact numbers, address and all that?" Tom queried a bit mystified. Carl laughed,

"Don't worry; I am sure they have that already."

Eventually they arrived in Dunkirk around five in the morning, Tom couldn't wait to get off, his stomach was beginning to sympathise with his fellow seasick passengers.

"Right, here we go Tom, follow me, we can get a train from here direct to Paris"

Carl darted off in the direction of what Tom discovered; was the local train station; it was clear this man really knew his way around. Finally they arrived in Paris around eight o'clock.

The Canadian told Tom that he was staying at the Ritz; and coincidently; 'or was it?' the thought flitted briefly through Tom's mind, as it just so happened that the Ritz, was directly opposite the Meurice Hotel where he was staying.

They parted in the middle of the square between their two hotels, with a warm handshake.

"Well, thanks for your company Carl, I enjoyed meeting you"

"You never know Tom" Carl smiled, "Perhaps one day we will meet again"

Tom booked into his Hotel; and asked the receptionist if a Miss Khoury had arrived yet,

"Yes sir,"

The receptionist wrestling with her English pronunciation continued,

"You may speek wis 'er on ze inter phone, I weell put you through,"

Maria answered, her voice unmistakable

"Hi Tom, come up, what room are you in?

"I am still in reception". He examined his key, "Room 239 it seems"

"I am in 339 just above you"

He followed the porter, put his case in his room, and tipped the young man, and then he quickly made his way up to Maria. He was delighted and just a bit surprised at the welcoming hug and kisses he got from her, she was obviously very pleased to see him. Tom realised that she must have only just woken up, as she was still wearing a pink knee length nightdress, with its matching loose flowing negligee. *'Thank you Carl, if it wasn't for you I would still be sitting at the airport.'* he thought, as he bent over to kiss her. He could feel her soft warm body against his; and could smell the familiar perfume on her neck. They didn't speak for quite a while, locked together in an embrace which neither wanted to be the first to let go. Tom thought he had died and gone to heaven, but eventually Maria broke away,

"What happened to you last night? I heard you will arrive in the evening, but when I checked at reception they told me that all flights were cancelled from England"

Tom, was feeling quite proud of the fact he had braved the weather, answered with a broad grin,

"They were. I came over on the boat to Dunkirk, and believe me, it was a very rough trip, but I had to get to see you. It's as if every time we get an opportunity to be on our own, something is put in our way"

"You are absolutely mad," She said hugging him tighter.

"No, more like desperate," He answered with a wry smile.

"We have a lot of things we need to discuss, especially now that you are on the move to the States for a while"

He stifled a yawn, trying not to let Maria see he was totally exhausted, but she looked at him concerned,

"Why don't you have a sleep on my bed while I take my shower"

He nodded in agreement; much to his annoyance he could hardly keep his eyes open.

"Are you sure you don't mind? We never got any sleep last night, it was too rough."

He lay on her bed, and could smell her perfume on the pillow as he drifted off to sleep. He only slept for a short while; waking just as she came out of the bathroom wrapped in a large white bathrobe. She leaned over Tom to see if he was still a sleep.

When she realised that she had disturbed him she kissed him fondly on the nose and said in a very soft voice.

"Sleep some more if you want. If not go and unpack, and I will get dressed and come down to you when I am ready. Is that Ok with you?

His eyes twinkled as he reached for her hand,

"You know, I have a far better idea"

She guided him gently in the direction of the door,

"Do you my darling?" she grinned; "now that is a shame"

Maria knew only too well his meaning, especially as she was still in her bathrobe and towel.

"Ok" he shrugged defeated, "I'll have a shower and unpack, and I'll see you there in one hour"

Exactly one hour later she joined him in his room, he had showered and changed and was waiting for her. *'Wow, she is beautiful'* his eyes were immediately drawn to the shape of her breasts where he could see her nipples pressing against the deep red satin blouse. He mentally blessed Carl once again.

Their elegant hotel was located between the Place de la Concorde and the Grand Louve, near the Tuileries gardens, and only a few yards from the famous Garnier Opera House. The area was well known for the surrounding jeweller's shops in the Rue de la Paix, and Place Vendome.

"Do you know they decorate the hotel every day with two thousand or so fresh roses andorchids, and it is all tastefully styled from the 18th century"

"Let me guess, you have been reading the hotel brochure" Tom laughed. "It looks like a very expensive Hotel, what made you pick this one?" Maria tossed her hair back indignantly.

"I didn't choose it. The travel agent booked it together with the flight,"

They walked to a little pavement cafe for a coffee, where they continued their conversation; there was so much they needed to say to each other. Tom told her about the rough weather on the trip over, and his meeting up with Carl, although he didn't mention anything about the 'spook' business.

"I'm talking too much" he laughed, "Tell me what did you do last night, while you were waiting for me?" For a split second, Maria looked distracted.

"What's up?" He asked

"Sorry Tom, I was just thinking about last night. I have a couple of friends living here in Paris, and with another friend we all went out for dinner. When we returned back to their apartment, this other friend wanted more from me, a lot more. He became very aggressive, so I pretended to go to the bathroom saying I needed to freshen up, just to get away from him, and than I escaped by a side door. I wasn't going to say anything, but he has already called this morning with threats"

Tom looked worried,

"Where were your friends while all this was going on?"

"That's the whole point" she was still very tense,

"The wife had gone to bed and the husband was in another room. I felt as though I had been set up"

Tom pulled a face,

"Some friends! Not one of your smartest moves, getting yourself isolated was it?"

"True," she said, "But I had no reason not to trust them, we were talking and next thing I knew the couple had disappeared. Anyway, this morning on the phone, he said that he would see me on the plane, because he knows my flight details." Tom's face changed to anger,

"He obviously knows your hotel and room number too"

"Don't worry Tom; I can take care of this, my way. Don't let it spoil our time together, let us go shopping this afternoon"

But Tom was still worried about it, and as they left the cafe he had an idea.

"The first thing we will do is to change your New York flight. I have to go back on Friday, so let's see if we can get an earlier flight for you before mine, so you won't be here on your own"

Maria linked her arm tightly with his,

"For an English, you are very smart, you know that"

"Englishman, not English," He laughed

They went to a nearby travel agent to check for an earlier flight, and found one that took off three hours before Toms, so they booked it. Tom didn't mind the extra time at the airport, and he felt better now that he was not leaving her behind.

When they got back to Maria's room they found a note slipped under her door. As she read it she was noticeably upset at the content, and slipped it quickly into the drawer of the bedside table, saying nothing. When she went into the bathroom, Tom quietly opened the drawer and retrieved the note, he had been very concerned by Maria's reaction when she had read it He took a quick glance; and saw the name Elie Sfeir at the bottom of the page.

When Maria came back in the room Tom was laying on her bed, she went over and kissed him.

"So, has the difficult trip been worth it?"

He propped himself up on one elbow looking very serious,

"I can't say at this early stage, ask me that at the airport. And by the way with this maniacfriend of yours on the loose, I'm not leaving you alone tonight,"

"Tell me, what's happening at home" she deliberately ignored his meaning, but he guessed from her question that she wanted to know the facts on his marriage, before she accepted his protection offer.

"We have agreed a settlement, for when I leave her. But its not rubber stamped yet"

"What means, rubber stamped?" Maria looked confused,

"It means that it is still up for discussion but not finally agreed I suppose, anyway I am leaving once I know where I stand with you," It was more of a question than a statement.

Her mood quickly changed, she looked at him anxiously,

"Tom, I don't need to tell you how I feel about you, do I? But I am not going to be seen or accused of being 'the mistress' in your life. It's not fair; you have to go with your feelings on this one. I am not going to persuade you on what you should do, or offer myself as a 'goat' as you say; for your wife's benefit"

"Scapegoat you mean." He gave a short laugh as he corrected her. "But it would be a shame to waste that double bed, especially now that you need my personal protection"

She couldn't help but smile at the expression on his face, but she retorted,

"It's also a shame to waste your room if you are sleeping here."

With that Tom went back to his room to get showered and dressed for dinner, not exactly sure yet what his position was with her.

When he went back to get her, it took his breath away. Her long dark shiny hair was dressed in a Grecian style with a gold braided headband, and one long plat hanging down her back. Her figure hugging ankle length black and gold backless dress was split one side to well above her knee, emphasized by gold high heel shoes. 'She really is a stunner' Tom thought proudly, he loved the attention they got as they went down to the restaurant. When they were seated he leaned across the table to touch her hand saying softly,

"Judging by the reaction here, I am certain you will need all the protection you can get tonight, and every other night."

Maria smiled, she knew coming from Tom that this was a compliment, but she also knew his second meaning.

They lingered at the table after dinner slowly sipping their coffee feeling totally relaxed. After a while Tom looked at his watch,

"It's getting late young lady, time for bed." They made their way back to her room; and as soon as they were inside Tom closed the door and turned to take Maria into his arms, but she slipped out of his embrace and headed for the bathroom.

"I won't be long Tom, I need to get changed"

He wasn't sure what to think, but he quickly stripped down to his shorts and sat on the side of the bed waiting.

When she opened the door the bathroom light shone into the darkened bedroom silhouetting her body shape through her thin pyjamas. She laughed nervously as she noticed Tom's expression,

"That's my side of the bed, if you are wondering"

Then she said in a very quiet voice, although she was still smiling.

"Who said I accepted your protection English?"

"See me as your bodyguard, this way I guard your body. So stop talking and come here"

He pulled her towards him to kiss her, but she pulled her head back from him.

"Tom please, I need to explain, I don't want an affair with a married man, and for me it would ruin our relationship. I do love you, and nothing would give me more pleasure than to have you between the sheets, as you English say. It is just as hard for me to resist you, believe me."

He wasn't sure what she trying to say, so he tried to pull her towards him again. She took a deep breath, her eyes filled with anxiety as she begged him,

"Tom be strong for me, I am truly sorry my darling, but it is really important to me"

His heart sank; he couldn't believe that she was still not ready to commit sexually after all these years. Maria could see the hurt and disappointment on his face. She searched for the right words to explain to him how she felt,

"Tom you must understand, our Middle Eastern culture is very different from yours, and a woman's mind is also very different from the way a man thinks about sex. I have had many boyfriends that I believed at the time were the only one for me, the great love. It is all part of growing up. But if I had given myself to all of them, I would be regretting it now I am older. Look at it like this" Maria took both his hands and looked beseechingly into his eyes, desperately wanting him to understand. "When you go into a grocery shop you do not take a bite out of every apple in the shop to taste it before you purchase it; do you? Because the next customer behind you would not buy the apple, would you want to buy an apple that had been bitten by someone else?

Tom was bitterly disappointed, but trying to make light of what in his eyes; was a straight refusal, he gave a short laugh.

"I would probably go for a nice 'pear' anyway"

She frowned not really understanding the meaning of his joke.

It was beginning to dawn on him; that this was how Maria wanted their relationship to remain, at least until he had sorted out his own life back in England. Although how the hell he was going to get through this night, he had no idea.

Although she realized how Tom felt, Maria still felt extremely happy that after such a long time they would both able to spend their first ever night together, even as restricted and conditional as it now was. She slid easily beneath the duvet, and snuggled up to him.

"Would you like me to get an extra blanket in case it gets cold?"

Tom wrestled with his emotions, "No, it's fine, the room's hot enough as it is. Why do they have to have the temperature so high?" He snapped irritably, but Maria didn't seem to notice. He immediately felt sorry, but he was very frustrated with the situation. He realized he must respect her wishes, but it was almost more than he could stand to be so close to her; and not be able to love her. He lay on his back staring into the shadows, clinging on to a vague hope; that she would change her mind during the next few days.

The next morning was extremely cold so Maria put on a deep red Cossack styled woollen suit, and a white roll neck sweater. As usual she attracted many admiring looks as Tom escorted her through the hotel foyer and into the street beyond; she was every inch Parisian chic. He felt proud just to be with her, even though it still rankled a bit when he thought about the previous night.

As they wandered hand in hand around the shops and little pavement cafes, Maria began to feel edgy; and kept glancing over her shoulder

"Tom I have a distinct feeling we are being followed" Tom looked around quickly,

"Do you think it is your so called friend from the other night? I can't see anyone, but let's take a few precautions just in case"

They moved in and out of various stores, up lifts down stairs, until Maria after several more backward glances relaxed. Satisfied they were on their own again, they continued shopping and gradually forgot all about it.

On the third and final day as they left the Hotel, Tom picked up both bills to pay, but Maria protested,

"No Tom, for now I pay my own way. I hope you will not be offended, but if you pay for my room it would give people the wrong impression." Then she grinned teasingly, "Anyway, I can claim the money back. But don't worry you will have a lifetime to make up for it, I don't come cheap."

He was beginning to recognize there was not a lot of point arguing with her, although her ways seemed to him old-fashioned, deep down he admired her for it.

During the short taxi ride to the airport, he enquired with a twinkle in his eye,

"How will you manage in New York, without me as your body guard?"

She gave a knowing smile,

"I have my own protection when I get there, don't worry"

"What do you mean, young lady? You're acting like an undercover agent"

She glanced at the taxi driver and lowered her voice,

"Well, some of my skirts have splits for pockets, without pockets, if you understand what I mean. In New York I carry protection that I have strapped to my thigh just in case, because in New York you never know."

That shook him a bit, but then he laughed, his mind going off in the usual direction.

"Very sexy, so if I put my hand in your pocket, it might locate the trigger?"

This time she understood his meaning,

"First Filsey, its too late, we already left the hotel and secondly, you would only get a handful of problems that you do not need right now"

Maria smirked, pleased at her own little joke.

Considering their very different cultures, the natural humour between the two of them was amazingly reciprocated. But then the smile left his face; he was actually rather shocked by her revelation.

"Seriously, you arm yourself in New York? Do you know how to use it? Do you do the same thing in Alabama? "

"No" Maria replied, "It's not necessary, it is just for New York, in case I am alone anywhere, like on the subways. It is legal, and my uncle insisted. And yes, I know how to use firearms it is all part of my training" she gave a slight grin "Does that really shock you?"

He shook his head very slowly,

"Nothing surprises me about you, anymore"

Tom feelings for Maria were even stronger now, having spent time with her, but he was also beginning to realise; that she lived her life constantly on the edge. His stomach knotted at the thought *'She could be here today, and blown away tomorrow.'* He had noticed during those last few days together, that she had been on constant alert, continually looking over her shoulder, and he knew he could not be there all the time to protect her. A shiver ran down his spine, it was a hard lesson to learn.

At the airport they clung to each other lovingly. After four years, they had just spent their first three days alone, and neither wanted it to end. As he watched Maria walk through to the boarding gate for her New York flight, he made up his mind there and then; that he would move out of his family home early in the New Year. He felt a sense of relief as he thought, *'I've no idea what the future will bring, but I have to start from here'*

CHAPTER 8

When Tom arrived back in England the first thing he did; was to go to the local florists and arranged for two-dozen red roses to be sent to Maria in New York. The second; was to send Nadia a telex; to say Maria had left Paris a day earlier than planned. The response came back almost immediately.

'HI TOM, THIS IS BAREFOOT'

He quickly typed,

'WHO IS ELIE SFEIR?' There was a short pause before she answered

'HE IS A FRIEND OF THE FAMILY, WHY YOU ASK?'

Tom rapidly tapped the keys.

'GOOD FRIEND OR NOT, HE TRIED TO RAPE MARIA BEFORE I ARRIVED. SHE WAS VERY UPSET'

This time there was a much longer pause, then came the message

'DON'T WORRY TOM, HER BROTHER GEORGE IS HERE, HE SAID NO PROBLEM, LEAVE IT TO HIM'

Still concerned, he typed back,

'SFEIR SAID HE WOULD GET HER IN NEW YORK'

He waited for her response but the machine went quiet, and then it whirred into life again,

'TOM FORGET IT. NOTHING WILL HAPPEN; SHE IS SAFE.PLEASE LEAVE IT TO US'

They closed the telex. *'That's easier said than done'* he thought. *'I feel so bloody useless so far away'*

A couple of days later he received a phone call from Maria.

"Hi Tom, thank you, your flowers were lovely. But" She emphasised the word *'but'* sounding annoyed,

"The other thing I want to talk to you about, what the hell did you say to George?

"Not a lot, I only asked who that creep was in Paris, the so called friend of the family. Why?"

Maria replied in a quiet voice,

"You could have caused me a huge problem, but as it is, Sfier now has the problem. I cannot say anymore than that. Tell me, how did you know his name?"

He hesitated, not wanting to admit that he had read the note.

"Don't ask"

Then it dawned on her,

"You took the note from my bedside table. Right?" she gave a little laugh. "Now you too act like an agent?"

'If only she knew about the proposition I had from Carl Johansson on the Ferry' Tom felt a bit guilty for a second as he retorted, "You're quite smart for an Arab"

"Lebanese Christians are not Arabs, she responded briskly, but her good humour was restored.

"Ok, lover" he said. "You can tell me what happened later. Personally I don't care if hehad his legs broken after what he tried to do to you,"

Maria gave an odd little spluttering cough, which rather suggested to Tom that he was very close with his assumption. He changed the subject,

"Did you realize how desperate I was to get to you the night I came to Paris on the ferry? Ifound out later that on the same night; the Penlee lifeboat was lost at sea with everyone on board. There was a force nine to ten gale blowing that night,"

She gave a little gasp

"Tom, that's terrible I didn't know. It didn't seem that bad in Paris. So you risked your lifeto get to me then?"

"So it seems, but all in vain" He replied in a woebegone tone.

By now Maria was getting used to Toms double meanings,

"Not if you really love me. Anyway, I am staying here until after Christmas; and then I will join my brother Joseph in Alabama for New Year. When I get there I will call you. So have a nice Christmas, I will be thinking of you"

"You have a lovely Christmas too" Tom answered "And let's see what the next year will bring. Take care." He replaced the receiver, his mind going over their brief conversation. *'Did she say, 'You too act like an agent?' and did that mean that she was one?'* His thoughts raced on remembering other little comments she had made in the past. It crossed his mind that he might be getting into something he could not control, but even so, he still felt a buzz of excitement.

New York at Christmas was exciting for Maria. Her aunt lived in Brooklyn; so she was able to show her all the Christmas sights New York had to offer. Maria was very close to her aunt, and one evening when they were sitting quietly together, she told her about how she had met Tom; and what he meant to her, but most importantly, her worries about him being married. Her aunt was quiet for a moment as she digested all that Maria had told her, and then she smiled gently,

"We all deserve real love Maria, and if your Tom was leaving his wife anyway, then I don't see too much of a problem for your conscience. You say he was considering a divorce even before he met you, so if that is true, why are you so worried?" She sat back in her chair looking serious as another thought struck her.

"But what you do have to consider; is that if anything comes of this relationship, you would be expected to move to England. Is that what you want to do, leave your family at a time like this?"

Maria had already turned this dilemma over in her head many times, "I do love him, and I realize that I still have unfinished business at home, but I can no longer ignore my feelings. Even though we have only had a few days together it was wonderful."

She sighed, "but I suppose only time will decide what we will do." And then she shrugged dismissively,

"Anyway, it has to be his decision as it's his life that is going to be upset."

Her aunt smiled and leaned over to take her hands, she gave them a squeeze saying,

"This one really has got to you hasn't he. Are you pleased you're not a Nun anymore?"

Maria chose her words carefully

"For four years I have resisted him, and he is still there. It has to be something special. As for not taking my final vows, that's something I may never know"

Maria enjoyed Christmas with her aunt, and she was sad to leave, but the time had come to travel on to Alabama to be with her brother for the New Year as planned.

Tom had intended to go to the States to meet up with Maria, but this plan had to be shelved because things on the home front moved faster that anticipated. He had decided it was time at last to end this farce of a marriage. And then finally, after a few nasty moments with Jane regarding the usual subject of money, and also custody of the girls, it was over. He moved out of the house and into a small apartment near to his office with a strong feeling of relief, tinged by sadness at being parted from the children.

It was not long after the move; that Tom received a formal message requesting him to come to a meeting at the M16 Headquarters at Century House in Lambeth, London. No reason was given, but the way it was worded; he correctly assumed it was related to the conversation he had had with Carl on that eventful trip to Paris. He tingled with anticipation as he noted the address and time, and made his arrangements accordingly.

On the day given, he arrived in London at a large unimpressive building overlooking the Thames, and gave his name to the girl on reception. With just the merest glance at him she checked her computer; and signalled for another young woman; who took him down the stairs along a badly lit twisting corridor to a large bustling antiquated office.

Tom was surprised to see at least thirty people working there, he wasn't sure quite what he expected, but it looked just like any normal busy office.

Then a very smart young man approached him with a smile, and directed him to a vacant desk in the corner, he then asked him to complete a long detailed form. Sitting down Tom reached in his jacket for a pen and looked around, but no one appeared to notice him, so he turned his attention back to the task of filling in the paper in front of him. When it was completed, he walked across and handed it to the young man sitting at his desk nearby, who again smiled politely, and indicted for him to sit down while he briefly scanned the form.

"Thank you. This will have to be checked thoroughly, and if it's all ok, you will be required to attend a two week training course either in the north of England or Scotland. This will include written and physical tests, also a full medical before and after. Have you any questions?"

Tom couldn't immediately think of anything to ask, except,

"Will I be given time to arrange things at work; and with my family?"

"Of course" The young man smiled.

"Now I must ask you to sign the official secrets act, as you realise this is all top secret"

Tom read carefully and signed the form, and then after a brisk handshake he was shown back to the reception hall. And in just over an hour he found himself on his way home feeling slightly nonplussed by the speed of the whole meeting.

Four weeks after the visit to London he opened a slim brown envelope; which contained the date of his training course. He felt his stomach lurch with excitement, '*And this time*' he thought with satisfaction, '*I don't have to give any explanation to Jane, although I'd better let her know I will be away for a couple of weeks*' He did however feel he should offer some explanation to Maria in case she tried to contact him. He phoned her, but her answer phone clicked on.

"Hi it's me, Tom, I just wanted to let you know I shall be away for a couple of weeks on business in Scotland, and I won't be able to phone again till I get back, Take care sweetheart, speak soon." He replaced the receiver relieved that he hadn't had to go into any details.

He had received instructions; that he was to travel to London by train and make contact at Liverpool Street Station with a young woman carrying a copy of the Cosmopolitan magazine. He was told to wear the brown overcoat that he wore for the interview, and to carry his brown briefcase in his left hand, so that she would recognize him. '*Very James Bond*' he grinned reading through the letter once more on the morning of his departure.

Later that day, on the bitterly cold March afternoon, Tom stood on the long draughty station waiting for the train from Norwich to London. He stamped his feet impatiently, the train as usual; was almost twenty minutes late.

When it arrived he settled himself down thankfully on the nearest seat; and spent the hour-long journey watching the other passenger's faces, wondering what they did, and what their reaction would be if he told them that he was going to Scotland to train as a spook.

When the train pulled in to Liverpool Street station; he stepped onto the platform wheeling his suitcase with his right hand and carrying his briefcase as instructed in the left. As he approached the ticket barrier, he glanced up at the station clock; and saw it was almost nine. He looked around, 'Now what do I do?' and then he heard a woman's voice behind him with a soft Scottish accent.

"Good evening, sir"

Not sure if it was directed at him, he turned to look. It was.

"Good evening to you, young lady"

She then gave him the prearranged password,

"It's been a nice day for this time of year"

Laughing at the ludicrous suggestion of it being anything like a nice day, he replied,

"Who dreams up these stupid passwords, it's been a bloody awful day for any time of year" She threw back her head laughing in agreement; it really had been a bitterly cold day with very strong winds, heavy thunder and rain.

"I have the tickets so let's go, the train leaves at ten thirty, and we need to get across London to Kings Cross Station"

They hurried out through the ticket hall to a waiting black Mercedes complete with a chauffeur. The man smartly touched the peak of his hat and lifted the boot for Tom to put his luggage. 'Not bad, I'm beginning to like this' he thought climbing into the back seat, while the young woman got in beside the driver. The car glided away noiselessly, and the young woman looked over her shoulder, and smiled.

"Are you looking forward to your wee winter break?"

Still there were no introductions and no names mentioned. Tom smiled,

"We shall see, and I will let you know later"

The young woman pointed out of the window as they were passing St Pancras Station, and said with obvious enthusiasm,

"I think that station is the most impressive in London, It's architecturally Victorian Gothic with its granite pillars. I just love that clock tower you can see that looks like a miniature Big Ben."

Tom eyes followed her pointing finger and thought the same. The entrance to St Pancras was indeed very grand. Although living only sixty miles away, it had been a long time since he had made any social visits to the capital; he had forgotten just how interesting it could be.

"Very impressive, even more so under the spot lights"

She nodded, her eyes scanning the building,

"I studied Victorian Architecture at University. But that's another story." She twisted around in her seat to smile at him.

"You have me at a disadvantage young lady, what do I call you" he asked.

She gave him a cheeky grin, which he noted, lit up her entire face.

"From your record, being disadvantaged hasn't happened to you that often has it?"

He grinned at her sarcastic tone; it was the sort of humour he understood.

"Don't believe all you hear, it sounds as though my soon to be ex-wife has been writing your reports for you"

She returned his grin thinking, *'I have a feeling I'm going to like this one'*

Five minutes later they arrived outside Kings Cross Station, the traffic had been unusually heavy for that time of night but they still had plenty of time.

They left the car and walked along the platform until they arrived at a first class sleeping compartment. As she stepped into the carriage, the young woman looked over her shoulder at Tom,

"Elaine Simpson, but they call me Lane"

"Nice name" He answered cheerfully.

She continued briskly, "We have plenty to do while we travel; we still have some more form filling to do. I am afraid I need more detailed information about your personal life"

Teasingly he enquired,

"Information of a personal nature! Is it for you; or for Her Majesty's Secret Service?"

She retorted sharply, trying to hide a smile.

"Don't delude or flatter yourself sir. The interest is purely MI6",

Tom studied her as she made herself comfortable in the seat opposite him, *'She must be in her early twenties,'* He thought as he admired her straight full-length blonde hair. He noticed she wore very little make-up other than pale pink lipstick, and a pair of very delicate spectacles, which at the moment were perched on the end of her nose. *'I wonder if she needs them, or if she uses them for a disguise.'* He mused.

He was bought back to earth when an aging porter arrived with their suitcases at the door of the compartment, and stood looking pointedly at him. Sorting out the change in his pocket he gave the man a tip, which he hoped was appropriate, and then looked around taking in the luxury of finding himself in a private first class train compartment, complete with its own mini-bathroom.

"Someone paid a lot of money for this trip" he commented to Lane.

"Don't worry, if you fail the course we will send you the bill"

She laughed seeing Tom's expression at her answer. He smiled back at her as he thought with amusement, *I'm going to have to keep on my toes with this young woman*

"Now, lets get down to business. Until you are accepted you are given and known to everyone on this course by a number, in your case 101. It's a little dramatic; but it's safer. When you're out with the others training I will be in the gym working out, or at the office in the communications department, if you need to contact me."

Tom nodded briefly, "Fine by me"

Lane looked at him over the top of her glasses,

"Do you understand the purpose of MI6?" She questioned.

"I've got a rough idea," then he grinned, "but I'm sure you are going to tell me anyway"

"It is to obtain and provide information relating to the actions or intentions of persons outside the British Isles and to perform other tasks relating to those concerning the interests of national security" .she quoted as if reading from a manual.

"Yes miss" he replied meekly, hanging his head like a small schoolboy.

Lane smothered a grin and continued briskly,

"I hope that you do. And another thing for you to keep in mind, I don't fraternise with operatives" She gave him an inquisitive smile, "The odd lunch maybe, if you're paying, but dinner is a definite no-no. So let's lay down some ground rules before we start."

Tom shook his head slowly, his face stretching to a broad grin

"You are a typical feisty Scot. Did you make those rules?"

She laughed,

"Of course"

He burst out laughing at her vain assumption; for once the thought hadn't crossed his mind considering his relationship with Maria.

Although it was getting very late, Lane continued to ask him various questions about his lifestyle, wife, children, business, which he felt she almost certainly knew already,

"I understand you have left the family abode?"

"Correct. Is that an official question, or did you add that one to the list?" He joked

She ignored his comment.

"Who is Maria Khoury?"

That certainly took him by surprise,

"A very beautiful Lebanese girl I met about three years ago"

"You know that we will have to check her out, providing you pass the course"

He shrugged his shoulders indifferently,

"Be my guest, maybe you can tell me more about her; when you find out"

She looked at him quizzically.

"I am sure that we have a file on her, 101"

"Now why doesn't that surprise me?" he laughed sarcastically.

The motion of the train was making Lane tired; she had already kicked off her shoes.

"I think that's all I need today" She yawned, stood up, put away her papers and made her way to the tiny bathroom. When she returned she had changed into white tracksuit bottoms and an army green coloured T-shirt, she pointed to the lower tier of the two small bunk beds.

"I will sleep here if you have no objection"

"Be my guest." He picked up his toilet bag and headed for the bathroom, "If you get cold in the night give me call, I'm a light sleeper"

"I am sure that will not be necessary." She snapped sharply.

He poked his head back round the bathroom door; not surprised by her hostile response,

"I meant I could get you an extra blanket" he grinned,

Lane flushed realizing she had jumped to the wrong conclusion,

"Sorry, I thought........."

He wanted to laugh out loud at her flustered expression, but thought better of it as he interrupted her apology,

"You can trust me, believe me, I was only teasing you"

Lane visibly relaxed, lay back and pulled the covers up to her chin.

"Oh good, then sweet dreams 101"

It turned extremely cold during the night, and Lane was very restless in her sleep keeping Tom awake. He got up very quietly and got another blanket from the overhead cupboard and, gently laid it over her, almost instantly she relaxed; and slept peacefully until morning.

The train stopped at Newcastle, which woke them both. Tom peered over to the lower bunk,

"Don't tell anyone that we slept together last night will you"

"Very funny. She yawned "Go and get us some coffee so we can wake up"

"Is that a request, or an order.........Sugar?"

Lane was beginning to like this man more and more, and his cheeky manner, but she kept a straight face.

"No not an order, a request. No sugar, no milk"

"I suppose you take your Scotch neat too" he joked

"As a matter of fact... " She started defensively.

"Oh dear," he raised his hands in submission. "I shouldn't have asked that one, should I?"

Just at that moment the train pulled in at a station, and a waiter knocked on their door with coffee and biscuits, "Saved by the bell, of rather the coffee," he laughed. Lane sipped her drink thoughtfully,

"Thank you for last night"

"Oh no, I didn't did I?" he said in mock horror; and then laughed. "Ok then, how many marks out of ten?"

Lane shot him a scornful look

"Very clever, I meant thanks for the blanket; I was freezing but too tired to get out to find one"

He gave a little bow,

"My pleasure, young lady"

The train eased out of the station and continued on towards their final destination Edinburgh. Lane in typical female fashion occupied the bathroom for the next half and hour, eventually reappearing looking fresh and ready for the new day,

"Be quick 101, we only have a few minutes before we arrive"

Grabbing his toilet bag, he replied,

"Typical, you hog the bathroom and then tell me to hurry. You women, you're all the same"

"And you are an expert so I'm told,"

Lane was getting into the swing of this word game now.

He laughed

"Ouch that remark was below the belt. I'll let you freeze next time"

"Next time? 101, aren't you being rather presumptuous? "

"You mean we are not going back to London together?" Tom queried innocently.

"Yes" She smiled, "But that will be during daylight hours"

It was still misty and quite dark when they finally arrived in Edinburgh. They then had a thirty-mile trip by taxi to a sleepy little fishing village, located on the outskirts of Dunbar, where they had been pre-booked into a hotel resembling a small castle.

Lane checked them in; and they were allocated adjoining rooms at the end of a long corridor with double connecting doors.

Tom left his bag on the bed and had a quick shower, before going down to the dining area to see if breakfast was still being served. Lane was already seated at a table dressed for a workout, she had her hair tied back, and was wearing a black tracksuit. Beside her on another chair was a woollen hat balancing on top of her ski-jacket. He crept up behind her,

"Its not dinner, so may I join you"

She smiled, and scooped her clothes off the chair beside her, dumping them unceremoniously on to the floor,

"Of course, you may. By the way" she said as he sat down, "I have been reading up on your file to date. And I think that I may have misjudged you"

He answered without hesitation,

"On that very point, we are surely agreed"

"Don't be so positive in making your point 101, you could hurt a girls feeling"

Tom smiled "Can't have you calling all the shots can we"

For the next few days Tom was engrossed in a mixture of weapon training and fitness tests.

The entrance medical was very thorough; and he was pleased that he passed with no trouble as he prided himself on keeping fit. The next five days were extremely gruelling, he started with light training, and if that went well it would be followed by heavier combat instruction.

During this particular bonding period he made quite a few new friends, although he only knew them by their number tags hanging around their necks. It became quite normal after a few days to address each other in this manner.

Before long it was time for the final exam, this was basic general geography, which he found quite easy having travelled a great deal in his business life. In addition to this, there was a test of mathematics and leadership skills.

The day before they were due to return home; each recruit was called individually for an interview with a high-ranking civil servant and given their results.

He was amazed; he had achieved a grade of ninety four percent. Lane showed almost as much pride in his achievement as he did; as she explained to him exactly what that meant.

"It's good Tom, you could now be considered for covert operations, rather than just a footsoldier. They were very impressed with you, so well done"

He was overjoyed with his results, although a bit embarrassed by all the fuss; he covered it as usual by joking,

"Ah, so I do have a name after all. I was beginning to think I was hatched, not born"

He laughingly continued

"How about dinner, all of us, you can pay if you feel so bad about it"

"You are a cheeky B…"

Tom raised his eyebrows, interrupting her unladylike description of him,

"Now, let's get the others together and make a night of it, agreed?"

"Fine, but you pay"She smiled.

He laughed out loud.

"A typical Scot"

The evening was a big celebration for all of them. They had all passed without exception, but as Tom was top of the class; he was nominated to buy the first round of drinks. After they had finished their dinner at the hotel, they went on to a nightclub in Edinburgh to complete the celebration into the small hours.

Tom found himself in Lane's company most of the evening; which he had no objection too; he liked her company, as she clearly liked his.

During one very slow dance, she snuggled up to him resting her blond head on his shoulder.

"If I recall; you made the rules?" he whispered jokingly in her ear.

"There are always exceptions to rules". She answered softly, "And by the way, the adjoining door in our rooms; may not have been locked on my side. But there you are; now you will never know"

He glanced down at her a little concerned, unsure whether to take her confession seriously or not, and thought it best to joke,

"Now you tell me"

Lane immediately regained her composure hoping that he had not seen how she felt. For the first time in her life, Lane had fallen for a man that she knew she could not have.

"Don't worry Tom, I'm only joking. That was certainly not on my agenda"

At that moment the music stopped to change tempo, she kissed him on the cheek, excused herself and fled to the ladies-room, she didn't want to embarrass herself in front of him; or the others. Tom watched her walk away thinking worriedly *'I hope I haven't given the wrong impression, that young lady is not as tough as she tries to make out.*

The next morning they were on their way back to London. Lane had bought a couple of newspapers at the station for Tom, and some magazines for herself.

Once they were settled on the train, she tried to ease the slight atmosphere between them over last nights little incident,

"I'm sorry Tom, if I embarrassed you last night, I don't usually react that way. Your Maria is a very lucky girl" She added anxiously, "I hope we will always be friends"

He was moved by her sincerity, and knew that he had to be ultra careful in his reply as she had just confirmed his thoughts from last night.

"Thanks Lane and you are a very beautiful and honest young woman who I respect very much. I too hope we can be close friends for a very long time to come."

Then he added with a grin to lighten the mood,

"It was a strange feeling last night, wondering if your door was open"

She burst out laughing, protesting,

"I made sure I locked it last night, so you didn't think I had made you an offer"

The tension now relieved they settled back to enjoy a relaxing journey home.

Lane as she had done in the outward trip slipped off her shoes and slept for a few hours, sometimes just half waking as the train pulled in to stations en-route. Tom read his papers from cover to cover until he too dozed off with the motion of the train.

They arrived back into Kings Cross during the early evening rush hour. Lane's chauffeur took them across London to Liverpool Street station for Tom to catch his train back home. As they were saying their good-byes he took hold of Lane's hand and kissed it, her bright blue eyes looked up into his,

"Can't you do better than that?"

Tom put his arms around her and pulled her towards him, kissing her on each cheek gently. She reached up and put her gloved hands firmly on either side of his face and gave him a delicate kiss, so delicate in fact that their lips barely touched. He looked down at her face, knowing full well that if he made a wrong move it could give out the wrong signals once again.

"Any better?"

She was clearly upset, but she managed to hold back the tears,

"A little bit, yes, but please take good care of yourself in the field, I will never forget you Tom Forster, and you better believe that. And I sincerely hope everything goes well for you and Maria, tell her from me that she is a very lucky lady."

Soon he was on the train home, thinking about the last two weeks and what it meant for the future. He knew once he was signed up there was no way back. He was also aware that one could never officially resign, and if you retired and remained a 'sleeper' they could always call upon you wherever you were in the world. *'Let's hope my first assignment will be a nice simple one.'* He thought as he closed his eyes and leaned back in his seat.

But Tom was soon to learn that there was no such thing!

CHAPTER 9

As soon as he got back home Tom phoned Maria, he didn't tell her anything about the past two weeks, except that all went well. But he did have a proposition to put to her

"Maria I have some business in Wisconsin in April, any chance of you coming up from Alabama for a few days?"

She answered casually, trying to hide her excitement,

"Maybe, fix your dates and I will check it out,"

But the next day things didn't go exactly to plan. The person he was seeing in Wisconsin was taken sick, and there was nobody else he could re-arrange the meeting with at the factory, so he had to call Maria back

"Maria, I am sorry, I have to cancel Wisconsin, but how about a couple of weeks in Bermuda? I need a break, and to see you. Can you get there?"

"I don't have a problem with that" She replied, "Will you organize the tickets or me?"

"Its ok I will" He wasn't going to leave anything to chance this time.

When he told his daughters what he was planning, they both got extremely upset. They didn't seem to want to let him out of their sight, even for a short while. This worried him more than he cared to admit, and his conscience got the better of him, so he rang Maria once again,

"I am so sorry Maria, but I can't go, the girls are very upset, I think this break up has had a worse effect on them than I thought"

She was very understanding,

"Don't worry; the girls must always come first Tom. I have told you that"

The next day after having a chat with the girls, he discovered that it was nothing to do with him going away; they were not bothered about that at all, so he changed his mind yet again.

'What the hell will she think' Tom thought, 'probably tell me to go to hell.' But to his surprise she understood his feelings very well.

"Don't worry Tom. Do whatever you feel comfortable with. But can I pack my bag now or not," she laughed.

"Yes, I guess you can, but you won't need a lot" He retorted

"Filsey buggers you English" came her quick response.

"It would appear you are really getting the hang of the English language," Tom laughed.

He loved the way she mixed up her English pronunciation with her Arabic accent, but he had to admit to himself; that all her descriptive words were most likely applicable.

Maria's flight to Bermuda from Alabama; even with a stop over in Atlanta, still got her to the airport an hour before Tom, and she waited in anticipation for his flight to arrive. They were both keenly aware that this holiday could be 'make or break' time concerning their future relationship.

Tom had booked the 'Elbow Beach' in Paget, a five star hotel with independent chalets spread about in secluded gardens. He was feeling very upbeat as he signed them in and picked up the room key. He grinned as he opened the door to their room, and whispered suggestively in her ear,

"One room, one bed for fourteen nights. You are going to be so tired"

"You're Filsey" She retorted

"I'm filthy, not filsey"

"So you recognize yourself then?" She quipped

"Oh dear a smart ass I see" he answered reaching out to take her in his arms. She kissed his lips briefly; and wriggled out of his embrace,

"Later my love. We only have time to get changed for dinner"

Dinner was the last thing on Tom's mind, but he gave himself a quick shake; and obediently did as she asked.

They made a striking couple as they made their way down to the restaurant. Maria wore a knee length white flowing cotton dress, with a wide gold belt. Her hair was platted into one dark braid, which reached down her back, set off by a gold and crystal headband. Tom completed the picture in a light grey suit, white shirt, and a typical English necktie. More than one head turned as they were shown to their table. Much later, after a leisurely meal, they strolled out to explore the gardens within the hotel grounds. Gold coloured lanterns illuminated their way, creating a romantic atmosphere as they wandered along the narrow paths. Tom slipped his arm around her waist.

"How do you feel now we have time to be together at last?"

"I will let you know in the morning," She laughed mischievously.

They made the way slowly back to their room, at long last it was going to be their first real night together. Maria was feeling a little apprehensive hoping they would not be disappointed, they had waited such a long time for this day.

She rather self-consciously removed her belt and un-zipped her dress, keeping her back to him and laid the dress on a stool beside the bed. He caught his breath as she turned and shyly smiled at him. Her heart raced; it was not that difficult to read his mind.

Tom didn't move, as Maria sat on the edge of the bed and carefully rolled down her stockings. And then just as he decided to reach out for her, she stood up and walked towards the bathroom smiling at him,

"I am going to have a quick bath. I won't be long Tom I promise"

'Oh God' he groaned inwardly, 'Surely it's not going to be a repetition of Paris'

In the bathroom she turned on the taps and poured a somewhat over generous amount of bubble bath into the water. Removing the rest of her underwear, she stepped into the bath and immersed her body in the bubbles. Teasingly she called out.

"Tom darling, what are you doing?"

He pretended he had not heard. She called out again this time in a soft inviting voice,

"Darling"

His heart started to beat a little faster as he answered her, trying to sound cool and casual,

"Is there anything I can do for you madam?"

Her voice was husky,

"Why don't you come and see. Bring the champagne from the fridge and two glasses"

Without any more hesitation he picked up the champagne and a glasses and joined her in the bathroom. Forgetting he was still wearing his boxer shorts; he stepped into the bath very carefully; and sat at the opposite end to Maria.

"This bath was certainly not meant for two." He laughed trying to wriggle out of the shorts,

"You sure put a lot of bubbles in this bath didn't you? It will take ages to disappear"

She laughed,

"Now you have to wait a little while longer to see me. I didn't see what I was getting for my money, so why should you? And you never know, I might want a refund".

Tom splashed a handful of bubbles at her

"You cheeky Arab"

There was no room in the bath to manoeuvre; and no words were needed as Tom finished his champagne and got out of the bath. Wrapping himself in a towel he returned with the bottle to the bedroom and waited. As soon as he left the bathroom Maria quickly dried herself, and massaged some oil onto her body before putting on her small bathrobe. She made her way back to the bedroom feeling far more relaxed as the champagne and warm bath took their effect. Still holding on to her empty glass she sat on the edge of the bed, Tom leaned towards her to refill her glass,

"That's a very nice smell, what is it?"

"It is baby oil, I always use it after my shower every night" she replied softly, seemingly unaware that the front of her robe had opened to her waist, so that her oily breasts were now visible to him. But a quick glance at her face told him she was very aware of the effect she was creating.

Before he had time to make a move, Maria slipped the robe off her shoulders and dropped it behind her; and in one quick movement she straddled him, pushing him back onto the pillow.

"Lay back English, I will put some oil on you, it will make you relax"

Reaching out she picked up a small bottle from the bedside table and proceeded to apply oil to his bare chest with gentle massaging movements, at the same time very slowly and seductively applying any excess oil to her breasts. She kissed his chest very gently, running her lips up to his neck, her teeth playfully nipping his ear before returning back to his lips. Her knees were on either side of him pinning his arms down; she was taking total control of their first passionate lovemaking encounter. Tom thought he had died and gone to heaven, he had never experienced anything like this before.

Maria gazed down at his face; all worries forgotten, she wanted to show him just what true caring love was all about. And now there was no going back, she was determined to provide all the love that he deserved. There was no more doubt in her mind.

Next morning she awoke, got out of bed and lent over Tom giving him a light kiss on the cheek, whispering.

"Hi sweetheart, are you awake?"

His head still buried in the pillow he mumbled back to her,

"Still want a refund?"

She gave him a playful smack on his bottom,

"You will learn, I suppose. I have to train you a little bit more. But," she gave an exaggerated sigh, "I think that it may take quite a while. However I do like a challenge"

He jumped up on the bed and made a grab at her, but she ran laughing into the bathroom

They spent their first full day sunbathing; Maria wore a bright red bikini, trimmed with gold braid on her hips, a very modern eye-catching design.

Tom layback on the sun bed; lazily watching the admiring looks she attracted from the other guests; thinking rather smugly, *'you can all look as much as you want. She is mine.'* He had never felt so contented in his life before.

. Later that evening after dinner they went back to their room, and as Maria took the key to open the door, he crept up behind her joking,

"If I put you in an arm lock like this, what can you do about it?"

Maria instinctively put her right arm around his waist then tipped her hip so that Tom was slightly lifted off the floor and off balance. She then turned him round holding his arm and threw him onto the bed backwards. With the speed of her reaction he bounced off the bed onto the floor and sat there roaring with laughter. Maria rushed to his side in concern,

"Oh Tom, I am so sorry, are you Ok?"

Although he was laughing, he was also amazed by her swift reaction

"I don't have to worry about you taking care of yourself, do I?"

She pulled a face as she explained,

"I was trained in the police force, although I am a little rusty, is that what you say?

"Are you rusty in all departments?" He grinned mischievously.

"Cheeky. She laughed; your memory has faded very quickly. That's old age creeping on"

"Oooh that hurt, Tom grinned, "But you must teach me some of those moves sometime"

Not wishing to go into more detail on the subject of her work or self defence, Maria decided to use her own feminine methods of distraction by slowly un-buttoning and removing her blouse. She then un-zipped her skirt and let it drop to the floor, waiting for Toms' predictable reaction to her seductive manoeuvre

"That's not the moves I meant, but don't let me stop you. Is this another lesson in the art of seduction?"

Maria laughed, and pushed him back onto the bed.

"No, because it is your turn to seduce me tonight, English!

The following evening as they lay on their bed, Tom decided it was time they discussed their future plans.

"Maria, give me some background. Why is it that only now you have accepted to come here with me as man and wife, when you have rejected the entire idea for four and half years?"

She thought deeply before answering,

"You were married, I know you still are, but now you have left home. I did not want to be the cause of your break up; you had to make your own decision. I could not to tell you my feelings until you did, because I did not want to have that on my conscience."

He interrupted her

"At what point did you have feelings? Because to be honest, I can't say I noticed any difference in your attitude towards me, especially through the earlier years."

Maria looked thoughtful,

"You mean, when did I have any love for you? She smiled gently, "Almost from the beginning I suppose,"

Tom interrupted again

"From my side, I think maybe I was rather too obvious, right?"

She nodded in agreement, as she searched for the right words in English to make him understand.

"But I still had to wait to see and test your real personality and this takes time"

He was still puzzled,

"Ok, but the confusing thing to me is that whatever your feelings for me, you were stillprepared to get engaged to that so-called boyfriend at one point"

Maria broke in indignantly before Tom had finished,

"Who said this, me? It was never on my mind to do that. Don't think life was easy for me. I was suffering too, and the more we contacted each other the worse it got for me. This is why I wanted to stop many times, because it was driving me crazy."

She paused for breath then continued

"Tom, I didn't see any hope for us until I got to Paris, then things changed. And as for poor Alain, he was my 'boyfriend' I suppose. But he was always restricted to kissing me on the cheek. For almost three years or more he suffered with me, that is why we argued so much, it was always about the same thing he must have been very frustrated, poor boy. Anyway in the end it was like going out with my brother, that's how I saw him the last year, and any sexual relationship would have felt like insect to me".

He burst out laughing

"You mean incest, not insect"

Maria laughed, "I know what I mean"

"Seriously though, what else do I need to know about you?" Tom asked with a smile.

"Need to know, is a very good question, darling," she retorted firmly.

He held his hands up in surrender,

"Ok, I understand I don't need to know anything, but you do have an air of mystery about you, what is it? Are you involved in some sort of undercover work connected in some way with this Phoenician person that Nadia told me about? Who is he? What does he do?"

Maria's chin tilted proudly as she answered,

"Believe me Tom, one day the Western world will have the Muslim fundamentalist problem that we have now, and then they will understand the hell we are going through. They will have wished that they had supported us. As for the 'Phoenician' you know I cannot reveal the identity of this person, or what he does, not even to you"

He felt a little hypocritical, asking questions like that, when he himself was just about to start working with MI6. Maria cuddled up closer to him,

"Why you are asking so many questions? Firstly you know I am in the army, which is linked to the airport police department. I am also head of a part-time ambulance crew, and I used to model fashions. The rest is on a need to know basis and you my sweet darling, do not need to know" She kissed his chest hoping he would now put it out of his mind.

"You don't trust me, I see" He sighed dramatically.

Taking his reply a lot more seriously than it was initially intended, she sat up and lent over him putting her hands on each side of his face; and looked earnestly into his eyes.

"Darling listen to me, trust doesn't come into it. Tell me, why put other people in danger? Just know I love you very much. I am here isn't that enough?" With a broad smile, she changed the subject. "Now, let's talk about you. What is your wife really like?"

'What a mood stopper' he thought. 'Here I am lying in bed with one of the most beautiful women in the world, and she wants to talk about my estranged wife.' Staring at the ceiling, he answered in a bored voice, not seeing the teasing smile on her face.

"Attractive, fair hair, five foot five, a little insecure, do you want more?"

"But you must have loved her at one time" She quizzed,

Tom thought for a few seconds,

"We were both very young when we met, and as we both became more mature I guess our goals and ideals in life changed, sometimes drastically. We are divorcing if that's your point, because neither of us can continue the life we have been leading over these past few years"

He paused again for a few seconds to think, as Maria remained silent, listening intently

And now, here I am," He turned to her, his face softening "In bed with the sexiest woman on earth"

She knew where this final compliment was leading up to.

"Sleep, filsey English"

She laughed softly reaching across him for the light switch, very slowly dragging her warm uncovered breasts across his chest. With a muffled chuckle she kissed him, and switched off the light whispering,

"You can see me in your dreams tonight"

"Ok but this time, behave yourself" he whispered back.

She giggled and slid down the bed with her back to him. They lay there in total darkness for a couple of minutes, then Tom remarked casually,

"You know, when Lebanese people mean 'yes' they shut their eyes tight and when they mean 'no' they raise their eyebrows,

"Mmmmm"

"I wondered how you manage in the dark."

She didn't answer the question as she guessed what was coming next. He waited silently for a few more moments; and then just as she was almost asleep, he kissed her ear and whispered,

"I will have to assume you now have your eyes tightly closed"

She burst out laughing, and turned over to face him.

They spent the next few days just sunbathing and swimming, and one morning when they were sitting around the pool; Tom noticed a big scar on Maria's shinbone, which was becoming more prominent as her suntan developed. He reached down and gently touched her leg,

"What happened to you?"

She instinctively put her hand out to cover the scar,

"Its nothing, it shows up more in the sun"

"Bullet wound?" he queried

"No shrapnel, I think you call it?"

"Yes, that's right. So tell me; how did it happen?"

"Do I have to Tom?"

"Well; not if you don't want to, but I'd like to know"

Maria hated talking about the things that had happened in the past, especially the War. But she realized that Tom needed to know about her life, as she did about his.

"Ok. It happened when the war first began, we were living over in West Beirut, and we had to leave in a hurry to get to the East. Women and young girls were being raped, and cut, you know where." She glanced at his face, he looked horrified, but she continued.

"George and I drove a jeep between East and West to bring all of our family out. And then we went back many times for other people. The last time however, we were forced to leave the vehicle in a hurry; and a mortar shell landed near me as I was running for cover, a piece of the road went deep into my leg." She shrugged "That's all, no big deal"

Tom was very quiet, his mind going over what she had just told him. *'Dear God! No big deal!'* His heart swelled with admiration for this woman that he loved more than he could ever have believed possible. He took a long slow breath, before saying quietly.

"You were lucky then?"

There were tears in her eyes as she replied,

"Luckier than a lot of the young Christian girls. They were terrible times"

She struggled to continue, her mind reliving the horrors.

"Ok, forgetting the house, that's not so important. We lost everything, our entire photo memories, clothes, everything. We had to leave with nothing. But at least we are all still alive." Maria shuddered. "They took our neighbours daughters into the street, tortured and raped them, then killed them in front of their families. So yes, I suppose I was lucky, very lucky"

He desperately wanted to comfort her, but wasn't sure how.

"One day I will make it up to you, when we are together for good."

With a lightning change of mood she looked up and grinned,

"Is that a proposal, then lover?"

The question caught him completely unaware, but he readily answered.

"I think its bloody fate," He kissed her and smiled "Probably mine"

"Then I accept, my lovely English"

She looked at him; her eyes wet, her voice choking with emotion,

"I do love you so very much, and always have"

He too was battling with his emotions, and for once remained silent as he took her in his arms; oblivious to the other people around them and held her close. After a few moments he queried,

"What did you do when you left school?" There was still so much he wanted to know about her extraordinary life, things he found hard to even imagine.

"More questions?" Maria sighed, lying back in her seat. "Ok, as soon as I left college I went into a Convent to become a nun, I was there for about six months. I used to take care of the youngest of the orphans, and I loved it. Then I heard that my mother was getting sick with the worry of loosing me to the convent, and desperately wanted me to come home" She paused deep in thought; remembering how her aunt had been persuaded to talk her into going back home. "I did not want to leave, but I loved my mother very much"

Once again she gazed into the distance: her mind going back to that heart wrenching decision of choosing between the convent and her mother's happiness.

"If you had, you would never have met me" he wanted her to go on with her story.

She pushed her thoughts to the back of her mind and gave a wry little smile.

"Exactly my darling, this is my thinking, would it not have been better for everyone, you, your wife, and your children?"

He ignored that last remark; he didn't want to go into that again.

"Then after the convent, what did you do?"

Warming to a subject that she clearly felt happier with, her face brightened.

"Oh I went back to college. It was in the good days; when we had both communities; Muslim and Christian at our college. I was the president of the Christian sector, but then the situation in our country got worse and eventually everything collapsed, including college". She paused, and lit up a cigarette. "So then I took a job in the Beirut office of Czechoslovakian airlines. I also did a bit of fashion modelling with Celine at the posh hotels in the evenings. It was fun, but the type. of people that hung around after the girls was not so good, so we packed it in".

He moved his head slightly as her cigarette smoke drifted across his face; it had always worried him that she smoked so much.

"Is this why you smoke? He queried "It's not good for you, or me come to that"

Maria shrugged her shoulders; she knew he didn't like her smoking.

"I'm sorry but you have to suffer this small bad habit until things calm down in my country." She glanced at him out of the corner of her eye and gave a mischievous grin; as she stubbed out more than half of the cigarette in the ashtray,

"Enough talking, or are you going to waste your days and nights asking me questions?"

Tom took that as a hint. He helped her to her feet; and they made their way back to their room, where they stayed for the rest of the afternoon until early evening.

He lay back on the pillow watching Maria as she slept; thinking about the oily massage she had given him; and sharing a bath, it was all so new and exciting to him, and he was eager to learn. It was this sort of intimate contact that he had never in his life experienced before. Even though he had been married for more than sixteen years.

He smiled as she turned in her sleep and cuddled up to him, *'This girl knows exactly what she wants from a relationship,'* he thought happily. *'There's no doubt about it. It's for life, or nothing.'* And he drifted off to sleep feeling very happy and content.

One morning a couple of days later he woke very early, the room was very hot and clammy, he knew there was no way he would be able to get anymore sleep. He just lay there watching Maria; not wanting to move for fear of disturbing her. The heat in the room was making her bare tanned back glisten with moisture. Reaching out he stroked her long dark hair spreading out over the pillow, his heart almost bursting with love for her. He couldn't even begin to contemplate his life without her now. She stirred half-awake. Barely opening her eyes she rolled over and lazily smiled up at him.

At that moment a shaft of bright sunshine broke through the open doors from the veranda, highlighting Tom's face. Maria just momentarily caught sight of his loving expression before closing her eyes to the bright sunlight. Puckering her lips she offered him a kiss, but before he could respond; she had once more drifted back to sleep.

He couldn't resist her any longer. Leaning over he kissed her on her neck, pushing her hair to one side, playfully nibbling her ear. He felt her body respond even in her sleep. Very lightly he kissed her neck and following the contours of her back down to the base of her spine, gently easing the sheet back to reveal her naked body. Maria stirred again and rolled over; trapping the sheet around her body, moaning softly she snuggled back down on the pillow. He could see there was no way she was going to wake up.

He gave in and glanced at his watch and saw that breakfast would be served on the veranda very soon, '*I had better have a shower before the waitress arrives*' he thought with a smile. '*Perhaps I'd better make it a cold one*' Pulling the sheet up to cover Maria, he crept out of bed and quietly went into the bathroom. A few minutes later Maria woke disturbed by the sound of running water, she slipped out of bed she went into the bathroom to join Tom in the shower.

Without saying a word she picked up the soap and sponge and started washing his back. He turned and took the soapy sponge from her and squeezed the sponge over her head, watching as the soap trail slowly descended down over her curves; and trickle around their feet into the shower tray. Gently he turned her around and continued to cover her back in trails of soapy bubbles. Maria took control of the sponge once again and squeezed the soap over Tom's chest. Then their eyes met and the mood was lost as they both burst out laughing at the state of themselves, they were totally covered in an excessive amount of soap. At that precise moment the doorbell rang, Tom choking back his laughter said,

"You go sweetie, I can't, and it will only be the waitress and I don't think she will want to see me like this,"

"But Tom, I am covered in soap and shampoo" she protested, "It will drip everywhere."

Still protesting she took a small towel and covered her-self as much as possible, wishing that she had her robe, which she had left in the bedroom well out of reach. She peered round the bathroom door but could see no one; so she tiptoed out. Suddenly a waiter, not the usual waitress appeared from the direction of the veranda, where he had just left the breakfast. He smiled at Maria; who was now stranded between the bathroom and the bedroom,

"Good morning madam, I am Steven, your waiter for today"

Tom on hearing voices; but not realizing it was a male voice, pushed the bathroom door closed.

A broad grin spread across the waiter's face, as he stood there looking at her. '*Oh God, I expect he wants a tip*' Maria thought, wandering how she could get to her bag beside the bed.

She didn't dare move; or adjust the small towel an inch as it was hardly covering her now, so she kept her bare soap covered rear facing the closed bathroom door. A small puddle of dripping soapy water began to spread over the uncarpeted floor. She smiled nervously,

"I am sorry I don't appear to have any change on me at this moment"

Still grinning he appeared to be looking past her. She assumed Tom had opened the bathroom door. "No problem Madam" the waiter replied and left the room smiling.

As he closed the door, she turned to go back in the bathroom and screamed in horror,

"Oh my God"

She had been careful enough to ensure that the towel was covering the front of her, but behind her the full-length mirror on the bathroom door had reflected her wet soapy rear. The waiter had had a full and most enjoyable view of her naked bottom.

Tom called from the bathroom,

"What's the problem?"

Maria, embarrassed and angry with herself went back into the bathroom holding her towel in her hand, only to find Tom drying himself with a full size bath towel.

"Where did you find that towel?"

He looked up surprised at her tone of voice, as she continued crossly,

"The waiter got a good view of my rear from that stupid mirror on the door, why did you close it? Didn't you hear that it was a man out there and not a woman? All I had was this silly little towel."

Although he thought it was hilarious he tried to keep a straight face,

"Don't worry, you have most likely made the poor mans day. And if you got it, flaunt it, that's what I say. And you my sweetheart, have got plenty"

Maria tried not to smile; she was still annoyed at herself, and ignoring his remark she protested,

"I don't like this idea of people just knocking and then letting themselves in like this, if it had been the waitress then that's not so bad, but a young waiter it is not nice at all"

"Ask him if it was nice or not" Tom said laughing as he left the bathroom. Maria showered and put on her cotton robe before joining him on the veranda.

They spent the rest of the breakfast joking about her partial exposure, and Maria was starting to see the funny side. After they had finished eating she lit up a cigarette and picked up the local newspaper,

"I didn't know you were at war"

Tom looked up surprised,

"Neither did I, with whom?"

"Argentina invaded the Falkland Islands"

She continued reading aloud.

"I never even knew you had a dispute that must have been a quick decision"

She handed him the paper and he glanced through the article saying in typically English fashion,

"Our boys will soon sort them out, that's for sure"

Maria raised her eyebrows, and checked the comment that sprung to her mind. '*Huh! The English, such confidence*'

That evening there was a party organized by the hotel for their guests, so they thought they should attend. Maria put on a very short mini-skirt, and a skimpy T-shirt.

"Wow, that's a bit saucy" he grinned. "Very nice"

She was not quite sure what he meant; but she took it as a compliment by the look on his face. But when they arrived the doorman wouldn't let Maria in; as the age minimum was eighteen years. Maria laughed and protested that she was well past eighteen, but the doorman was serious, the only way in was for her to produce her passport.

"I expect they think you are with your father" Tom remarked ruefully as they walked back to their room to get the required proof,

She smiled at his expression,

"I don't think so. But it's a nice compliment for me, reducing my age by eight years. I hope they do that when I am forty"

"Anyway" He grinned. "Now I know what happened, the waiter knows the doorman and he passed the word, that you have a butt of a sixteen year old"

She laughed and kissed his cheek,

"Now you really have made me feel good, filsey English"

The rest of the evening went very well and they finished the night with their usual slow walk along the white sandy beach lit by a beautiful full moon, back to their room.

The next morning, to Maria's relief, the waitress was back on breakfast duty.

That evening they decided to eat away from the hotel at a fish restaurant in Hamilton. After they had been shown to their seats Maria looked around,

"Tom, look over there. That man sitting in the blue shirt, I am sure it's that breakfast waiter"

Tom glanced round to where she was looking.

"Well they must pay them well to be able to eat here. Don't worry about him"

But Maria was curious, there was something about him that disturbed her, she decided she would try to find out more from the waitress in the morning.

The next day when the waitress delivered the breakfast, she quizzed her

"Tell me, how often does Steven bring the breakfast to this room?"

"We do not have a Steven, Miss" The girl replied politely.

"Are you sure? The day you were off this week we had a waiter, and he said his name was Steven"

The waitress looked puzzled

"But we do not employ male breakfast waiters here Miss, for obvious reasons. Sorry"

"How can that be?" Maria persisted, "We most definitely had a male waiter that morning"

"I will ask my friend in the kitchen Miss, and let you know." She replied as she left the room.

About thirty minutes later the young girl came back with the explanation looking very worried.

"My friend told me a man came up to her just as she was about to knock on your door, and said it was his room and he had left his key inside. He then said he would take the breakfast because his wife was asleep, and he did not want to disturb her"

Maria was angry that security was so easily broken in the hotel, but before she could say anything the girl continued anxiously,

"Please Miss, don't say anything as my friend is new here, she is only learning and needs this job very much. I will make sure she never does it again"

Maria was very concerned at this intrusion, but she felt sorry for the girls, and she didn't want to alert Tom, so she agreed to say nothing. After the girl had left, she discreetly made a phone call to her contacts in the USA. A few seconds later a top ranking security officer came on the line and apologised for not informing her, but reassured her that this was a security move arranged for her own protection. She quietly put down the phone and decided not to mention it to Tom for the time being, as she knew he would be concerned, and she reasoned, it could also lead to having to having to explain too many other things. And this she was not yet quite ready to do.

The rest of their holiday went very quickly, with no more problems.

They had had a wonderful time, and when the day came for them to leave for their separate destinations, Maria to America, and Tom to England, they had made many plans for their life together, as soon as Tom was finally divorced.

CHAPTER 10

It was expensive for Lebanese families to send their sons to America to study, and Maria's job was to make sure they were settling down, working hard, and on course to completing their studies in the allotted time given.

After a couple of months in Alabama with her brother and the other students, advising and checking on their progress, she was quite happy with what she found. Although she was enjoying her time with the students, her thoughts once more turned to home.

She sent a telex to Tom telling him of her plans to return to Lebanon, and immediately received an answer asking her to stop off in England on her way home. This she was more than happy to do, and rearranged her plans accordingly.

When the day of her arrival dawned; he drove to the airport feeling like an excited teenager. Laughing they fell into each other's arms the minute she came through the arrivals gate, and then quickly made their way to the car, and the long drive back home.

About a quarter of an hour into the journey, Tom noticed that she seemed rather quiet,

"Are you ok, darling?"

Maria looked up at him thoughtfully, "Yes I am fine, except I have been thinking," she hesitated.

"Tom I don't think it would be a good idea for me to stay in your apartment, it might be better if you can find me a hotel near to you instead"

That was the last thing he expected. Seeing his disappointment she tried to explain

"I am thinking of your daughters, and I would rather not meet them like that. And we must be careful Tom, you don't need any extra problems with your wife, especially not now"

His heart sank, he knew it made sense, Jane would make a big thing of it especially with the children, and it could also make for legal complications, and that he did not want. He sighed and reluctantly agreed.

"You're right I suppose, but after Bermuda it's going to be difficult"

She squeezed his hand understanding his frustration,

"Don't worry when you are divorced we will enjoy the rest of our lives together"

It was the quiet season, so it was quite easy to get a room in the local hotel. He booked her in; and drove back to his apartment alone trying to console himself 'At least she is only round the corner, and no Jean to cause problems.' With that cheery thought he felt much happier as he arrived at his apartment.

Maria lay in bed that night thinking about Tom's children, and hoping they would like her. She wanted to ask Tom what his feelings were on starting a family of their own once they were married, but kept putting it off. She drifted off to sleep thinking 'perhaps I will get the chance to talk to him while I am here, if I can find the right moment'

The following day Tom took her to meet the children and his parents, and to his delight they all took to each other straight away. At first the girls were shy, but it was only a matter of minutes before they were all chattering as though they had known each other all their lives. His eyes met Maria's over the girl's heads, they could both see the relief in each others faces, and it was quite a momentous occasion for them all.

Later that evening while they were having dinner alone at the hotel, and heartened by the fact that all had gone well today with the girls, Maria decided that the time was right to ask him about starting their own family.

"Tom, what is your opinion about us having children?"

His hand froze midway between the plate and his mouth; then he quickly regained his composure and joked,

"You mean now; or when we are married?" But on seeing her expression quickly added,

"To be honest, I hadn't seriously given it much thought; I suppose I always felt my two daughters were enough for me, why?" He searched her face feeling a bit nervous, wandering what had brought this on. She looked very serious.

"Well, it is important for me to know how you feel" she replied, "So please think about it"

Then her eyes twinkled, " I think I would like to have a baby that will grow to look like you" She smiled mischievously, "Tall, handsome, blonde with blue eyes."

He felt a slight sense of panic; he didn't want to say anything that might be misconstrued as a promise to have more children.

"I feel bullshit in the air." He smiled trying to make light of it. "But honestly, I had never really considered having any more children"

Maria looked crestfallen; but retorted firmly,

"Don't you think that is a little selfish? Maybe you should reconsider. You still have plenty of time"

Reverting to his usual response to a difficult moment. He joked,

"Should I take that as a requirement for marriage?"

Maria still looked very serious,

"Not in that way, but if it means you're only thinking of yourself. Then that is a problem.

"And," she continued, "I would never use blackmail under any circumstances"

Although he had begun to realize how deadly serious and very determined she was, he continued to joke,

"So I still have an opt out clause then?"

She smiled and slowly leaned towards him; looking straight into his eyes.

"You couldn't bear to lose me sweetie, you love me far too much, so face it, you have a problem that needs to be thought out, haven't you?"

He could think of no answer to give her at this precise moment, and she never mentioned it again as they continued eating their meal, although they both had plenty to think about.

But Maria was concerned, it would be a major problem for her if Tom seriously thought only about his own position and was not prepared to consider hers. She loved children, and always dreamt of having her own someday, But for now she was content to have planted the seed in his head and let it grow for later when the time was right.

During the week; Tom took her into the office to meet Sally, where in the course of conversation with her and Tom's father; the idea came up that she might like to work in the family business.

"Brilliant idea! We are looking for somebody to work in the office in Cyprus."

The company had recently set up a new generator sales office in Limassol and they weren't too sure of the people out there running it, they needed somebody they could trust twenty-four seven. He looked at Maria excitedly

"What do you think darling, would you like it?"

The more he thought about it the more he warmed to the idea. He had also been wandering how he could get her away from the problems of war.

"We also have the Nightclub and the Restaurant over there, you could keep an eye on those at the same time."

Maria laughed,

"Slow down Tom, I really need to think about it before I can say yes" But he could see that she was interested.

Eventually she accepted, but only on the condition that she could return to Jounieh as often as deemed necessary, because as she pointed out to him,

"I cannot completely abandon my commitments there".

After an enjoyable week together, and getting to know Tom's family, Maria finally left for home. She stopped over for a few days in Lebanon to see her family, and to make her arrangements, before travelling by ferryboat across the short stretch of the Mediterranean Sea to Cyprus to start work in her new appointment.

She booked herself into the Palace hotel where many of her Lebanese friends either stayed or congregated, until she could find somewhere more stable. It didn't take her long to settle into a routine, but after just a couple of days she started to feel uncomfortable in the hotel, she had a strong feeling that she was being watched.

On the third day she came up from the pool to find her room and baggage had been ransacked. More disturbing, her underwear had been left in neat piles on the bed, but nothing as far as she knew had been taken. Someone clearly wanted her to feel uneasy and to know who she was and why she was there. When she reported the incident to the Manager he replied that if she had any complaints, she should leave. It occurred to her that he might be involved in some way by his unhelpful if not slightly aggressive attitude; but also the way he avoided looking directly at her

Maria was furious, threatening to pass the word around to her influential Lebanese contacts exactly what had happened. It was obvious to her that someone had had access to her room with a key, but nobody at the hotel was interested. There was no point contacting the local police, she knew from past experience that the Cypriots would always stick together against the Lebanese, upholding the long-standing resentment between the two communities, but she decided it was time to move.

Later that night when Tom phoned her, she told him what had happened,

"Right that's it. Get out of there straight away. I will be over on the next flight"

"Don't worry Tom I have already checked out. But it would still be nice to see you."

Late morning the next day, Maria took a taxi to meet Tom at the airport, and on the way back he bombarded her with questions

"Have you any idea what they were looking for? You said you thought you were being watched? Who by? Someone is obviously spooked by your presence here. Do you think it is from the Lebanese side or from here?"

Already ahead of Tom in his thinking she replied

"Who knows? But it's strange that just my underwear was laid neatly on the bed, everything else was a mess." She pulled a face and gave a little laugh. "Maybe I have a secret admirer with a fetish for underwear."

But Tom was worried.

"That's serious in itself. But I think it is deeper than that, especially if you feel that the hotel is involved. My thinking from what you have said is that it was a woman, not a man; a man wouldn't lay out your underwear like that." He felt his stomach lurch. "Unless like you said; he really was kinky."

Maria shrugged impatiently,

"Let's forget it for now Tom, and continue where we left off in Bermuda"

Tom was quite happy to go along with that idea, although it didn't stop him thinking about it. Maria had booked them into the Apollonia Hotel a little further along the coast, and they spent the next few days looking for an apartment for her to live in permanently.

During their stay at the Apollonia and without exactly stating his relationship to Maria, Tom introduced her to one or two business associates who called to see him. One of these was an old friend, an American called Clive now living alone in Cyprus, who Tom had known for many years. Clive was a bit of a womaniser and couldn't take his eyes off of Maria. He sidled up to Tom and whispered out of the corner of his mouth,

"What do you think Tom, do I stand a chance?" Tom laughed, and looked across at Maria.

"Not a hope mate. She is head over heels in love with a real nice fella"

The American looked crestfallen

"What a shame she is gorgeous, and smart with it, where the hell did you find her? I can'tbelieve you missed the opportunity to try yourself"

"Well that's another story" Tom laughed, "I'll tell you about it one day." At that moment Maria walked over to join them, and Tom was relieved that he didn't have to continue with this conversation, he didn't want any more interference in his love life.

The most suitable apartment they could find for Maria; was a very impressive sixth floor penthouse situated in the town centre. The rent was reasonable considering its size, and it was big enough should she want her family to come over to stay. This would be easier than her having to travel back and forward to Jounieh, and it would be good for the family to escape from the war situation for a few days. So they decided to take the apartment as soon as the papers could be completed.

Maria still worked in the mornings, but spent the afternoons with Tom relaxing by the hotel pool. Each day she wore a different coloured bikini and high-heeled shoes, emphasizing her long beautiful tanned legs and figure.

Tom rather enjoyed the attention she received from the other onlookers around the pool, he had a theory that there were bets taken as to what colour she would wear each day. He would send her to get drinks and ice cream just so he could watch the effect and attention that her walk around the pool created.

Sometimes she would over do the wiggle so much that even he became a little embarrassed from the looks she got from the other guests. Maria knew exactly what Tom's game was, and she certainly knew how to handle him.

"All old men like to see the young girls wiggle their butts, so I knew you would like it"

He laughed and swiped at her butt with his rolled up newspaper,

"You cheeky Arab"

"Well; you are nearly as old as my mum," She grinned

That thought had not exactly escaped him.

Lying back on her sun bed, she gazed up at the deep blue cloudless sky her eyes deep in thought.

"Tom I have a delicate question to ask you"

He propped himself up on one elbow and gazed down at her,

"Go ahead "

She started a little hesitatingly,

"You love me I know, more than anyone has loved maybe, but I hope you don't see me as a prize possession do you? Someone you think is nice to have on your arm to show off to your friends, because in time I will not always look like you see me now"

"Yes I am guilty of all those things." He admitted, trying not to smile.

Maria shot him a startled look. He had intentionally paused long enough to see her reaction before continuing.

"You are a very attractive woman, and naturally I am very proud to have you on my arm. Any man would be over the moon to have a beautiful, highly intelligent woman to love him. You are a dream come true for me, and have been from the first day I saw you. And no matter what time brings, you will always be beautiful to me."

Maria was deeply moved by his loving words said with such sincerity. He had delivered the most reassuring reply that she could ever hope to hear, she felt happier now than she could ever remember being in her entire life.

Later as they made their way back to their room Tom noticed a unisex hairdressing salon, tucked to one side at the entrance of the hotel

"I really need to get a trim. Why not have your hair done for this evening, sweetie?"

"Ok why not?" Maria agreed, "We can make an appointment before we go up"

They stepped inside the salon, where a very efficient receptionist informed them that there was nothing available for at least another two hours. So they made their appointments, but just as they were about to leave, the girl called to Maria.

"Excuse me Miss, why not experience our newly promoted massage area while you wait. It's half price full body massage for female treatments today. You will find it is extremely relaxing"

Maria turned to Tom,

"What do you think should I give it a go? We have plenty of time, and my neck has beenhurting all day. I took a painkiller earlier, which hasn't worked but this might help"

Tom was surprised that she was keen to give it a try, for some reason he didn't think she would like that sort of thing.

"Why not if you feel like it," he replied

The receptionist picked up the phone and spoke quietly for a few seconds, and then she smiled.

"The masseuse is free at the moment. If you wish sir you can go straight to the Jacuzzi or sauna and wait there, your wife can join you afterwards"

Tom winked at Maria,

"How do you feel about that, wife?"

"No problem, husband"

Before committing herself Maria went to view the treatment area. There were four cubicles two on either side of the room facing each other, it all looked very clean and professional, and so she went with the young assistant to the changing room.

"Your robe and towel are on the door. Please remove your necklace and watch. You can leave your underwear on if you prefer; but for full body massage most people don't."

Maria weighed up her options; she was not sure about being completely naked, so she slipped off her damp bikini bottoms, and quickly changed into her black stretch shorts, which she always kept in her beach bag.

She put the robe on and waited feeling a little unsure about what was going to happen; she had never been to a professional masseuse before, and the room temperature was extremely hot which didn't help either. The curtains parted, two women came in and introduced themselves as Eva and Viviane. They seemed pleasant enough so she felt a little more relaxed. The younger of the two women asked her to remove her robe and to sit on the edge of the massage table.

Then she heard a distinctive American female voice coming from a cubicle opposite followed by a deep male voice. Instinctively Maria reached out for her robe again, but the elder of the two women noticing the concern on Maria's face, said reassuringly,

"Don't worry, that's our male colleague, he won't be coming in here. Would you like a drink before we get started? Only it's going to be very hot work as the air-conditioning is not working today, hence the half price offer"

Maria gratefully accepted an ice-cold drink, and drank it down quickly,

"Today you get two of us for the price of one. Isn't that a good deal," Eva said.

"Even more so when you are half price" Maria smiled,

"That's right my dear, that's better isn't it? Now you just leave it to us and relax"

Wearing only her mini-shorts she lay face down on the table with the towel underneath her. Using plenty of oil and a nice smooth but firm action, both women started work on her back. *'This is absolute heaven'* she thought.

Only three or four feet separated the curtained cubicles, leaving just enough room for the masseuses to work, and the heat in the room was becoming unbearable. Within a few minutes the two women had stripped down to their black shorts and white sports bras. The massage and the extreme heat were making Maria feel very drowsy, and most, if not all of her earlier inhibitions were completely forgotten.

The women concentrated on the backs of her legs, mainly her calf muscles and thighs, working upwards until the older woman's manipulating oily hands were at the base of Maria's bottom.

"Would you mind if we slipped your shorts off, otherwise they will be ruined with this oil" By now Maria was so relaxed she had no problem with that request. The older woman Eva chatted on in a soothing voice,

"I have a clinic at the hospital when I am not working here, and Viviane is training to be aphysiotherapist. But the pay is so bad; we have to moonlight a bit and take on extra work, it makes a nice change for us. I am also a fully qualified chiropractor but I still have to work to make up my money"

Maria was only half listening to her as she drifted in and out of semi sleep.

"Our male colleague is a doctor at the hospital, so you see you are in good hands and youdon't need to feel embarrassed; so just relax."

Maria jerked back to reality with a stab of pain at one point as Eva pushed into her back. Viviane suggesting to her colleague,

"We need her to stand if she can"

The two women helped her off the table. Maria struggled to concentrate; and made a vane effort to retrieve the towel as it slipped to the floor, but she felt strangely light headed.

"I need your hands straight down by your side please" Eva's voice broke into her woolly brain. She responded very slowly to the request. The two women then murmured something to each other, and then Eva said to Maria

"You appear to have a problem in your lower back, or it could be a pelvic disorder, but I will check with the doctor when I finish with you. I noticed you were wearing very high heel shoes when you came in, this often causes a problem"

Maria tried to protest in an incoherent voice, which they totally ignored as they eased her back onto the bed so that she was lying on her stomach. And then Viviane left the cubicle to attend to a new arrival.

Applying more oil on her hands Eva proceeded to work on Maria's back, which successfully released the tension from in her body, allowing her to once more drift off into a relaxed state of semi sleep.

Eva continued to work intensely on Maria's neck and shoulders in rather caressing and delicate circular movements. Gradually Maria felt herself becoming aware of her surroundings, she had never had her body treated like this before; it was unlike any beauty massage she had ever heard of.

Realizing her client was now partially awake Eva asked her to stand once again. Which she did, swaying slightly against the side of the table, she put her hand out to steady herself slowly moving her head and neck in a circular and stretching movement

"This is a lot better, my neck and back feel great now"

Maria could hear her own voice slurred and felt as though it was coming from a long way away. Somehow she eased herself back onto the table.

"Good, but you must lay down again we have not finished yet"

Eva left the cubicle for a few minutes, and returned with another drink,

"You must drink this one slowly, and then please lay down on your stomach"
With that she once more left the cubicle. She returned a minute later with an instrument coated with small rubber spikes that she ran very slowly up and down the full length of Maria's body. Although at first it tickled her, it also disturbed her, and her unconscious reaction was one of ultimate pleasure. Laying the instrument down on the bed, Eva shook her slightly to wake her, Maria struggled to concentrate but felt far too tired and lethargic, her whole body was oily and soaking wet in the unbearable suffocating heat.

"Ok that's good" Eva said wiping her hands on a towel.

Maria was not fully in control of her speech or her movements, she didn't want to move or talk, all she wanted was for the treatment to continue. Eva excused herself saying

"One moment please I need to speak to the doctor"

She threw the towel over Maria as she left the cubicle, leaving the curtain half open. Maria closed her eyes. After a while Eva returned pulling the curtains back wide, saying briskly.

"Ok please remain lying on your stomach for a moment,"

Maria was still drifting in and out of sleep blissfully unaware of her appearance or how long she had been there. She was just vaguely aware that somebody else had come in the room with Eva.

The male colleague who Eva had referred to earlier surveyed the woman lying on the bed and impatiently removed the offending towel covering her, throwing it onto the chair. Realizing his patient was not fully awake, he commented to Eva,

"I have seen this ass wiggling around the pool along with the rest of her equipment"

Maria became aware of much stronger hands gripping her calf muscles, slowly up towards the base of her spine. The oily intrusive hands appeared to know no boundaries. When they arrived at the area that had previously given Eva concern, Maria responded in a tone indicating pleasure rather than pain.

"Oohh Ummmm………… Ummmmm ……ahhhhhh"

"Seems like she is enjoying this as much as I am"

Maria could hear a distant male voice and a woman answering, but understood very little or where it was coming from.

"She really does have a cute ass," he said running his hand caressingly over her bottom.

"Later, be patient" Eva smiled, whispering, "I think we have done all we can for her today"

"You may have, but I could do a lot more for her" He boasted

Before leaving the cubicle she placed the towel across Maria's glistening bottom. Ten minutes later she returned, surprised to find Maria lying on her back with the towel neatly laid across her waist, with no sign of her male colleague.

A concerned Eva helped a drowsy Maria to sit on the edge of the bed. Her mouth was so dry that her tongue felt swollen, and was sticking to the roof of her mouth. She was now very hot, dehydrating, and dripping with a combination of oil and perspiration.

"Would you like another drink?" Eva asked

"Please." It was hard to get the words out. "It's so hot in here and I am so dry, thanks"

Eva brought it over saying with a smile,

"Ok now you can get dressed and I'll see you in a couple of days. And leave off the heels for a while" As she turned to leave, she looked back saying," What time is your appointment at the hairdressers?"

Maria struggled to think,

"No idea, still another hour I think"

She looked up at the wall clock trying very hard to focus on the clock's dial.

Then Eva suggested.

"Why not try our Jacuzzi before you get dressed. We also have a couple of saunas in that room, but I think you would enjoy the Jacuzzi better. After all you are already prepared for it" she nodded towards Maria's naked body with a broad smile.

Maria looked round for her shorts and spotted them lying on the end of the table. Still feeling slightly shaky on her feet she managed to put them on, and then took the towel Eva was offering her and draped around her neck; arranging it to cover part of her breasts and followed Eva to the pool. At first she didn't notice that there was another person already in the Jacuzzi, until the woman called out to her,

"Come on in my dear girl, don't be shy"

Maria clutched the towel tightly around her chest, feeling a little concerned; she thought she would be alone. She tried to focus on the hazy figure in the pool, and could see that the woman appeared to be topless maybe even naked.

A bigger concern however was the closer clearer vision of a man sitting in white shorts by the poolside wearing dark tinted glasses. Lying beside his chair was a thin white stick, a bottle of cola and a local newspaper.

'Where the hell is Tom' she thought feeling slightly panicky, 'He said he would be here' gradually she was becoming much more aware of her surroundings.

Maria turned to Eva saying,

"Where the hell is my boyfriend?"

"Maybe he is in one of the saunas, don't worry, relax" Eva smiled at her reassuringly.

Maria approached the edge of the Jacuzzi, her left hand holding on to the brass handrail as she stepped very cautiously down the three small steps into the cool water, turning her back to the man who although portraying to be blind, appeared to be transfixed with her movement. Eva reached out and eased the towel from Maria's shoulders, but luckily her hair was long and thick enough to cover her breasts. With her experience as a dancer, she had never been self conscious of her body, but something made her feel very uncomfortable in front of these strange people

"Are you ok now, Maria?" Eva asked, "Be careful you don't fall when you move, as the pool can be slippery sometimes". Adding with a smile, "I will join you if neither of you mind?"

The woman in the pool nodded her permission, and Maria just smiled, but she didn't like the way they were all looking at her. And it also crossed her mind that the man sitting by the edge might only be partially blind for all she knew.

Maria looked at the other woman in the pool, taking in her bottled blonde hair and noticing the dark roots, an American judging by her accent. Glancing up at the man, she thought he looked a lot older; he was slightly bald, heavily built with a very hairy chest, and of course those dark glasses. Eva took off her robe to reveal her heavily tanned body; naked apart from her tiny bikini bottoms, she was older and a lot heavier built than Maria, but she was in proportion for her height. She walked confidently into the water and sat between them, the American turned to Maria,

"You have a very nice figure my dear, a lovely shape, nothing to be embarrassed about at all. You should be proud to show it off"

Her eyes still wandering over Maria's body, as she asked,

"Where are you from?"

Maria felt irritated; she didn't need this woman's opinion of her body, and ignored her remarks. Coldly she replied,

"My name is Maria, I am from Lebanon."

"I see. My name is Marlene, I'm from New York"

Then she indicated to the seated man,

"That's my half brother Louis. We just love it here."

Not really wanting to continue with this conversation, Maria said "That's nice."

"I have just had a massage too, in fact I was opposite your cubicle. So very sensual and relaxing, don't you agree"

"Sure" Maria could not disagree with that, in fact she had enjoyed the treatment much more than she had originally expected. She never thought she would enjoy another woman's caressing hands as much as she had, especially towards the end of the session.

Maria was still feeling a bit self-conscious at the way the man sitting by the pool seemed to be staring at her, so she folded her arms across her chest. Following the direction of the young woman's gaze the American woman tried to reassure her.

"Oh! My dear, don't worry. You don't have to cover yourself; we are all women here. My brother cannot see you" she lowered her voice, "he is totally blind"

Feeling a bit more comfortable on hearing this from the sister, and noticing that Eva wasn't concerned, Maria unfolded her arms. Noticing her change of attitude, the two women smiled to each other. The American woman teased

"I see you feel much better now dear, but you are so beautiful, it is a real pity my brother cannot see you"

Eva was becoming a lot more carefree as she untied the strings of her bikini bottom; she pulled them from beneath her and threw them to the side of the pool laughing loudly. Turning to Maria she insisted

"Go on Maria, be bold, those shorts must be killing you and very uncomfortable ".

Maria hesitated, but remembered the newspaper beside the man's chair. *'Someone had clearly read it, and maybe it was him.'*

Then the man finally spoke, having heard what his sister and Eva had said, and he appeared to be staring straight at Maria, as he joked

"Maybe I can see, maybe I can't, but I have a good imagination, what do you think about that young lady?"

Maria felt troubled, she had heard this voice recently but she couldn't remember from where. His sister thinking that his comment alone had unsettled the young woman, replied directly to her brother,

"That's not nice, even if it was a joke. Anyhow just so you know, we have two of us totally naked and one still thinking about it I feel sure. Right my dear?"

"No, I don't think so," Maria quickly replied,

"My brother used to be a glamour photographer, before he lost his sight" That struck Maria as hilarious, and she couldn't help grinning, as she leaned over to whisper to Eva,

"Perhaps that was the reason he went blind"

Eva burst out laughing, and slid down in the water to gain control. The American woman moved around the pool to be closer to Maria and placed her hand on her thigh,

"You really don't need those shorts, do you dear?"

Maria edged away from her towards Eva, but the woman moved too lifting her arm and running her hand across Maria's back.

Feeling extremely uncomfortable at this sort of behaviour, she glanced at Eva for some support, but Eva had her eyes closed.

"What lovely smooth skin you have my dear." The woman remarked.

Maria turned to Eva, once again and whispered in her ear,

"She sounds like the big bad wolf from Little Red Riding Hood"

Eva nearly choked with laughter as the same thought had crossed her mind. The woman then placed her hand back on Maria's thigh, gripping it in an even more suggestive manner.

"We are staying in the hotel, so maybe we can spend some time together you and me"

With that the she rose quite quickly from the Jacuzzi and left the room. After a few minutes she returned to collect her brother and without another word, or glance in their direction, the odd couple left the room. Maria turned to Eva,

"What the hell was all that about"

Eva looked up totally unconcerned; she was lying back deep in the water enjoying the Jacuzzi,

"Relax Maria, there is no problem, did you enjoy your massage?" she giggled.

"Yes that was great, I have never felt so relaxed, but as for that weird couple, hopefully we will never see them again. She was so obviously ogling my boobs all the time, and as for the brother I am not sure he was really blind" She looked across at Eva who was still giggling helplessly as she bobbed up and down in the water, and couldn't help but to join in. Eventually they both recovered and went in search of Tom.

Still dripping wet they finally found him alone in the sauna. With still fifteen minutes left before their hair appointments. She asked him to come back with her to the Jacuzzi, on the way back she told him about the 'blind man'. When they entered the pool area; Maria surprised Tom when she threw her towel at him; slipped out of her shorts and calmly walked stark naked into the cool water. He whistled in admiration,

"I think maybe the old man really was blind, otherwise he would have shown more reaction if he could see what I can see"

She laughed a little self-consciously as she said,

"It was embarrassing when my nipples touched the cool water, I felt very awkward at thatpoint, and tried to keep my arms folded across my chest, which was very difficult if not impossible"

Tom roared with laughter at the very thought. They had ten minutes in the Jacuzzi before their hair appointments, and had to rush to dry themselves. Maria pulled on her thin white cotton dress over her still damp naked body, and although Tom admired the wet T-shirt scenario, he did not want other males in the hotel to enjoy the view as well, so he felt that he had no alternative than to enlighten her of the fact. Once again it left Maria struggling to keep her arms wrapped across her chest as they crossed the hotel foyer to the hairdressing salon.

After dinner that evening, back in their room, she started to tell Tom about the massage,

"You know darling, that tablet I took when I came out of the pool for my neck, together with the massage made me very sleepy. I was so relaxed! I was dreaming that I was with you; I could feel you touching me all over my body. It was so weird; but I loved it, I felt as though I hadn't a care in the world, you were wonderful my darling" She confessed as she slipped off her underwear. She then gave a wicked grin at Tom as she teasingly unzipped her strapless evening dress, letting it slide gently down her naked body and onto the floor.

"But I'm not dreaming now, and I still feel so-o-o-o wonderfully relaxed."

Wearing nothing more than a seductive smile and high heels, she threw her arms around his neck.

"I think I had better be more careful in the future, what do you think darling, do you want me to be more careful?"

Tom laughed, as he slowly guided her towards the double bed, her legs now wrapped tightly around his waist.

"As long as you tell me the next time you're going to take a tablet," he replied as he laid her gently down on the bed.

"You filsey boy" She whispered in a husky voice, "Why wait until the next time?"

CHAPTER 11

After Tom had returned to the UK, Maria continued her visits to the beauty salon. It was the same routine, except she made a point of never taking pain- killers again before a session. As much as she had enjoyed the total relaxation of her first visit, she would rather be in control. Eva wasn't always present at the salon, but when she was there; she occasionally joined Maria in the Jacuzzi and Sauna, sometimes they stayed after closing hours enjoying the facilities without interruption. Maria found her company very pleasant, but strangely that first appointment was never a topic discussed, for some reason Eva didn't want to talk about it, Maria assumed that she might have been embarrassed by the way she had behaved, so she didn't pursue the subject.

She was also settling in well at the Cyprus office, but finding out that things were not going as well as they ought to be. It was not long before she discovered that Panicos Nikolaidis the man the Forsters had employed as a salesman, and a relative of Tom's lawyers Tony and Paul Zannaras, was extremely lazy and incompetent. Although he was taking a good salary, he was either sitting behind his desk all day reading newspapers, or could be found sun bathing on the beach with his young family.

The sales records revealed that during his first three months working for them, he had not made or attempted to make one Generator sale. Maria immediately advised Tom that he should be removed as soon as possible, explaining to him the situation she had found. When Nicolaidis heard about this he was furious, and vowed to get even with her.

One afternoon shortly after his dismissal, Maria had a visit from the police and the immigration department. It appeared somebody had reported her as not having a work permit, and it didn't take a lot of working out who it was. But apart from the inconvenience, it didn't cause too much of a problem; and she was cleared of all charges. What Nicolaidis, who she correctly assumed was responsible, didn't realize was; that a foreigner working for a company that was foreign and offshore owned was exempt. Tom was fuming, and telephoned Tony Zannaras one of the Lawyers that had recommended him to the company,

"What the hell is going on over there, I want that bloody idiot Nicolaidis out. Why the hell did you recommend him Tony, you must have known what he was like."

Tony swore under his breath,

"Sorry Tom, it's my fault, but he is family and he needed work, when he got back from the UK, the Cypriot army were after him for not doing his national service. We thought he could get lost in the system if he had a job. But the bloody idiot blew it, I am so sorry"

Tom didn't trust himself to continue the conversation with Tony and slammed the phone down. A few minutes later he picked the phone up again, dialled a number and passed the information he had just received from Tony to the Cypriot authorities. He was assured on full authority that Nicolaidis would be given thirty days to leave Cyprus, or risk being taken into national service for two years. He replaced the receiver with a satisfied smile and settled back down to his work. It was game set and match.

During the next few months Maria went back to Lebanon several times, the situation had worsened considerably, and she was needed for duty. Although Tom was not happy with her returning to the war zone so often, he had to accept it was on those conditions that Maria had agreed to take the job in the first place. It made life extremely busy and tiring for her trying to juggle her life in Lebanon with her job in Cyprus, and she had very little time to herself.

On her trips back home, often the only route available to her was to take a freighter from Larnaca.

There was no passenger cabins on board, so she had to sleep on the deck, usually accompanied by a mixed bag of assorted travellers; mainly military; who were also looking for the cheapest; although the most exhausting way to travel.

It was not long after one of these visits that Tom made another trip over to Cyprus to see her.

Tony Zannaras volunteered to take her to the airport, but Maria really preferred to go on her own.

She wanted to explain to Tom privately why she had changed her hairstyle since he had last seen her, she knew how much he loved her long hair the way it had been and he was not going to like it. But no matter how much she protested; Tony insisted on driving her.

When Tom came through the barrier towards her he looked shocked when he saw her, he opened his mouth to comment but Tony stepped in front of Maria his hand outstretched,

"Ah Tom welcome to Cyprus, it's good to see you. Please come this way we have to hurry, I have the car parked outside waiting in a no waiting area"

Maria was furious; he hadn't even given her a chance to speak.

Once they were settled in the car Tom turned to Maria in dismay and muttered under his breath,

"What the hell have you done with your hair?"

She shook her head glancing anxiously at Tom,

"I will tell you later,"

But he persisted and repeated his question again a little louder.

Maria frowned,

"Leave it Tom, I said I will tell you later"

They had no more time to argue as Tony rudely interrupted them,

"Tell me Tom; how was the flight, did you have a good trip?"

The last thing he wanted to do was to listen to a conversation on the subject of Maria's hair.

When they got to the apartment, Maria rounded on Tom,

"Why did you not wait when I asked you, I did not want to discuss my hair and what happened in front of Tony, or anyone else. Surely you understand that, especially after my room was ransacked at the hotel"

Tom was confused,

"Your hotel room? What's that got to do with it?

She sat down wearily to explain,

"My people have investigated and they are positive that he and his brother had something to do with it, but they cannot prove it as yet. But I can tell you the brothers don't want me here reporting on what they are doing, even more so, when it involves the nightclub business"

Tom was even more confused,

"What do you mean the nightclub business?"

"Well" Maria continued, " The Phoenician is almost sure that they are involved with quite a considerable contraband set up and are using the nightclub as a cover. They thought as you were overseas you could not check on things easily. It's made it harder for them my being here, but the manager; who I know I can trust is keeping me informed".

Tom tried to get his head around what she was telling him,

"How long have you known about this?"

She paused, her face expressionless "Quite a while, but I was not free to talk to you about it. But I can tell you Tony and his wife have been spying on me. They are getting very nervous, they very rarely let me out of their sight, that's why he insisted on driving me to the airport."

Tom nodded in agreement; it was all beginning to make sense. Maria continued,

"As for my hair, you know that I am member of an ambulance team in Lebanon. Two weeks ago when the heavy bombing started again, we were called over to West Beirut. On the way we passed an apartment building on fire, people were screaming and waving us down for help. I soaked a towel, threw it over my face, and went up the stairs to help a Muslim family who were stuck on the first floor."

She did not really want to talk about it, but appreciated that Tom had the right to know.

"When I went through the fire some of my hair escaped from under the towel and got severelysinged, so I had to have it re-shaped at the hairdressers"

She paused and looked at him defiantly,

"At least nobody died".

Then she gave him a little smile,

"How could I tell you all that in front of Tony, I did not even want to tell you, but you are so bloody persistent."

He didn't know whether to laugh or apologise, but the pride and love he felt for her that moment took his breath away. He shook his head in disbelief,

"Those people you saved are your sworn enemy every other day of the week, but you still risked your life for them. Don't you sometimes feel like taking revenge?"

She shook her head sadly as she searched in her bag for her cigarette case.

"No Tom, they are human beings like us, and they were a family with young children, its no more their war than it is ours. If you stopped to think and analyse a situation, then you could easily die yourself. It has to be spontaneous"

Taking out a cigarette and lighting it, Maria felt she had now exhausted the subject, but Tom's head was still reeling,

"I am so very proud of you. If you were in the U.K, you would be seen as a heroine, and without doubt you would have received a commendation."

She shook her head impatiently,

"What for? Just to show off? You should understand Tom, that life is the most important thing of all. When you have been in a war situation as long as we have, you appreciate human life more than those silly material things, believe me."

Again she wanted to leave the subject; she really did not like talking about her other life. Realizing this, Tom said no more, but he didn't stop thinking about it. Then after a few minutes she took out another cigarette and spoke quietly.

"You know Tom, you don't always have to take revenge. I believe God takes care of things. I had a cousin who was abducted mutilated and delivered back to the family dead. We all knew who was responsible for this act. Then about a week later that man also died. He was sniping from a third floor building and slipped, he fell from top to bottom, isn't that justice enough? You don't need to have blood on your hands when you have God by your side"

He looked at her face; reading the passionate conviction in her eyes, he had no answers for this type of reasoning. But he loved her all the more for her belief and her strength.

The next evening while Maria was in the shower getting ready to go out to dinner, the phone rang; it was Maria's brother George.

"Hello Tom could I speak with Maria please, it's urgent"

111

He called out to Maria and she picked up the phone in the bathroom, he heard them greet each other and then silence. He realized they were waiting for him to replace the receiver.

When she had finished her shower she dried herself and went into the bedroom, she put on her underwear and started to dry her hair. Tom wandered in and sat on the bed watching her get ready, she had such a precise routine. He found it fascinating the way she applied her makeup, something he had never had any interest in before now. She looked in the mirror to Tom saying anxiously.

"Tom, I know I have only just returned from Lebanon but I may have to go back soon, as Ihave some family problems to sort, but first I have to wait for another call"

Tom was beginning to have a lot more understanding with her situation, and knew there was no point asking questions.

"Ok don't worry, I can catch up with Clive, that American friend of mine who you met briefly when we were at the Apollonia, He called me earlier; maybe I can meet up with him for a drink, if you leave here before me"

She stood up, slipped on her dress and kissed him gently.

"Thank you darling, you are a lovely boy"

"Yeah, I know" He grinned "And I like the boy part"

Nothing happened until two days later, the day before Tom was due to return to the UK. He received another call from Clive, asking him if they could meet for an urgent discussion, at the local restaurant,

Clive was originally from Ohio, but had lived in the Middle East for more than two years; he was also very active in the CIA under the guise of an engineering salesman. Tom was the first one to arrive at the meeting point so he ordered a drink and waited, eventually Clive appeared nearly fifteen minutes late.

Tom watched him walk over to the table, he was a well-built man about six feet tall with short blond cropped hair, and his whole demeanour just oozed confidence.

"Hi ya buddy, how are things going. Sorry I'm late; got held up"

"I'm fine, how is life in Cyprus? Tom replied as he stood and shook his hand warmly.

Clive then sat beside his friend.

"It's fine. I am with a nice Cypriot girl now called Anna." He snapped his fingers at the waiter indicating he wanted a drink.

"I didn't ask you to meet to talk about my love life." He grinned. "We have an urgent assignment. It will only take a couple days"

Tom looked surprised,

"What do you mean, we, I thought I was only supposed to be a look out for you boys?"

Ignoring that remark Clive continued

"We have to be ready to go over to West Beirut tonight; there are no other agents available.

All I know is that it's very urgent, although I don't have details yet"

Tom, blew his cheeks out and cursed,

"Blast! I'm due back in the UK tomorrow"

"No chance buddy, you're needed here"

Resigned to his fate, Tom asked

"What's the score then?"

"No idea," Clive replied with a shrug,

"We have to meet at the port around nine tonight. The Christian LF is running the show and we are there to see fair play, so I was informed"

"What interest does the CIA have in Lebanon?" Tom queried

Shrugging his shoulders again Clive replied,

"The same as M16 I guess, that's why they need us both. You watch me and I watch you, isn't that how it goes these days?"

"I see" Tom answered, not really seeing at all, but he supposed it would all be explained fully later.

Clive swallowed the rest of his drink in one go and pushed back his chair,

"Drink up, buddy I'll drop you off"

Tom was not prepared to rush things; he needed time to think,

"Let's eat before we leave. We don't know when we will get the chance again do we?

Clive sat back in his chair,

"Good thinking my friend, so you own this joint?"

"Yep" Tom replied as he beckoned the waiter "Can we have the menu please",

After they had had a couple of beers and had eaten their meal, He was now ready to leave; and Clive stood up to join him, but he waved him back down.

"Stay, finish your drink, don't worry I need a walk. I'll see you around twenty hundred hoursat the main entrance to the Zoo"

Tom needed the extra time to think about how he was going to explain to Maria, that he didn't need her to take him to the airport. Also he had to organize a ticket change, *'and that would also need some explaining'* he thought as he went into the travel agent and re-booked for the following week.

When he arrived back at Maria's penthouse he found a note pinned to the inner door, which read; 'Darling I got the call I was waiting for. I will be back at the weekend try to stay on for some extra loving' It was signed 'M'. In a way he was relieved; at least he didn't have to tell his first lie to Maria.

He packed a small holdall with a few essentials and set off to the meeting point.

Once again Clive was fifteen minutes late, however they soon made up the lost time and arrived at Larnaca Port on schedule.

They were met by a young Lebanese man, who miraculously steered them through customs and onto the ferry, well before any of the other passengers.

The young man waved his arm with a sweeping gesture indicating their tiny quarters at the end of a long corridor.

"You have a cabin to share,"

"I hope you don't snore Tom" Clive said throwing his bag onto one of the bunks.

"The vessel will sail at twenty three hundred hours, and I am to tell you to be ready to move at that time" The young man bowed his head in their direction and made his exit.

"Man of few words" Tom grinned as they unpacked their few things, and settled down for the long wait.

"I understood from my earlier briefing there will be five of us," Clive remarked casually.

 Tom turned to his friend saying sarcastically

"How very reassuring"

Clive grinned,

"Cheer up old boy, let's go and find a stiff drink. I'm gasping" Still feeling a bit apprehensive; Tom muttered as they made their way up the steps to the buffet deck,

"Any idea what sort of shitty mess you've got me in to my friend?"

"Don't blame me partner" Clive laughed "Your controller nominated you because you werealready here in Cyprus chasing skirt"

Now it made sense. 'Lane, you- - -! Just wait until I see you again' he thought, following his friend into the bar.

They only had time for one quick drink before returning to the cabin. They did not want to take the risk of mingling with the other passengers who were starting to come on board.

"Hello, looks like we have had company" Tom remarked, he walked over to his bunk and picked up an envelope lying on top of the assault kit folded neatly on the bed. He ripped open the envelope and read out loud,

'Be ready to move as soon as the ferry sails. You will be contacted in your cabin and escorted to a waiting dinghy at the point of departure by one of our team. No questions' Tom raised an eyebrow questionably at Clive, who just shrugged,

"You read the order old son, no questions."

They managed an hours rest and then fifteen minutes before the nominated time, they changed into their combat kit. The numbers printed on their kit was now the only means of recognition. Tom noticed Clive had a Number five printed on his lapel, and twisting his head slightly he saw that he was listed as Number four. He gave Clive a wry smile,

Does this mean I have to jump before you?

They sat quietly waiting for the ferry to sail and the imminent signal, each man deep in his own thoughts. Then after what seemed a never-ending wait there was a tap on the cabin door, and the young Lebanese man appeared who had briefed them earlier. He too was dressed in the same style, on his lapel a Number three. Hearing a noise outside he put his finger to his lips and peered out of the cabin door, seeing no one there he beckoned them to follow him. Their timing was calculated to the exact moment that the ferry slowed to a stop. Number Three climbed in and steadied the dinghy and the rope ladder as it was carefully and quietly lowered over the side. The other two silently scrambled down the ladder, and once on board they rowed swiftly away; and waited until the ferry had moved on before starting the outboard motor. At this point they were now about a mile off the east coast of Beirut. Tom strained his eyes through the inky blackness all around them, happily he could see no sign of any other vessels, but they knew a makeshift customs or police could stop them at any time. Eventually they got within half a mile of the West Coast, and Number Three cut the engine. In the distance they could pick up the lights on the distant shore twinkling faintly. Silently they picked up the oars and started rowing once again.

One of the men pointed ahead, Tom screwed up his eyes; he could just make out the shape of a boat moored but not a light anywhere. Shortly after they arrived at the rear of what he could now see was a half submerged wreck. The young man who he remembered was Number three, indicated for them to tie up on the far side out of sight from the beach. This was to be the first part of their destination.

The wrecked vessel was part submerged and tilted at a slight angle; it had been left to deteriorate on the breakwater since the civil war began. But there was still a dry cabin or two where they could wait.

"Shit!" Clive muttered, "Can't say I like the look of this, one slip and we would be down that slope and in the water before we knew it"

The slope of the wreck looked like it was going to be a problem, but once on board it didn't seem so bad. They were approached by another member of the team, identified by the number two on his lapel, and judging by his manner he was a senior ranking officer,

"Get some sleep gentlemen as much as you can," He greeted them briskly "We move out at twenty hundred hours, so make the most of it. We are waiting here for our commander to arrive, she will be here as soon as possible"

Clive looked astounded,

"You mean we are being led by a bloody woman? You must be nuts"

"This woman is like no other," The officer replied giving Clive a quick look of appraisal.

"She has planned this operation to the last detail, I will brief you later. But you must do exactly what she tells you to do without question, if not you will die for sure, she is a very experienced high ranking officer"

He gave a slight smile still watching the expression on Clive's face,

"Believe me she is the best and extremely professional, as most of her male colleagues would testify "

Tom butted in before Clive could say any more,

"Do you know why the British are involved?"

Switching his gaze to Tom the officer replied somewhat sarcastically.

"Because the CIA want to take the credit as usual and we know they always need the British to hold their hands. But the fact that you are a friend of Number Five influenced the choice,"

Clive interrupted angrily,

"That's a load of bullshit"

Number two smiled, shrugged his shoulders in dismissal of Clive's outburst,

"We are not dealing in bullshit number five; if we were we would not be here. The only reason we are; is that one of your pansy boys got himself caught, so remember that"

Tom interrupted quickly again before Clive could retaliate,

"Do we know if he is still alive?"

"Well he was yesterday," the man replied, "but that's a chance we have to take because since then; we have not been able to make contact.

"Who is he?" Clive asked having now calmed down a bit.

"Stephen Matheson, a so called diplomat of yours. But most Americans don't know the meaning of the word diplomacy, do they?

The dig at his fellow countrymen slipped unnoticed as Clive whistled through his teeth in disbelief.

"You mean Razor Matheson, that sadistic bastard. Why are we risking our bloody necks for that piece of shit?"

Tom shook his head asking with a wry smile,

"You boys love to give bloody titles to everyone, why Razor for Christ sake?"

"Because he's a murderous maniac" Clive answered spitting out his chewing gum, "He kills women for fun; and is an expert with a blade, and his sons are no better from what I hear He has been turned more times than a pig on a spit,"

With that the room fell silent as the men sunk back to their own private thoughts.

A few minutes later Clive stood and stretched his back,

"Well there's not much we can do while we are waiting for this bloody wonder woman to turn up. I'm going to get some sleep" '*Sleep*' Tom thought, '*How the hell does he think we can do that*' But to his amazement they slept soundly until mid afternoon, and when he eventually opened his eyes the only noise he could hear was that of the creaking vessel and water lapping up against the side of the wreck.

Once they were all awake; one of the men produced a pack of cards and they played poker until dark. The small space they were crammed into was thick with smoke, as both Lebanese officers were heavy cigarette smokers, with Clive added to the pollution by chewing gum and smoking cigars. About an hour and a half later they were handed a small tin and told to blacken their faces. Tom and Clive were then stationed on lookout duty, one on the port side the other on the starboard. Within minutes, Number three spotted their leader signalling and coming towards them by speedboat. There was a splash some fifty yards from the wreck, and the little boat turned sharply and sped away.

The woman swam the rest of the way until she arrived at the lowest point of the wreck where Number two lifted her onto the slippery sloping deck. Not a word was spoken just a thumbs up sign. She went straight to the small cabin that had been prepared especially for her. Although there were no doors a torn curtain had been draped across the entry for her privacy.

Carefully she lit a small candle for minimum light. Clive who was positioned on the deck immediately above her cabin could not believe his luck as she peeled off her wetsuit. With her back towards him he could just see her flickering silhouette. Once she moved towards the candle he could see she had long dark hair that hung loosely down her back. He waited with baited breath for her to turn into the light, but she moved into the shadowy part of the cabin away from the candlelight.

"Aw shit" he muttered under his breath, and turned his attention back to the sea.

The men were called together again in the main cabin for a last minute brief, and when she appeared she was like the rest of them; unrecognisable except for the Number one on her lapel, her face blackened and hid under the balaclava of her assault kit. The woman stood silently observing in the background while her second in command primed the two now unrecognisable foreigners. He was showing them a hand drawn map of the target building, detailing their positions, and what was expected of them,

"Please memorise what you are seeing gentlemen, it could save your life"

He gave them a couple of minutes; then folded the map and slipped into a small hand case, which he was leaving on the wreck.

"We will have cover from a land bombardment for thirty minutes, fifteen minutes than a break and then another fifteen, that should give you time to get off the beach, into the building, and out again. After that the shelling will stop, that means no cover. Any questions?

Clive spat out his gum,

"Yeah, supposing something goes wrong and we need more time, thirty minutes seems to me cutting it a bit fine"

"That gentlemen is something we must make sure does not happen" He looked at the small group in front of him and saw there were no further questions.

"Right gentlemen you know what we have to do. We go in ten minutes, once we are in the dinghy its silence all the way. Did you get that Number five?" Clive ignored the taunt.

One last quick check of their equipment and they were ready. Clive gave Tom a thumbs up as he climbed over the side and lowered himself into the dinghy; Tom gave a return thumbs up and silently slid into the seat behind him, within minutes they were rowing to the shore. As per schedule the moment they hit the beach, the shelling started. Sliding over the side of the dinghy they crawled on their stomachs until they reached a point where they could see the target building.

Number one gave the signal to move forward. In front of him across the shell-damaged road Tom could see the outline of the building, in front was a large open square partially lit. They swiftly made their way one by one across the road avoiding potholes and into the shadows bordering the square. Keeping well within the cover of the shadow they approached a narrow stone stairway leading up the side of the building.

Number one indicated with her finger that she going up first, and they were to follow closely. In dashes of ten metres or so they silently moved up the steps dropping off Number three on the first floor, Number two on the third, as cover. Clive and Tom went with her to the fourth floor. Just as they reached that point, a stray shell hit the building with a tremendous thud and the explosion knocked them off their feet.

"Bloody hell that was near" Tom hissed at Clive. He looked around for the woman, she was picking herself up and wiping dust from her eyes, but otherwise they were all ok.

Number one indicated that they were to stay here while she made her way alone along the narrow corridor and up a short flight of stairs to the designated holding area. She knew her way around the building post war; and the intelligence organization had confirmed this to be the room where they were holding the American. She felt bitterly disappointment to find no evidence of occupation; she retreated down the steps and decided to go further along the corridor. Then from nowhere and before she had chance to react, a group of dishevelled soldiers surrounded her. She now found herself staring into the menacingly barrels of the guns pointed at her.

She realized she was totally isolated and trapped; it was clearly obvious they were expecting visitors, as there was no element of surprise. Back on the stairwell Tom and Clive heard the slight scuffle, Clive put a finger to his lips for silence; and indicating that he was going to take a look, he crept along the corridor and peered up the short flight of stairs, but he soon realized he was totally outnumbered and retreated back to Tom. Breaking the silence he whispered hoarsely,

"They got her. At least half dozen Arab soldiers, I didn't understand a bloody word. What's our position now? They told us not to go back for anyone including her."

Tom grabbed him by the arm,

"For Christ sake Clive, we are not leaving anyone, especially a woman in the hands of thosebastards. Lets get back down to the others, and we can decide what to do"

They ran swiftly back down to the next floor to where the Lebanese officer was waiting, quickly they told him what had happened. The officer was clearly upset at this turn of events, but offered no solution or action. Tom looked at him in amazement,

"For Christ sake man, what do you think we should do?"

When no reaction came from him, Tom took charge,

"Can we get onto the roof at all; it must have an air-conditioning conduit, in a building of this size"

The man regained his composure and nodded his appreciation to Tom,

"Wait, I'll get Number three he knows the lay-out of the building,"

He headed for the stairs saying,

"If we don't get her out quickly they will take turns in screwing her, then they will torture her to death. They are bastards with our women, and I know she won't talk"

When they returned with the information, the officer still seemed quite happy for Tom to take control.

"Ok, I'll go with Number five into the overhead ducting. Hopefully they are on the top floor, and we can find the bloody room where they are holding her. Number two, you take the stairs, and Number three; you take the main entrance. Do what ever you have to do, just give us time to get her out"

He loaded his pockets with some of the ammunition they had brought with them.

"Come on pal, let's go. Six tear grenades should be enough to cause a distraction"

Then he nodded in the direction of the Lebanese officer,

"Give us ten minutes to locate her then I want you to start causing a diversion with thegrenades you have, Ok? "

Clive and Tom made their way through the air-conditioning shaft. Very slowly they inched themselves along the cramped space, Tom hoped the building layout given to them by the Lebanese soldier was correct.

Faintly ahead of them they could hear raised angry voices and they followed the sounds until they came to a mesh screen through into a room where they had expected to find the commander.

Unfortunately the room was empty although they could hear voices much clearer. Tom felt his mouth go dry, his heart was racing and the pounding in his ears was so loud he felt sure Clive could hear it as well. He glanced at his comrade; and one look at his face told him that he was feeling the same. Communicating by hand actions only, they silently continued their search along the duct; peering into each room as they passed, and all the time the voices grew louder until at last they came to the room where she was being held.

Tom twisted his head his eyes scanning what looked like a small gymnasium. The air hung heavy in a thick film of dust lit by thin streams of light coming through the dirty roof lights. It had been stripped bare apart from a table and chair positioned in the centre, which the commander now occupied.

She looked as though she had been roughly handled by her captors, and now sat on the chair with her head bowed and her hands tied behind her back. Her feet firmly tied to the legs of the chair, her jacket now unzipped to the waist that had been pulled back over her shoulders revealing her black combat vest. For a split second Tom felt an odd feeling of familiarity at the sight of her bare shoulders, but his thought was interrupted by a sudden outburst of angry excited shouting in Arabic, and a lot of confusion.

Then just as sudden; silence descended as someone entered the room, and a man's voice snapped out an order to the men. From the chair in the centre of the room the woman gave a sharp intake of breath as she recognised the deep southern American accent. It was Stephen Matheson. This was the man they had come to rescue

Matheson was in his late-forties; he had light brown hair fading into grey at the side, and thick bushy eyebrows over close set watery grey eyes. With his long face and pockmarked complexion he was certainly not a handsome man. He made his way slowly across the room towards the woman in the chair, his beer bloated stomach hanging over his trousers; and at six foot two he towered over the other men in the room, he stopped inches from her feet. Bending over he poked her with the small stick he was carrying,

"Very nice to see you at last commander. Perhaps you would like to tell me, how manymore of you are there? "

The soft menacing voice continued,

"It was kind of you to come to rescue me, but as you see I don't need your assistance. He leaned in closer to her his expression contorted in a sickening smile,

"I have been informed that you know the identity of this bastard, the one they call the Phoenician. Who is he my dear, and where are the rest of your men? Answer me bitch," he screamed, his mouth almost touching her ear. Grabbing her hair he jerked her head backwards. She made no sound. Tom caught his breath; although he couldn't see very clearly he again had that same sense of familiarity. Clive sensed the sudden tension in his friend, placed a firm hand on his arm to restrain him.

"I have it from very good authority that you didn't come to rescue me, but to eliminate me. How close to the truth is that, bitch?

When again she didn't reply, he turned to the guards shouting to them in Arabic

"Ok boys let's do it. She will be happy to talk once she has had the full treatment, get her ready, I am first, you can all have her afterwards" He smiled sadistically.

Number one fought to control a wave of panic gripping her stomach. She knew from past experience that her survival depended on showing no outward sign of fear, even though she realized that Matheson was almost out of control.

From their position behind the mesh screen they strained to see what was happening,

Tom was beginning to feel the fear tightening inside him, he whispered to Clive,

"I can't see a bloody thing now, but I can hear a yanks voice"

"Yep, sounds like a southern drawl to me" Clive replied reaching into his pockets. These few stunners should give us some cover when we go in"

At that moment the group parted slightly and they saw Matheson with what looked like a double-edged dagger approach the commander and hold it against her throat, and then slowly direct the point of the knife towards her chest. As he did so he cut her, and blood started to trickle down between her cleavage. Both men watching were tense waiting for the right moment.

Number one felt sick with fear but she did not flinch or utter a sound.

121

Matheson gave a deep-throated laugh; and with a flick of the wrist sliced her black vest straight down the centre. The guards surrounding them laughed and jeered. They could see that the American was getting more and more agitated, he waved the knife in front of her face.

"It's your last chance bitch; these men are just waiting to have a little fun with you"

He touched her cheek with the point of the blade,

"When I have finished, of course"

But although her heart was pounding, she still maintained her silence. She felt him come right up close to her and put the knife to her throat once again, she could smell his hot foul breath as he pushed the hair off her face and kissed her, she wanted to be sick as his slobbering wet mouth covered hers.

She was terrified but refused to let him see her fear. He stood back looking down at her, and her outer coolness incensed him even more.

"Put her on the table. Let's see how many she can take before cracking"

Two of the Arab soldiers stepped forward and roughly untied her, they dragged her to the table; pushing her flat on her back with her legs positioned so that her bottom was right on the edge. One man tied her legs whilst the other tied her hands to the table above her head so she was spread-eagled on the table; rendering her terrifyingly vulnerable to whatever sadistic action she knew very well this man was quite capable of performing.

Her heart almost stopped with fear, she was on the verge of fainting but still she knew she must not let him see it, as this was exactly what he wanted, 'Please God; please help me' she prayed over and over again in silence.

Realisation hit Tom like a bomb; when for a split second he saw her face; and knew what was happening,

"Jesus Christ Clive, we have to get down there now"

Clive gripped his arm, holding him down as he glanced again at his watch,

"Hold on buddy, thirty seconds to go"

Matheson picked up his knife again grinning as he indicated to the others that he was about to dispense with the rest of the woman's clothes, piece by piece. This proved to be too much for one of the young soldiers; he made a movement as if to defend the unfortunate victim, but he was instantly overpowered by the other guards who wrestled him to the ground, but, it bought Number one a few more vital seconds of extra time.

Exactly on cue the diversion started, as the first explosion ripped through the air, Tom yelled, "Go, Go, Go." They simultaneously kicked out the mesh grill, jumped through and hurled a couple of tear gas grenades into the room.

There was chaos as the guards panicked and rushed for the exit, Clive fired at the retreating figures dropping two of them as they scrambled for the door.

And then as the smoke cleared they saw one of the young soldiers had remained behind and was now calmly pointing his gun at Matheson.

Matheson still screaming obscenities at the retreating guards turned back to see the barrel of a gun from one of his own men aimed straight at his heart, he looked around wildly but discovered he was now alone to face the consequences. Tom called out to Clive,

"Cuff the bastard Number five. We are going to take what we came for, dead or alive, and believe me I don't bloody care which way it is"

Directing his conversation to Matheson he said,

"And if you want to resist or run go ahead pal, I am badly in need of some serious target practice"

He went over to the commander who was still tied to the table, her hair still covering her face and cut her free. She was coughing from all the tear gas and her eyes were watering and stinging. Turning her back to Tom she reached down for the balaclava which had been carelessly slung on the floor and pulled it quickly over her head, and then she ripped off the tattered vest and pulled her suit top back over her shoulders. Tom had already retrieved her boots and as she finished getting dressed, he bent over her and whispered softly in her ear. His voice gruffly distorted with the emotion he was feeling.

"How are you doing, sweetheart"

Although still dealing with the effects of the gas, her whole body stiffened.

"Why you address me like this, I am your commander"

He gave a quiet laugh,

"I would recognize that cute little ass anywhere"

She gave a gasp of surprise; whispered inquisitively "Tom?" she spun round and looked at him in

horror. He reached out to steady her, as it looked like she was going to faint,

"Right"

Her knees gave way and she clung to his arm for support, as her words came out in a strangled whisper,

"Oh my God"

Tom saw Clive approaching them; he squeezed her arm in warning,

"Later"

Oblivious to the situation between them, Clive interrupted with a grin,

"Nice underwear, ma'am"

The Commander replied sharply

"This is not the time, or the place Number five.

"As you say ma'am, but no problem; I have seen it all before"

She picked up her equipment not looking at him, but knew he was referring to the wreck.

"I know that's why I didn't turn around"

He laughed, realizing he had been clocked. He indicated with his head towards Matheson who was on his knees with his hands cuffed and the young soldier standing over him.

"What should we do with him, ma'am"?

Maria pursed her lips together grimly; and thought for a second,

"We should terminate him, which was the general idea. The purpose of this operation was to stop him buying military equipment and passing western secrets onto the Russians. But now I think he would enjoy a trip back to the States instead, don't you?"

Tom looked around the room checking that they had all their equipment,

"So was it a rescue mission, or not?"

Maria didn't respond, seeing it was more of a statement than question. Then reverting back to her role position, ignoring the fact she was now speaking to her lover, she snapped out an order.

"Move out, Number four we can discuss the politics later"

She turned to the young soldier who was still standing guard over the restrained Matheson, she could see that the young man was no more than seventeen to eighteen years old, she questioned him in Arabic,

"Why did you put yourself in danger for me?"

He hesitated before he answered, his eyes full of emotion

"Partly because, I cannot accept to see a woman raped, but when he revealed your face, I recognised you as the woman that had saved my family in Lebanon when my house was burning"

She breathed deeply, her mind rushing back to the incident where she had singed her hair.

"My God! You must come with us, you can't stay here; they will know you betrayed them"

The young man shook his head sadly,

"No I must stay" He looked nervously over his shoulder as he heard the gunfire getting closer.

Maria held out her hand to him,

"You must come they will kill you" Reluctantly the young soldier changed his mind and followed her to the stairs.

Swiftly they made their way back down the stairs; meeting their two Lebanese comrades crouched just inside the exit reloading their guns. All of the retreating guards were now dead, lying on the stairwell or in the open square. No mercy had been shown.

Making their way out of the building they kept as tight as they could to the shadows bordering the open square, and then just as they thought they were safe; a single bullet from the rooftop dropped the young soldier to the ground, he lay there motionless. Tom bent down to feel his pulse. He looked up at Maria and shook his head. For the first time that day Maria showed some emotion.

"He is dead?"

"I'm afraid so." Tom sighed, " What a bloody waste of a young life"

Maria knelt beside the young mans body and mumbled a small prayer and gave the Catholic cross, even though he was Muslim. Then she stood, her face blank,

"He isn't the first, and he won't be the last"

Tom knew behind the calm exterior she was very very angry. She snapped out an order to both of her Lebanese comrades

"Get back up there; and make sure you don't leave any of those bastards alive, we cannotmove from here, they can pick us off too easy. We will give you cover. Be quick, we don't have much time"

The two men ran to the base of the building, as the others fired at the point where the gunshot had come from. After a short while there was sporadic gunfire that lasted little more than three to four seconds, then cold silence.

The trio on the ground anxiously waited for their comrades to return. Suddenly both men appeared silently from the shadows; they were unharmed, and in very good spirits. Number two spoke to Maria in Arabic,

"No problem commander, three dead. You said take no prisoners, so we didn't" He turned to his comrade laughing and put his arm around his shoulder.

"Right my friend?"

They silently moved on in single file keeping close to the shadows as much as possible, knowing there was still the possibility of sniper fire.

They covered the distance to the beach in short time, dragging Matheson with them, to find the dinghy waiting exactly where they had left it. Silently they manoeuvred the boat into the water, climbed aboard and cast off. Nobody said a word until they were far enough out to relax.

They looked at each other in relief, now all they needed to do was get back to the wreck as fast as they could.

"Well done every body," Maria whispered, "but no more talking until we get back on board"

125

CHAPTER 12

It was now complete darkness; the moon had disappeared behind heavy clouds as they arrived back at the wreck. Silently they climbed aboard, Clive and Tom supporting Matheson between them.

"Ok, everybody make sure you have left nothing below, I want absolutely no evidence left behind that we have ever been here" Maria said briskly, "Make it as fast as you can, I have a feeling they will be looking for us. I'll watch him." She added nodding in the direction of Matheson. Within minutes they were back and assembled on the sloping deck ready to return to the inflatable. No time for modesty as they hurriedly changed, and boarded the dinghy, however this time they had no hesitation about using the engine; they needed to get far away from the western area of Beirut as fast as they could.

Twenty minutes later they were able to relax, another task was almost completed.

Tom urgently whispered,

"Cut it the engine quick. Patrol boat ahead."

They waited silently their hearts pounding for the patrol boat to move away, Tom glanced at their prisoner. In spite of the situation he smothered a grin when he saw Clive practically sitting on Matheson's lap with his hand clamped over the man's mouth.

Maria looked at her watch she was worried, she knew they had only one hour to catch the ferry before it left the port of Jounieh, and now they had lost considerable time.

Eventually the patrol boat went away and Maria breathed a sigh of relief, luckily they hadn't been spotted. They waited a few moments longer before starting the engine, and finally arrived at the pickup point with less than a few minutes to spare. The Lebanese officer gave the signal for the rope ladder to be lowered. Speedily they climbed aboard, half pushing and half-dragging Matheson between them.

Very soon the vessel was well on its way to Cyprus with Matheson safely locked below in the cabin next to Maria's cabin. Back in their quarters, Clive confronted Tom indignantly,

"Why didn't you tell me that Number one was the girl with you at the Apollonia?"

Clive's statement caught Tom off guard,

"I hadn't a clue, it came more of a shock to me, than it did to you"

Clive laughed accusingly,

"Yeah? You bloody MI6 mob think everyone else is stupid but you.

Then he grinned,

"Anyway there is no way I could mistake that cute ass man, and if we had waited another fewseconds............"

Tom laughed uneasily

"Don't even go there my friend," he warned. "She didn't know I was in, and I certainly didn't know she was operational, although I suppose I'm not really surprised,"

Clive gave a dramatic sigh,"

"You're a lucky bastard. Oh, and yeah, I forgot she had a boyfriend, very nice chap if I recall, you lying bugger"

With that, they laughingly went up on deck for a few cold beers. That was a big mistake.

It had only taken a short while for Matheson to convince the young Lebanese soldier who was guarding him, that he was ill, and in desperate need of the 'bathroom.' As soon as the handcuffs were unlocked, he overpowered the guard rendering him unconscious before tying him up and gagging him.

With vengeance on his mind, he took the keys to Maria's cabin from the unconscious man; and quietly let himself in; he could see she was sound asleep in bed. Silently he searched the cabin for his knife, and then his eyes alighted on the bedside cupboard. Without a sound he slid open the drawer, and stifled a snort of satisfaction as he saw his knife. Very slowly he picked it up and turned to the bed where she lay on her back with her head turned towards him.

'Right bitch, its pay back time' with one hand he held the blade to her throat, sliding the other hand deep under the sheet checking to see if she was armed.

Maria woke with a jerk, and stared straight in to the ugly face of Matheson. She froze, resisting the urge to scream, as she knew she had to stay calm. His face contorted with satisfaction of what he was about to do,

"I've come to finish what I started, so enjoy," He hissed into her face.

Her blood turned to ice as his chilling words quickly sunk in, and she felt his hand roving over every part of her warm body. She looked at him with contempt,

"You will not get away with it; the authorities will be waiting for you when we dock in Larnaca"

Her apparent calmness infuriated him; he swept back the bed sheet, his eyes bulging at the sight of her flimsy camisole top and brief shorts.

"Shut up bitch. Now very very slowly, get up, on your knees."

Maria had very little option other than to do as she was told. She rose slowly to her knees and pulled the sheet up to wrap around her waist. Matheson's cold watery eyes watched her every move as he sat down heavily on the bed.

"No, that's no good. On the floor, kneel and face me"

Maria manoeuvred herself off the bed still clasping the sheet. Sitting on the edge of the bed his knees either side of her he ran his fingers around her throat saying in a soft menacing tone.

"Ok, so maybe they will get me, but I'm gonna screw you first" His tone changed. "So get rid of that fuckin sheet."

She knew from her earlier encounter with him, what a dangerous psychopath he was, and could guess the consequences if she disobeyed any of his sick demands. At the moment she had no alternative, so reluctantly she stood, dropped the sheet and knelt back on the floor.

Matheson leant towards her as if to kiss her neck; but instead he just laughed and slid the double-edged blade under a strap of her firm-fitting camisole. She dare not move, knowing what he was capable of from the cut on her chest. Convinced that now he had total control of her he laughed sadistically.

"How are you feeling bitch? Perhaps you would like to be a little more comfortable"

Demonstrating the sharpness of the knife he sliced one strap of the camisole, looking at his victim's face for a response. He stared straight into her eyes, grinning as he cut the other strap. Maria fought to stay in control, her mind sharpened with the fear; but she knew that she had to wait for the right moment.

The camisole slackened from her shoulders, and suspended evenly on the tips of her breasts. Matheson moistened his lips, his breath quickening. "That's better, now get up. It's here that the fun starts."

Trying to play for time, she spoke softly.

"Why all this anger, we have plenty of time if you really want me that badly,"

He leered at her knowingly,

"I'm not fuckin stupid, or falling for that one. Get on with it, nice and slow face the wall; Iwanna see that entire cute ass of yours, and baby, I really mean all"

Maria slowly did as she was told, the clinging top immediately slipped from her breasts and on to her waist.

She could sense him becoming more sexually aroused, as he stood close up behind her, so close she could again smell his hot stinking breath on her neck. He sliced the loose camisole in halves as it lay on her hips, ripping it away from her. He then sat heavily on the foot of the bed and whispered hoarsely,

"Now that's better"

Her heart was thudding with fear, but she needed to buy more time. She had to stay focused if not she knew it would be the end for her. He had nothing to lose.

Maria then had an idea, and took the risk. With her bare olive skinned back towards him; she lazily reached out to the shelf directly in front of her and pressed the switch on her portable radio. She was sure that it would be tuned in to the LF music station. 'Please God,' she prayed, 'let it work.' Before he had time to react, she very slowly started to move around the cabin swaying exotically to the music as only she knew how. Matheson stared mesmerized; but he didn't move. Gradually she evolved her dance routine, ensuring her back was towards him at all times.

"Very good" he breathed, "Now turn, and come over here"

But she continued to dance with her back towards him acutely aware that he was becoming more and more frustrated at her continued concealment. Judging by his breathing she knew she would not be able to put him off for much longer. Maria was banking on Tom coming to see if she was still asleep. Matheson sarcastically applauded,

"Very nice" He jeered "But don't play fuckin games with me bitch, lets see some ass and then turn around and let's see what's so special about you"

'Please Tom, hurry, for God's sake' Desperately she changed her tactics and started playing with the elastic on her shorts, hoping that one more extra effort to distract him would spin out the time with a limited but controlled striptease routine. Bending forward suggestively, she moved her shorts slowly up and then down further each time, revealing as much as she dare. She knew she was playing a very dangerous game, but she was fast running out of options.

She also regretted turning off the air conditioning before she went to sleep, as the room temperature was now soaring to more than 35 degrees centigrade. Eventually having displayed most if not all of her rear, she stopped dancing as if defeated. Seizing the opportunity he stood up and moved towards her with the knife still in his hand.

"Ok, so you've proved you got a nice ass, turn round; I won't ask again."

With her arms folded protectively across her breast, and dripping with perspiration she turned, in spite of her exhaustion; her training told her that she had to remain totally calm and focused if she was to survive such an ordeal.

"Now unfold your arms bitch, let's see your tits," he said, his voice soft and sinister.

Maria lowered her arms down by her side; the perspiration trickled down her body with fear, and the addition of the room temperature.

But once more the fear sharpened her mind, she realised that with her dance she had managed to position herself close to her 9 mm Browning pistol, it was now only inches away from her right foot. She had placed the gun on the floor near the head of the bed before she went to sleep; it was now hidden from sight under a newspaper Matheson had knocked from the bedside table when he searched for the knife.

The American unbuckled and dropped his trousers, before taking a step towards her,

"Now, on your back."

That gave her another idea. Calmly she sat on the edge of the bed and slowly lowered herself backwards, her left arm dropping casually off the edge of the bed, but still she could not bend her elbow round enough to reach the floor where she had placed the pistol. It was too risky.

Maria knew that she was taking a chance with this sadistic psycho, but she continued to tease him, as she needed to be on her stomach in order to reach the pistol with her right hand.

Trying to acquire some control of the situation she looked up at him making sure she had his full attention, and whispered huskily,

"Tell me, why you are so obsessed with me,"

Kneeling at her feet, he ignored her remark reached forward with the knife, and deliberately cut up one side of her satin shorts, and then slowly he sliced the other side, until they were only held together by the tiny band around her waist.

Maria saw that his face was streaming with sweat, and the pulses in his neck pounding fit to burst. Dropping down beside her he put his right hand on her exposed bare thigh before running it up the full length of her slender body arriving at her throat, then slowly progressing down to her left breast, his clammy index finger circling her nipple.

It took every ounce of her training and self control to stop herself from panicking. Encouraged by her submissive attitude he continued running his hand down her warm body barely touching her delicate skin. Briefly he circled her diamond pierced navel, before resting his wet clammy hand at the top of her shorts. She felt sick, as she knew there was nothing to stop him from exploring even further. *"Tom please; please come, hurry,"* She prayed silently.

He glanced at her face for a reaction of some sort but there was none. Maria kept completely still, it would be too dangerous to taunt him or let him see her fear whilst she was in this vulnerable position.

He applied pressure on her flattened stomach, putting the back of his thumb full length deep inside her shorts, running it slowly backwards and forwards. She flinched as his sharp bitten fingernail dragged across her delicate skin.

Matheson was infuriated that he was not getting the sort of reaction of fear from his victim that he expected. His face contorted with frustration,

"Turn, with your face down". He ordered harshly.

Maria hesitated slightly, although this was what she needed to do in order to reach the gun, her stomach knotted with fear at his constant change of mood. She knew that most assassins couldn't look their victims in the eyes before they execute them. She twisted onto her left side rather than on her stomach, which agitated him even more. He pushed her shoulders forcibly and snarled,

"I said face down bitch"

Making an awkward effort she turned very slowly; still trying to buy as many seconds as possible although she was beginning to give up hope that anyone would come to her aid in time.

Eventually she succumbed to his brash order, but kept her face turned so that she still had some visual contact. He lent over her forcing both of his knees in between her legs.

Leaning forward he dragged his slobbering lips across her lower back, licking the sweat from her tormented body. Then in one violent movement he ripped away the rest of her flimsy tattered shorts, saying hoarsely,

"Yeah! This ass is what I want, and this time honey you're going to get it."

Excitedly, he mauled her with sexual intent, now fully prepared to keep his latest promise. He then leaned back pulling his T-shirt over his head with one hand, and started removing his under shorts with the other, which was proving to be even more difficult.

For one split second his guard was down, and taking this opportunity Maria reached down with her right hand and retrieved her pistol. She quickly turned over, pointing it straight at his head, and waited. He did not immediately notice she was now armed; his eyes firmly fixed on her naked glistening body. Then she spoke in a deceivingly quiet voice,

"Now you have a choice, live or die I don't care which. You decide asshole. Get down on the floor.................. and do it now!"

His head spun round, his face contorted with fury as he starred down the barrel of the pistol. Cursing he moved away from her.

"Shit! You bitch, you will pay for this. If I don't get you, someone will, I can promise you that"

Maria smiled more in relief, as she reached down for the sheet to cover herself, never taking her eyes from him for a second.

"If I ever feel your stinking breath on my face again, it will be the last one you ever take"

He didn't reply; he was well aware from her reputation that she was very capable of carrying out her threat. Maria indicated with the pistol,

"Drop on the floor face down, and spread your legs. One false move and you are history"

As he stretched out on the floor there was frantic banging on the door. Maria swung her legs off the bed holding onto the sheet with one hand while aiming the pistol at Matheson's head with the other. She slipped on a pair of briefs with one hand and carefully stepped behind the spread-eagled man to open the door to her Lebanese second in command, and the still dazed young guard.

"Where the hell was everyone? " She questioned angrily.

"Secure him Number two, and this time make sure of it"

Tom and Clive had also arrived along with the rest of the team, and Maria became acutely aware that more than her identity was now being exposed to her comrades. She tightened the sheet around her as she caught sight of Clive's appraising eye; and said sarcastically,

"You missed the big show Number Five. What a pity "

Clive laughed, as his eyes continued to wander over her body,

"I don't think so ma'am."

Tom threw him a warning look as he put his arm around Maria's shoulders. For all the bravado she was showing he could feel her trembling beneath his arm.

Turning to Matheson, Clive threw his clothes at him.

"Get dressed asshole, you're coming with me"

Then he slipped some cuffs on him and removed him from Maria's cabin, this time to a more secure lock-up, where he was bound hand and foot. Clive nodded to the soldier left to guard him,

"I don't care if he craps all over the floor, there is no way you untie him. Get it?"

A short while later Clive received a ship to shore message that read,

"Cargo unwelcome, dispose immediately"

He went back into the lock-up cabin and dismissed the guard. Matheson watched warily as Clive untied his legs,

"Come on my friend," Clive smiled, "Let's get some fresh air, you can tell me all about yourself and what you think of our Commander's sexy bits"

The two men went up to the deck above the cabins.

Now that Maria's identity had been revealed, Tom decided he would take no more chances on leaving her alone,

"Now my darling, I will be staying here with you for the rest of this voyage"

Maria opened her mouth to resist, but saw the look in Tom's eyes and knew there was no point in arguing.

"Ok. But first I must have a shower; I need to wash away every trace of that maniac.

Maria looked refreshed and more relaxed when she returned; she pulled out the little stool under the dressing table and started brushing her hair. Tom got up and stood behind her, watching her in the small wall mirror.

"Do you want to talk about it?" he asked with a gentle smile. Maria nodded and began to tell him. She explained how she had danced, and how she had prayed for him to come, and how she had nearly given up hope. When she finished; she just sat quiet and looked at him in the mirror waiting for his reaction. Tom bent down and put his arms around her and drew her over to the bed. He was seeing another side of this extraordinary woman, he knew she was a strong, but to go through all this under such threat, and twice in twenty-four hours was more than he could conceive. He sat on the edge of the bed smoothing her damp hair gently,

"Try to get some rest for a while"

"Tom, lay with me"

She fell back on the bed physically exhausted and closed her eyes. Then just as she was dozing off to sleep, she jerked awake as she heard a noise,

"What was that Tom, it sounded like something went over board?"

It didn't take a lot of imagination on Tom's part to guess what had happened.

"I hope he can swim better than me" He smiled wryly.

"Oh my God," she gasped.

Maria wanted to get up to see what had happened, but Tom restrained her,

"Leave it Maria it's not our problem. You were going to kill him anyway"

"You knew?" She looked at Tom solemnly

"Sure" He replied smiling, adding,

"It's America's decision now and nothing to do with us. He was not worth saving, don't forget he was quite prepared to rape and kill you. There is no need to feel sorry for him"

"I feel absolutely nothing for him, definitely not when his treason risked hundreds of our operative's lives" Maria retorted scathingly,

Tom shrugged,

"Its better the headlines read, "Diplomat lost overboard" rather than "Lebanese slay American Diplomat" Far better all round don't you think?"

"Yes, I am sure you're right" Maria replied, as she lay back down and closed her eyes once again.

Soon they were back on dry land where Maria and Tom said their goodbyes to the team. Maria gave Clive a quick kiss on his cheek and smiled,

"Maybe we will see you again soon Number five"

"Well ma'am," He winked at Tom, "I could say I hope to see more of you, but I think I've seen all there is, and it really was worth the wait"

Maria had at last begun to understand his sense of humour, so she laughed and replied in the same manner,

"Thank you, but remember you have to bite the fruit, to taste the flavour,"

"That's a very good answer Commander, It's one that I won't forget" he smiled

They clasped hands warmly and he kissed her twice, once on each cheek. Then he shook hands with Tom,

"See you soon, old buddy, and take good care of this young lady"

"I will, not so much of the old, and try to keep your head down"

Clive grinned, gave a mock salute and disappeared into the crowd.

Tom and Maria returned to her apartment to finish their interrupted holiday. They were able for the next two days, to spend some quiet loving time together before he had to return to England.

On the last morning lying in Maria's king sized bed, Tom got to thinking about all that had happened. He propped himself up on his elbow and looked down at Maria,

"I'm curious. As a Lebanese woman, how come you got to hold such a high rank?"

"How come you are involved with British Intelligence?" She retorted, answering a question with a question.

"Touché" Tom laughed. But then another thought struck him,

"Now I know why, when I asked for security clearance for you, it came back accepted within forty-eight hours. I always understood that those things usually took months"

"You see, even your MI6 know I am a good girl," She laughed.

They wrapped their arms tightly around each other, each understanding that they both had another life, and knowing that to a certain extent there would always be some things that they would never be able to share openly.

About two weeks later, in the U.K, Tom picked up the National Newspaper, and on page five, a small headline caught his eye, it read

US DIPLOMAT MISSING FEARED LOST AT SEA.

CHAPTER 13

With Christmas fast approaching, Tom arranged another short trip to see Maria. Once again he had to go by boat, as the airports were closed due to the currant situation in Lebanon.

When he arrived at the Port in Jounieh, he spotted Maria and her brother Joseph, waiting for him.

'Mmm, that looks interesting' he thought as he noticed the battered BMW Joseph was leaning on. Then he caught sight of the two burly men accompanying them, he raised one eyebrow to Maria. She smiled as she noticed his enquiring expression,

"Don't look so worried Tom, it's just that the foreign hostage situation has got a lot worse, and we cannot take any chances of you being taken. As you know Christmas does not mean anything to the Palestinians and Muslims."

She linked her arm through his and laughed,

"And of course I would have no one to get married too, would I?"

"Now that is very true" Tom replied smiling back at her, but at the same time he was a little concerned at the high profile reception. He put his bags in the boot of the car and noticed several loose grenades in the empty wheel arch and an AK 47 automatic. *'Oh great, so much for a peaceful break.'* At first he felt a bit shocked, but then putting it into perspective he thought, *'I guess this must be normal to them by now, I just hope they know what they're doing'*

He soon realized that things had changed since his last visit to these shores, security was certainly a lot tighter, but at least this time he had been invited to stay at Maria's home, which was deemed a lot safer than the hotel. But after a couple of days he began to feel a bit on edge, everywhere they went, one bodyguard would walk in front and one behind.

His British training had taught him to adopt a low profile at all times; making him even more anxious about the attention that these obvious guards were creating. Every meal they had out, two armed men accompanied them, even though they sat on another table, the implication was obvious.

"Maria, is this all necessary, do we really want to attract this much attention?"

She glanced quickly at the two guards, and replied in a quiet voice,

"I cannot explain to them that we don't need it, can I? Just go along with it Tom"

Adding anxiously

"No one in my family knows about my undercover work, and they certainly don't know about yours"

Looking at it from that angle, he reluctantly agreed,

"I suppose you have a point"

"I do, darling, trust me." She smiled

. "Do I have a choice?" He grinned

As that moment a young man came up to their table smiling politely,

"Excuse me Sir, I couldn't help overhearing you speak, are you English or American? Tom looked up surprised, but before he could answer the two bodyguards had the man restrained in an arm lock and rushed him out of the restaurant. The other diners looked up startled for a brief moment; and then carried on eating as before with just the odd curious look in their direction. Maria gave a little grin at Tom's surprised expression, and said,

"Just imagine if he had been a suicide bomber, or had a gun concealed"

He soon recovered his composure, and returned to his meal,

"Yes, I suppose so, but in a restaurant isn't that a bit unlikely?"

Maria shook her head sadly,

"If anything; it's the obvious place these days, nowhere is safe."

After a short while one of the bodyguards came back and whispered to Maria, before joining his partner back at their table. She leaned across to Tom and said quietly,

"You were lucky. He was carrying"

That threw him completely, but it certainly bought the local situation home to him with a jolt.

"Jesus" he breathed out slowly and looked around the room; everything was so normal. Maria watched his face,

"Do not worry about it, I am sure that he has been dealt with. It may have been nothing, people often carry weapons these days for their own protection."

He studied her face for any sort of expression, but there was nothing he could relate to. 'Is she just trying to put me at ease?' He really couldn't tell. Tom realized he still had a lot to learn about her undercover activities in this country.

When they had finished their meal they left the restaurant accompanied by the bodyguards. This time he had no objections.

After this very short but quite eventful visit he returned to the UK, promising to come back for the New Year, and spent the remaining few days of the holiday with his girls.

As soon as Christmas was over he returned to Lebanon, and soon after he arrived; he sensed Maria had something on her mind. Later that evening they went out together to a local restaurant; and all through the meal she still seemed quiet, so as they walked back to the car after the meal; he asked,

"Are you going to tell me what's wrong?" She looked up surprised,

"It's just," she hesitated and smiled at him ruefully.

"It's you, I have you in my head all the time, and I can't concentrate as I should, I am making mistakes, and that is dangerous for me in my work as you know."

"Oh, I see" He was not sure how to respond, but he knew what she was getting at.

"I should be divorced in a couple of weeks; if that's what's worrying you, so where do we go from there?"

Maria looked relieved, now she had the opportunity to say what she felt,

"My mother keeps asking me what is happening, and she says people are asking her awkward questions, like when we are getting engaged etc. She cannot say you are already married awaiting a divorce, because everyone will think that I am the reason for the break up, and that's not true" She paused, and looked up at him with a little smile, "At least not totally true."

Teasing her as usual, he said,

"Did you tell them you haven't asked me yet?"

She laughed, and he continued,

"I expect they don't want to see you getting too dusty on the shelf, so I suppose we had better do something about it" He stopped walking, turned to face her, and taking her hands he smiled,

"Ok let's do it"

He was rewarded by the look in her eyes as he pulled her towards him, gently kissing her lips. Maria slipped her arms around his neck her eyes shining,

"Oh yes please Tom, I love you so much" He laughed; and kissed the tip of her nose,

"And I love you too"

He knew that the marriage question would crop up sooner rather than later. However it had come a little earlier than he had anticipated, as he was still married in legal terms.

Maria suggested excitedly,

"I guess we had better visit the jewellers tomorrow. What do you think?"

Tom shrugged his shoulders nonchalantly, but with a twinkle in his eye,

"Ok, if it keeps everyone happy,"

Maria looked crest fallen,

"Please don't say it like that, even if you are joking"

He looked at her worried face and grinned,

"Therefore I accept your proposal"

"Very funny darling" She answered sarcastically, adding anxiously,

"Can I tell everyone you asked me?"

This time Tom laughed out loud,

"Anything if it makes you happy "

The next day they bought two identical narrow gold band rings; that as custom dictated; they would wear on their right hands until the wedding day.

Although she was very happy for them both, Maria's mother felt a pang of sadness, she had grown to love her intended son-in-law very much, but she knew her daughter would most likely go to live in England, a country that to her seemed so very far away. George her eldest son, noticed she seemed a little quiet in spite of her smiles. He slipped an arm around her shoulder,

"What is it? What is the matter?" When she confided her fears to him, he laughed,

"Don't worry, even if she does go, England is only a short plane ride away. You will see her often I'm sure." His mother smiled, although she wasn't quite so sure, she knew she must not spoil their happiness by showing how she felt.

The next few days were lost in a round of congratulatory visits from family and friends, and then it was time for him to leave once more. It crossed his mind as he landed in the UK that now he was engaged to one woman while still married to another! However it would only be a formality before he was divorced, at least he hoped that was the case.

The following day he went to visit his friend Rick to tell him the news; and ask him if he would like to be his best man.

Rick was delighted, he was already planning to take his annual holiday with his wife Babs in Cyprus, and once he had managed to re-arrange his travel dates around the proposed wedding date, he happily accepted to go across to Lebanon for the two days,

The day finally came; and Tom flew into the reopened airport at Lebanon, where George met him with a warm handshake and a huge smile.

"Welcome Tom, I am pleased to see you, I hope you are ready for the big occasion?"

"As ready as I will ever be" he replied with a grin. They climbed into the battered car and George filled him in with all the family news on the drive home.

The next couple of days were extremely busy, as they needed to get approval from the Orthodox Church, and complete all the paperwork involved, before the wedding could go ahead.

Saint Nicholas Church where they were to be married was situated a few hundred yards from the so-called 'Green Line' the strip of no mans land between the Christian East and Muslim West. Secretly Tom would have preferred it to be in a safer area, but Maria had her heart set on being married in the Church she had attended most of her life.

The evening before the wedding a large party had been organised. Traditionally the bride's family, and the groom's family held separate parties, then at midnight they would join together at the bride's home. But due to the fact that the groom was from overseas without his family attending, just a single party was held at Maria's home.

The party was going well and everyone appeared to be having a good time. But in the distance Maria could hear the sounds of distant explosions,

"Turn the music up louder," she whispered to George, "We don't want to alarm the visitors, at least not yet" But gradually through the evening the shelling intensified, and by now everyone was aware of the situation, Rick sidled up to Tom who was also looking a bit anxious,

" I say Tom, Is it ok to stay here? Shouldn't we be getting into an air-raid shelter or something?" Tom laughed uneasily, saying with more bravado than he felt,

"Don't worry Rick, they will tell us if its necessary." He looked around at everyone laughing and dancing, "Nobody else appears to be bothered do they?"

The party finished around two in the morning, and by this time the shelling had stopped; so they made their way back to their hotel for the night.

They had just settled down in bed when it all started again, and this time their hotel was in direct line of the shelling barrage. Tom could hear shells dropping within two to three hundred yards of the building onto the nearby shoreline. He lay on his bed unable to sleep and not sure what to do, *'The family know where we are, and if they think we are in danger, I'm sure they will send someone to get us,'* he thought anxiously. In the other room however Rick was pacing the floor. He looked over at his wife; she was already fast asleep *'God I wish I could be like that, nothing seems to disturb her.'*

After an hour the bombardment stopped; and Tom drifted off to sleep, but for Rick sleep was impossible.

Dead on five o'clock, exactly an hour later, the shelling started once more; but this time much closer. Tom woke with a jerk, quickly dressed and went to call Rick only to come face to face with him outside the bedroom door, with Babs close behind him.

"Christ Tom, what a night, we have to get out of here"

"You're right, let's go down the back stairs to the basement. We can ask the hotel staff what to do"

When they got down to the ground floor, there was no basement, and no hotel staff to be seen.

"Where the hell is everybody?" Rick shouted above the noise of the incoming fire,

"I'm getting out of here." He headed for the door dragging Babs by the hand.

"Wait Rick don't go outside; it's better we stay here." But Rick wasn't listening, so Tom had no choice other than to follow.

They had only just got outside when George arrived in his car, clearly risking his own life. When he saw them all out in the open he shouted angrily,

"Tom what the bloody hell are you doing out here. Surely you know to stay undercover by now"

There was no time to argue as the shells and explosions were coming in fast, and to stay and have a conversation on the rights and wrongs of survival procedures was not a consideration at that moment. They jumped in the car and left the area at high speed leaving a trail of dust and stones flying behind them.

After a few short minutes they cleared the worst of the shelling, and George relaxed, he turned to survey his rather shaken passengers,

"You will all be safer with us. Sorry Tom; for shouting at you"

Tom responded in his usual manner,

"Don't worry George, I clearly understand. You were worried that your sister would not be able find another English husband. Right?"

George laughed,

"You should be safer with us, the shells are going over our house and onto the area of your hotel. We just hope they don't send one in a bit short"

They all laughed nervously,

"Bloody Hell George, how you live with this" Rick commented. George just shrugged.

When they arrived back at the house everyone was waiting for them, looking very worried. Tom put his arm around Maria and said with a grin,

"In England; it is considered bad luck to see your bride on the same day before the wedding."

"It could have been even worse luck to stay where you were," she replied with a wry smile. She looked around at her family and added,

"I do not think anyone will sleep now, I will get dressed then we can talk. I think we may have a problem if this continues this afternoon."

Tom grinned

"If this continues I may be the one with the problem tonight"

Everyone laughed at his joking innuendo, relieving the tension all round.

They spent the next few hours laughing and joking, especially jokes about wedding days and nights, until they suddenly realized the noise had stopped. Maria laughed delightedly,

"You see we didn't even notice the shelling had stopped. Would you all like to walk down to the local coffeehouse for breakfast now?" Everybody was quite happy with that suggestion; it felt good to stretch their legs after the long anxious night.

As they sat on the balcony drinking their coffee, overlooking the waters edge at Jounieh, they noticed that there were a lot of dead fish and debris floating, or washed up on the shoreline.

"That was heavy last night" Maria exclaimed, "The worst we have had for a while".

She looked around at her English friends,

"Now you know what we have to put up with," adding with a note of relief, "but I am so pleased that it has stopped, especially for today"

When they left the coffeehouse Maria linked her arm through her sisters,

"Celine and I must leave you now; we are already late for the hairdresser,"

She gave Tom a little kiss on his cheek,

"See you at church sweetie don't be late, I know what my brothers are like."

Even after that warning they were very close to being late. Maria's younger brother Joseph, who was responsible for getting them to the Church, got caught up in the aftermath of the previous night's bombardment, and it would take a racing driver with attitude to get to the church before the bride. Joseph rose to the challenge, took their lives in his hands, and managed to overtake the bridal car only two minutes before it arrived at the church.

"You know Tom," he said as he pulled up in front of the church shaking his head woefully,

"Although people get depressed with the war, there is very little suicide in our country." He laughed at Tom's puzzled expression. "All they have to do is drive on our roads"

Disappointingly, because of the bombing situation, a lot of the invited guests found themselves stranded on the other side of the 'green line', unable to get to the church. From the five hundred guests invited, less than one hundred and fifty managed to attend.

Tom was worried as he waited outside of the Church, they had had no wedding rehearsal, and so he was a bit unsure about what came next. *I suppose I'll have to play it by ear, or as they say back home, go with the flow*. He thought smiling nervously at Rick.

There was a buzz of excitement as Maria arrived with her Father. They walked towards Tom; and in the local tradition; the two men formally shook hands, and then Maria's father gave his daughter's hand over to him. She was absolutely breathtaking in her long white lace gown, her eyes shining with happiness. She looked at Tom in his white suit, maroon bow tie and cumber-band, and thought how handsome he looked; and read the love in his eyes. She could hardly believe that at last they would be together always.

Holding the hand of his lovely bride, Tom led her through the entrance of the church, pausing to cut the white and yellow ribbon that was traditionally placed across the aisle. Then he escorted her up the long aisle to the Alter.

The ceremony should have lasted one and half-hours. But the intense shelling the previous night had left everyone on edge including the two priests, also there was still a risk of a rocket attack at any time, and so it was reduced to just forty minutes. After the ceremony they quickly lined up to shake hands with all the guests, followed by a very short photo session, and then the entire ensemble disbursed as soon as possible.

Rick breathed a sigh of relief as he shook Tom's hand,

"Christ boy, that was the most nerve wracking wedding I've ever been to, but you're a lucky man all the same"

Everyone piled into their cars and headed in a convoy to Maria's home, at least two-dozen vehicles, all blasting their car horns. When they arrived the champagne was poured and a toast was made to the happy couple, and then the cake was cut. Tom took her in his arms and whispered jokingly in her ear,

"Not bad, I get the girl of my dreams, and you get a British passport"

"You cheeky English!" He stopped her unladylike expression with a kiss and laughed.

"Anyway" Maria tossed her head haughtily, "In my line of work, I don't need an English husband, to get one of those.

After a very long tiring day, they left with Rick and Babs to spend their first married night in the hotel.

"I hope we don't get a repeat of last night." Tom said gazing up into the dusky sky,

"What the hell are those four red lines in the sky, Maria?"

"Don't worry" she replied with a slight grin, " They are either Israeli aircraft, or ours flying over"

Once back in their room, Maria wrapped her arms tightly around her husband, kissing him gently she said,

"That was exhausting"

"I agree" he replied. "But I expect it was made worse by the worry of everything that happened over the last twenty four hours"

Maria started to undress, revealing her white lacy underwear, white stockings and suspenders; she had a blue garter around the top of her leg, which she had borrowed. She glanced over at Tom saying with a grin,

"You see I am very traditional, I have something old something new, something borrowed and something blue"

He looked up curiously,

"I see something new, something borrowed and blue, but where is the something old?"

As soon as he spoke he knew what she meant. Maria burst out laughing, unable to get the words out to explain, she just pointed her finger at him.

"You will pay dearly for that remark Mrs Forster" he promised with a grin.

"Don't make promises you can't keep Number four," She said seductively, as she slowly rolled the garter down her tanned leg. Tired or not, that was a promise he was definitely going to keep

Early next morning they all met up in the hotel lobby, George was driving Rick and Babs back to the airport so they could continue their holiday in Cyprus. They all piled in the car for the short journey, and after they had said their goodbyes, they decided to go for lunch. While they were eating their meal, Maria decided it was time to have a little laugh at Tom's expense for once,

"Tom, you know you asked me last night about the four red traces in the sky last night?"

Tom looked suspiciously at the laughter in Maria's eyes.

"I don't think I want to hear this do I?"

Maria, and her brother and sister could hardly speak for laughing. They had thought it hilarious; that even after watching such a heavy bombardment the previous day, he was still ready to believe that what they saw were synchronized aircraft rather than actual in-bound rockets. Tom felt a little embarrassed considering his training, and tried to justify himself by saying,

"Ok Ok. Maybe we believe what we want to believe, but I'm learning"

Recovering from her laughter Maria said,

"And don't you remember Tom, Lebanon does not have its own fighter aircraft, only helicopters, and not many of those either.

He had always had problems understanding the internal situation of this war, and it was even more difficult when trying to explain it to his European friends.

After the first night at the hotel, Maria and Tom planned to spend the rest of their honeymoon week at the family home.

Having arrived back at the house, they found that Joseph, being the artistic one, had prepared the bedroom with ribbons and flowers. They were both thrilled; it was a lovely thought, and Tom had to admit he felt much happier to be with the family, even though it was their honeymoon.

The following night something woke him in the early hours of the morning, he looked at the clock it was three a.m. and then he felt the room moving,

"Maria!" He whispered shaking her urgently, "What the hell is happening now?"

"Go to sleep darling" She said in a sleepy voice "It's only an earth tremor, and you woke up on the third one"

"Jesus" He breathed deeply "First bombs, now this. How often does this happen?"

"Not that often, stay and you will get used to it," Maria replied already drifting back into sleep.

There were a few more small tremors causing the bare light bulbs to swing gently. Tom lay on the bed nervously waiting for the next one, until he eventually went back to sleep.

The next morning he couldn't resist joking,

"You know lover that must be the third night running the earth has moved for you."

She yawned, trying to keep a straight face,

"No, only last night, and then I had to wait until three o'clock, while you slept"

"I see" Tom laughed "Well, we just have to see what we can organise for you tonight then"

Maria laughed and shook her head,

"You are getting too old for all this excitement, I think you need a break tonight."

After breakfast they drove to the nearest telephone exchange to book a call to Tom's parents in England. They waited thirty-five minutes before they were given a line through. Then just as his father answered, there was a massive explosion,

"What the hell was that?" his father asked.

"Its ok dad, Tom replied, "I'm not sure at the moment, but after the past few days I can well imagine"

"Are you both ok?" his father sounded very worried.

Tom could hear the glass breaking all around him, and then Maria opened the cubicle door, and said urgently in her best Commander's voice,

"Don't be too long. We need to move, and quickly"

"I've got to go dad, we're ok. Don't worry I will call again soon. Bye"

Maria was now operating in full official mode,

"Tom, we have to get back to the house. This area is under attack. I think it may have been a very large car bomb."

Then there was another massive explosion, shattering more windows around them. She grabbed Tom's hand and ran swiftly with her head bowed and keeping her back down low behind the parked vehicles for protection. Tom copied her action realizing there may be snipers around.

All the windows around them had been blown in and there was thick black smoke coming from the next street. They found their car, luckily it was undamaged, Maria had the car started in seconds and drove away from the area through back streets at high speed, screeching around the corners on two wheels.

When they arrived back home, they were welcomed with much relief by the family, who had realized that they were in the area that had been targeted.

To Tom's relief, the rest of the week was reasonably uneventful; but it went very quickly, and soon they were packing their many bags to make the trip back to England.

Maria had accumulated a large amount of bags and packages containing her new wardrobe, and most; if not all of their wedding gifts. She had already advised the airline that she would have excess baggage.

As soon as they arrived at the airport they booked their cases and packages in at the check in desk. The airline had arranged for the baggage to travel without charge as a wedding gift to Maria. Tom raised his eyebrows,

"You certainly have friends in high places!"

"Of course" Maria retorted with a grin.

When they arrived at Heathrow they elected to go through the red zone and be prepared to declare everything. Maria had all the relevant invoices for most of the expensive gifts. The English customs officer was very pleasant when she explained that they had just got married and were returning from their wedding. He took details, disappeared for a few moments to make a phone call and then returned with a beaming smile and said,

"You may go through, please accept this as a wedding gift from Her Majesty's government"

Tom could not believe his ears. No cost from start to finish. He whispered quietly to Maria,

"Do you think that the governments' generosity was anything to do with my little sideline?

Maria laughed, and linked her arm through his,

"Well, sweetheart, if it wasn't; mine definitely was, and believe me all governments talk."

Within three hours they were back in Tom's apartment. As soon as they had unpacked, they went to see Tom's parents; who welcomed them with open arms. He told them most of the events of the past few days but not all, knowing only too well that if he told them everything, they would be worried every time he went to Lebanon.

CHAPTER 14

There was a lot of thinking and reorganizing to do now that they were married, Tom and his father had already decided to dispense with the lease of the showroom in Cyprus, and to sell the freehold on the restaurant and nightclub in Limassol. Things had not worked out as planned, mainly due to the underhand dealings of the two Cypriot lawyers. And as Maria had already given up the lease on her apartment before she left, there was nothing to keep them in Cyprus

Tom's young daughters appeared to have accepted the new situation quite happily, but Maria always knew there were going to be bridges to be built, and she also knew it would be difficult being a foreigner, when dealing with these two very English teenagers.

The girls were spending most of their time with them now, until eventually they both declared that they wanted to stay with their father for good. Much to their surprise Jane agreed, so they had little choice other than to look for a larger home.

One day a couple of months later after they had just moved into their new home, Maria put the phone down after a call from her mother,

"Tom how would you feel about my mother coming over to stay for a while? I think she is missing us dreadfully."

"Of course, why not? It would help you with the girls, and I can understand that she wants to see you." Then he grinned, "A mother-in -law that doesn't speak English, who could ask for more? She can stay as long as she wants."

She gave him a withering look,

"Very funny." She replied sarcastically,

Then she laughed,

"Well I have bad news for you; she is going to learn English so she can communicate with you, this is what she told me"

For Maria it was ideal, for two reasons, one, she loved her mother very much, and the other being, that she did not particularly enjoy housework, and any help running a large house with five people would be very much appreciated, especially with two teenage daughters that were definitely not

domesticated either.

The family settled down into a comfortable routine, as a few happy, and thankfully uneventful months passed. Maria's mother had been with them for a while now; she was learning English fast and getting on well with Tom's daughters. So Tom decided he would take Maria on a belated honeymoon in the South of France.

He rang the travel agent, and luckily managed to book for the following week, it was all a bit quick, but Maria's mother was more than happy to take care of the girls while they were away, and the girls didn't seem to mind at all. So they packed their bags and left with a sense of freedom for a well-earned break.

They arrived early in the morning at the hotel 'Martinez', in Cannes situated close to the famous Carlton Hotel, and spent the next day relaxing on a totally secluded beach near St.Tropez.

"Oh this is heaven," Maria murmured stretching her body luxuriously as the sun warmed her skin. Tom opened one eye; squinting against the sun and looked at his beautiful wife,

"I agree, aren't you glad I thought of it."

He felt so completely content with his life now; Maria was every thing he could ever wish for. She was beautiful, thoughtful, and passionate. He was so proud to be with her, and still could not quite believe that she had eventually chosen to be with him.

Although coming from Middle East culture Maria had travelled a great deal. In doing so she had become more liberal and open minded about western life in general. She would laughingly point out to Tom various topless girls on the beach that she thought he might appreciate or had missed. Something most girls of her upbringing and culture would never dream of doing.

Very early the next morning they went back to the secluded beach. Maria removed her beach-wrap, revealing the most daring yellow and gold bikini he had ever seen in his life. '*Wow! She- - looks - - gorgeous,*' he thought giving a little wolf whistle,

"I dare you to remove your top, anyway you might as well now we are alone, no one can see you; and you can get some sun to your body" he suggested, never thinking for one minute that she would take the dare on.

To his surprise she removed the top without a second thought. She took the sun oil out of her bag, tipped it down her chest and very slowly rubbed the oil into her stomach, arms, and breasts,

"Are you happy now" she joked as she lay back on her towel.

"Not really, that was my job"

After looking around he exclaimed casually,

"I know why no one is here, it's because it's a nudist beach"

She gave a little laugh, knowing exactly what he was getting at,

"Well my darling, you can go to hell, that, I am not doing. Don't forget I am not European, we don't even go topless on the beach in my country"

After about half an hour of intense sun bathing, she was now extremely hot and burnt. She sat up and looked to the sea.

"I need to cool off darling; I think I'll take a swim"

Maria stood up, stretched, adjusted her briefs and tiptoed across the burning sand to the waters edge, and then waded in until it got deep enough to dive under the waves, she then swam out to a floating raft moored about five hundred yards away. She climbed up onto it and lay down flat on her back. Tom sat up to watch her, wishing he were a better swimmer so he could join her.

Settling herself into a comfortable position her legs dangling in the water she closed her eyes for a few minutes and let the sun warm her body.

A few minutes later she was abruptly disturbed when she heard someone approaching. She knew it couldn't be Tom, he would never swim that far, but it was clear to her that someone was about to join her on the raft. *'Oh God my top!'* She rolled off the raft into the water, holding onto the edge.

"Hi, may I join you madam?

It was a handsome young Frenchman, in or around his mid twenties; he was treading water at the opposite end of the raft. He spoke to her in French and she replied in his language.

"Sure, but can you please give me a moment?"

She eased herself backwards, lifting her bottom with her arms onto the raft, then sat feeling a bit awkward her back towards the young man, remembering what Tom had said about this being a nudist beach. The raft rocked with his weight as he climbed on board. Maria kept her head turned away from him just in case he was not suitably dressed, she said hesitantly to the stranger,

"We were told this was a nudist beach, is that right?"

"I don't think so. I live around here; and I have never heard of this before"

She swore under her breath, *"Bloody Tom! I will kill him"*

"Do you mind, Madam? He asked in a hand gesture requesting to move closer

"Oh, no it's Ok"

The young man then came and sat along side her. She felt a tinge concerned being out here alone with a complete stranger. She didn't mind being topless with Tom, but she was not comfortable displaying her breasts to yet another man. She turned herself slightly trying to keep her right shoulder towards him.

"Are you on holiday "The young man queried politely,

"Yes, just for a week with my husband, that's him on the beach," she felt more confident now she had made him aware that she was not alone.

After a short while and a dive into the sea to cool down again, she started to relax as they sat chatting amicably about his life living in St Tropez, compared with her life in England, all the usual things tourists talk about. He glanced up at the sun,

"Ah well, it's time to go, it was nice to have met you." He stood up; gave her a brief nod; and made a clean dive into the water and swam strongly back towards the shore. Maria watched him disappear almost out of sight. With her legs still dangling over the edge of the raft she lent back again on her elbows, she could see Tom sitting up on the beach and gave him a wave, but he never saw her, as she got no response.

It was mid-day and the sun was beating down on her, there was now a strong warm mistral wind. She realized she could get quite burnt, especially under these conditions, so she stood, stretched her body, and dived into the water to cool down, and then swam back to the beach.

Tom watched her rise majestically out of the water and smiled at his own thoughts. *'She looks just like that girl from the James Bond movie.'* Maria walked slowly and confidently up the beach, her dark tanned body glistened under the intense heat of the blistering sun. He continued to daydream until he was rudely brought back to earth when she got close enough to kick sand over him pretending to be cross

"You are telling me stories, you filsey boy this is not a nudist beach"

"Oh isn't it?" He grinned and brushed the sand from his chest. "My mistake"

She went on to tell him about what had happened,

"A very nice looking young sexy Frenchman appeared from nowhere and asked if he could join me on the raft"

"Are to trying to make me jealous"

"I know you very well, you're not the type, but I felt a little awkward at first, but no problems thank God, It's a pity you don't swim better darling, you would have loved it out there".

Gradually the beach was filling up as more and more people came to cool off from the heat of the day, Maria glanced around and relaxed, she no longer felt self-conscious; as it appeared that all of the girls and women without exception were sunbathing topless. She lay down and slowly applied more oil to her body while watching Tom out of the corner of her eye, and then she smiled suggestively,

"If you had been a good boy, you could have done it for me, but you were bad"

She continued, "But it was just as well I did not strip right off, otherwise it could have made it very difficult out there on the raft, wouldn't it?"

"Stop talking" he whispered leaning over her, and closing his lips on hers. Her damp body rose to meet his and then collapsed back onto the sand-covered towel. He followed her movement down their lips still remaining firmly pressed together.

"Shall we go, back to the hotel?" He murmured, as he nibbled her earlobe.

"Filsey mind" she giggled in response "So, don't start what you can't finish"

The short break revitalised them both and they returned home ready for a new start, but a few weeks after they got back Tom complained of feeling unwell, and Maria was worried he was heading for a heart attack or a stroke, he was working so hard.

"Tom, you must see a doctor, this is not right" For once he didn't argue.

She immediately called in the doctor who organised tests at the hospital. A couple of weeks after the tests, they received a letter from the specialist. The diagnosis was not good. It had eliminated all other known possibilities, but it said the symptoms indicated very early signs of Multiple Sclerosis.

Tom refused to accept the diagnosis; convinced the doctors had got it all wrong. But Maria took a more positive attitude. She read up on the disease and recognised the symptoms, and soon realized that there was no cure or treatment; so positive thinking was required for Tom's sake. Gradually as time passed, she thought he was beginning to come to terms with the situation, but in reality Tom had convinced himself that there was nothing wrong with him. So what if he was half-blind in one eye for a few months, and then in the other for a while, he could live with that.

Maria didn't push too hard, as she knew it was his way of dealing with his illness. She encouraged him to continue playing cricket, as it was now his main sporting pleasure. This seemed to take a lot of stress off of him especially with a game or two each week. But at the same time she made sure he didn't do too much, knowing that if he overdid the exercise it could lead to a heart attack or a stroke.

Tom wasn't always happy to be restricted in this way. He always wanted to do more; it was as if he needed to prove to himself that there was nothing wrong with him. But Maria was very firm,

"I want you to have as much physical pleasure as possible, but I need to see you too. Share me with your cricket team. I am sure they won't mind"

Tom, still finding her English to be quite comical, burst out laughing as he retorted

"I am sure they won't mind, and I am all for physical pleasure. But sharing you with the cricket team is a bit much to ask, isn't it?"

But Maria was not laughing although she wanted too. She ignored his joke and kept her face serious. Although Tom knew what she meant, he continued with his jovial manner,

"We can start now if you want. I am all yours for pleasure, where would you like to start?"

At last she gave in to her laughter, she could never resist when he teased her like this.

"You are still just as much a filsey bugger"

He reached out putting his arms around her waist kissing her tenderly,

"I know, but you wouldn't have me any other way, would you?"

Despite all the problems that surrounded them both, they had not lost their passion for each other or more importantly their sense of humour, and they would need both, if they were going to get through the problems that lay ahead.

CHAPTER 15

As the weeks passed Tom gradually pushed the problem of his failing health to the back of his mind, and although Maria kept a close eye on him she didn't make a big issue of it; she knew he had to handle it his own way.

One morning he arrived early in the office to find an official looking envelope lying on his desk, it was an urgent request from the Libyan government; requiring his presence in Libya to complete a visual survey of their Patrol Boat fleet; that had engines aboard that had originally been supplied by British manufacturers. He gazed thoughtfully at the letter, and then picked up the phone and dialled the M16 Head Quarters in London.

A couple of hours later he received a fax requesting him to attend a meeting at eleven a.m. the following day.

He arrived precisely at eleven o'clock, and was shown into a small side office. A senior officer explained to him exactly what MI6's expected from him whilst he was in Tripoli.

"Any questions 101?" The officer gazed at him searchingly.

"No, that's fine"

He shook Tom's hand,

"Good man" Tom could see that the meeting was over, 'Well they certainly don't waste time around here' he thought as he closed the door behind him.

He walked down the corridor and entered the main office. To his surprise and delight he spotted Lane talking animatedly to an associate. Swiftly he worked his way across the room and approached her quietly whispering softly in her ear.

"Excuse me, can I have a word with you Miss?"

Lane smiled and turned around slowly, she knew instantly the owner of this strong Australian sounding Essex accent. Her heart pounded as her eyes met his.

"Tom how lovely to see you." She kissed him on both cheeks warmly, "I'm just about finished here, how about lunch, I know a nice little Italian restaurant, not too far from here. Have you got time?"

"For you I will make time" he grinned. Lane laughed, "You never change do you"

As they made their way to the restaurant, Lane took his arm,

"How are you keeping Tom?"

"I'm fine, and you? Did you ever find a man worthy of you?"

"Sweet Tom, no, I am still single. But I noticed you finally married your Maria"

Tom shot her a quick look; remembering the last time they had met, but could tell nothing from her expression. How on earth she was not married; he would never understand.

When they were seated in the restaurant; Lane commented,

"I noticed you have had a lot of success since we last saw each other, especially the Matheson operation. Not a nice man" she shuddered. "And it was quite a coincidence that the operations Commander just happened to be your Maria." She smiled innocently as if it had been a total surprise to her.

"Yes I want to have a word with you about that" he nodded with a knowing smile. Lane ignored the implication and continued,

"She certainly made a big impression on the CIA attachment. How she managed to get the drop on him whilst he had a knife, I'll never know"

"Me neither" Tom smiled, "I guess it was just bare cheek that did it"

Lane smothered her laughter with her hand, and changed the subject

"Does she know about your plans to Tripoli?" She asked

"Not yet. I didn't know myself what they wanted from me until today"

"You can tell her Tom, she is MI6 cleared and still operational. You knew that of course?"

"I guessed as much," he nodded in agreement, "but we don't discuss these things unless it's necessary"

Then she told him something that he was not aware of,

"Well, I can tell you she is closely linked with us at a very high level, and she has already been briefed on what is required from you on this trip"

Now that really surprised him, Maria had shown no awareness of this when he had told her he was going to Head Quarters.

"Oh I see. Is there more to this brief than I have been told, do you know?"

Lane looked as though she was going to say more, but hesitated,

"Of course, but later. Let's, just enjoy this meal for now. Ok?"

After their lunch they strolled back to the office, Lane with a bounce in her step put her arm through Toms once more.

"Now I am going to surprise you again Tom"

He shook his head

"I doubt that very much"

Lane laughed,

"Perhaps not, I was just going to say, I have met Maria on a few occasions, and I really like her very much"

"No, it doesn't surprise me" Tom said shaking his head, "I don't think anything really surprises me in this business"

Lane continued,

"Very sensible. By the way, we have a young French agent; who thinks Maria is very intelligent, and that she has a very nice figure"

"South of France, last June right?" Tom retorted.

She laughed at the look on his face,

"Spot on, sir"

He laughed, the very thought of Maria being checked out whilst she was on that raft and half naked, was quite something. *'Just wait until I tell her'* he thought. *'Although I expect by now she already knows'* He was beginning to realise that his wife was way out of his league in these matters.

Another meeting had been arranged at three o'clock, and at least six key MI6 personnel were there. Lane chaired the meeting.

"Gentlemen, you all know, or have heard of our agent 101. So let us get down to what we need out of Libya during his arranged visit" She looked down the long boardroom table at the group in front of her and smiled, "At the request of the Libyan Navy would you believe?"

Turning to Tom, she instructed.

"Please 101, give us a brief outline of your official objective, as required by the L.N.O.C."

Tom stood and walked around the table confidently.

"My company has been asked to survey four fast patrol boats, and the one and only dilapidated submarine, plus our old friend Colonel Gadaffi's flag ship the 'Dats Awari.' This could eventually mean two or three visits to the Libyan shipyards in Benghazi and Tripoli surveying the spare parts stores, and general condition of the vessels"

At that point the operations commander interrupted loudly,

"Needless to say we do not want the Colonel's vessels made seaworthy 101"

"Well, sir" Tom replied, "We should all understand that if 'WE' don't do it, then the Germans will, sanctions or no sanctions"

Lane intervened quickly,

"Then you will have to see to it that your survey is as misleading as possible. Right 101?"

"Fine, no problem" He raised his eyebrows at Lane and shrugged, "Only twelve million pounds worth of lost business"

"You don't need to change your Jaguar just yet do you 101?" she retorted with a sympathetic smile.

He shook his head in resignation

"I guess it can wait a bit longer"

After they had discussed the technical issues the meeting closed, and Tom was ready to catch the train back home. He kissed Lane goodbye and left London at four thirty, arriving back home around quarter past six.

Maria greeted him with an apologetic kiss,

"Sorry darling, but you know I wasn't free to say anything until you had been briefed"

"It's ok, I understand, but it's hard sometimes, knowing your wife knows what is happening before you do. Not good for my ego" he grinned ruefully. Maria laughed,

"That will do you no harm at all"

He told her that he was flying to Malta at the weekend, she knew the dangers if he was caught, but she said nothing. They both knew the rules. *'But it is just as hard for me,* Maria thought, *'I sometimes wish I didn't know the dangers involved'*

It had been pre-arranged that he was to meet an undercover Maltese agent called Max. He remembered Max from the training course in Scotland and looked forward to seeing him again.

As soon as he had cleared customs in Malta, he went to find his colleague who he was told would be waiting for him in the coffeehouse. They greeted each other warmly and made their way to the Hilton Hotel where Tom had pre-booked. After arranging to meet later for dinner, Max left him to unpack.

"By the way" Tom remarked later that evening. "Lane sends her kindest regards and hopes you are well"

"Thanks. You know Tom," He smiled, " During those couple of weeks in Scotland, we all thought you and Lane had a thing going on"

"Rubbish" Tom protested, but with a hint of a smile, "There was nothing like that, she is a nice girl, more like my young sister"

Max laughed "But you don't have a sister"

"Ah" Tom grinned, "Well if I did, that's is how we would be together"

"Ha Ha, very good" Max retorted "But why do you think she didn't marry anyone else?"

Tom was getting a bit uncomfortable with this conversation

"No idea, anyway lets discuss the arrangements for tomorrow"

Max got the message.

"Ok, Ok, I get the picture, lets leave that subject then"

Next morning very early Tom boarded the plane for the short flight to Tripoli.

It was extremely hot and airless as he worked his way through the arrivals terminal. The Sun was beating down through the dirty glass windows. *'It looks as though this place has not been cleaned for months, if not years,'* he thought mopping the sweat from his brow. He stopped at the customs desk to have his luggage searched and visa checked, and then made his way to currency control.

There was a strict law stating that you had to change a minimum of five hundred dollars at the airport customs at a very poor exchange rate, one US dollar to one Libyan dinar instead of the usual three Libyan dinars. A result of tit for tat measures imposed by Colonel Gadaffi in response to the UN imposed sanctions on Libya.

Tom checked in at his hotel; and then made his way to the reception hall. He had arranged to meet the military officer responsible for arranging all the high-level contacts he needed, for the required survey, and the possible overhaul of their six stricken vessels.

Two days later, having visibly inspected the engines, and made all the necessary notes, Tom had obtained enough information for a second visit. And this would require two of his engineers coming over to do the full survey on all the vessels.

In the morning on his last day, he was driven to the procurement head quarters of the Libyan armed forces, to submit his report and quotation. A surly young soldier showed him into a bare dirty high ceiling hall rather than a room. Tom looked around wandering what to do next, there was a motley selection of chairs scattered around the perimeter, and a table in the centre that was being used as a reception desk. He sat down on the nearest rickety chair about half way along one side of the hall.

Half an hour later he was still sitting there totally ignored by the man at the reception desk. Tom shifted in his seat uncomfortably, *'I have just about had enough of this,'* he thought angrily. He walked over to the man at the desk,

"Excuse me, I have an appointment with the head of procurement. How much longer will he be?"

"Please wait sir, we shall have someone with you soon" the man replied curtly without raising his head from the papers in front of him. A few minutes later the dirty black telephone on the desk rang, the man spoke very quietly into the mouthpiece shielding his words from Tom, not that he would have understood anyway as the man was talking very fast Arabic. Then he looked up,

"Why are you here, Mr......... ummm. ......Foster"?

"The name is Forster" Tom corrected "And I'm here to see the head of procurement"

"Why" the official enquired in the same curt tone.

"To discuss the British machinery used within your Navel Department." He was beginning to feel a little uneasy. Something wasn't right.

"Most irregular," the man looked agitated "Who made the appointment?"

Knowing full well that he couldn't mention Hassan's name, he replied,

"My office in London"

"Give me the papers on your Company, and wait here,"

The official spoke softly into the phone before replacing the receiver, and held out his hand in a nonchalant manner for the papers.

Tom's anxiety increased,

"Look, my friend, I can only give you five more minutes as I have a plane to catch,"

The man ignored his remark and left the hall. Tom looked around the gloomy room, the silence was almost deafening, he realised that something was seriously wrong. Although he understood very little Arabic, he had managed to pick up the word 'police.' He knew he had to get out of here. As casually as he could he walked slowly out of the room; and headed for the main door trying not to attract too much attention.

With his heart in his mouth he nodded briefly to the two guards guarding the entrance of the premises with rifles crossed. They looked at him briefly; and then straightened their rifles, and moved back slightly to allow him to exit. Controlling the urge to run, he walked away from the building knowing that his back was making a rather large target. His legs felt like jelly, and the hair on the back of his neck prickled, but he kept focused on the main gates about twenty metres away; across the concrete compound, all the time waiting for some sort of alert to be sounded. With a sigh of relief he reached the gates and walked quickly away out of view. Almost immediately a taxi drew up along side of him.

The driver beckoned him to get in quickly. By now Tom was wary of everybody, he hesitated, glancing back at the compound where he could hear voices getting closer.

"It is ok Mr Forster, Hassan sent me to keep an eye on you" The taxi driver leaned over and opened the car door, "Please get in, it is not safe here"

Tom didn't need telling twice, at the mention of Hassans name; he threw himself into the car and the man drove off before he had chance to close the door.

"Hassan said to take you straight to the airport, and don't worry about your bag" he grinned jerking his head to the back seat.

Tom sat back in his seat hanging on for dear life, as the young man drove like a maniac to the airport, once there they shook hands; and with a cheerful grin he departed at the same breakneck speed.

When he got through customs, he sat and waited in the departure area for his flight mulling over the last few hours. He was deep in thought, when he looked up to see Hassan striding towards him full military uniform. Tom rose to greet him,

"That was close, what was the problem at the procurement department?"

Hassan shook his hand,

"Sorry about that. I have since found out that the head of procurement is under investigation, which explained why there was all the extra interest in you"

"Great" Tom replied with a slight note of sarcasm in his voice,

"Anyway my report is with them now, one way or another"

"That's ok, no problem we can track that" Hassan reassured him "The Government will need your team in three months time, can you still manage the full detailed survey?"

"That's Ok with me" Tom agreed,

They shook hands warmly

"Fine and I will be in touch," Hassan answered firmly, shook his hand once again, turned and strode briskly away. Tom boarded the aircraft with a distinct feeling of relief, and sat back for the short flight back to Malta, and within one hour he had connected with his flight to London.

CHAPTER 16

Maria put down the telephone and glanced at Tom, she had been waiting for this call from HQ. She smiled at him apprehensively,

"Darling, I need to go to London for a couple of days, do you mind?"

"You mean you want me to keep an eye on the girls and take a couple of days off work?" he grinned. Maria gave a wry smile; putting her arms around his neck,

"You know me only too well darling but there's no need, my mother can manage"

"Sure, any particular reason?" He inquired warily.

"Well, yes there is," she looked serious. "But I cannot say right now, are you Ok with that?"

He felt a pang of anxiety; it was ages since this sort of situation had arisen; life had been so normal and quiet, so much so; he had almost forgotten the business they were both in. He put his feelings to one side, and tried to act unconcerned,

"Fine, no problem"

By the time Tom arrived home from the office the following evening, Maria was packed and ready to go. She planned to take the early morning train to London.

"I called Lane and told her I was coming up for a day or so. She was over the moon, she wants me to stay with her." Maria said as she busied herself preparing dinner.

"Good, at least I can get you on the phone if I need you" he smiled relieved; at least she would be with Lane.

The next morning Maria left very early for the train, to her relief she managed to get a seat despite the usual rush hour traffic. Just after nine, she arrived in London to be met at the barrier gates by Lane. The two women greeted each other warmly, and drove directly to the newly designed offices of MI6 at Vauxhall Cross, but well within easy walking distance of the old building at Lambeth.

"Very impressive" Maria commented nodding her head in approval.

A high level ministerial meeting had been arranged to discuss and collate the top-secret information that she had recently obtained from 'The Phoenician' while Tom was in Libya, and also to re-arrange her line of communication.

A couple of hours later, after the meeting had finished, Lane and Maria took a taxi into the city centre, where they found a nice little French restaurant in one of the small back streets in Hammersmith.

"I feel quite exhausted," Lane said dropping down in her seat, "Tell me, why are most foreign office politicians total prats when it comes to standing up and being counted?

Maria grinned,

"They are the same all over the world, I can assure you of that."

The meal was delicious; and after they settled the bill; Lane asked

"Shall we go back to my place now, or would you like to hit the shops?"

"Oh shops please." Maria laughed delighted; she was dying to see what London had to offer. Later that afternoon they returned to Lane's apartment by taxi, with more bags than they could carry, retail therapy well and truly satisfied

Maria looked around her; she was instantly impressed by the décor, and tidiness!

"This is very nice" She exclaimed, you have a lovely apartment. I do love London, far better than the end of the world place where we live.

Lane smiled,

"Thanks. By the way, how is your Tom? I enjoyed seeing him when he came to the office a while ago. You are very lucky with that husband of yours, he is a real gem"

"Yes I know, Maria replied, he is lovely, but not the usual type for this undercoverbusiness"

Lane gave her friend a quick look,

"Is there a type?" She asked. "That's a strange thing to say when you both do the same type of work"

Maria laughed,

"I suppose it was an odd thing to say, but you know what I mean."

"Yes I suppose I do really, he's certainly not like some I've met"

Maria sat down on Lane's expensive looking leather sofa and rubbed her aching feet, hoping they would stand up to the night out that had been planned for later with some of Lane's colleagues.

Lane disappeared into the kitchen and came back with two glasses and a bottle of red wine,

"We have ages before we need to get ready, let's just relax and have a good chat"

"Mmm good idea" Maria said kicking off her shoes and curling her legs up in the chair. "Ever been in love, Lane" she quizzed,

Lane grinned, as she reached over to pour the wine,

"Yes, once but you already had him"

Maria smiled; she had half guessed that Lane had a thing for Tom,

"You know" she replied, "In a way he loves you too, and I don't mind that one little bit"

Lane was relieved that Maria was not jealous in any way.

" It must be so reassuring to have that sort of trust in each other. I just hope one day I can find what you both have."

Maria nodded her head in agreement.

"I suppose it is unusual, considering that we come from two different worlds almost"

"Yes it is" Lane peering at her empty glass, "I would think almost unprecedented."

A couple of glasses later; Maria stood and yawned;

"Would you mind if I had a rest for a while before we get ready, I'm afraid that wine has made me sleepy "

 "Me too, I will set the alarm for one hour, which will leave us plenty of time to get ready."

Lane woke with a start when the alarm went off,

"Maria, time to get ready. Would you like to use the shower first or second, you choose"

"I'll go second" came the sleepy reply"

Soon they were showered dressed and ready to party. Both young women looked exceptional. Lane wore a fashionable short black tight fitting dress with a high back and plunging neckline, set off by a pale green belt, shoes and bag.

Maria was dressed in a red calf length figure hugging pure silk oriental dress; in complete contrast to Lane's, as hers had a high necked Chinese collar at the front and a very; very low plunging back and a deep split up one side.

They walked around admiring each other's dresses

"Oh dear" Maria exclaimed looking anxiously at herself in the full-length mirror,

"I think I can see the top of my underwear at the back, can you?"

 Lane laughed,

"Yes, I am afraid I can see your knickers"

"Knickers? Maria repeated, "Oh, you mean my briefs. Oh God, what will I do now"

Her face looked comical with her dismay,

"You only have one option, and that is to go commando" Lane laughed.

Maria looked puzzled

"What is it? I never heard this expression before" Then it dawned on her. "You mean don't wear any!"

Lane remained silent just watching her friend's facial expression in amusement.

"Oh I can't, no way, no, no, no," Maria exclaimed, beginning to laugh.

"You have no choice if you want to wear that dress" Lane laughed. When she thought back to what Maria had been through on that last assignment, *'It was odd; that she should be so worried about such a little thing as going commando'*.

"Oh and a word of warning Maria, be careful of Terry tonight. He thinks he is Gods gift, and with you in that dress and no knickers! But he is a dear; and a damn good reliable agent"

Just then the taxi arrived; and within twenty minutes they were at the Mayfair Inter-Continental Hotel, where Lane's colleagues; three men and one woman greeted them. Maria whispered out of the corner of her mouth to Lane.

"Somebody worked out the numbers"

Lane waved her hand roughly in the direction of the group; and with an almost unnoticeable wink said,

"Maria, this is Terry, I have told you all about him,"

Then she nodded in the direction of the others saying,

"That's Brian, and Peter, and this is Emma.

Maria quite liked the look of Emma; she had a very open friendly smile. She turned to greet the other two men, they were a lot younger and seemed a little reserved as they shook her hand. And then it was Terry's turn,

"I hope Lane hasn't been telling you untruths about me Maria?"

She smothered a grin as he took her hand and raised it to his lips and kissed it,

"Are there anymore in Lebanon like you?"

Lane gave an imaginary yawn; she had heard Terry's chat up line many times before,

"No there is not, she is unique, so be careful you randy old sod"

There was much laughter at Lane's comment, as they went in to find their table for dinner. Terry as expected positioned himself between Lane and Maria. He was a tall rather good-looking man in his late thirties early forties; well-groomed and obviously very fit, with dark hair, and sporting the latest fashion of a one day's growth of beard. Maria's first impression was that he was pleasant enough, but she had been warned.

He smiled at Maria,

"I hear your old man is in the business"

She found that slightly irritating,

"You mean my husband, who is not old, and yes he is; but part-time mostly"

Totally oblivious to her rebuff, he continued

"I have also heard excellent reports of you"

"Really" Maria replied coolly. For a brief second she was tempted to tell him of the reports she had heard of him. She glanced around at the others, she would have liked to talk with Emma, but Terry continued to monopolize her attention.

"I hear you're running the Middle East for us with 'The Phoenician.'

"Then you heard incorrectly" she retorted, "I am only assisting your organisation, as and when I can"

He was rather enjoying the verbal banter with this feisty young woman, and continued with a mischievous grin,

"The raid to rescue that ugly Bas…" He quickly corrected himself; "Yank in West Beirut was for us wasn't it? And apparently so I heard, a first class exhibition"

She couldn't hide a slight smile, but didn't respond, allowing him to make his point.

"Did you know you are quite famous for being the mother of all belly dances, I read your file, and you're very cool under pressure, I like that in my women"

He smiled to himself waiting for the obvious backlash, which was not too long in coming,

"I am NOT one of your women," Maria retorted sharply. "And you should not believe everything you read"

Terry laughed, "Ah but I know what I see." His eyes roved over her body, he couldn't resist teasing her further,

"I was also wondering how the hell you got into that dress tonight," He saw the look in her eyes and lifted his hands up in submission, "but of course, I'm not complaining"

Maria opened her mouth to answer, but changed her mind; she was having the same thoughts about the dress herself. *'One thing for sure, there is no panty line showing'* she thought.

When the band started playing the 'Lambada' Terry stood up, put his napkin beside his plate and bowed to her in a very gentlemanly manner, holding his hand out for her to join him.

"This will be an experience," She whispered to Lane as she rose to follow him onto the dance floor.

Terry soon realized Maria knew how to dance the 'Lambada,' which he was well aware that if danced correctly is very raunchy, and he was rather enjoying the movement of her body as it moulded to his.

Fortunately for Maria the music changed to a waltz, Terry held her a little too close for her liking. As they glided around the floor his left hand was still at the base of her spine, pulling her closer again. At that point, and knowing his history Maria suspected that he was trying to take advantage of the situation as his hand strayed slightly below what she considered to be an acceptable level. Considering how she was dressed; or not as the case may be, she slowly reached up very close to his ear as if she was going to kiss him on the cheek; and whispered,

"Remove your hand my friend or you will not be able to walk back to the table"

He instantly obliged his face showing no reaction, but still kept her very close to him. Maria smiled to herself. Then the lively music changed to a smooch 'The first time ever I saw your face' this was Tom and Maria's special tune. She apologised to her partner,

"I'm sorry Terry, but I would like to sit if you don't mind"

She walked back to their table; she knew that she could never dance to that tune with any man other than Tom.

Lane had been watching them on the dance floor and smiled at Maria raising her eyebrows questionably as she took her place back beside her at the table. Maria smiled back with a very slight shake of her head indicating there was no problem with Terry.

Terry leaned across the table and poured them both another glass of wine,

"As a matter of interest, you and I have a joint assignment in Cyprus"

"Are you referring to me?" Maria queried, realizing that he was looking directly at her.

"Of course, how do you feel about that?" he replied

"Where exactly in Cyprus?"

"British airbase at Akrotiri near Limassol,"

Confirming Terry's announcement, Lane interrupted,

"That's right; I was going to tell you later." She gave Terry a withering look. "We need to brief you on the assignment before you leave,"

Not one to miss a chance, he laughingly winked at Lane,

"Briefs she has not"

Maria rolled her eyes, and looked at Lane in mock horror, Lane shook her head in despair as she said sarcastically,

"He is a man of the world, and has been taught to spot all these little points" The two women burst out laughing.

Terry continued to pester Maria, he realised that he was getting nowhere with her, but he more than liked a challenge.

They sat drinking and talking for another hour and a half, mainly about the Cypriot assignment, until Emma stood and yawned,

"It's late Terry, I think we had better get going"

Terry glanced at his watch, and looked up in dismay realising that he had no option, he had promise to escort her home. Reluctantly he rose out of his seat,

"What about you two ladies, can I give you a lift?" Lane shook her head grinning, she knew he was waiting for her to invite them back to the apartment, but there was no way she going to sit up half the night while Terry flirted with Maria. He knew when he was beaten.

"Ok, but I will see you two ladies tomorrow"

After Terry and Emma left, Lane phoned for a taxi, and as soon as they got home they both wearily went straight to bed.

Next morning they awoke quite early, had a quick breakfast, showered, and dressed. They had made an arrangement to meet Terry in Hyde Park to discuss in more detail when and where in Cyprus the operation was to take place, and the exact nature of the problem. Lane being the perfect organiser had already arranged everything they needed for a picnic.

By the time the women arrived; Terry was already waiting. He kissed them both and gave a dramatic sigh,

"You both look just as ravishing as you did last night, I really thought you would have invited me back to your apartment last night Lane, we could have had a delightful end to a delightful evening"

Lane laughed and patted his cheek,

"You old flatterer. You couldn't manage one of us, let alone two"

Terry pulled a face, "Now you have really hurt my feelings"

Although they were all laughing and joking, Maria wondered how much truth lay behind his joking remarks, she wasn't at all sure if she would trust him on a one to one basis.

"Now, perhaps someone will tell me, why am I required in Cyprus?" Maria questioned

Terry looked meaningfully at her,

"We are after a particular British Army officer; who is running a very nasty game out of Limassol, and he has a strong preference for dusky Arabs.

Maria's eyes flashed with anger at that statement, she responded sharply,

"Lebanese Christians are not Arabs"

He raised both his hands in his now familiar act of submission, still smiling,

"Ok Ok but he won't know the difference"

She still hostile, felt irritated by Terry's ignorant attitude,

"He will unless he is bloody stupid. Why, what has he done?"

Terry stopped smiling, he realised he may have gone too far,

"Sorry Maria. We suspect he is collaborating with Russian outlaws. Women are disappearing, and we don't know how. Ten have disappeared in the three weeks; we believe they are being used in the sex industry, and we need to get someone in there quickly, to find out who is involved and what is happening to these women."

"When?"

"Tomorrow," he replied, "everything is booked"

Maria frowned, deep in thought, then after a long pause answered,

"Right, Ok. I suppose I had better go home today and get packed"

"Bikini's are an essential part of your assignment kit," Terry continued with a glimmer of a smile, "The more revealing ones you have the better"

Maria looked sharply at Terry's face, then at Lane,

"Are we talking entrapment here?"

Lane nodded sympathetically,

"We might be, but we are not sure if it will work"

"Then we will have to make sure that it does work." Maria confidently replied, standing up to brush some crumbs from her short skirt.

"We had better get back I have a lot to do"

Terry looked at her with undisguised approval, realising that all he had heard and read about her was correct. As soon as they had cleared up, he drove both women back to Chelsea where Maria collected her overnight bag, before he took her on to Liverpool Street Station.

She arrived back home mid-afternoon, and partly briefed Tom of her mission, purposely leaving out the bikini requirement.

"How long do you expect all this to take?" he enquired anxiously. And then Tom being Tom joked,

"If it's Cyprus; you had better pack all your bikinis"

Maria smiled at the mention of bikinis rather than a bikini, but on the question of, 'how long', she could not say, a time limit on any covert operation; was an unknown factor, and she knew Tom knew that anyway, before he asked.

"I really don't know, a week perhaps, hopefully no more, but don't worry if it turns out to be a little longer"

Trying to sound far more casual than he actually felt, he replied,

"Fine, I'll drive you to the airport"

"No need," she replied, playing the same casual game "They are sending a car for me at seven o'clock"

Making an effort to keep the anxiety he was feeling out of his voice he said calmly,

"Then I think we had better get an early night"

Maria knew how much an effort this was for him; she slipped her arms around his neck.

"What would I do without you, darling?" She whispered placing a gentle kiss on his cheek.

Tom hugged her very tight struggling with the lump in his throat; he knew the dangers for an attractive woman like Maria in this business, especially as he knew only too well that she was never one to leave things to others.

"Why not give Clive a look when you're there, he may be able to assist you"

She pulled a face at him, wrinkling her nose,

"I am sure he could, but not in the way you mean. Anyway, I already have one man coming with me who is on an ego trip, I really don't need another, especially not a CIA"

Maria's car arrived next morning just before seven, she was dressed ready and waiting. She had said her goodbyes to Tom's girls the previous night, and to her mother earlier this morning, and now she held him tight for a brief moment and gave him one last tender kiss, then got in the car willing herself not to look back.

Very soon she would be on her way to another very tricky assignment.

CHAPTER 17

Tom stood at the door and watched as Maria's car turned the corner and disappeared from sight, already the house felt empty without her. He could hear her mother busying herself in the kitchen preparing the children's breakfast. Slowly he made his way through to the kitchen trying to put his anxieties to one side before the girls woke up. Suddenly the shrill ringing of the telephone interrupted his thoughts. He picked up the receiver.

"Forster!"

"Good morning, 101 this is HQ, we need you to report to London immediately, something rather important has cropped up"

"Blast! Not very good timing" Tom cursed, "Ok I will be there as soon as I can sort something out here"

"That means today, 101, there is an urgent briefing at 1400 hours" There was a sharp click; the phone line went dead.

Tom looked at the receiver still in his hand,

"Oh Shit!"

He went through to the kitchen to speak to Maria's mother.

"What is it Tom? You have problem?"

He gave a wry smile,

"Yes in a way, I have to go to London this morning on important business, would you be able to manage the girls on your own for a while? I don't know for sure how long but I'll let you know as soon as I can."

"Of course," she smiled happily, "That is no problem. They are always good with me, I am happy with them". Tom gave a sigh of relief, and quietly thanked God that she was still here; at least he hadn't got to involve anyone else in the family for help, who might well want to know where he was going

After breakfast, Tom explained to the girls that he too had to go away for a short while, which to his surprise didn't seem to worry them at all, especially when he said he would bring them back a present if they were very good for their step-grandmother.

There was a train at noon that would get him to the London office easily by two p.m. He arrived at the HQ with only minutes to spare. Once security cleared, he walked down the corridor to the Head of Departments office; he tapped lightly on the half opened door, the officer looked up,

"Right Forster, I have a sealed envelope here, no time for a detailed briefing we now have to move quickly." He handed it to Tom.

"You will only open this when you are on board the aircraft, and," he gave a slight grin, "as usual; it's a 'D' and 'D' (*digest and dispose*). There is a car waiting outside; and your ticket will be ready for you at the British Airways desk as soon as you arrive."

Tom opened his mouth, but before he could say a word the officer picked up his telephone and dialled a number, and then almost as an after thought he reached out with his hand.

"Good Luck 101"

Within a matter of minutes Tom was being driven at high speed to Heathrow airport, still with no idea why or where he was going.

As soon as he was dropped off he went to the British Airways ticket desk.

"First class, very nice, but why Malta for Christ sake?" He muttered to himself, looking at the ticket in front of him.

Checking the flight times he saw his flight was now being boarded, so he made his way quickly to the boarding gate. Once on board and settled in his seat he looked around, there were only four passengers in first class, two men opposite, one in front and a woman's well manicured hands clasping and reading the 'Times' directly opposite him. When the plane had taken off and levelled, Tom opened the envelope he had been given, and started to digest the contents. He was interrupted,

"Champagne, sir?' A pretty young airhostess smiled down at him.

But before he could answer, a soft female voice from behind the newspaper said,

"I think you will find this gentleman doesn't drink"

Tom laughed.

"He most certainly does." He took a glass from the slightly bemused hostess and leaned back on his headrest,

"I hope you are not trying to pick me up young lady?"

"You wish" she replied lowering her newspaper, a little embarrassed as the hostess shot her a questioning look.

"You pig, she will think I don't know you." Lane grinned and got up to sit beside him, he laughed and kissed her on the cheek.

"Where the hell did all this come from?" he asked; waving the envelope he had just opened. "It doesn't say a lot except something is brewing that will affect the whole western world"

Lane answered quietly.

"From the Phoenician, and so far he has been top drawer with his information, so no reason to question it. The information I received; is that it's about an unknown group preparing to sabotage oil installations"

"Who the hell benefits from blowing oil wells, all it will do is push up the price of oil"

"Exactly. The U.K. has limited North Sea oil I know, but the west in general couldn't survive without imported oil."

Tom nodded in agreement.

" I suppose so, but why me?"

"You won't be alone, Max; our Maltese agent will be with you, he has been working on this for a couple of days, and will update you when you arrive."

Tom was relieved at least he would have some back up, and although he didn't know Max very well; they seemed to get on ok, but more importantly; he trusted him.

"What about you, where do you fit into this?" he asked. Lane smiled,

"I will be coordinating the whole thing from Valletta"

"Mmm, the easy bit as usual" He remarked, waiting for the verbal backlash.

"Yes" she grinned, for once not biting back. "Here is my phone number and room number, call in every four hours and that's an order 101"

They stopped talking as their meal arrived. The hostess smiled politely at Lane,

"Would you like your dinner served here madam?" she asked, and then gave Tom a questioning look.

"It's ok" Lane laughed. "We do actually know each other."

"But not very well" Tom laughed

Once the aircraft had landed they collected their luggage and left the arrivals hall separately, Tom was booked into the 'Excelsior Hotel' and Lane was in the 'Hilton'

Shortly after he had finished unpacking, there was a tap at the door, peering through the spy hole he could see it was Max so he opened the door.

Striding confidently into the room Max shook hands with Tom.

"Nice to see you again 101, this time I've brought you a little gift" he held out a gun wrapped in a duster. Tom raised his eyebrows.

"That bad, eh?"

Max opened the hotel mini bar and took out a whisky offering one to Tom, who declined.

"So I understand," he answered throwing his head back and swallowing the drink in one go.

"What we need to know is who is behind the plot and when it's going to take place. You know of course its oil don't you?"

Tom nodded,

"Lane confirmed it, yes. Have you any idea where?"

"Not as such, but pretty damn sure. We need to get inside their organisation. I have a meeting at 10.30 tonight with someone who I think may be ready to help"

"Right" Tom answered, "Where do we meet him?"

"Sorry old chap" Max grinned. "Not you, this one I meet alone. If he sees anyone else it will scare them off" Tom wasn't very happy with that; but he had no choice other than to agree.

"I guess so, but I will expect you to report back here before midnight, either by phone or in person. Because if I haven't heard from you by that time, I will come looking."

After Max left Tom went down in search of a meal, thankfully there were only a few people in the restaurant so he was able to eat his dinner in peace. When he had finished he went back to his room to wait for Max to contact him. He glanced at his watch and saw it had only just turned ten o'clock; so he switched on the TV and absently flicked through the channels, and then lay back on the bed watching a local wild life program. About an hour later the phoned rang,

"Hi Tom, it's me, we are on, I'll be with you in a few minutes"

Max arrived within fifteen minutes and sounded quite jubilant.

"I understand from my contact that it's a hit on the oil rigs in Saudi."

"Christ" Tom replied. " Where the hell do we start?"

"Can you bring Lane and meet me in the morning downstairs in the hotel lounge about 9.30? We can discuss it then." Max headed for the door,

"I can't stop my friend as much as I enjoy your company. I have better things waiting for me down stairs" He winked at Tom and grinned as he closed the door behind him.

Tom sat for a moment trying to digest the enormity of the job ahead of him, and then he picked up the phone and dialled Lane.

"Lane, I've been in contact and your information is correct, it is the Saudi oil installations" He relayed to her about the arranged meeting with Max but avoided telling her any further details over the phone.

"My God Tom, this one is going to be difficult, there is a very thin diplomatic path to walk here."

"We should know more in the morning. I feel a bit useless at the moment with Max doing all the leg work"

Lane gave a short laugh,

"Don't worry about him; your time will come, and it won't be easy." There was a slight pause then she said softly, "Good night Tom, and take care"

"I'll try. Goodnight now." He put the phone down and lay back on the bed deep in thought.

Next morning, after breakfast Tom made his way to the hotel lounge and was surprised to find Max accompanied by an extremely attractive young woman. Within a matter of minutes Lane joined them. Max rose to greet Lane giving her a kiss on each cheek.

"Lane, Tom, this is Leila."

Leila smiled and shook hands with them both. "Pleased to meet you" Lane sat down next to her and poured a coffee, while Tom pulled Max to one side,

"This is your contact?"

"Indirectly yes. It was her who set it up for me last night."

Tom grinned and raised one eyebrow. Max laughed,

"Don't worry she is well connected'

"So I can see" Tom laughed, they turned back to the women, who were chatting and drinking their coffee.

"Right Leila, I will leave it to you to explain" Max sat down and leaned back in his seat

"Ok, I have been accepted into a little known terrorist group based here in Malta whose sole aim is to raise the price of crude oil world wide, causing massive escalation of prices. This will cause chaos in Saudi, and imagine what it will do to the West. Also it satisfies their personal grievances of being exploited"

"Oh I see, that old chestnut. But why Saudi?" Lane asked

"Because Saudi are the ones over supplying, and refusing to stick to their Opec quota, therefore keeping the prices low to the West, and the poorer countries just can't compete with them"

"Do we know which Saudi installations are being targeted?" Tom asked

"No, but I understand there are four or five in total"

Lane looked thoughtful,

"OK, thanks for that information. We need to get into their organization, can you help?"

Leila grinned,

"I can try, and I will let Max know tomorrow"

"Tonight would be better, join us for dinner around nine o'clock, we need every minute we can get" Lane replied firmly.

"OK, I'll try my best." She stood, shook hands with Lane and Tom; smiled at Max and left the hotel lounge.

Lane continued discussing tactics with her two operatives

"Any suggestions gentlemen?"

"It will need a lot of thought" Tom replied

Lane turned to Max,

"How well do you know Leila, Max?"

"Well enough I feel, I was introduced to her by the department a couple of weeks ago, she is highly intelligent for her age, which incidentally is twenty three, her mother is English, her father is French, and she works undercover as a receptionist at the Regency Hotel"

"How did she make contact with the terror group" Tom queried

"They are staying at her hotel, and from their actions she suspected that they may be up to no good. She was chatted up by one of them, and during the past few days she spent a lot more time with him trying to find out what they are doing in Malta"

"OK" Lane replied, "Let us see what else she can give us this evening. What I need you to do Max is to hang around the Regency, check a few things out. We need to find out their real names, origin, room numbers and so on, and then we can ask London if they have them on file"

"I doubt they will be using their own names" Tom intervened "So I am thinking why we don't organise a function away from the hotel. Leila can invite them through the one she is friendly with"

"Good idea Tom" Lane responded.

"Right, Lets start to get it organised"

Max turned to Lane,

"Do you want a lift back to your hotel?"

"No thanks, you get off, I'll hang around here, but keep me informed of any progress, and we will see you and Leila later this evening"

After Max left; Tom gave Lane his room key and went out of the hotel to avoid using the hotel communication system, and put in a call to London,

When he arrived back to his room he tapped on the door, Lane took her time opening the door.

"I have been thinking about your idea of a function, we can get one of our local boys to be the photographer, then whether we have names or not they might be able to identify them in London. This way we will know a lot more, what do you think?"

"Good idea. I have just requested some surveillance equipment from HQ; and it will be here tomorrow lunchtime. When do you want to arrange the party and where?"

Lane grinned,

"I too have been busy, we can hire a yacht in Sliema for tomorrow late afternoon"

"Good, that's a start. Do you fancy a drink before you go?" he asked her opening the drinks cabinet.

"No thanks, I need a clear head and I had better get back, I have a lot of thinking to do, and some reports to write"

Lane then kissed him on the cheek and left the room to return to the Hilton.

During dinner Lane laid out her plan,

"I have booked the 'M.Y.'Misty Moon' for four o'clock tomorrow in Sliema harbour, she can take thirty persons. Leila, we need you to make sure that the four suspects are on board"

"Ok, I think I can manage that, and I have many young friends that would appreciate a little party too, if you need them,"

"Fine, try to arrange for more girls then men to balance the numbers." Lane replied. "And remember dress code will be very casual, if possible tell the girls to wear bikini's, we need to keep these four scumbags occupied." She turned her attention to Tom, "I am afraid you and Max will miss out on the party girls" She glanced back at Leila. "Will you be able to get a master key for their rooms after the cleaner has been?"

"No problem, I can do that" Leila replied.

Lane turned back to Tom,

"As soon as your surveillance equipment arrives Tom; you and Max need to get the key from Leila, and get it set up, then you can join us later. Now; does everyone know what they have to do, or are there any questions?" Nobody answered. Max rubbed his hands together briskly.

"Right my friends, lets get it done"

Next morning around midday, Tom and Max went to the airport to collect the equipment, and returned to the hotel room to check it out. The phone rang, it was Leila confirming that everything was arranged; and she would call in at the Excelsior around three o'clock to give Tom the key before going back to pick up the suspects and take them to the harbour.

They were ready to go when Leila arrived with the key. They drove directly to the Regency. Slipping in the back entrance they made their way up the stairs to room 204 and 206. They worked silently fitting a motion-sensitive two-way spyglass to the dressing table mirror, and then fitted bugging devices in the bathroom and overhead lights. Still working silently and methodically they searched the cupboards and suitcases and found detailed maps of Saudi installations with four crosses outlining their soft targets, two crosses marked at Ras Tanura terminal and two at Ju'aymah terminal, both located on the Persian Gulf.

They also found United States identification documents, and two rucksacks containing US emblems and US dog tags. Tom took out a mini-camera and photographed the documents and maps.

They closed the door quietly after checking that the room was left exactly as they found it. Moving on to the next room they repeated the search, and installed the same devices as before. Once more double- checking that this room also was left undisturbed they walked calmly back down the staircase and out into the car park. Tom looked at the note he had made of the suspects car number plate,

"Just one more thing Max, keep an eye out while I fit this tracking device, that's their car over there."

"Ok dear boy, but get a move on, we have some very expensive champagne waiting for us" Max replied grinning.

"Unfortunately not you, my friend, you need to be here to set up the monitors in 205 opposite. Leila had arranged for this room to be posted as 'out of order' to avoid cleaners entering while we occupy it, and we cannot leave this room un-attended at any time."

"Oh great, you get to party, and I have to work. You owe me one big time chum"

"Don't worry" Tom laughed. "I won't be there long, I'm only calling in to pick up Lane"

The party finished around eleven. Leila dropped off her guests and went home as Lane and Tom returned back to room 205 to listen in on the four suspects. Max looked up as they came in,

"Nothing to report so far, just small talk. I will leave it to you." He got up and stretched.

"I'll see you guys in the morning, goodnight"

Lane and Tom took their place at the monitors.

"Here" Tom said passing Lane the film from his camera "You better get this over to London, its details of their target, plus it looks as if they plan to shift the blame onto the US."

"I had a feeling that might be the plan." Lane answered as she slipped the film into her bag. Their attention was taken up instantly when they heard the phone ring on the monitor, and one of the men answered.

"Hello" he paused "Speaking, OK what time he arrive, OK" He then closed the line

Another voice in the room asked,

"When do they arrive?"

"Our man is bringing the detonators in the morning flight OA 556"

"How will we recognise him"

"By password, which is………"

The password was drowned by the sound of the two other men entering the room.

"Damn them", Lane cursed, "We needed to know the password"

"What great news you have for us Abdul?" one of the men asked,

"Our man is travelling under the name James Smith, and will be here at Eleven o'clock," Abdul replied, "and the password is Barracuda" Lane and Tom grinned at each other in delight. The man continued, "We will pick him up from the airport; he will be wearing a red shirt and necktie, we can't miss him"

The men sat for another twenty minutes or so; discussing the young women on the yacht and what they would like to do with them. The two men who had recently arrived in the room; got up and went back to their own room.

Lane looked thoughtful,

"We need to switch the courier, and replace the detonators with dummies, and then we could pass Max off as the courier. What do you think Tom?"

"I'll do it, not Max, he is much too local, they may well recognise his face but they don't know me. I avoided them on the yacht when I came to pick you up; just in case of a situation like this"

"OK, if you're sure, but remember Tom it could be very dangerous, if they catch you that's it for you"

"Don't worry I don't plan to get caught. We need to get some dummy detonators early morning, and I need to acquire a red shirt etc. Also arrange to get this Smith fella lifted as soon as he gets off the plane, or better still while he is still on it"

Lane yawned, "We had better get some sleep Tom, we will both need it. I hope you don't mind sharing a room with me tonight."

"No problem, we have done that before if you remember" he grinned. "Anyway it looks as if our boys have crashed for the night. If there is any movement, there is an alarm built in to the circuit, it will wake us immediately."

Lane slipped of her short skirt, and got into one of the single beds.

"Goodnight Tom"

He stripped down to his under shorts and took the other bed. He lay there for a while listening to Lane's gentle breathing, and thinking of the job ahead, until eventually he too drifted off to sleep.

The following morning Max arrived at seven o'clock ready for his shift on observation. Lane had dressed and quickly filled him in on the plan. He nodded in agreement at their decision,

"You were right Tom, I would never have got away with it they most certainly know my face" He looked around the room,

"Glad to see both beds were used last night" He said winking at Tom, Lane gave him a look of distain; but chose not to answer. Tom grinned at the look on her face,

"Of course. I am a perfect gentleman, aren't I Lane?" Lane decided that the best way to finish this conversation was to ignore them both.

"We must get going Tom. We have a lot to do in a very short time"

After a brief stop at the local menswear shop to get his shirt and tie, they arrived at the airport with little more than an hour to prepare their strategy. Lane called Max for an up-date.

"Max, any movement from our boys?"

"They woke up at 0823hrs, but all four are still here at the moment"

She put down the phone and turned to Tom a bit anxiously.

"Are you sure you are OK with this, Tom, I didn't get clearance for you from London, so we are taking a bit of a risk"

"Don't worry I'll be fine"

"By the way, you look very nice in red" She joked looking at his brand new shirt and neck tie.

"Make sure it isn't permanent"

James Smith was detained on arrival by customs, as arranged Tom took his place and made his way out of customs hall with dummy detonators. Immediately after he walked into the arrivals hall he heard a quiet voice behind him.

"James Smith?"

Tom slowly turned and stared at the man, recognising one of the men from the hotel, he was obviously anticipating the password.

"Barracuda" Tom saw a flicker of satisfaction in the man's eyes,

"Come with me, you have everything we need with you?"

"Of course, did you expect anything else?" The man looked at him cautiously,

"Where are you from, you sound Australian"

"Close" Tom replied curtly.

"A man of few words, I see. No problem."

He escorted Tom to the waiting vehicle directing him to the passenger seat. From distance Tom had already noticed three others sitting in the back.

He felt a wave of relief when he thought of the tracking device under the wheel arch, he knew Max would be tracking him, just in case they had decided to go somewhere else other than back to the hotel.

But his luck held; and forty-five minutes later they were back in room 204. One of the men held out his hand,

"You have something for us my friend"

Tom handed over the package; they eagerly tore it open. The detonators were then laid out on the bed and counted. After checking the number again they appeared to be happy. One of the men stood up and stretched out his hand to Tom,

"Welcome James Smith. I am Abdul Khan, this is Albert Maskaj, that is Artan Blushaj, and over there is our youngest Iyas Frasteri,"

"From where?" Tom asked

"Does it matter, my friend?" Khan replied, "Just remember these names, they will be very famous soon" he laughed. "Now my friend, you will teach us all we need to know about these little beauties"

He picked up one of the detonators and examined it closely. Tom held his breath, but then relaxed, they obviously had never seen this type before. The next twenty minutes was taken up with Tom's instructions, which were reasonably simple once they got the hang of it. It was clear that Khan was their leader when he outlined the next part of their deadly plan,

"We have everything now to complete the task, I have booked four tickets for tomorrows morning's flight to Rome, it leaves at 0745"

"Very nice" Blushaj said, "Are we going to see the Pope?" Khan shot him a disdainful look.

"We do not have time for stupid jokes" He continued "We will then get a connecting flight to Riyadh. But first we have to get the equipment out of the hotel"

He turned to Frasteri,

"Call your girlfriend at reception, and ask her up here"

Frasteri rang down to reception but was informed she was not at her desk, and would call him back. As soon as Leila got the message, she rang room 205 to make sure that they knew what was happening,

"It's ok, but phone them Leila, you don't need go up there, I am recording everything so don't worry".

The phone in room 204 rang and Khan answered.

"I am sorry sir but I cannot leave the desk at the moment. How may I help you?"

"Good afternoon Miss Leila, I just wanted to say thank you for a great party, we really enjoyed meeting all those nice people, especially the lovely girls"

"You are most welcome, Sir" She replied. Khan continued in a soft persuasive voice,

"I wondered do you have an idea where in Valletta I can get the lock on my suitcase fixed."

"I will make enquiries for you sir; and call you back in a few minutes"

Two minutes later she rang back and gave him the address of a local locksmith in Velletta.

"What the bloody hell was all that about" Maskaj asked.

Tom never said a word; he was not there to question their tactics. But he too wondered what Khan was up too.

"Well" Khan replied, "We have to get a suitcase out of the hotel, without anyone thinking we are leaving for good."

He laid the largest of the suitcases on the bed, opened it and placed the packed rucksacks inside together with the other items concerning the mission.

Khan turned to the young Frasteri

"You must take this case down to the car, but don't show that it has any weight in it, and if anyone asks, you are taking it to Valletta to the address Leila gave you to get it repaired"

Tom remained silent, thinking *'Just as well we have all this on tape, at least we know now what to look for'*

Khan continued with his instructions,

"Take the car and get lost for a couple of hours, then come back here but leave the case in the car, OK?"

Tom waited for the young man to leave before saying casually,

"I have booked a seat to return home in two days, so I will see if I can get a room here in the hotel"

"That won't be necessary "Khan replied "We are leaving around 4 a.m. and we are not taking the boy, so you can stay in his room with him."

"Fine" Tom replied. "But why four tickets"?

Khan ignored Tom's question,

"Iyas has been told, that if anyone asks for us, we went on a fishing trip and will be back at the weekend. And in case they wonder why he didn't go, he can say he would get sea sick walking on wet grass"

They all laughed at Khan's humour. Tom stood up and stretched,

"If it is OK with you, I would like to take a walk and do a bit of sightseeing. I have not been to Malta before"

"That's fine, but if you're late coming back this evening, make sure you use room 206,"

Tom left the Regency and walked briskly up to the main highway in search for a taxi, when a car pulled up beside him. It was Lane.

They took an indirect route back to the Excelsior; just in case Tom had been followed, where they sat and discussed their next move.

"I think I had better call London and put them fully in the picture." Lane decided.

"Be my guest, I'm taking a shower"

When he came back, Lane was just replacing the receiver. She advised him of HQ's instructions.

"Sorry Tom, I have to return to London. I have an appointment with my boss at the Saudi Embassy"

"Great" Tom replied smiling "We do all the work and you get all the bonus points"

"Don't worry, I will tell them you did a little more than just sleep in my room," she laughed

"Your room?" He grinned continuing the banter,

"I know, I know. But it will be charged to my credit card"

"I can't win with you," He laughed "Come on," he pulled her to her feet "Let's go out and find some dinner, then we can see what else we can charge to your card"

Lane laughed,

"Now don't get carried away, I have to account for all this you know"

Over dinner Tom explained the plans that Khan had made for him to share a room with young Frasteri.

"I don't think he trust me, by his actions"

"So be careful,"

They ate their meal leisurely, and then sat talking about old times almost forgetting the reason why they were there.

Lane glanced at her watch,

"I had better get back now Tom; I have some packing to do."

Tom nodded his head in agreement,

"And I think it might be a good idea if I take a Taxi back, rather than be seen with you" They stood up to go, Tom kissed her cheek gently, "Goodnight, see you back in dear old London in a couple of days"

When he returned to the Regency, he was just about to enter room 206 when Abdul Khan barred his way.

"Mr Smith, I need to talk to you, please come with me"

'Oh Christ' Tom thought. 'I hope Max is awake' He followed Khan into room 204.

"Please sit down Mr Smith, I am afraid our plans have changed a little, and we now need you to come to Saudi with us"

Tom was not at all happy with this turn of events. Thinking, 'He is lying, I was always the fourth ticket'

He questioned

"Why? I have taught you all you need to know",

Khan looked at him sharply,

"I know, but we have decided that we need you to be there in case anything should go wrong, as insurance you could say"

"Oh shit!" Max muttered under his breath as he listened to all that was taking place in the other room.

"That's put the cat among the pigeons." He picked up the phone to call Lane.

"Christ that's the last thing we wanted" she exclaimed in horror. Then she pulled herself together.

"Right Max, here's what I want you to do."

Next morning while Frasteri was at breakfast, Max removed the bugs from both rooms. And later after breakfast when Frasteri went back to his room he found Max sitting calmly on the bed waiting for him.

"Good Morning young man" Max grinned as he pinned him against the wall and frisked him for weapons.

"My name is Max. M16." The young man's face turned white.

"I want you to take a good look around this room, I think you will find absolutely no sign that your three friends are ever coming back for you, look here."

He opened the wardrobe "Nothing," He continued opening all the drawers and cupboards.

"You see, gone." He turned and smiled at the young man. "You have been well and truly hung out to dry, my friend"

Frasteri started to move around tensely around the room, Max added casually,

"Don't think of doing anything silly, you won't get far," he added. "You're wanted by British Intelligence and your friends by the Saudi authorities. You are luckier than you think. Our prisons in England are slightly better than those in Saudi, plus as a bonus you get to keep your head"

The young man's shoulders sagged; he knew that he was beaten.

"Now you have a choice, you can come quietly with me back to the UK, or you can stay in prison here until we get an extradition authorization signed, which may take a year or more.

"It's OK, I'll go with you, but can I pack my things and say goodbye to Leila"

"No chance" Max answered grimly.

Max phoned for a taxi to take them to the airport, and then he escorted the young man down the corridor to his room to pick up his own bag. He smiled quietly to himself when he thought back to Lane's instructions, when he had asked her what he should do if he tried to escape

"With the size of you, against the size of him, I don't think you will have a problem, do you? But if it happens, break his arm, then leg, then neck, but not necessarily in that order"

+ + +

Tom sat in the aircraft his mind in a whirl; as the plane circled for landing in Rome, he hadn't planned for this to happen. He took a sideways glance at his travelling companions; they were all deep in thought. All he could hope for; was that Max had contacted Lane, and if the system worked, as it should, they would already have someone in place in Rome by the time he arrived.

Thankfully Abdul Khan and his compatriots were not the talkative types, so he had been able to think, or at least try to think of how he was going to get out of this situation. He decided that at the moment it was best to sit tight; and hope that MI6 would come up with an answer.

The plane landed on time and they made their way through customs and out into the arrivals area. It crossed his mind that if he had been searched he would have had a hard job explaining the gun strapped under his arm.

Abdul put his hand on Tom's shoulder,

179

"This way Mr Smith; we have tickets for the next flight out to Riyadh, we must hurry"

Tom followed Khan to the check-in desk; where a small neatly dressed man standing near by caught his attention. The man looked up and gave him a brief almost undetectable nod. *'Thank God! Well done Lane'* Tom felt a wave of relief sweep over him; at least he knew he was not alone.

About an hour into their journey to Riyadh, Tom stood up to go to the washroom, almost immediately one the terrorist stood up to follow him. Tom grinned at the man,

"You to eh' Blushaj? I couldn't wait any longer either."

Blushaj half smiled and grunted his agreement; and then followed Tom down the centre isle. *'I think perhaps they don't fully trust me after all'* he thought. A couple of rows behind him he noticed the agent from the airport. As he passed his seat the man looked up at him, and with just the smallest flicker of his eye Tom managed to acknowledge that he was aware of his presence.

The rest of the journey passed uneventfully, and once again he was pleased that his companions were not inclined to talk. They went through the airport system with no problems, and when the scanner didn't react to him or the agent carrying weapons, then he was convinced that the Saudi airport authorities were almost certainly aware of the situation.

"This way Mr Smith, we have a car waiting, it's a long drive to our hotel in Dammar" This time Abdul Khan kept close by his side.

After driving for almost five hours they eventually drew up outside one of the smaller hotels on the outskirts of Dammar, and Tom found himself sharing a room with Khan.

"We have a long night ahead of us Mr Smith, and tomorrow is a good day for us don't you think?"

"You are right Mr Khan, and if you wouldn't mind I would like an early night"

"That is no problem, but you must call me Abdul, and I will call you James."

Tom could see that Khan was feeling very confident as he continued in the same buoyant tone.

"I hope you don't mind but I have to talk to my friends, I will not disturb you when I return"

Tom laid his bag beside his bed and slipped his gun under the pillow before going into the bathroom to shower. When he returned he got into one of the twin bed, but he knew he must not sleep. About an hour later he heard Khan creep quietly back into the room, he feigned sleep. Khan walked softly over to Tom's bed and stood motionless for a moment.

When he was satisfied that Tom was asleep; he carefully unzipped Tom's bag and checked the contents, and then he searched his clothes. Satisfied that he had found nothing he threw himself onto his bed and within minutes he was snoring. Tom let out a sigh of relief. *'Thank God I left nothing in my bag or clothing that could have given me away'*

In spite of his efforts he dozed off to sleep; and woke to hear Khan in the shower. His first thought was to check that his gun was still in place, it was. Khan came back into the bedroom,

"No need for you to get up yet James, we won't be needing you today, but I would appreciate it if you did not leave the hotel"

Tom looked surprised,

"I thought you wanted me to come with you to the target site?"

Khan looked around as though the walls could hear,

"We do not talk of this James. We can manage by ourselves. You must stay here, and I must warn you; the hotel will be watched."

Half an hour later Khan and the others left the hotel.

Tom now knew that the reason he had been brought along was so that he wouldn't talk, and he suspected that they had no intention of letting him leave alive either.

He knew the dummy detonators would soon be found to be useless, and glancing at his watch he realized he might only had a few hours. He sat on the edge of the bed wondering if the agent from the airport had followed them to the hotel, and whether he was going to make contact, when a light tap on his door interrupted his thoughts. Drawing the gun from its holster he went to the door and listened,

"Tom, it's me, Max"

He opened the door

"What the hell are you doing here, are you nuts?"

Max laughed

"Orders, my friend, orders, I'm sure Lane doesn't want any harm to come to you because she said you still owe her for dinner."

"Very funny, so what's the plan now?"

"No plan, its your shout"

"OK, what sort of back up have we got?"

"Well, we have two of ours armed downstairs in the hotel lobby as well as the agent who followed you here, and outside there are forty or more well armed Saudi guards stationed on every conceivable building and rooftop you can imagine"

Tom nodded thoughtfully.

"Ok. Well by my reckoning we have about an hour and a half before they discover the detonators are duds, and I should imagine it would take them approximately thirty-five minutes to get back here to me.

"And when all hell breaks loose. What do you plan to do Tom?"

Tom slipped his gun back into its holster.

"We are not quite sure if they are going to attack, but I want you to go down the back stairs to the reception desk, to give me cover from behind. I will go down the main stairs; as it's me they want. Hopefully he will just want to talk, although I don't think it's likely.

"For Christ sake Tom, talk will be the last thing on their minds" Max protested.

"Don't worry Max, I'm not about to commit suicide yet. Make sure the order is out that there will be no firing until I give the order. Is that clear? If it turns into a battle, as Lane would say, we take no prisoners"

Right on cue they heard a vehicle screech to a halt immediately under their bedroom balcony, and then heard Khan's raised voice,

"Where is that bastard?"

"I have a strong feeling he means you Tom" Max grimaced.

Then came a single shot as a Saudi guard open fire before any signal was given.

"Shit" Max cursed. "That does it"

There was loud gunfire and a lot of commotion, Tom and Max darted out of the room, Max headed for the spiral staircase that led to the door behind the reception desk, and Tom made his way to the main stairs keeping tight against the walls for cover. He could see two men either dead or unconscious on the floor behind the reception desk.

Khan had a young receptionist around the neck holding a knife to her throat, and the other two were holding guns to the heads of male hostages. The other terrified staff and guests were huddled in a corner.

"Mr Smith please show yourself otherwise this young lady will join her friends over there" Khan shouted waving his gun at the two men lying on the floor.

He calculated that by now the Saudi guards would have surrounded the building, and Khan would also know that there was no possible escape. Tom knew that they had absolutely nothing to loose, they were dealing with very frightened dangerous men. He waited until he saw the door behind the desk move open a fraction and signalled to Max to make his move.

Max fired twice at Blushaj hitting him in the head. He fell instantly pulling his hostage down with him. Maskaj and Khan were taken by surprise; giving the captive held by Maskaj his chance to escape his grasp. The two men fired wildly around them, Tom saw Max go down but he was not sure how badly he was hit. Tom fired a direct hit at Maskaj who dropped instantly. Khan was the only terrorist one left, and he was still holding the receptionist at knifepoint.

Tom walked slowly towards him.

"You're finished my friend, put the knife down"

"Go to hell" He screamed. He moved himself and the hostage closer to the desk where Max was laying.

At that moment the Saudi guards stormed the hotel,

"No body move, lower your weapons" Tom shouted to the guards.

Khan shuffled ever closer to Max, Tom realized his intention was to grab Max's gun lying on the floor beside him. As Khan bent to pick it up, the young woman slipped from his grip and got away.

The desperate man eventually made a lunge for the gun, but before he could reach it a single shot rang out and he dropped like a stone, falling down beside Max.

Tom checked that he was dead; and then checked Max, who was still bleeding profusely from a shoulder wound,

"Max, are you ok buddy?"

Max opened one eye and gave a weak grin.

"Even I couldn't bloody miss from there."

The ambulances arrived and took the dead and wounded away, and Tom accepted a lift from the Saudi officer back to his hotel.

The following day Tom made his plans to return to London and then went to the hospital to say farewell to Max. Both men very pleased with the outcome of the operation, apart from Max getting shot. They talked for a while and then Tom stood up to go,

"I will leave you to enjoy your rest, but as soon as you feel like it you are welcome to come over and stay with us in England, Maria would be pleased to see you"

"I may well take you up on that" Max replied with a smile. "So long my friend"

The following day Tom flew back to London to attend HQ for a debriefing, during which he was informed that the young man Frasteri had been most co-operative. He had given them the identity of the country behind the plot, which would now be reported to the United Nations Security Council.

The senior officer smiled across the desk at Tom.

"The Saudi Ambassador has relayed the Saudi Kingdoms extreme pleasure and eternal thanks to the British Intelligence Services for their excellent work." He leaned back in his chair, "As you know the three members of the terrorist group wanted to give the Saudi authorities the impression that they were American citizens." He paused, and his smile widened. "So they were buried together with their rucksacks and dog tags"

After the meeting Lane escorted Tom back to her office, and just after they arrived the phone rang, Lane picked it up. As she listened her facial expression tightened.

"Oh dear, I am so sorry to hear that" She replaced the receiver very slowly, and turned to Tom, "I have some very bad news, that was Leila, Max was killed yesterday in a hit-and-run as he was leaving the hospital"

"Oh Christ! Tom sat down heavily on a chair. "The Bastards! So we never got them all?"

He sighed, "He was a bloody good reliable operative, he will be missed in the field, and I will miss him as a friend"

Although Lane was sympathetic, they all knew it was part of the job. She reached out for Tom's hand,

"You have to consider the fact that both of you could have easily been killed in that operation. You did a brilliant job, but Max was unlucky. Between you, you may have saved many innocent lives if those bastards had succeeded, it could so easily have led to a war. You also saved a hell a lot of embarrassment for American-Saudi relations.

"OK" Tom replied pulling himself together. " I'll take my reward now, you can take me out to lunch on your expenses"

"That sounds good to me," she laughed picking up her bag.

After they had lunch, Lane hailed a taxi, and went with Tom to Liverpool Street train station, Tom kissed her goodbye and got out of the taxi, Lane wound down the window, and called him back

"Tom" she said, "You know, I really liked your sexy underwear"

He looked puzzled,

"What do you mean?"

"Just because you heard heavy breathing that night in 205, didn't mean I was sleeping" She winked and laughed as the taxi drove away.

He sat on the train thinking about all that had happened over the last few days, and his thoughts turned to Maria, he wondered where she had gone for her assignment. It seemed like a lifetime since he had waved goodbye to her on the morning he had received the phone call from HQ. But it was only a few days, and so much had happened.

CHAPTER 18

That same morning Maria settled back in the Taxi after she left Tom and tried to concentrate on the task ahead. She had found it particularly hard to say goodbye this time, but she felt easier knowing that her mother would be there for Tom and the girls.

By the time she arrived at Heathrow's terminal two, Terry was already at the check in desk waiting for her.

"First class?" she commented, "I see MI6 has money to burn"

"Of course," he grinned. "Only the best for the dancing queen." Terry picked up her hand luggage and they made their way through to the departure lounge,

"Let me tell you, for this operation, I am the envy of all the chaps in the department"

In spite of her reservations, she smiled at his comments,

"Don't you ever give up?"

"Certainly not, but it is true" He replied grinning back at her.

The flight to Larnaca airport in Cyprus; took four and a half hours arriving on schedule. They had no problem finding a taxi, and within one hour they were at their hotel in Limmasol, which was situated about two and a half miles from the British airbase at Akrotori.

They were allocated adjoining hotel rooms on the first floor. Maria put her case on the bed and looked around the traditionally furnished room, it seemed pleasant enough. She kicked off her shoes and started to unpack, jumping nervously as Terry walked through from his room,

"Sorry, I did knock but you were pre-occupied," *'It couldn't have been much of a knock'* Maria thought suspiciously. He strolled across the room and sat on the edge of her bed,

"It appears we must move very quickly. A table has been arranged for us tonight at the restaurant that our friend uses on a regular basis. They play Arabic music; which as you know he has a liking for. So we want you to be prepared to take the floor after dinner to catch his attention. But," He looked very serious, "Please, this time no stripping, you must control yourself"

Maria opened her mouth to protest, until she noticed the twinkle in his eye, she was beginning to understand his English dry sense of humour; it was so very similar to Tom's.

"Very funny. Are you sure he is going to be there, or is it just a rehearsal for your benefit"

"I am sure, don't worry." He confirmed with a wicked smile.

"And from what I hear Matthew Grainger, is a self-declared 'gay' medical doctor, so you should be perfectly safe from him as well."

She ushered him out of her room

"Ok, now I need to shower and get some rest. What time do you want me?"

She knew the minute the words left her mouth; that this was a silly question, but before she could re-phrase it; she got the answer she expected.

"Anytime; day or night sweetheart, my door will remain unlocked"

Maria glared at him,

. "Ok, Ok." his hands went up in the now familiar gesture. "Around nine ok, I'll see you in the bar"

As soon as he retreated back into his room Maria locked her side of the adjoining door, just in case.

It was a very hot almost unbearable evening, she lay on top of the bed in her underwear pondering on the evening ahead. After a while she dozed off and woke up about twenty minutes later feeling very hot and sticky, and decided to take a cool shower before changing for the night ahead.

An hour later Maria sat at the dressing table applying her makeup carefully, when she caught sight of her eye-catching dress hanging on the wardrobe door. It was a very daring extremely tight fitting dress in dark red silk, 'Oh God; I hope it's not too much' she thought, 'But they did say the object of the exercise was to get Grainger's attention."

Terry sat in the bar waiting for Maria, when he heard a murmur circulating around the room and a low whistle from one of the young men sitting near him. He turned his head to watch as she walked across the floor to join him, savouring the envious looks from the other men in the room. 'I am going to enjoy this, even if it is only an assignment.' He thought rather smugly.

"You look a million dollars sweetheart, what's your poison?" he smiled at her. She smiled back appreciating the compliment.

"Good, Glad you approve, it should catch his eye then. Dry white wine please"

The evening was still very hot and humid, with no sign of it cooling down. A sultry Maria knew she had the men's attention as she took an ice cube from the bucket on the bar, lifted her long hair and rubbed it slowly around the back of her neck, and then just inside her cleavage.

There was a detectable stirring from the men in the room; who were unable to take their eyes from her, her body language and pouting lips drawing them in like a magnet. This was exactly what Maria had intended. She glanced at Terry with just the smallest flicker of an eye, he was satisfied; he knew it was a rehearsal for later.

As soon as they had finished their drinks they left the hotel, and made their way to the restaurant, but when they arrived there was no sign of Grainger or his friends. The headwaiter escorted them to a corner table, Terry had purposely booked this corner, so he could watch all proceedings, and nobody could get behind him.

They settled themselves into their seats and ordered some drinks, then patiently waited as the restaurant quickly filled. About half an hour later they heard a rather loud pompous English voice,

"I say, my good man do you have the jolly old Arab musicians here tonight?"

Terry watched as the headwaiter explained to the man that the live music would arrive later. Musicians toured different bars and restaurants throughout the evening, covering quite a wide area, spending a couple of hours in each one.

"That's him the jolly old boy over there, on that table near the bar. The colonial prat" he muttered in a low voice.

Maria glanced discreetly around the room, taking in the table location that Terry had mentioned.

Grainger was mid thirties clean-shaven, *'very handsome; if you like the sun bleached blonde hair type'* she thought. He was well over six feet tall and acting like a typical British army officer based overseas.

"Once I make contact, what next?"

Terry took a sip of his drink, hesitating before answering,

"We need to get inside his apartment to see if there is any evidence of any sort"

Maria's eyes narrowed as she protested firmly,

"Oh no, that's not my way. I am not sleeping with the enemy. I am very happily married and much too old for this sex bait game" But remembering that she had agreed with this mission, she gave a rueful smile. "Ok maybe not too old," adding as an afterthought, "Will I be fitted with a wire?"

Terry smiled reassuringly,

"Not wired as such, because there is a strong possibility that you will be frisked, especially with a gorgeous body like yours, but we are prepared"

"I'm still not happy with this." Maria murmured, she felt very apprehensive; it had been a while since she had been in this sought of situation.

"You don't have to do anything you don't want too," he replied. Reaching into his pocket he brought out a slim jewel case, Maria opened the case and found it contained a small gold wristwatch.

"If things get too heavy; press the winder button in on the side once, I will be monitoring it at all times. I won't ever be far away" he smiled, "providing of course you make the connection with him. But don't ever let the watch out of your sight."

At that moment the band arrived, and within a few minutes the music started. At first the drumming was soft then it gradually became louder, and then the other instruments joined in building up the atmosphere. Maria waited, not wishing to be too obvious.

A small group of young girls got to their feet, starting to sway to the music as people gathered round the floor to watch. She knew she had to make her move soon.

She gave Terry a brief nod; rose seductively and glided onto the dance floor. Slowly she started her dance routine. Grainger's attention was immediately caught; he leaned forward and sat on the edge of his chair, his eyes following her every sensual movement.

The other girls left the floor in admiration leaving Maria to dance alone as the crowd watching outside clapped and cheered her to the beat of the drums. Maria worked her way across the floor, swaying to the hypnotic rhythm, gradually closing the space between her and Grainger. She was giving a similar performance to the one that she had used to tease Matheson on the ferry crossing, although this time, she was fully dressed.

Terry watched Grainger's face, seeing he was well and truly snared. When she finished her routine; Grainger made his predictable move towards her before she could return to her table,

"My dear that was the best dancing I have ever seen, and believe me I am an expert. Would you like to join us? Or are you with someone else this evening?"

She paused before answering, making a deliberate point of looking around the room for Terry, but he was nowhere to be seen.

"Well, my brother was here, but he wasn't feeling well; so I guess he left"

"Never mind my dear" he smiled warmly offering her his arm, "Come and join us and have some champers."

He snapped his fingers at the waiter.

"Another drinking vessel over here for this gorgeous young lady"

She didn't reply to his obvious flattery, so he continued,

"What is your name my beauty"

"Salwa" Maria answered giving him a flirtatious smile.

He pulled out a chair for her to sit, casually brushing his hand across the back of her neck as he took his seat beside her,

"Are you staying at a hotel my dear, or do you live here?"

The slight touch had not gone unnoticed, as she answered,

"I am in a hotel nearby with my brother, but he has not been well all day, so I think he has gone back to rest, I am a bit worried about him."

'This *hopefully should kill any idea of him coming back to the hotel, and of my going back to his apartment*' she thought.

"My dear, where did you learn to dance so beautifully" Grainger enquired silkily topping up her glass with more champagne.

"I trained as a dancer when I was very young" she smiled coyly taking a small sip of her drink, she didn't want to drink too much, she needed all her wits about her tonight.

But a few minutes later she began to feel quite intoxicated, but she was sure she had not had that much to drink, she stood to excuse herself for a moment; but felt quite dizzy. Grainger discreetly slipped his arm around her waist.

"Are you alright Salwa? I was hoping you would come back to my apartment for a nightcap, but perhaps you would like my driver to take you home instead."

She tried to clear her head, feeling vulnerable and no longer in complete control,

"No thank you I will be alright, but if you would like to call me tomorrow then maybe"

He was clearly unhappy at her rebuff,

"Oh but I insist my dear. My driver will drop you back to your hotel"

Maria could see he was annoyed at her refusal, so agreed to the lift, as she didn't want to lose the contact she had just made.

The car pulled up outside, Grainger walked forward and opened the rear door, helping Maria in, and to her dismay he got in and sat beside her. She was struggling to maintain her concentration, as he placed his hand on her thigh.

"Ouch!" she gave a little squeal, "I think something has just stung my leg"

She felt as if the car was spinning before she passed out. Grainger called out to the driver

"Take us home my man, I think the young lady has had too much to drink. I will make her some black coffee"

Upon arrival at his apartment Grainger ordered the driver to pick Maria up; and carry her up the stairs.

"Put her in the red room" He commanded briskly with a wave of his hand.

The driver hesitated

"Again? Are you sure that's wise sir?"

"Are you questioning my orders?" Grainger snapped at the man "Just do as you're told and keep you mouth shut"

"Yes sir" The driver replied, he knew better than to push Grainger too far.

The next morning, Maria woke late with a splitting headache. She was shocked when she realized she was in a strange bed. Lifting the sheet she was horrified to find herself naked except for her satin and lace briefs.

She gingerly sat up and draped the dark red silk sheet across her chest, and looked around the room. She could see her evening dress and shoes lying on the chair, neatly folded army style.

There was a faint tap on the bedroom door; and the door opened; it was Grainger carrying a breakfast tray. He approached the four-poster bed smiling broadly.

"Good morning my dear girl, I do hope you slept well" He put the tray on the bedside table "You passed out on me, and I couldn't drag you through your hotel like that now could I? So I brought you here"

"Who undressed me?" she enquired anxiously,

He laughed

"Would you be very upset if I told you I had?"

"Very much so" She replied firmly. "What happened last night? I am sure I didn't drink that much. Where am I?"

He sat down on the edge of the bed,

"You are in my friend David's apartment, but I live here most of the time"

Maria was trying to remember, she vaguely recalled coming round at some point; and seeing a blurred vision of a dark haired woman in green, then a few flashes of light, after that she must have passed out again. But she didn't mention this to her host.

"You said something stung you just before you passed out. I checked, but found nothing on your leg or thigh, and don't worry my housekeeper undressed you. Oh, and I phoned your hotel to let them know you were Ok," He smiled at her reassuringly and then continued. "I must go now, I've had an urgent call from the base but I'll be back around two o'clock, then I can take you back to your hotel. Make yourself at home my dear; there is a shower along the corridor. I've put a robe in there for you; it will save you wearing your evening dress during the day" As he went to leave the room he stopped and said confidentially,

"It is the housekeepers' day off so you are all alone, go have a swim and enjoy yourself."

As Maria sat up in bed and finished her breakfast, she heard a car drive away. Dressed only in her briefs she got out of bed and went to find the bathroom.

She turned the temperature down so the water run quite cool, it helped to sooth her still muzzy head. Feeling refreshed; she put her lace panties back on and the white bathrobe that he had provided; however it was very small and there was no tie or cord to keep it closed. She cursed as she made her way back to the bedroom, 'I hope there is nobody else around as this damn thing is totally useless'

She looked around the beautifully decorated bedroom, wondering what she could do until he came back, she picked up her bag went down the stairs and ventured outside. After walking about the garden for a few minutes, she sat beside the pool dangling her feet in the water; it felt gloriously cool. Glancing around to make sure she was alone and not overlooked in any way, she dispensed with the ridiculous robe and dived into the water; swimming lazily on her back enjoying the coolness on her skin. Maria chuckled as she thought of Terry; 'I bet he would like to be here now'

After a while she climbed out of the pool and sat on the edge letting the sun warm and dry her body. 'I need to make contact with Terry to let him know what is happening, before Grainger returns,' she thought. She then decided to take the opportunity to investigate the rooms while she had the chance, but in her mind she knew that if there were any incriminating evidence to be found, Grainger would not be stupid enough to leave a total stranger alone in the apartment.

To Maria's surprise she found an unlocked drawer in the study containing pictures of a dozen or so nude or semi-nude women all photographed in this apartment, in fact most in the same bed she had slept in the previous night. Also letters and documents that confirmed him or his friend were copying classified information concerning the air base and that Grainger was indeed gay.

She gave a sigh of satisfaction, 'Right Mr Grainger, I think this is no longer an M16 operation. I am sure the British Army will be pleased to hear about this'

She reached into her bag for her powder compact containing a tiny camera, copied the photos and placed them back in the same order with the papers as she had found them; and quietly closed the drawer.

Moving on to the master bedroom she opened the wardrobe door, "Oh my God," she gasped. Hanging in the wardrobe was the green overall and black wig, together with a large assortment of women's erotic clothing, handcuffs, and whips. Now she began to feel very uneasy.

'Shit, not only is he gay, he is a cross-dresser or transvestite. It was him who undressed me last night' she thought feeling a bit sick.

Maria called Terry

"Can you come and get me, and bring with you my casual shoes, shorts and any top you can find in my suitcase".

By the time Terry arrived she had put her evening dress back on.

"I've brought you some clean knickers just in case, you never know" he smirked

There was no time for modesty, "Turn round" she ordered. Reluctantly he did as he was told; and she quickly changed into the clothes he had brought. She wandered whether to leave Grainger a note or not but decided against it. *'It could be used as 'inciting entrapment' if ever the case came to court'* she thought.

As they drove away in Terry's car, Maria told him what she had found.

"That man is so sexually mixed up, and I also think someone else, maybe the apartment owner; who is called David has control over him. There were pictures of what I believe to be the missing women in the drawer. And I also believe that he or the man David, is passing information concerning the airbase and its operations etc"

Terry replied thoughtfully,

"You sound as if you feel sorry for him, but remember the life style he is living is not on an Army officer's wage. But, he may be being blackmailed because of his confused sexuality"

"I agree," Maria nodded "But we should formally hand this over to the base"

"No, not yet" Terry argued "Let's wait and see what we get from the photos first"

They took the film to the base to be developed, and glancing through them Terry chortled with delight, and raised his eyebrows at Maria saying,

"Did you study all these women in detail on the originals?"

"Not in detail; it's not my thing, more like yours I reckon, why?" She queried

Terry was still grinning,

"Wow babe, what about this one"

Maria leaned forward to look,

"Which one?"

"This one." He held it out to her "Nice tits"

"Don't be so crude" she said taking the picture from him.

She gazed at a picture of herself unconscious lying on the bed, naked from the waist upwards. She gasped in horror,

"The flashes! I remember now, he must have taken those last night"

Terry looked serious,

"Looks like you to have become another of their intended victims"

Then he grinned,

"I didn't know you had a tattoo there"

"Very funny" Maria replied scowling at him, trying not to smile.

Terry was quiet for a moment, all joking put to one side, because he knew he had to convince Maria to continue with the operation.

"These people are perverted Maria, but you are going to have to go back in I'm afraid, we need all their contacts. You are right; someone else must be involved from the base. So I want you to call Grainger and make arrangements. After all you are safe with him, you know his sexual preferences, not even you could turn him" he smiled wryly. "And you will need to be prepared for all eventualities, do whatever it takes. We must get an idea why and where they are holding these women. We know they are looking for attractive women who can be persuaded to........"

Maria interrupted protesting,

"No way, I don't like it, supposing him or his 'David' pal hang both ways?"

"Swing both ways, not hang," he roared with laughter. "I know, not a nice thought; but it's also very possible. But you must go back, and you need to be able to convince them you're up for anything"

Maria glared at him, clearly unhappy with the developing sordid situation,

"But I am not. I set the limits not him, not you, and not bloody London, Ok."

"Maria" Terry replied firmly "You were chosen for this assignment for many reasons, firstly for your attractive dusky looks and your dancing, but most of all for your alert brain." He continued, "Also you are at ease with your body; you've got it, and by all accounts you know how to use it. We cannot afford for you to have any prudish inhibitions now"

Maria breathed in deeply as she folded her arms,

"My God, what the hell have you people set me up for?"

Terry's expression softened, as he heard the anxiety in her voice,

"But don't worry you will have complete control, and we will not be far away. You have already proven that you know how to handle these situations. These men like a challenge, and they don't give up easily, and you may have to go further than you would perhaps wish. We need someone to go that extra mile.

Maria interrupted him indignantly,

"So M16 believe that I would be prepared to go this extra mile, as you call it, do they?"

"Yes, they do," he grinned.

"Ok, flashing a bit of flesh, that's never been a big deal for me. But no sex, I am not a prostitute, and don't forget I am very happily married," she strongly re-affirmed.

"Absolutely right" Terry put his arm around her shoulder giving her a comforting squeeze,

"It's all in your hands. You make the decisions" He turned her to face him, "so are you ready to make that call?" Maria lifted her head and gave a deep sigh, nodding her head slowly in acceptance, still not completely convinced by his explanation.

She made the call to Grainger just after two o'clock; he wasn't there; so she left a message on his answer phone,

"Hi Matt, this is Salwa I had to come back to the hotel as my brother's sickness got worse. He has flown home leaving me here alone for a few days, so if you get bored or lonely give me a call"

Almost instantly he picked up the phone,

"Then check out and stay here until you're ready to leave"

"Are you really sure?" She laughed girlishly, pretending to be excited.

"It will be nice to have the company, and tomorrow night we have a masked ball at the base, so you will accompany me" Grainger replied, making it sound more like an order; rather than a request.

"Ok, great. I'll check out and be over in a while," she replied

Terry and Maria had to quickly set up a line of communication, which they knew was not going to be that easy, and she still had the watch.

"So while I am working, what will you be doing?" Maria asked with a wistful smile,

"I will get invited to the masked ball tomorrow, and in the meantime I will catch up on my suntan" Terry added, returning her smile, kissing her gently on her cheek. "So I'll see you at the ball, sexy"

+ + +

The early afternoon had become extremely hot and humid with the temperature soaring into the high nineties when Maria arrived at Grainger's home. Her lemon coloured button through dress was now uncomfortably clinging to her body. The perspiration glistened on her darkened skin, her hair now sticking to the back of her neck.

She was feeling more than a little apprehensive about this particular assignment as she pressed the rather ornate doorbell. Although she never heard it ring Grainger had seen her through the glass panel and instantly answered the door, wearing only a pair of army shorts.

"Come in my dear, I am so pleased you came back."

She smiled at him coyly,

"Thank you for asking me Matthew"

"That's a cool little number you're wearing my dear" he commented, immediately noticing the way the dress clung to her as he led her into the hallway.

"I have put you in the same room as before" he smiled, "but before you settle in my dear, I must explain our strict house rule." he smiled again; the same silky smile that didn't quite make it to his eyes.

"We don't like to see our guests overdressed at anytime in our home, especially in this unbearable heat wave, it is so unhealthy. It is just one of our little quirks, you must try to humour us my dear. Meanwhile; please treat this apartment as your own"

"I have no problem with that" She replied with a less than convincing grin.

"If you really enjoy your stay with us; we may be able to offer you a little job, but of course that depends on whether we think you are really really suitable, if you get my drift"

Maria noticed the continued plural rather than singular in his conversation.

"Oh that would be nice" she smiled "But when you say overdressed, I guess you prefer shorts and tops, right?" She questioned innocently, although she knew his meaning.

"Shorts; yes if you really insist, but no tops" He replied with a suggestive grin before adding "Or as David would say, we prefer a one piece bikini".

She smiled calmly; but had now begun to wonder '*has Terry really read the script correctly about Grainger being gay*',

As though he had read her mind he laughed and said,

"I have to admit I really do enjoy the sight of a beautiful naked body. In fact I feel I must warn you I am quite obsessed with my little camera. I hope while you are my guest you will not object to my little odd requests"

"Whatever rings your bell" she responded sarcastically.

He smiled at her, looking pleased '*at least she hasn't refused to be photographed*'.

Maria felt again the perspiration beginning to trickle down her neck; making her feel extremely uncomfortable, as there was no air conditioning working in the apartment.

"I would love to take a nice cold shower if that's ok, I feel so sticky and hot"

"Why not take a swim my dear girl," He suggested jovially, "The water is so beautiful today".

"Why not? That would be really nice. I'll just go and change, I've brought my bikinis"

Grainger frowned,

"Don't be silly dear girl; you don't need a bikini so you might as well get undressed here.

She smiled at him with an unbelieving expression, hoping that he was joking, but his tone of voice told her the opposite, when he firmly suggested

"Come on dear," he coldly suggested, "Take your dress off"

'Oh my God', she thought, panic sweeping over her as she quickly assessed what she was wearing underneath, wishing she had had the forethought to wear a bra.

Grainger's attitude changed as he noticed her continued hesitation.

"Do you have a problem with that?" he asked in a more reassuring and softer tone, "I'm sure your underwear will serve you just as well"

"I would prefer my bikini; if you don't mind" she answered lightly. He took a step towards her, firmly reiterating his earlier demand.

"Oh; but I do mind, so take your dress off..................Now!"

Maria was startled at his continuous change of character.

"Perhaps you need some help my dear girl, it will be my pleasure to give you a little supporting hand or two," he leered at her.

'Surely he isn't serious' she asked herself, taking a small defensive step back from him. But she immediately realized that it was no longer just a suggestion.

She drew and held a deep breath unwittingly expanding her chest as he started to undo her top button, *'What the hell do I do now'* she thought. *'Smile and accept, or kick him where it hurts'* she gritted her teeth and stared straight ahead trying not to show her distaste.

Grainger smiling purposely took his time feeling his way down her shapely curves, and it immediately occurred to her she was being frisked rather than abused, so she controlled her initial impulse to protest.

As he released the last of the buttons, the dress hung slightly open revealing a little more than her fine white lace knickers, Grainger turned her around and stood behind her, showing no outward interest in her near nakedness.

Defiantly Maria stretched out her arms horizontally to show that she was not concealing anything.

With her back still towards him, his intrusive hands continued to search. She grimaced as she controlled the urge to push his hot clammy hands away. *'I just hope that his only interest in checking me over is for a wire and not for my cup size as it would now appear'* she thought angrily. *'Whichever way it is, I need to be accepted into their sordid organisation before I can infiltrate their seedy and perverted network'.*

She had been made aware by Terry's briefing that she would have to endure some bizarre sexual behaviour like this, but even so, she thought *'There has to be a limit on how far I am expected to go for the sake of MI6.'*

Once he was satisfied she was not wired, he eased the dress back off her shoulders letting it drop to the floor, and in spite of the late afternoon heat, she shivered with trepidation.

Although he had undressed his beautiful guest the night before, he was still filled with admiration at the sight of her shapely svelte like physique.

"Very nice" he softly murmured, gently running his hands down her bronze back before gently squeezing the cheeks of her bottom. "You have a lovely firm rear, my dear,"

Maria gave a little chuckle at his un-intentional rhyme.

"No don't move." he instructed as she bent to pick up her dress from the floor. Then from behind she heard the rapid clicking of a camera. She smiled and waited for his next lured instruction. Holding her breath, she waited for what appeared to be an eternity expecting more groping, but to her surprise, he just fondly patted her bottom.

"Ok Salwa, you can go and have your swim now"

Maria scooped the dress up and elegantly walked the few paces through the open patio doors; trailing the dress behind her; her head held high, wearing little more than a tight confident smile. '*My God, Tom would go crazy if he knew that I am parading around like this for the department*'

She went outside and without turning or saying a word, threw her dress onto the nearest chair, kicked off her sandals and dived into the pool where she swam leisurely for a while, trying to gather her thoughts. After about ten minutes she climbed out of the water and sat on the edge looking around, there was no sight of Grainger or anyone else, so she relaxed and let the sun warm her skin, thinking '*at least it looks as though they have taken the bait*'

It didn't take long for her thin lace knickers to dry in the hot sun; so she slipped the dress back on; picked up her sandals and went inside.

There was still no sign of Grainger or her suitcase, so she made her own way up the stairs to the same room she had used the night before. When she entered; she found her case had been unpacked and her clothes hanging neatly in the opened wardrobe

She took a change of underwear from a drawer in the dressing table; picked up the robe lying on the bed and went into the shower room to wash off the chlorine. Within a matter of minutes she returned to the bedroom to find Grainger sitting on her bed still wearing his army shorts. Maria smiled at him surprised; but strangely felt no threat by his presence. He returned her smile saying casually,

"My dear, I really do admire your taste in fashion so before you get dressed I would love you to show me exactly what you would wear with each garment"

She said nothing as she went to the wardrobe to show him, '*I suppose that's not such an unusual request considering his sexual preference*' she thought.

"I would wear this with this and with those shoes," she said holding up one of her dresses.

"Very nice my dear, but I have a better idea, show me what you would do with these"

He stood up, walked across the room, unlocked a door to a walk-in wardrobe revealing a huge range of women's shirts, casual tops, blouses, skirts and dresses, almost every colour and quality material imaginable. On the shelf below there were racks of matching shoes, and to complete the display, there were scarves, sexy lingerie still on hangers, with rows of beads, bracelets and belts to use as accessories

Maria gasped with typical feminine delight at what she was seeing, but at the same time she felt more than apprehensive, 'What the hell does he expect from me now?'

"Very nice, some look a little erotic for my taste though" she smiled.

He leaned back on the bed, a half smile playing around his face,

"Is that so? Anyway I want you to try them on, with all the required accessories; I do so love a one to one fashion show"

Her uneasiness increased; this didn't feel right. She tried to reason with him,

"Wouldn't it be better if it was a surprise for you whenever we go out?"

In another lightning change of mood, his request became a command,

"No, I insist, try them on now"

Taking one or two of the dresses off their hangers, she looked around for somewhere to change.

"Surely you're not shy anymore, are you Salwa? You know you can change in front of me. Perhaps you need to relax, come on sit on the bed"

Sliding his hand into his pocket he took out a cross and chain; and started to swing it slowly backward and forwards in front of her; as his voice softened.

"Now my dear try to stay calm, just follow the cross and you will soon feel totally relaxed"

This was not what she had expected. 'I mustn't look at the cross I must resist' she thought as she tried to concentrate on something else, reciting in her head over and over 'Don't look at the cross, think of Tom, think of anything.' She had no intention of being hypnotised by this unpredictable man if she could help it.

Eventually he placed the cross back in his pocket, with a satisfied smile convinced she had succumbed. Maria took a sigh of relief; letting her head slump forward, although she felt very relaxed; she still felt she was in control.

"Now you will do everything I ask you to do upon my command. Now; put this facemask on, get rid of your gown and let the show begin"

Immediately she reacted to his instructions, she put on the facemask, stood up and slipped the gown off; dropped it on the floor and commenced the 'fashion show' quite calmly.

"That's right my dear, very nice," Maria could now hear his voice fading slightly as she frowned trying with difficulty to retain her concentration. Grainger noticed the vague look on her face and spoke in a softer but firm voice,

"Now try the yellow silky wrap-over mini-skirt on for me," He smiled at her, waiting to see how she would interpret his order. 'That request should confuse her' he thought

Then as instructed she slipped on the skirt, twirling in front of him. In spite of the fact she was convinced that she had resisted his hypnosis, she felt completely relaxed and willing to comply with any request. Taking full advantage of his power, Grainger asked her to pose lying on the bed in just her underwear and shoes as he took glamour photographs at every opportunity while continuing to direct her. She happily complied without the slightest hesitation.

Eventually some normality began to return and she was beginning to feel be very tired. *'Under any other circumstances I would have been happy to model such sexy underwear and these beautiful expensive clothes'* she thought wearily

"Give me that little bit extra; you have modelled before that's obvious, so improvise a bit,"

Maria thought for a few seconds of the most popular pose that all models use, and walked across the room and sat on the dressing table chair so the panelled backrest faced the camera. Spreading her long slender legs either side of the chair. She smiled having noticed that this raunchy action had an immediate effect on Grainger; who was now breathing rather heavily,

"Wow, that's better, very nice, keep going young lady, keep going."

His over-reaction was confusing; *'This is the first time I have ever had this effect on a gay guy,'* she thought. *'Maybe this was how he gets his kicks.'* And then a worrying thought struck her, *'Oh God, perhaps he isn't'*

"Wait, I have an idea," he instructed. "Stand up just as you have been sitting,"

She stood with the chair seat still between her legs, supporting herself by putting both hands on the backrest of the chair.

"That's right, stay exactly like that, now put one knee on the chair"

She held the awkward stance as he rose from the bed hastily reloaded film in his camera, and started taking more snaps of her from all angles capturing every position. *'Thank God for this mask, at least nobody will recognise me if these photos ever become public,* she thought, and then a little smile crossed her face, *' only one man would ever recognise me'*

Grainger loaded another film into his camera,

"Ok, now you can carry on, put on those little red panties and suspenders, you will find some black stockings in the drawer," He sighed dramatically, "I just love red, and it's my absolute favourite colour"

Her eyes widened *'Oh shit'* she thought, *'Prancing around in next to nothing is one thing, but blatantly baring all is another,'*

"Come on, come on put them on" he impatiently insisted

Feeling pressurised she turned her back towards him; trying to find a diversion. She had an idea.

"Was that the doorbell?"

"I didn't hear anything, carry on!" he muttered, he got off the bed and cracked open the door to listen.

"But I am sure I heard it" Maria insisted. Grainger looked slightly irritated,

"I suppose I'd better check, stay here; I won't be a moment"

The minute he left the room she hurriedly changed into the red lace underwear, but she was only just in time before Grainger reappeared smiling.

He picked up the camera and continued to take photos as she was adjusted the suspender belt around her waist and sat on the bed to pull on the stockings.

"Now I want you to slowly remove them one by one while I catch the mood," he ordered with a little smile. She reluctantly did as he asked

"Ok, perfect. That's enough for now, take a break"

He put down the camera and leaned back on the bed as though he too was exhausted.

'Thank God for that' she muttered under her breath. She picked up the robe, all pretence of hypnosis put aside, waiting for him to protest, but he could see she was no longer under his influence. Speaking in a normal voice as though nothing out of the ordinary had happened over the last hour, he asked.

"As a special favour may I choose your clothes for the masked-ball tomorrow night?"

She looked at him warily remembering his rapidly changing moods.

"If you wish" she replied as she sat on the edge of the bed.

"Oh I do wish my dear," he whispered softly "I want you to wear the full length black and gold dress; the one with the very high thigh split and a very low back, and those goldie coloured sling back sandals"

"Fine, anything else" She sarcastically enquired, her confidence swiftly returning.

He replied this time much more briskly.

"No" and gave her a meaningful look as he ran his sweating hand down her back, gently squeezing her bottom. "Absolutely nothing else!"

Maria raised her head and gave him a slight inquisitive smile, soon realizing from his expression what he meant, especially as the expensive designer dress he had chosen was very tight and revealing.

Before Grainger left the room, he left her with a very unsettling thought.

"We have invited some friends round tonight for cards; and they insisted on meeting you, they are all from the base, and strict house rules will eventually apply," He sniggered. "You will see why later"

Once she was alone Maria mulled over the afternoon events, Grainger had an unstable sexual appetite that she found to be quite distasteful; yet non-threatening for some reason. However she didn't trust him at all; maybe he was really straight, or bi sexual, after all he had certainly responded in a more heterosexual manner during the afternoon.

Now she was very concerned about what type of friends he was planning to introduce to her tonight. She had a strong feeling that there was a lot worse to come.

Maria deliberated for some while about what to wear that evening, she had a feeling that she needed to impress these people coming from the airbase tonight, *'perhaps it's another test'* she thought shrewdly.

+ + +

199

Eventually she decided to wear Tom's favourite Grecian styled white and gold knee-length dress with slits up both sides with a gold coloured corded belt, she then piled her hair high on her head and wove tiny gold silk flowers into a long plait which hung down over one shoulder. Looking in the mirror she smiled to herself remembering; that whenever she wore this dress at home, it would be all she wore - - - - - But, she was not at home!

After one last look she slipped on her gold high-heeled sandals and made her way down the stairs to the lounge, to find Grainger waiting patently with a glass of red wine already poured for her.

"Wow Salwa come sit, you look absolutely stunning, I really do approve of that lovely dress," he said as he handed her the glass, Maria acknowledged his compliment with a smile and sat down in the chair facing the door. She wanted to be settled before his guests arrived, as she had no intention of drawing any more attention to herself by making an entrance.

A few minutes later Grainger answered a knock at the door. She heard laughter and footsteps approaching, when they appeared there were three men; two of them were young soldiers escorting two rather vulgarly dressed but pretty young women. However, it was the other much older male in particular who caught Maria's attention. Grainger called her over.

"Salwa allow me to introduce you to David Hines, he is the owner of this beautiful apartment" Maria smiled and held out her hand.

Hines grasped her offered hand, and lifted it to his lips; she felt an involuntary shiver of fear run through her.

Grainger poured them all a drink, Maria felt slightly uneasy as they were all looking in her direction, the two women looked her up and down in jealous admiration, and the two young soldiers openly ogled her figure in anticipation. She felt as though she was slowly being stripped naked.

"I really love your dress" one of the women giggled, "You look so sexy"

And the both women collapsed in a fit of giggles.

"I see you are all going to get on famously," Hines laughed as he signalled to Grainger and they both disappeared into the study.

She turned her attention back to the others, they were all laughing and drinking heavily, and by the look of them they had started long before they arrived.

After a particularly heavy burst of laughter one of the young men suggested a game of cards.

The two women giggled excitedly as they positioned themselves around the large card table,

"Come on Salwa, come and play, its called 'Twenty One Dare" one of the young women called to her.

"Never heard of it, I'll just watch" Maria smiled; she guessed by the woman's attitude that it would be another version of strip poker. And she had had enough stripping for one day.

"I'm really not in the mood"

"Oh, no, Salwa, you must play, don't spoil the fun for the rest of us, it's why we came, Matt said you would be more than happy to play.

But Maria was adamant,

"No really, not at the moment, but I will watch while you play."

Then from the study she heard a voice that was definitely not Grainger's.

"Young lady, if you want to stay here, then you cannot disappoint our guests, I suggest you re-consider, and join in."

Maria now firmly believed that she was being set-up, as she walked slowly towards the table,

"Ok, but you have to tell me the rules"

One of the women chose to explain,

"Right, two cards are dealt, the person with the lowest cards looses a garment or item of some sort, and the choice is given to the person with the highest cards. Also if you win the round, you can take any other item that's on the table and put it on. That's all there is to it."

Maria was now regretting her choice of clothes and she was worried that she had very little on underneath to lose. The cards were dealt, and for a while although not winning, she was not losing either. But she didn't have to wait much longer for her first loss.

One of the young men rose from his chair, came over to Maria, and removed her shoes; she smiled at him thankfully as he went back to his seat.' *That could have been worse*', she contemplated. So far all the others had been reduced to their boxer shorts or briefs so she was lucky. But then she lost the next round. The woman sitting beside her laughed,

"I claim your bra." She said, grinning as she saw the panic on her neighbours face.

"But I don't have" Maria protested.

"Then we will have your panties. I assume you are wearing some" She sniggered.

"Of course" Maria replied

"Then please stand"

"Let me help," one of the men laughed rising from his chair.

"You, stay where you are," The woman responded sarcastically; slipping her hands under Maria's dress, gently easing them off *'Thank God it was a woman'* Maria thought as she stepped out of the briefest of satin panties.

A few minutes later Maria lost again, this time it was her belt.

There were now just three left in the game, two of the others had already lost all they could.

The next round saw the departure of the last woman, leaving just Maria and the younger of the two soldiers, who was now looking extremely nervous.

By now the noise from the game had drawn both Grainger and Hines out of the study, and they all gathered around the table watching as they waited for the soldier to deal the next hand. The young man looked worriedly at Maria unsure what to do.

"Ok soldier, if you have lost your nerve, I will deal" Hines pushed the young man to one side. Maria looked at the expression on the dealers face and saw pure lust. She watched with baited breath as he dealt the cards.

The soldier had a total of seventeen in his hand; slowly she turned her cards over, revealing the first card to be an ace of diamonds, she smiled confidently, but her expression immediately changed as she revealed a six of clubs.

There was a sharp intake of breath from the others watching, Hines walked slowly around the table and stood directly behind her. He leaned over her, placing his thumb inside the top of her dress pulling it forward and peering down at her bare breasts and beyond. Everyone knew he was trying to intimidate her, but she just leaned back and looked up at him expressionless.

He then surprised everyone by unclipping her earrings and placing them on the table.

"The next time she loses it should be fun, especially after all I've just seen" He gloated.

No one responded to his taunts.

"Right" he continued rubbing his hands together looking at Maria "Let's get on with it, your dress against his boxers, are you both ready"

Maria felt sick.

"Are you both ready?" he repeated, looking from one fact to the other.

The soldier nodded his face very pale; he knew he had got into something he didn't quite understand.

Maria glanced at Grainger, who raised his eyebrows. She took a deep breath and quietly replied,

"Yes I'm ready as I ever will be, get on with it."

"A gutsy woman, that's good" Hines nodded with approval.

Unexpectedly Grainger stepped forward,

"I'll deal the last hand,"

He took the cards and shuffled the pack, before dealing two cards to each player. Maria turned her cards over slowly, a four of diamonds and five of clubs, she gasped, and took a deep breath as she patiently waited for the young soldier to reveal his hand. His first card was six of hearts; Maria closed her eyes and held her breath in anticipation. Then silence prevailed, followed by hearty laughter; she slowly opened her eyes and saw the soldier staring at a 'two of clubs'. She glanced quickly towards Grainger, their eyes met. Hines face contorted with fury; he pushed back his chair tipping it over and stormed out of the room.

"Go on Salwa, do your duty" Grainger insisted; without turning a hair at his friends sudden departure, "It's your treat, you are the winner"

She slipped on her shoes, picked up her belongings and walked around the table; the young soldier stood watching her, his pale face beginning to turn a rosy red. Maria stopped behind him and with one hand pulled his shorts half down, and without waiting for any reaction from the audience she turned and left the room.

As she made her way to the bottom of the stairs still clutching her underwear and belt, the other young soldier stepped out in front of her saying,

"I saw you dancing the other night in the restaurant. You were very good"

"Thank you, I enjoy dancing" she smiled politely.

"Just as well" he grinned,

"What do you mean?" she looked warily at him

"We were promised a special audience tonight. Isn't that right, Sir?" The soldier said looking at Grainger who had just come into the hall. Maria tossed her head defiantly,

"In your dreams soldier, I don't do specials"

He laughed ignoring her protest; and went back into the lounge producing a tape from his pocket and put it in the cassette player. Maria recognised the familiar music as the drums started to beat. Grainger signalled to Maria to respond but in a show of continued defiance she refused to move. He went over to her, got hold of her hand and whispered quietly,

"Come on Salwa, I think you owe me a small favour, just one dance for our friends"

Maria knew she owed him a favour; he had certainly saved her back at the card table, so she agreed to dance. She was rather concerned with the fact that she had not had chance to replace her underwear, and thankful that her loose flowing dress concealed most of her body. Her audience was spellbound, and when she finished the dance they cheered and clapped, but she shuddered as she noticed the expression on Hines face as he re-entered the room. But before he had chance to approach her she made her excuses to Grainger and escaped to her room. She needed a cold shower.

Maria had just slipped off her dress, when she heard them calling her,

"Salwa come on, it's lovely in here." Holding the dress in front of her she stepped onto the balcony; she could see that the pool was now brightly lit, with everyone, including Grainger and Hines sitting on the edge or in the pool.

"Come on Salwa, a swim will help you cool down" Grainger called up to her

She hesitated for a moment; she was tired but realised she really had no option other than to join them if she wanted to complete this mission. She called back,

"Ok, give me a moment; I will come down"

She put on a tiny yellow bikini and beach wrap and went down the stairs and out to the pool. She knew she was defying the house rules, but she was going to make the effort to cover up as much as possible in spite of their demands.

All the others were stripped to their waists, and when Maria slipped off her wrap and stepped towards the edge of the pool, Hines called out to her.

"One piece bikini, remember? And of course we don't mind which piece do we guys?"

They all laughed, '*These people are sick, and obsessed with nudity; and the damn women are just as bad*' she thought, her eyes flashed angrily. Hines rose from his seat and came towards her,

"You choose which part, or I will" He sneered as he got hold of her arm. '*What an asshole*' Maria thought, she shook off his hand and turned to leave the poolside. But he caught hold of her arm again, twisting her round to face him,

"It seems to me you are loosing your nerve, may be you had better leave."

For a brief moment their eyes locked, it was a battle of wills. The others noisily joined in to persuade her to comply.

"Go on Selwa"

"Get 'em' off gal,"

Maria still with her eyes firmly fixed on his, calmly unhooked her bra top and dropped it on to a sun-bed, and with a look of pure contempt directed at Hines, she walked haughtily to the edge of the pool and dived in; leaving him outwitted once again. Grainger smiled quietly to himself at the expression on his friends face.

A few minutes later the others realising nothing else was going to happen, got out of the pool and ambled over to the bar for a drink, chatting to each other and laughing.

Maria now had the pool to herself; she could see Hines and Grainger in a deep heated discussion, so she swam as close to them as she could, trying to hear any part of their conversation, but all she heard was the words 'Island' and 'Phoenician.'

A short while later the party broke up, with the arrival of a taxicab to take the others back to the base. Maria had no option other than retire to her room for what turned out to be a restless night's sleep.

The following day she intended to have a lazy day sunbathing. Grainger was not expected to return from the base until two o'clock at the very earliest, so once again she had the place to herself.

She relaxed by the pool in her skimpy red bikini bottoms and a large floppy straw sun hat. Her own thin cotton robe was lying beside her sun bed just in case she received any unexpected visitors from the previous night. She felt drowsy in the warmth of the sun and what with her restless night; eventually she drifted off to sleep

Grainger unexpectedly came back early whilst she was sleeping, and stood at the end of the sun-bed looking down at her. She woke sensing she had company; half opened one eye and tipped her hat slightly. She knew it must be Grainger she could see his silhouette in the glare of the sun,

"Is there not one part of you that isn't perfect? It's enough to make an old queer go straight"

She sniggered finding this remark very comical especially coming from him, although she was not totally convinced about his sexuality.

"Really! That much? "

He smiled as he sat on the edge of the sun-bed and picked up the sun oil, poured some into his hand and applied it to her feet and calf's, totally oblivious as to the liberty he had bestowed upon himself. His eyes briefly scanned her upper body as he massaged her thighs,
"You really should put some of this on your tummy; it looks as though you have already burnt part of your chest."

She immediately became alert, and sat up holding out her hand in a gesture of defiance, just in case he intended to apply the oil himself to her breasts.

"Please Salwa, relax," he said with a limp wrist and brandishing a broad boyish smile" I have no intention of getting covered in oil at this moment, in spite of your gorgeous sexy body"

Maria smiled at his compliment, although she was still on her guard. She glanced at her watch, then changing the subject she suggested,

"I think I had better go up for a shower and cool down a bit"

"Good idea, I will do likewise," He answered, but made no effort to leave.

He continued looking at her, with an expression she could not quite fathom, it made her feel a bit uncomfortable. And then all of a sudden he stood up, and with a little smile strode off into the apartment.

Although Grainger was now proving to be more of a gentleman than she had originally thought, she wasn't about to take any undue chances. She waited for a while before going up to her bedroom and before taking a shower. As soon as she thought the coast was clear she wrapped a large towel around herself and tiptoed along the corridor to the bathroom

As she got closer, she heard the sound of water running as she opened the door. To her dismay she found Grainger standing with his back towards her in the other shower, it hadn't occurred to her that he would be using the other cubicle at this time. Unconcerned she unwrapped the towel and hung it on the hook just outside the shower door. She was about to slip into the shower cubicle, when Grainer, realising that he now had female company, called out over the noise of the water.

"I didn't heat the water this morning so it is quite cold, hope it's Ok for you"

"No problem, I will manage" Maria shouted back. She was beginning to get used to his odd feminine ways and was not too concerned by his naked presence.

When he left the shower room she took her time and rinsed off with what was now ice-cold water. Feeling exhilarated from the cold water she slipped on her robe and made her way back to her room, only to find Grainger lying on her bed with just a towel wrapped around his waist.

She acknowledged her host casually as she sat at the dressing table; her hair wrapped in a hand towel. She filed and painted her fingernails hoping he would get bored and leave, and then she turned away from him to paint her toenails.

"May I" He called out eagerly.

"That's Ok thanks, I can manage" She hastily replied.

He took no notice, rose from the bed, tightened his towel around his waist and took the varnish from her hand and sat down on the stool beside her. Her hands defensively dropped onto her lap holding her gown in place as he lifted her left foot onto his knee and put cotton wool between each toe. Her body tensed; *'Surely he must know that I have nothing on under this gown'.*

He started to apply the varnish with painstaking artistic care. *'Hmm, he has certainly done this before'* Maria thought starting to relax a little.

After he had finished he moved back to the bed grinning,

"There; that wasn't too bad was it?"

He lay back on her bed totally relaxed, chatting about the evenings Masked Ball that he was taking her to, until he fell asleep. She smiled to herself as she looked at his boyish face totally relaxed in sleep. Against any earlier judgement, she was slowly beginning to understand this rather mixed up but likeable man.

She lent over him and called his name softly to be sure he was really asleep, then she took the moisturising cream from the table untied her gown and applied it to her body, arms and legs. She turned her back just in case he woke, but strangely no longer felt under any sexual threat from Grainger; as to her it was no different than being with female company

Just as she was wondering whether to switch on her hairdryer or not; he woke up and without a word got up and left the room. She loosened the cord from her gown and sat on the bed to dry her hair. She then lay down and fell asleep almost immediately.

Maria woke with a start about two hours later to the sound of the telephone ringing. Sitting up on the bed, her gown now loosely covering only part of her. She looked around, and was very surprised to see the black and gold dress that Grainger had insisted that she wore, and the shoes and mask laid out very neatly on the bedside chair.

She went to get her underwear from the wardrobe only to find it securely locked. *'Blast, they obviously expect me to go commando, as Lane calls it '*

Maria felt a new wave of apprehension at the actions of these very changeable and peculiar people; they appeared so unpredictable in every sense of the word. Fortunately she had a little habit that Tom found very amusing. She always carried an emergency g-string with her; it was skin coloured and so fine it was almost undetectable, she slipped it on under the dress smiling with partial satisfaction.

Grainger arrived back at the apartment to collect Maria. His eyes roved over her,

"You look absolutely stunning my dear, I hope you didn't mind the maid laying out your clothes for you, I told her not to wake you, as you looked so peaceful,"

"Not at all, I am glad you approve" she smiled coolly; she wasn't going to give him the satisfaction of mentioning the shortage of underwear. *'And, If he thinks I believe that stunt again about a maid, he has certainly underestimated my intelligence'* she thought grimly.

When they arrived at the Ball, Grainger now masked as she was; proudly escorted her down the spiral staircase into the ballroom. Maria looked around the room; everybody was dressed in style, all wearing facemasks without exception. *'How the hell will I find Terry in this'* she thought, *'they all look alike'*

The tables had been set for groups of eight; and she had been placed on the table between Grainger and to her dismay David Hines. Maria got the impression that they were not going to let her get too far from their sight. The evening meal was first class; and the music was provided courtesy of the Air Force Swing Band; which was considered to be one of the best swing bands in Cyprus. It was a very impressive occasion all round.

After the meal finished, Grainger and Hines went over to the bar to speak to some of the other guests, and the dancing began. For a brief moment she was left alone at the dining table, and then she felt a gentle tap on her shoulder,

"May I have this dance young lady?"

Maria recognised the voice instantly, Terry stood beside her, his face covered by the mask.

"Of course" Maria replied without giving any sign of recognition.

She noticed her two escorts standing at the bar watching her every movement so she knew she had to be very careful. However before she could speak, Terry whispered

"In case you're wondering, I would recognize that cute ass of yours anywhere" adding, with a quick glance towards the bar, "I need to quickly de-brief you"

"You do have an unfortunate way with words," Maria commented dryly, before she continued, "These people are sick. Grainger got me to practically strip naked whilst I try on sexy clothes in front of him, then he tried to hypnotise me while he lay on the bed taking photos. Also someone locked up all my underwear so that I should come here without any"

Terry smothered a laugh,

"Wow, droughty out tonight was it, and not for the first time if I recall' he joked,

Maria gave him a chilling look

"A lady always has an alternative so keep your hand above my waist line or else"

"I know" He grinned, "Otherwise I won't be able to walk back to the table"

"You got it"

She manoeuvred Terry around so he was again facing the bar.

"The one standing on Grainger's left is not the boyfriend; I think he may be more senior. And he is the owner of the apartment. His name is David Hines. They left me last night to play a game; which was really a faster version of strip poker, while they chatted together in the study. That's where I found those photos".

Terry was distracted at the thought of Maria playing strip poker.

"How far did you go?"

Maria at first ignored him, continuing

"I refused to join in at first, but in the end I had no choice, but with a little extra help I didn't lose, or perhaps I should say I didn't lose everything, but I was left wearing just one item"

"Which one" he asked

"You guess, you have a vivid imagination" she joked.

Terry laughed at her observation.

"Be careful," she warned manoeuvring him around again, "They are looking at us; I think they are coming over. Take me back to the table now"

Terry couldn't resist adding as they slowly walked

"By the way we have occupied the apartment next door, with a very nice view" he chuckled.

Maria drew a deep breath, realising that he must have been watching her around the pool.

"You pig" She smiled through gritted teeth.

Terry escorted Maria back to her seat and returned to his table; where the undercover police party were waiting for the information that she had passed on.

They immediately identified the officer with Grainger as Captain David Hines a man who they had had under surveillance for quite some time, but they had never been able to pin anything on him. Meanwhile Hines was not looking very pleased; he didn't like her dancing with strangers.

"Do you know that man"? He enquired testily

"No, but he sounded quite pleasant" She replied wondering why he was so concerned, she hoped he was not getting suspicious about her in any way.

He looked at her keenly,

"He seemed to be quite familiar with you whilst you were dancing"

Maria looked at him coldly,

"Don't all men try it on given the chance, especially those that can't be identified, anyway what's it to do with you who I dance with?"

"A lot if you want to work with us," he replied sharply.

That was the first time he had spoken about the job, Maria tried to look unconcerned,

"I don't even know what the job is, maybe I don't want it"

He ignored her remark, and finished his drink.

"The next waltz you are dancing with me" He informed her arrogantly.

Not wanting to push him to far she shrugged,

"Fine"

Eventually the music changed to a waltz; he stood up and without a word tipped his head in the direction of the dance floor. She rose slowly, placed her napkin beside her plate and walked in front of him to the edge of the dance area. As soon he had put his arm around Maria's waist she knew she had a problem as his left hand went directly towards her bottom and was very near to being inside her dress.

"I like a girl who lives dangerously" He leered as he held her even tighter.

"Oh yes, in what way?" She replied sarcastically. He laughed,

"The maid told me what you would and would not be wearing tonight, on my orders of course"

For once she replied without thinking.

"Oh really! You really cannot believe anyone these days"

That remark she soon realized was a silly response. He was holding her very tight with the right arm as his left hand went on to investigate further.

She tried to pull away but he was far too strong for her. His mauling hand was now completely inside the lower part of her dress and she could feel him touching her bare bottom.

Anger rose up inside her. She would not tolerate this creep under any circumstances and was preparing to knee him in the groin if he went any further, assignment or not.

Just at that moment he released his grip on her, he appeared to have missed the tiny waistband of her g-string. As he relaxed she managed to break free, she turned and left him on the crowded dance floor and walked back to their table.

Terry had seen all this from where he was sitting, and although it was a very tense situation he dare not interfere, anyway he was sure Maria was experienced enough to cope without blowing her cover. 'Thank God' he thought, 'she should only have one more night of this sexual harassment to suffer'.

Grainger, who had also watched the action from the bar, was now furious and ready to leave. He called for the car and they were driven back to the apartment in stony silence.

As they got out of the car Grainger whispered to Maria sarcastically,

"I am sure that you will really be very pleased to learn that David is staying here tonight"

She wasn't sure if he was warning her; or tormenting her; but her stomach lurched; that was the last thing she wanted to hear. She knew she had to stay alert, as God only knows what plan they had for her this time; considering that they seemed to have easy access to all the rooms and doors in the whole of the apartment.

Maria went straight to her bedroom. To her dismay Hines followed her within three to four minutes, pushing the door wide open without a knock or an apology. She had her back to the door; and had already slipped the dress off her shoulders leaving it hanging loosely suspended around her waist. She was aware that if it had been a few seconds later; he would have certainly spotted her scanty underwear. He perched himself on the edge of her bed, and looked her up and down saying.

"Continue my dear. I just came to ask you downstairs for a small night cap, with or without your clothes on" he laughed

She remained static with her back towards him, her hands now clutching her breasts, almost a pointless exercise considering the wall-to-wall full-length mirrors in the room.

"I would rather not, I am very tired" She said trying to think of an excuse,

Not content with her feeble answer, he replied, still believing she was naked under her dress as he looked past her now studying her refection in the mirrors.

"Ok, fine, carry on if you prefer. I think I will enjoy this more anyway"

Maria quickly changed her mind and adjusted her dress; he stood and she followed him down the stairs to the lounge.

He came and sat very close to her on the settee, putting his arm around her shoulder and forcefully pulling her towards him.

"Relax my dear, move over a little and let Matt sit down too"

Maria felt like a butterfly trapped in a spider's web. Hines handed her a glass of whisky, which she accepted and drank far quicker than she intended. Within a few minutes she felt the room beginning to spin. She cursed herself for being so stupid, as she realized too late; that her drink had been spiked.

Hines laughed at her dilemma as she weakly tried to push him away. She made a great effort to stand holding onto the settee for support. He laughed and clasped his hands together in anticipation, not noticing that his friend was not sharing his excitement.

Somehow she made her way to the stairs stumbling a few times as she held tightly onto the twisting rail; making a vain effort to get to what she thought in her drugged state of mind; would be the safety of her bedroom. A grinning Hines followed her a few paces behind as she climbed to the top of the stairs and into the bedroom

He could see that she was semi-conscious as she lay on her stomach across the bed. He spoke over his shoulder to Grainger who had followed them.

"She danced with that guy who was sitting all evening on the military police table; I need to check out if she really is who she says she is, if not we are in trouble"

He searched through her handbag, suitcase and wardrobe, but found nothing. He then searched her make up bag and wash bag in the bathroom, but after going through all her belongings, he still drew a blank.

"I'm going to give her a full body search," He snarled; his face contorted with lust.

Grainger was not happy with that suggestion, he was no angel, but even so he had limits. But before he could make his objections known; Hines had swiftly un-zipped her dress and pulled it down to her waist. Maria was vaguely aware that her body was being violated but was not able to offer any defence.

Kicking her discarded shoes out of the way, he knelt on the floor frantically ripping at her dress. In his perverted lust, he had not noticed the tiny G-string, however Grainger had.

As Hines pulled himself up from the floor, Grainger swept the red silk sheet across her body to hide the offending garment.

Maria now barely conscious, groped at the sheet with one hand in a vain attempt to protect herself, but in doing so, she again exposed the tiny waistband of her underwear.

"See, see what she is wearing. Hines screeched almost hysterically,

Putting his hand on her hip he raised the tiny elastic waistband with his little finger,

"This is what I mean, my friend, she disobeyed us."

He ran his rough hands over her smooth un-protected body,

"What do you think Matt? We could have a threesome tonight and have some real fun with her. What do you say?"

Grainger shook his head placing his hand firmly on Hines shoulder,

"I don't think so my friend, that wouldn't be a very good idea at the moment, you can have her later. Remember our orders were to persuade her to work with us, not against us. I am sure that HQ would not like to hear that you couldn't wait".

Hines struggled to regain his composure

Grainger was well aware of his friend's psychopathic sexual appetite. Angrily Hines got off the bed his face like thunder, he brushed past him almost knocking him over; and stormed out of the room. Grainger looked down at Maria and gently pulled the sheet up to cover her, turning off the bedside light as he too left the room.

+++

Early next morning Maria woke dazed, with a parched mouth; her head throbbing. She got out of bed, opened the double doors to the balcony and stepped outside to enjoy the early morning breeze; shivering slightly as a fresh puff of cool air brushed her warm body. She stood barefoot on the glass-panelled balcony leisurely exercising and stretching her lean bronze frame to its full extent; gently easing the stiffness out of her neck and body.

Somewhere in the depth of her mind she felt very disturbed, and struggled to clear her head in a vain attempt to remember. In a flash it came to her, 'the bastards drugged me!' She shuddered as the blurred memory of Hines mauling her came clearer, but then her mind became confused, as she was aware that Grainger had also been there.

Suddenly she felt the desire to take a cool shower to wash the disturbing thoughts out of her mind and to ease her painful head. She walked back into the bedroom, slipped on her robe, and laid clean underwear out on the bed, before picking up a towel and creeping along the narrow corridor towards the bathroom, 'I just hope to God they are both still asleep' she thought nervously.

Once safely in the bathroom she gently closed the door behind her, hung the towel on the hook beside the cubicle along with her robe, she hesitated for a moment before deciding to keep her tiny string briefs on, just in case.

Then as quietly as she could she stepped into the shower and turned the water on. Almost immediately the bathroom door opened. It was Hines; he could see Maria's full length shapely form slightly distorted by the steam and the frosted door panel. He stood just inside the door watching; not making a sound. Maria was oblivious to his presence as she stood with her eyes closed washing her hair with the warm soapy water. He quietly closed the door behind him, and leaned against it, savouring her every movement. Gradually and silently he moved closer towards the cubicle.

She sensed a presence and froze; she felt a sharp stab of fear in the pit of her stomach. Slowly Hines opened the soap-splashed cubicle door; both parties remained silent as he observed the slender bronze rear of the near naked woman in front of him.

After what seemed like eternity to Maria, he spoke in a low sinister whisper,

"Very nice indeed" he laughed. "The view is good from this angle, but what about the rest of you?"

She remained static with her back towards him; the only movement came as she screwed up her eyes to avoid the shampoo as it slowly dripped down her flushed face.

"I'm waiting" His chilling voice cut into her nerves like a knife.

Maria's mind darted in all directions; it was no use calling for help, nobody would hear except perhaps Grainger, and she wasn't too sure about him. 'Think Maria think' her mind whirled, she was well aware of the seriousness of her predicament. 'Don't let him see your fear, that's what turns mad men like him on.' She fought to stay calm. Somehow she had to find a way to distract him, if not she knew what was going to happen. Opening her eyes she turned her head very slightly,

"Oh it's you, can't a lady get any privacy in this house?"

"Ah you forget my dear, it is my house, so I can do as I please" He sneered

The powerful shower spray splashed off her back and shoulders directly onto him. He laughed excitedly; and stepped inside the cubicle,

"Now I am wet; I might as well help you"

"I don't need your help"

He ignored her rebuttal and grabbed the sponge from her hand, liberally poured the liquid soap onto it and started to rub it slowly over her shoulders, back, all the time moving lower towards her buttocks.

"Put your hands above your head, flat on the wall and keep them there" he ordered breathlessly, pushing her arms up as he spoke.

She did as he asked, not saying a word, hoping that if she remained silent it would confuse him. She knew this type of deviant pervert fed on the fear factor of others. But instead of putting him off he seemed encouraged by the lack of objection.

His breathing got louder and faster as one hand moved round her waist towards her stomach, pulling her to bend towards him Maria knew that she had to quickly find some other sort of diversion tactic, *'Whatever I do now, it's going to be a massive risk'* she thought worriedly, *'especially if he thinks it's a come on.'* At that moment he briefly moved a step backwards and lowered the sponge;

"Now my dear, we will now see how good you really are, but first, take these bloody things off." He said referring to her string briefs. She lowered her arms to her side, and closed her eyes; with her chest heaving and her heart pounding profusely she took a deep breath. And turned to face him, *'Like hell I will'* she thought.

Placing her right hand against the shower wall and her left hand on her hip, she looked directly into his wild staring eyes challenging him confidently.

For a brief moment Hines was caught off balance; confused by her boldness. Then an expression of triumph spread across his repulsive face. Encouraged by her reaction; he grinned and reached up to turn off the shower, moving closer to her he held the sponge and squeezed out the excess soap over her breasts; watching intensely the white trickle of bubbles descending slowly down every visible contour of her shapely statue like body.

It took every ounce of her strength to control the urge not to resist as she maintained her rigid stance. He slid the sponge slowly from her breast down her body towards her jewel-studded navel and beyond. Hooking his finger through the tie of her now transparent string he pulled it slowly until it slacken just enough to slip slowly from her hips, before dropping to her feet. He became visibly more and more stimulated as he caressed her body unchallenged, shaking with excitement.

'Enough' her mind screamed, she could stand no more, her whole body tensed as she frantically searched for a solution

She slowly lowered her hands, placing them protectively in front of her before breaking her silence. Looking him straight in his eyes she said in a quiet determined voice.

"Now you have seen all there is to see. Let me finish my shower,"

Something in the way she spoke, reached deep down into his mind and his mood instantly changed. His face registered a catalogue of emotions, as he strove to regain some self-control.

Without a word he handed her the sponge, picked up her string panties and stepped out of the cubicle. The door slowly closed behind him as her legs gave way, she sank slowly to the shower floor. Now she fully realized what she was dealing with. Hines was an extremely unpredictable and very, very dangerous man.

Maria only had one thought on her mind, she needed to get to the wristwatch, if she could activate the alarm; support from Terry would be only a few minutes away.

Still shaking she stepped out of the shower and realised immediately that her towel and robe had been removed. *'Oh my God '*she thought, *'what the hell do I do now?'*

Frantically looking round the bathroom to see if there was anything she could find to cover herself, she noticed a small white cotton sheet in the top of a cupboard. Hurriedly she wrapped it around herself, it was far too narrow to cover her totally, so she draped it around herself the best way she could. She had a dreadful sinking feeling that she hadn't seen the last of Hines as she made her way back to her room.

Hines was lying in her bed smoking a huge cigar. She noticed his wet shorts lying on the floor beside the bed, so she was sure that he was naked under the thin silk sheet. She deliberated briefly before resisting the urge to turn and run as he eyed her up and down.

"That bloody sheet. Get rid of it," He demanded tersely.

"Go to hell." She snapped back at him, still dripping wet from the shower.

Hines raised his eyebrows,

"You disappoint me. Have you lost your nerve? We thought you would be perfect for the job."

She was once again alert, perhaps at last she would find out what she wanted to know.

"What is this job exactly?" She asked curiously, trying to distract him by keeping him talking.

"Get into the bed first; and then I'll tell you" he said softly. But then once again his mood changed. "That's no longer a request. And get rid of that bloody sheet"

Maria glanced at her fresh underwear lying on the end of the bed; she reached out casually to retrieve it.

In one swift move he swung his legs over the side of the bed and grabbed her arm,

"I don't think so, you won't need them," he said with a leering smile, as he placed his smouldering cigar in the ashtray on the bedside table. She glared at him defiantly holding on tight to the soaking wet sheet and trying to release her arm from his grip.

Maria was now very worried and a bit frightened as the situation developed; she wondered how the hell she was going to get out of it this time without blowing her cover. But having come this far; she needed to know just what their plans were. Hines pulled back the bed sheet whispering menacingly,

"I said get in"

She had no choice; she dropped the wet sheet to the floor and quickly slipped into the bed positioning herself up close to the headboard, and securing the bed sheet tightly under her arm.

"That's better and far more comfortable isn't it?" he said breathlessly easing up close beside her.

"Be a good girl, be nice to me, and then you can have this back".

To her horror he held her wristwatch in his hand. 'He knows about the watch. How?' Her mind panicked, but she forced herself to stay calm.

Looking at him trying to appear unconcerned, she shrugged her shoulders and said.

"Go to hell. Keep it if you want it"

She was praying that he didn't know the true purpose of the wristwatch; otherwise she was in big trouble. Seeing that she was not bothered about the watch he dropped it onto the bed. As casually as she could she picked it up and slipped it onto her wrist avoiding his eyes; hoping that he could see no sign of the relief she was feeling. She kept talking to distract him,

"So, this job. What do you want from me?"

He ran his index finger along the top of the sheet, Maria's heart thumped as she tightened her grip.

"We want you to teach your erotic dance routine to a bunch of sexless foreigners"

She looked at him surprised, "Dance! Where?"

"You ask too many questions. But I can tell you it's on a little unknown island; controlled by some outlaw Ruskies. Interested?"

"Tell me more," She answered, still desperately trying to keep him talking.

He breathed harshly; he had no intention of wasting any more time.
"Later"

"Dance routine?" She asked desperately, "Is that what all this is about?

He shifted his position until he was leaning heavily against her, his hand trying to grasp her thigh.

"You are still asking too many questions. I said later."

Gathering her thoughts together she decided this was the end; this was as far as she was prepared to go. The information she had gathered should be enough for the time being, and now she needed to get out of here. She decided to take a gamble, as she looked him squarely in the eyes.

"I will co-operate, but only on one condition. You keep your filthy groping hands off me, or I walk" Maria held her breath wondering exactly how he would react to her blunt ultimatum.

His face contorted angrily,

"You are not exactly in the position to bargain" he retorted,

But then he remembered Grainger's warning; he knew his superiors were depending on her expert services to help them with their plans.

"Ok. This time you win," he snarled, "but one day very soon; you will pay dearly."

She reached out to pick up her underwear.

He re-lit his cigar, making no attempt to leave the bed, but just layback on the pillow watching her between his half closed eyes.

Standing with her back towards him, Maria slipped on her dry underwear. But Hines unable to resist, lunged out at her, pulling her backwards onto the bed kissing her neck. To Maria's relief they heard Grainger calling.

"David are you coming, we have to be out of here as soon as we can"

"Damn the bloody man" Hines said angrily, ignoring him.

Grainger called again, but this time a lot louder,

"For Christ's sake David, get down here and get Salwa, we need to talk"

Hines hesitated for one moment, and then pushed her to one side

"Ok Selwa, you may have got away with it, but next time it will be different"
Hines snarled.

Maria got off the bed and hurriedly dressed before following him down
the stairs to meet Grainger

"I understand David has spoken to you; and you want this job. I hope you
are a good sailor," Grainger asked her, glaring at Hines.

"Not bad why?"

Ignoring her question, he started to walk to the door,

"Good' and then he turned and looked at her,

"We have to go down to the port. So be ready in one hour. You will be
away for a few days, so don't pack much you won't need it. I will send a car for
you".

The two men then left the apartment. As soon as she heard them drive
away, she crept cautiously down the corridor to phone Terry,

"Maria, are you ok, what's happening?" Maria interrupted him,

"Listen Terry; I have to be quick as they are waiting for me. I have found
out that they are working with the Russians training women as sex slaves and
I suspect; selling classified airbase secrets for cash. They are sending a car for
me in one hour, and then we will be travelling somewhere by boat."

Picking up on her urgency he replied,

"Remember, you have the watch, just pull the winder out once when you
get to your destination, or when you want us to come in. The mechanism works
as a tracker, we will monitor everything from here twenty-four-seven, but don't
pull it too early, because when activated it only has a six-hour battery life, and
Maria, don't worry" He added "I will be with my boys at the port to get some
clear photos of all the bastards. Best of luck sweetheart"

With that the phone went dead.

+ + +

Exactly one hour later the car drew up at the door ready to take her to the
port, and within minutes they had arrived in front of an extremely expensive
looking motor yacht, Maria calculated that it must be at least twenty metres
long. The driver of the car came round and opened the door and escorted her
on board, and almost immediately they cast off.

She walked towards the front of the boat and looked around to see if she
could see Terry on the shore, although she knew he was far too professional
to be spotted, even by her.

On board as far as she could see were three rough looking burly men
making up the crew, silently going about their work. Nobody spoke a word
to her, but from the odd word she over heard; Maria assumed they were of
Russian origin. Looking over towards Hines she asked him,

"How long will it take us to get there?"

"Four hours, maybe five" He replied as he scanned the shore with his binoculars,

"We have full cargo today so I expect nearer to five"

"Where is Matt?" She questioned in order to distract him, praying he had not noticed Terry or any of the others on the dock.

"Don't ask so many questions," He snapped turning away from the shore to stare at her.

Maria sat alone at the forward section of the boat, troubled thoughts chasing around in her head. She could only count three crew and Hines at the moment, no other obvious passengers, but she guessed from the way they were acting, there was someone else down below in the galley.

The journey was uneventful, and as Hines had predicted the trip took almost five hours, until finally the yacht arrived at a remote but beautiful romantic looking island.

She was proved to be right about more passengers below, when two very frightened young women were brought up to the deck with their hands tied behind them. One of the young women looked at her in disgust. Maria knew what she was thinking, but she could say and do nothing for now. She glanced at the other young woman; who had her head down obviously in tears.

The girls were hustled off the yacht onto the white sandy beach, where they were soon surrounded by a dozen or more Eurasian looking women all scantily dressed, which didn't seem unusual to Maria at the time; as it was extremely hot; and only the slightest whisper of a breeze. She also noticed none of the women appeared to be showing any sign of being upset or worried in any way.

She looked up as more men arrived on the beach pushing their way through the women, shouting to them to get back. Hines spoke to one of the men in their own language, which was as she thought, Russian. He then turned to Maria,

"You have one week until I get back. I expect to see these women trained and ready to perform"adding with a threat, "If I don't think you have made the effort, then you will join them and we will get someone else"

Maria looked at him defiantly,

"You forget I accepted this job; and I will do my best, but that depends on their ability also. If they are not up to it then I will resign. NOT join them." Hines gave a cynical sneering laugh, and turned his back on her and walked away. It was at this point that Maria realised that she was as much of a prisoner, as the other women were.

Apprehensively she stepped down off the boat and looked at the women standing there watching her, *'How the hell am I going to do that in just one week?'*

The surly crew unloaded the weekly provisions; Maria watched as the engine warmed up to full power then with Hines having now boarded the craft they departed from the Island. Her hand wandered to the watch on her wrist, and then thought better of it; she decided to wait until the morning before activating the watch signal, she needed to get a far clearer picture of what was going on.

Two heavy butch Russian women untied the two new girl's hands, pushing them roughly to a makeshift shower area on the beach, indicating to them to strip to their briefs. The older of the two girls refused, and received a sharp slap on her face from the one of burly women, who also ripped her blouse from her. Maria watched helplessly as the poor girl struggled to hide her tears, whilst the men hung around pointing and laughing at their humiliation.

The stone-faced Russian women sadistically hosed the two new hostages down with cold water. When they had finished they threw them a small towel each, and the girls hastily tried to cover themselves as best way they could.

None of the other women on the beach seemed concerned with this performance; they continued laughing and chatting as before, completely ignoring the scene in front of them. It reminded Maria of a case study she had read once, where a large group of people had been brainwashed to act in an un-characteristic way, although not such a large group as this.

One of the Russian men came over to Maria and got hold of her arm saying in perfect English,

"You don't need a watch on this island" He pulled it from her wrist before she had chance to resist,

"Time means nothing here, and you wear only what we tell you and nothing else."

'Oh God', Maria thought. 'I hope Terry meant what he said about following me; otherwise I have a big problem. Somehow I have to get that watch back'

Then with the other two young women from the boat, she was taken to a large Marquee about two hundred metres back from the beach. As they entered the open side, her first impression was that it had all the hallmarks of a well-organized harem.

She stood just inside the entrance of the Marquee and looked around; at the far end there was a row of low beds, each one surrounded by a flimsy mosquito net. Beside each bed was a small cupboard and a mirror, and to her amazement; hanging from a rail at the side of each cubicle she could see a single exotic dance costume. As she went further in she noticed several small beacon lamps giving out a warm glow even though it was still bright sunshine outside. Opposite the bed area behind another thin net curtain, she could see an extremely large cushion seat and a selection of small exotically coloured day beds. There appeared to be little or no privacy from the inquisitive eyes of the male guards that patrolled the grounds around the marquee.

Maria also noticed that the area in the centre was clear of all furniture, and looked as though it might be used for entertainment. The whole Marquee was highly perfumed by several small incense burners, adding to the hot humid atmosphere.

One of the hostage women smilingly showed them which cubicle was theirs; and gave them the information as to when to change from their daywear into their dance costumes. Maria looked at the costume hanging beside her bed, and had to admit to herself that it really was beautiful. She fingered the fine chiffon material with sensual pleasure,

"Why don't you try it on" the woman smiled encouragingly. Maria couldn't resist.

Although she could only see part of herself in the tiny mirror provided, the thought flickered through her mind '*Whoever chose this; knew I was coming, and has picked the colour which suits me best'*. The dress had red and gold chiffon leggings, and a gold tasselled beaded headband with a red chiffon veil that floated down to a red and gold half cupped fitted bra. The colour flattered her olive skin perfectly. But as she twirled around trying to get the feel of the costume, what she didn't realise was; that she had attracted the attention once more of the same Russian guard.

Looking around at the others, she saw they had all changed into their costumes, she observed that all the other women wore pale green and yellow; she was the only one in vivid red. The two new women were dressed in pale blue, which she learnt later was to identify them as novices.

Maria counted about fifteen to twenty women hostages; who she assumed had been abducted over the past weeks and months, and was rather concerned that these women appeared to accept their situation, unlike the two latest arrivals.

The girl, who had protested on the beach and looked to be the older of the two, came over to Maria.

"Who the hell are you?" She demanded angrily, "Why are you working for these scum?"

Maria looked at the girl undecided; she didn't really want to explain to anyone what she was doing there, at least not yet.

"What makes you think I am working for them? I am as in the same position as you are"

"No I don't think so" the girl replied, "I heard what you said to that man Hines"

"Then you must also have heard his reply" Maria retorted.

"Please, can't you help us?" the young woman pleaded reaching out for Maria's hand.

"Quiet" Maria whispered sharply looking over to the doorway, then looking back at the distressed girl in front of her she asked,

"How did you get caught up in this?"

The girl looked down,

"We came over to be dancers, they told us we could earn good money, so we came, then soon after we got here all our money and passports were stolen. That man they call Hines said he would help us get them back, but he said it would take a while and why not work for him while we were waiting" She looked up into Maria's face,

"I know it was pretty stupid, but I can't explain; it seemed ok at the time. And then when we realised what was happening, they got tough; and here we are"

Maria made an instant decision.

"Maybe I can help you, but you must do as I say; and listen"

The girl looked at Maria her face alive with hope.

"What is your name?" she whispered

"Salwa" Maria replied gently.

"I am Karen" she beckoned to her friend, "and this is my friend Samantha. We have to get out of here. There must be some way we can escape"

Samantha smiled shyly,

"We thought you were one of them"

Maria answered with a rueful smile,

"Well I suppose I am in a way, but not in the way you mean. They asked me to come here to teach Arabic dancing to the women in one week, which is more than likely impossible. Otherwise I am a prisoner too"

The women looked astonished

"Why did you accept?"

Glancing quickly at the opening in the Marquee Maria shook her head,

"That's a long story, which will become clear to you later. But at the moment you must treat me as though I am one of them, it's in your best interest that you don't let them see you speaking with me too often". Then she added firmly,

"But don't try to escape on your own, there is no way off this island and if you try they will torture and without doubt rape you. The people running this camp are all obsessed with sex. They are dangerous psychopaths. Do you understand?"

The two girls looked at each other in dismay before nodding in agreement.

The Russian guard who had taken her watch earlier; stood in the entrance of the Marquee and called out,

"You Salwa, come"

She gave the two women a warning look, and followed the English speaking Russian to his quarters. He was very tall man in his mid thirties, with an air of self-importance, quite nice looking in a rugged sort of way. He appeared to be well educated as his English was near perfect to her ears.

"You start work in morning, you sleep here tonight"

"I accept I start work in the morning" She protested firmly with a confidence she did not feel, "But tonight I sleep alone"

At that he grabbed her around the waist and pulled her towards him with one arm, turned her around, and started kissing her neck and bare shoulder

"I could force you, you know?"

She twisted her body away from him, and looked at him coldly.

"You could, but then I don't train your women. That's your choice"

He thought of what his superiors would do if he jeopardised their plans and reluctantly dropped his arm to his side,

"Very well then later when you become desperate for a man"

"I never have, and never will get that desperate" she replied with a mocking smile.

He gave her an appraising look of admiration,

"I see I'm going to have a problem with you"

She turned and walked away. He made no attempt to stop her, but she could feel his eyes on her back as she left the tent. '*I hope that's not going to be the only way I can retrieve the watch*, she shuddered, *and 'That's if he still has it of course'.*

Maria stood at the opening in the Marquee deep in thought; the evening had become cooler with a slight breeze from the sea. She could see a fire burning in the centre of the camp; giving light rather than heat. Cones lit by flames; highlighted walkways from the campfire to the various primitive accommodations.

The whole setting resembled a medieval army camp, with its campfires; and men gathered around drinking and talking. Maria sighed as she looked around, '*It's hard to believe what is really taking place on this beautiful Island.*'

Next morning she woke early, and called for the women to be on the beach; ready for their first lesson. The women seemed eager to learn, but after showing them a few basic moves, she knew she was going to have to work extremely hard to achieve even the slightest standard Hines required. But a couple of hours later the women had mastered the first basic moves.

"Right ladies, we will take a short break, I know you must be as hot as I am"

The women laughed happily and stripped off to their briefs; unconcerned at the watching guards and ran into the water.

Maria noticed that even Karen and Samantha had joined in, and in spite of their plight they looked relaxed as they splashed each other to cool down. It was so hot she was very tempted to join them. And then she heard a voice coming from behind her.

"Why are you not in there? I insist. You deserve some relaxation," He laughed

She didn't need to turn around; she knew it was her Russian admirer. Without replying she removed her top and threw into the air, and then walked towards the waters edge until it was deep enough for her to dive into the sea. A cheer went up from the onlookers, then three of the men laughing like schoolboys; gathered up the women's clothes and took them away.

When the women came out of the water, the guards made a pathway and sat waiting for them to walk the 50 meters back to camp. It was clear to Maria that the childish game was nothing new for these women; they walked through totally unconcerned; one or two of them even smiling at the men. However she could see that both Karen and Samantha were clearly embarrassed, they walked through the lines of jeering guards with their heads down and their arms folded covering their breasts

As the days went by the same ritual was acted out, and after a couple of days even the two newest recruits ignored the men's behaviour. But apart from that slight annoyance, they were left to their own devices. But for Maria, wherever she went and what ever she did, she could feel the eyes of her Russian admirer upon her.

After a few days intensive work, the women had improved their dance co-ordination immensely. But the only way to find out if they were really ready to perform as a group was to arrange a full dress rehearsal.

That evening in the main arena of what Maria had christened the harem marquee, she gave a faultless demonstration, which had all the women and even the Russian guards clapping and dancing. Maria smiled and thought, *'Terry would have really enjoyed the atmosphere here tonight, and especially with all these pretty women'* Then she thought of Tom, and how he loved to watch her dance. She had tried not to think of Tom too much, as she knew she would lose her courage, although she realised he would be very worried about not hearing from her for such a long time. She pushed all thoughts of home out of her head; it was one of the golden rules when on any mission.

It was now time for the rest of the women to perform their combined routines. She went between each one of them adjusting their movements. They were doing well, in fact she was pleasantly surprised, as it seemed that they were almost ready for the exhibition due at the weekend.

She didn't know whom the mystery audience would involve, but she knew Hines would be there, and the feeling of anticipation around the camp led her to believe that the big boys were coming as well. Maria realized time was running out, she had to contact Terry. It was vital to get the watch back, and soon.

After pondering on the situation for a while, she decided that she would have to take a risk. Over the past few days, although she knew he had been watching her, the Russian had given her no further trouble, if anything he had been very pleasant and polite.

Putting on her seductive dance costume, she slipped silently out of the Marquee making sure that she kept out of the reach of the campfire light, and went in search of the Russian in his tent. She was hoping with a little flirtation she could strike some sort of deal to get the watch back without suggesting sex. She skirted the backs of the smaller tents keeping on constant alert. *'The last thing I need is to run into a lone guard, especially dressed like this'* she thought nervously,

When she finally found the right tent, she took a deep breath and stepped through the opening to find him sitting on a floor cushion smoking a "Hubble bubble" pipe.

The air inside the tent was thick with the smoke; and although she was accustomed to smokers around her in Lebanon she found this to be extreme. She knelt beside him but before she could speak, he questioned lazily,

"You stay tonight; we have a good time, yes?"

Maria smiled up at him seductively, letting one strap of her bra top slide carelessly off her shoulder,

"Tomorrow night after the show, I come here, that's a promise"

"But tomorrow all the English, American and Russian clients will be here" He protested.

"What time are they coming?" She quizzed placing her hand on his knee and immediately getting the response she expected, as she felt him quiver with excitement.

"Around early to mid- morning, so I was told why are you bothered?" He answered running his fingers along the base of her neck.

"I have to know the exact time so that I can get the women ready in case it's early. But I need my watch" Maria held her breath waiting for his response.

"Ok, you can have it back later tonight if you come here alone, I will be waiting."

He gave a lopsided grin, "Tomorrow is no good, as you will be busy with the dancing and getting the women ready to entertain our guests," He winked, "Both sexes. You know what I mean?

"Yes I do. You mean anything is acceptable"

"They are paying a lot of money for these women to dance erotically, the more they do; the more they will bid for them. Do you understand?

Then as she lent forward his huge hand traced the curve of her deliberately exposed breast as he added,

"But not you, you are mine"

Maria forced a smile as he slid the other bra strap from her shoulder.

"You understand, I want you in my bed for free"

"Yes I understand" she whispered seductively, "Tell me are there any special requests for tomorrow night?"

He took his eyes from her breasts and looked at her, one eyebrow raised meaningfully.

"Special requests? I will let you know those; when you come back later"

Maria giggled coyly,

"I meant for the dancing"

The smoke from the pipe drifted around his head as he layback on the cushions,

"I know"

She rose and left the tent; aware that she would have to go back that evening, she was desperate to have the watch back before the guest arrived; so she could set it the six hours Terry needed.

A few hours later having changed out of her costume she strolled casually over to Karen's bed; where she was sitting with Samantha. She knew what she was about to do was extremely dangerous, and she hoped she could handle things without endangering herself or any of the other women. She spoke quickly to the two girls,

"If you want out of here, you must do everything I say"

They instantly agreed without any hesitation and Maria explained her plan.

Later that evening, having dressed again in her dance costume, she made her way cautiously once again to the Russian's quarters. He looked up as she entered the tent, and with out a word motioned to her to sit on the cushions beside him. The tent was lit with many candles, and as she looked around she could see that the whole floor was decorated with the large soft multi coloured silk cushions.

The air was pungent, with incense and smoke, and she soon realised from the smell that he was smoking Marijuana. It didn't take long before the effects began to make her feel quite dizzy. She had already observed there was a bottle of Vodka on the floor beside him half empty, and presumed that he had consumed the rest, so he was already quite high. She felt this gave her a good advantage, providing she didn't come under the same influence herself.

Without warning he lunged at her putting both of his huge hands on her shoulders trying to pull at the tiny straps on her costume, but the Marijuana and the drink coupled with his large awkward hands made it difficult if not impossible. Cursing he spluttered,

"Take that bloody thing off"

"Nothing off until I get my watch" she said in a very quiet controlled voice.

"Two can play that game. No watch until you do" he replied reaching out to take another swig of Vodka,

She considered his demand '*I suppose I don't have much of a choice*' she thought unhappily. But before she could act; he muttered his speech now slurred.

"Alright, find it yourself it is under the cushions somewhere. Here take this"

He handing her a Marijuana joint, and made another grab for her, pulling the front of her bra top down. Maria had predicted his intention and managed to turn away from him, causing his hand to slip, and lose his balance.

While he steadied himself she re-adjusted her bra, and turned to face him again. He was still holding out the joint to her, leaving her no option other than to take it from him. He watched as she put it to her mouth and drew on it trying not to inhale, but having already absorbed a considerable amount of his smoke, plus the effect from the incense it quickly took effect.

She felt as if her whole body was floating on a cloud of silk. She could hear herself giggling as she started to crawl on all fours searching under the cushions for the watch. It was difficult keeping her balance on the soft silky surface, and she eventually toppled over and lay on her back giggling uncontrollably. He handed her the joint; she happily took it drawing heavily until it was nearly finished He took it from her and put it to one side.

Seizing this opportunity he made another lunge towards her landing with his full weight on top of her, she was powerless, completely trapped beneath him. She fought to regain her concentration as he smothered her neck and shoulders with kisses, his hands firmly clutching both her breasts.

He then raised himself from her body before making another clumsy effort to undo her bra; but his fumbling fingers couldn't manage the damaged fastener. The Russian was becoming more and more frustrated and agitated as he pulled at the offending garment, pleading with her hoarsely,

"I'll give you the bloody watch if you take that fucking top off now," He reached his hand under the cushions he held up the watch. She knew it was a small price to pay.

She laughed teasingly as she slipped the bra straps off her shoulders and put her hands behind her back releasing the fastener. He watched her transfixed, his body swayed slightly as he moistened his lips in anticipation.

The drug continued to have its affect on her, and soon she began to hallucinate, she stared at the Russian in horror as his face slowly dissolved, but then smiled happily as Tom appeared before her.

"Where have you been my love" She reached out to touch him "I want you so much,"

"I am here my lovely, I want you too" The jubilant Russian replied.

"Make love to me my darling" she whispered kneeling down in front of him willingly

The Russian not waiting for a second invitation grabbed her hand and pulled her closer to him; laying her back on the bed of cushions he kissed her passionately before burying his rough unshaven face between her heaving breasts. She sighed with contentment as he fumbled excitedly with the remainder of her delicate costume.

Some time later, following the plan they had made with Maria, Karen and Samantha slipped quietly into the tent. The exhausted Russian sensing company raised his head very slowly and stared at them for what seemed like minutes unable to comprehend them being there. And then he exploded; his face scarlet as he screamed in frustration at the two young women for their interruption.

"What the bloody hell are you two doing here? Get out. Get out."

"We thought you could handle some extra company" Karen replied huskily, as she seductively slid off her top as she swayed her hips the way Maria had recently taught her. She then lay down on the cushions close to the Russian running her fingers up and down his arm trying to attract his attention away from Maria. Samantha hung back not quite so brave, but eventually came forward and sat down beside her friend.

The man ignored their advances, so Karen turned and began to help Samantha remove her top,

"See; you could have so much more fun with all three of us," she smiled enticingly running her hands gently over her friend's bare shoulders, still trying desperately to lure him away from Maria. For a brief moment she thought he was going to respond but to no avail, he was only interested in the woman who had teased him with such promise.

The frustrated Russian turned his attention back to Maria, who was now kneeling in front of him moaning softly as she cupped both hands teasingly supporting her breasts, before sliding them down her gyrating hips.

"You like?" she whispered seductively leaning towards him.

The two women stared wide-eyed at Maria's provocative gesture; they had no idea that what she was seeing in her drug-induced state was the image of Tom.

"Oh, yes I do like" he gasped, swaying unsteadily his lustful expression of satisfaction contorting his sweaty face. But just as he stretched out to embrace her he gave a loud groan, his eyes rolled as he collapsed unconscious in a heap in Maria's lap. For a moment nobody moved, Karen and Samantha stared at the tableau before them.

"Now that is what you call divine intervention." Karen said as she crawled over to help Maria; who was giggling helplessly still trapped under the weight of the Russian She shook Maria's shoulders and rubbed her face and hands until the effects of the marijuana began to wear off. Gradually Maria regained some composure and looked around her in alarm as her mind became clearer, she groped around in the cushions to find her discarded costume to cover herself,

"Listen" her head jerked suddenly; her mind instantly crystal clear.

They could hear the sound of voices approaching, there was no time to get dressed, and at this moment they were more concerned in finding the watch which the Russian had dropped as he fell. They could hear the voices getting closer and closer as Karen put her hand under the unconscious guard's shoulder; and there it was.

The three women looked at each other in delight, and then Maria whispered urgently,

"Quick, lie down, pretend you are asleep, hurry they are coming in here"

The men looked into the tent and saw their leader asleep with three beautiful women lying naked and semi naked draped over him; said something in Russian and laughed, and to the women's relief; they left.

"Well done girls" Maria smiled at them, "Now let's get out of here. Get back to your beds as soon as possible, and make sure nobody sees you."

As she was putting her costume back on, she looked down at the unconscious Russian, who still had a smile on his face.

"With any luck he won't remember a thing in the morning"

"With any luck, she won't either" Karen winked to Samantha.

Maria watched as dawn slowly filtered through the canvas roof of the Marquee, she had been awake most of the night planning her next move. Finally she decided not to release the signal winder on the watch until she was absolutely sure that everyone involved in this diabolical scheme was on the island. And she was rather concerned; that for some of these women it may be already too late.

But a far greater concern worried her; she didn't know how far away Terry was. She had to assume at the worst scenario that he could still be in Limassol, which; if he was following the tracking device by sea he was going to be a minimum of four to five hours away.

The other women began to wake up; and there was an air of expectation rippling through the Marquee as they chatted to each other excitedly. Maria glanced over to Karen and Samantha sitting quietly on their beds, they were both looking pale and very worried, she would like to have gone over to reassure them, but she only had a few minutes to make sure that all the women were dressed and ready to go. After they had had breakfast, one of the guards burst into the Marquee shouting,

"You all hurry now. Quickly; on the beach"

Hurriedly glancing around to do the last check, Maria hustled the women down onto the beach. She could see three boats in the distance approaching the shore as she arranged the women in a straight line. They made quite a sight, twenty or more women all wearing dance costumes, standing on a beach in the middle of nowhere; nervously checking that their veils covered their faces. But the atmosphere was electric.

Maria could make out three motor yachts about two maybe three miles off shore. She felt her spine tingle, every nerve in her body alert. She glanced quickly at the Russian leader; he appeared to have completely recovered; and showed no sign that he remembered what had happened the previous night as he preened himself ready to greet his guests. Just as the boats were about to land, he turned to Maria saying,

"Make sure they do as they are told. Anyone stepping out of line will be harshly punished"

Within ten to fifteen minutes the guests were on the shore.

Maria watched as they came up the beach towards her; she roughly guessed that there were at least fourteen men and five women in the group, and then she caught her breath in shock as she recognised one of the women as the American from the Jacuzzi in Cyprus, accompanied by her 'blind brother' who clearly wasn't blind now. *'Thank God I have my veil on'* she thought, praying that she would not be recognised. Then came another shock; when she heard the obvious leader of the group introduced to the Russian senior guard as Mr Matheson Jnr.

This Matheson looked no different than his pig of a father except that he was a bit shorter. Looking over at the line up of women, he whispered to the Russian guard. The guard threw back his head and roared with laughter, and then called out to the girls,

"Ladies prepare yourselves"

Matheson Jnr walked towards the women tapping a small cane against his thigh, Karen and Samantha looked at each other in horror; and then towards Maria for some comfort. She could offer none; she was more than a little concerned with the situation herself, and knew if the son was half as perverted as the father, they were in deep trouble.

Judging from the expression on his face, she also guessed what the consequences would be if they did not obey. Hines, who was standing just behind Matheson, looked at Maria and intimated for her to step forward. As she complied she casually put her hands behind her back and pulled the winder on the watch and prayed with all her heart that Terry got the call.

Matheson walked along the line with the cane still in his right hand, closely followed by the American woman and her brother. They stopped at each woman removing their veils; the American woman touched some of them in away that made them flinch with embarrassment. This was not what they expected. Then they came to the two newest recruits dressed in their novice blue, Matheson leant forward and peered closely into Karen's face, she flinched and tried to pull her head back from him, but then he walked behind her squeezing her firm bottom trying to intimidate her. Karen stared straight ahead struggling to show him no emotion. Maria felt a wave of admiration for the terrified girl. He then moved on to Samantha who by this time was visibly shaking, but to Maria's relief although obviously terrified; she remembered her advice and remained calm. Then it was her turn. He stopped in front of her slowly looking her up and down.

"So, you are the Queen Bee. There is obviously something special about you. So what do you have that the others don't?"

When she didn't reply he ripped her veil from her face and leaned towards her, she almost choked as his fowl breath hit her mouth, and then he walked behind her. She tensed waiting to feel his groping hands on her rear in the same way he had to her two friends; however this time it was different, she gave a little gasp as he put the cane between her legs; and moved it harshly backward and forward in a sawing action. She felt a surge of anger rise up, but she managed to control it. He then made a great show of walking around her inspecting her body poking and squeezing intimately, much to the amusement of his laughing audience.

"Mmmm very nice" He said as he stopped and ran a stubby finger down her face.

Maria stared over his shoulder and focused on the American woman who was now looking straight at her and whispering to her brother. They called the Russian leader over, who turned and looked at Maria, but nothing else was said. But Maria knew that she was now in severe danger.

The girls on the beach were confused, this was not what they had expected to happen, they were here to be dancers, why were they being prodded and pawed as though they were cattle? The Russian leader came over to Maria,

"Salwa, prepare the women for their first dance in two minutes"

Maria nodded; and told the girls to replace their veils and commence with their welcoming dance routine. The visitors gathered around to watch the show pointing out the girls they preferred, obviously making their selection for the evening.

When the welcoming show had finished, the guests made their way up the beach to the main Marquee. Hines appeared at Maria's side,

"I thought you would like to know Salwa, we have decided that you will stay here on the Island for a while longer. We have a lot more work for you to do."

This statement filled her with trepidation; especially at how he emphasised her name Salwa, the Americans had obviously told him that she had used the name of Maria when they met her in the beauty Salon.

Then came the reaction she was expecting. Two of the Russians guards grabbed her and took her to the main Marquee, all the guests were sitting about on the day beds drinking and eating and being waited on by the dancers. They pushed her over to where Matheson was sitting. He looked up at her; she gave an involuntary shiver as she met his eyes. They were as cold as ice.

"So your real name is Maria, the famous Lebanese belly-dancer. Now isn't that a coincidence. I understand from my father you danced for him. Maybe you can remember the occasion"

His expression turned to pure hatred as he added,

"Now I wonder what you are doing here. By the end of today you will disclose to me all I need to know, isn't that right my dear?"

She looked straight into his eyes her heart pounding, but gave no reaction or reply. He lazily gestured to the guards

"Give her the water wheel treatment that should help her memory and loosen her tongue"

As two guards grasped hold of her arms, Maria straightened defiantly and looked directly at Matheson,

"Go to hell"

They whole party rose to their feet and followed them down to the beach as a large wooden wheel was brought out from behind the trees. It was then dragged into the sea and positioned so that it was two thirds under water.

Tying her to the wheel by her hands and feet, two burly Russian guards turned the wheel slowly as Maria's head went under the water. She surfaced without a word, gasping for air. Matheson shouted from the beach

"Stop, hold her there. Why are you here, who sent you? Was it the Phoenician?"

Again she didn't respond but her mind was working fast, 'Why does he think I have any knowledge of the Phoenician? What does he know?'

"I see, no reply. Turn it a lot slower this time. I will tell you when to release her"

The Russian leader translated Matheson's instructions to his men. They hesitated and looked at each other in disbelief as they turned the wheel again.

There was a deafening silence from the watching audience, and it seemed like an eternity before Matheson agreed to let her up. Maria was now semi-conscious but still uttered no sound. At this point Matheson's face was almost purple with rage.

"Ok again; this time longer," He screamed hysterically.

The Russian leader knew he had to intervene; the situation was getting out of control,

"You will kill her," he shouted trying to penetrate Matheson's violent fury. "Then you will never find out what she knows." He saw Matheson hesitate, so he continued

"And anyway I thought you wanted her tonight"

Matheson deliberated for a while; his face contorting, and then just as suddenly the fury left him.

"You're right, bring her in. We can all have her tonight. Meanwhile leave her in the sun to bake."

Maria was brought ashore over the shoulder of one of the guards, who lowered her onto the beach, who removed her wet costume leaving her in just her bra top and briefs. He then tied her hands together above her head; securing them to a small wooden stake, and tied her ankles to another one; leaving her absolutely no protection from the burning mid-afternoon sun.

Maria lay for more than an hour still semi conscious, until one of the guards appeared with a bucket of seawater and threw over her. She gasped as she came round and twisted her head to avoid the glare of the sun. Her eyes gradually focused, until she became aware of Hines standing looking down at her, and she could just make out the other guests hovering in the background silently watching. Her mind struggled to focus on what was happening, she tried to move; and realised they had tied her to the stakes.

'Oh God help me. Terry for Gods sake hurry' For the first time since she had started this assignment, she felt real fear.

After a while, one by one, the spectators became hot and bored and started wandering back to the Marquee. As they came in Karen and Samantha looked for Maria, and they were distraught to see she was not amongst the group. They had heard the shouting and could only imagine what was going on. Terrified and believing the worst they clung to each other in despair.

Meanwhile out on the beach Maria was burning up as the sun beat down on her exposed body. Every so often one of the guards would appear with another bucket of seawater to throw over her. She lay there for what seemed like an eternity, her mind drifting in and out of consciousness. For a moment she thought she saw Tom walking towards her, *'Oh Tom I do love you'* and then as he reached out his hands towards her; he faded away. Another bucket of seawater hit her; and she shook her head trying to concentrate. She thought of her family, and wandered if she would ever see them again. Then to push those thoughts out of her head she concentrated on Terry, trying to imagine where he was right now, and how long it would take him to get here.

The American woman and her brother appeared from behind and stood looking down at her. The woman knelt down and put her face very close to Maria's and ran one hand caressingly over her burning body, till obsessed with Maria's breasts

"Hi my dear, Do you remember me, it's Marlene; and of course my brother Louis. I see your lovely body is still in one piece. Why are you being so stubborn Maria? You must be either very brave or very stupid which is it?" She asked, a hard smile twisting the corners of her mouth.

Maria felt light headed, she was burnt and dehydrated; but managed to whisper a few slow words,

"You're a sick bitch. What pleasure do you get from this sort of humiliation to your own sex?" The woman didn't answer, but for a brief moment the smile left her face. She moved away and positioning herself on the sand beside Maria and watched as her brother knelt down on the other side.

"Now it's my turn," He whispered sadistically as he started to caress her body, his sister laughed enjoying Maria's plight.

He leaned forward and kissed her damp stomach, working his way up between her breasts to her throat; relishing her helplessness. Then as he went to kiss her lips, she turned her head away trying to avoid the rank stink of his breath. Angrily he forced her face back and kissed her full on the mouth forcing his tongue between her teeth. Maria felt her stomach heave in revulsion, and she wanted to be sick. And then Marlene laid her hand on her brother's shoulder and he leaned back breathing heavily.

"To answer your earlier question my dear," she smiled, "we get a lot of pleasure from our job. It's so very easy to find beautiful ambitious girls. Your dear friend Eva supplies us with all their details and David Hines and his friends do the rest"

Spitting out the taste of that disgusting slobbering kiss, Maria whispered,

"My God, not Eva too."

Marlene smoothed back her greasy lank hair; and reached into her pocket for a handkerchief to wipe her forehead.

"And by the way my dear, did you not notice my brother's help during your massage at the salon?"

The woman laughed at the expression on Maria's face,

"Oh, of course not. I forgot you had been drinking Seven-up; so you didn't feel a thing, but he certainly did" She sniggered, "He enjoyed it very much, and he thought you did also, didn't you Louie dear?" She patted her brother's arm.

Maria's mouth was so dry that she had a hard job speaking, but the memories of that day flooded back to her.

"How the hell did Eva get involved with the likes of you?" She whispered hoarsely.

Marlene shrugged

"Money, she owed us a lot of money, and she couldn't pay"

"Dear God" Maria whispered, "Poor Eva."

The brother and sister smiled at each other in a way that sent a shiver of fear down Maria's spine.

The woman stood up to leave; and looked down at her with distaste.

"I will leave you to enjoy yourself with my dear brother" She then turned and walked away. As soon as they were alone Louis leaned over to kiss Maria again, his hands roaming over every inch of her scorched body.

"Leave her alone, you animal"

Louis looked up startled.

"What the hell are you doing here?"

It was Karen.

"Cut her free, you bastard or I will"

She produced a knife from under her top and dropped to her knees, frantically sawing at the ropes in an attempt to release Maria. Louis swung back with his arm knocking Karen off balance.

"You will have to try harder than that bitch." He laughed slapping her across the face and kicking the knife out of her reach.

Marlene had not got very far when she heard the disturbance, and she screamed for assistance. Two guards came running along the beach and hauled Karen to her feet, Marlene picked up the knife and handed it to one of the men and snapped,

"Take her away and deal with her"

Maria looked on helpless as they dragged Karen away, *Terry; where the hells are you, for God's sake hurry*' she prayed. The two Americans were in deep discussion. '*They are obviously talking about me*' Maria thought, '*what now?*' But to her surprise; with one last look in her direction they walked away; leaving her alone on the beach. Maria rested her head back down on the sand, she knew they wouldn't leave it at that, '*It will be Matheson next or Hines, or may be both.*' The thought filled her with further trepidation, as she knew neither would be pleasant.

She guessed at least five of the six hours must have passed since she had activated the winder on the watch, and didn't want to think of what would happen if Terry had not received the signal.

Matheson was the one who arrived first, bringing with him a terrified Samantha. He roughly pushed her down on the sand and took Karen's knife from his belt.

"Now bitch, how would you like to watch me having a little fun with your friend," he said slicing through the straps of Samantha's top. He then proceeded to run the knife down the front of her chest cutting her bra top through stitch by stitch "Now bitch, for the very last time who is the Phoenician?"

Samantha screamed in panic.

"Tell him for God's sake, tell him."

Maria forced her head up from the sand she could hardly speak,

"Leave her alone you pig, I will tell you nothing if you hurt her" Matheson thrust Samantha to one side and approached Maria with the knife.

She froze. She knew he would not kill her as he wanted the information, but she was terrified of what he might do to extract it from her. She was unable to take her eyes from his face as the knife came nearer.

Samantha pleaded with him to stop; but he just laughed as he put the knife to Maria's throat.

The young woman was sobbing helplessly, realising that this animal was about to show Maria no mercy. He then tipped the knife expertly into Maria's exposed left breast, which instantly caused a gentle flow of blood to trickle down her breast and under her arm. Matheson moistened his lips; he was going to enjoy this interrogation.

"So you really thought you had killed my father,"

He laughed slightly hysterically; his eyes were glazed, the pupils like pinpricks.

"No fuckin bitch will ever get the better of him or me"

'My God he's completely insane' Maria's heart thudded in her chest.

Then his mood instantly changed, his neck and head jerked up as they heard the thumping roar of a large helicopter coming from the north side of the island. Almost instantly two smaller attack helicopters appeared from the opposite side.

There was chaos on the beach as the guards ran to get their guns dodging the incoming warning shots from the helicopters overhead.

The hostage women started running and screaming in panic, as the down draft from the helicopters blew the sand into a storm whipping at their flimsy costumes and blinding their eyes. Within minutes thirty or more armed soldiers in black combat uniforms came from behind the trees and surrounded the camp. Maria looked up at Matheson, defiant as ever,

"I think your game is over asshole"

He raised his arm, but before he could plunge the knife into her, a single shot was fired hitting him in the shoulder throwing him back onto the sand. Above the chaos the voice rang out that she had been praying for, Terry; had made it.

"Put it down Matheson, and stay on the ground. Or the next bullet will be at your head"

Matheson dropped the knife and lay on the sand as instructed. Samantha crawled over to Maria laughing and crying with relief.

Terry ordered two of his men to take charge of Matheson, and then he came over to Maria bent down and picked up the knife looking at the double edge blade,

"That looks quite nasty; you are a very lucky woman.

Then true to form he grinned.

"Nice outfit. Is that the fashion in this part of the world? Should I cut you free or do you want to get an all over suntan?"

She smiled ruefully at his ill-timed humour; the cut on her breast was becoming quite painful

"Pig"

"That's not a nice way for a lady to treat her knight in shining armour. Is it now?"

He cut the rope from her hands and feet and gently picked her up in both arms joking tenderly.

"I waited a long time to get you in my arms. I told you that one day you wouldn't be able to resist me"

Maria smiled weakly at him trying to steady the spinning in her head at being upright, Terry handed her a bottle of water,

"Here sip this slowly, and pour some on that cut" he added gently

His men had rounded up and arrested all the Russians and their 'guests,' and although there were many injuries, there were no fatalities. It was a good result all round, although Maria knew she had been only seconds away from certain death herself. She was worried about Karen though; she could not see her anywhere.

"Terry please can you find a girl called Karen, she tried to save my life. I am frightened of what they might have done with her"

Terry sat Maria down carefully under the shade of a tree; and left the beach for a brief moment. When he came back, he was shaking his head sorrowfully.

"Bad news I am afraid, they have almost killed one woman, I think it's her, dressed in blue?"

Maria struggled to her feet swaying slightly,

"Oh my God Terry, please not Karen, she tried so hard to help me"

It was Karen; and she had been badly beaten; still alive but only just. Maria begged tearfully to Terry

"You must get her to hospital right away"

Then she got angry.

"My God I hope they pay for what they have done to these women"

Terry left her for a short while to arranged for Karen to be airlifted to hospital, and when he returned he sat down beside her, looking totally confused,

"Can you honestly believe that half of these women don't want to leave the Island?"

Maria replied with a grin.

"I am not surprised, especially if it will now be man free"

Terry raised his eyebrows, looking even more confused, She smothered a laugh; as she knew what Terry was thinking, *'How can any woman want to live 'man free'* Then she tried to explain to him why they felt that way.

"Some of the Eurasian women came to Cyprus hoping for a better life, or at least better than where they had come from, only they got caught up in the sex world, a world they thought they had left behind. But this time we must make sure they get a fair deal when we get them back to the mainland"

A couple of hours later the helicopter was ready to take them back to Cyprus, Maria put out her hand to Samantha and together they climbed aboard. All of the other women were already seated clutching their few possessions on their laps; looking slightly dazed but excited.

The engine started and the rotor blades began to turn; and they were off. Maria gave a huge sigh of relief; she had never been so pleased to leave any place, as she was to leave this Island. As they settled down for the short journey, Samantha smiled shyly at Maria,

"Salwa, Maria who are you really?"

Maria turned and smiled back at her, raising her voice a little over noise of the helicopter.

"I am only a simple housewife; with a lovely adorable sexy husband that I would die for"

She looked pointedly at Terry. He just laughed.

Samantha reached out and squeezed Maria's hand gently saying,

"Simple housewife you are definitely not. Undercover cop or intelligence; you most likely are. But whatever you are I will always be grateful to you, even though I think you are totally and utterly insane taking all those risks for us,"

Maria laughed self-consciously, and again turned to Terry saying in a low whisper,

"Seriously Terry, she is right, I am getting past all this, I'm really thinking of calling it a day"

Terry raised his eyebrows in mock disapproval, and leaned over and whispered back in her ear,

"You know you can never retire from this business, they won't let you, once a spook always a spook" Then he smiled affectionately at her; "And you know very well that you are still the best we have"

Maria was now totally exhausted, she closed her eyes saying quietly,

"We will discuss it another time. For now, I am going home, and the sooner the better"

When they arrived back in Cyprus, Samantha said a tearful farewell to Maria, and left for the hospital to be with Karen with a promise that they would keep in touch. Terry and Maria boarded the bus with the other women to the accommodation waiting for them at the Airbase

After a few days rest; Maria went to see Terry at his office, and enquired

"What happened to Grainger? How much was he involved in this?"

"Well actually he is one of us" Terry stood and opened a cupboard and offered her a drink,

Maria took the drink absently trying to digest the fact of Grainger being on the same side.

"We couldn't tell you, it had to seem genuine. In fact he is not a gay doctor, and has never practiced medicine. He is army though, and has high-level connection at M16. He reckons you take a good photograph especially the ones in your bikini" he gave a slight cough and grinned, "bottoms"

"You B........." Maria looked at the drink he had given her; and resisted the urge to throw it over him. Terry reading her mind, interrupted her, while laughing at her expression.

"Now, mind your language, however, didn't you wonder about his continued intervention especially when you were in difficult situations, such as dealing you a good hand to avoid you loosing your dress having no knickers, or from Hines molesting you in the bedroom. Although you were not aware at the time he also stopped Hines from sleeping with you the night following the masked ball. They were no coincidences,"

Maria shook her head,

"I suppose not, I did change my opinion of him from time to time, but I didn't believe for one moment that he was working with us."

Terry went on,

"Don't forget that Matt Grainger was also under cover, he had managed to become Hines trusted friend, and therefore permanent guest in the apartment. You were also being watched on CCTV at all times by Hines, so he had to follow the perverted line," Maria interrupted him scornfully,

"Which I am sure he didn't mind one little bit". She sipped at her drink as she sat back listening intently at his explanation,

"It was Matt that arranged things so you could find the papers. He had to convince you he was gay and party to what was going on and to make you believe him and play your part"

"Well he certainly convinced me," she said sarcastically, the more she heard the more uncomfortable she began to feel.

"The bad news was," Terry continued, "every room without exception had hidden cameras. In fact we found eighteen to be exact, including in the shower, around the pool and underwater in the pool. Hines had set them up to watch and record everything twenty four seven, but Matt found the viewing monitor and erased anything that might have embarrassed you; or would have blown your cover with Hines. He was then able to protect you. And you can be sure no film was retained," He gave an over exaggerated sigh, and added, "Sadly"

Although smiling at his last remark, she was clearly not happy,

"I still cannot understand why was I never told about Grainger? Did you not trust me?" Maria was getting angry now.

"Anyway he is still a pervert. You knew he tried hypnosis, and got me to strip for photos wearing little more than a damn facemask. God knows what else he would have made me to do if I had been completely under his influence"

"You were fully under, even if you thought you were not," Terry laughed, as Maria continued to vent her anger at him. Eventually she calmed down feeling a little weary,

"I don't think it is at all funny. If he was protecting me, why did he leave Hines to go as far as he did, a few seconds more and I would have blown the whole operation"

Terry raised his eyebrows and shrugged,

"You were being tested by Hines all the time and up to a point; so was Grainger. Hines wanted to push you to the limit to make sure that you were up for the job. Your full frontal exposure in the shower convinced him, and us, so well done"

"Huh, not quite" she replied showing her first glimpse of humour,

Terry laughed,

She relaxed a little; she knew that their strategy was more or less correct considering the circumstances

"Ok, but I did not like being mauled by that creature. And if Grainger is not gay, I do not appreciate the way he so obviously enjoyed the strip show." She added indignantly.

Terry took the opportunity to tease her,

"His report indicates he thought the video of you facing up to Hines in the shower was almost beyond the call of duty, in fact he headed his report the 'Ultimate Exposure' and said you were extremely professional"

Before she could respond angrily, which he could see she was going to, he followed up with,

"Let me ask you this, if you had known that he was not gay and not a doctor would you have gone along with all his antics?"

"Definitely not" Maria replied sharply.

"However it was your natural response to Hines that gave us a chance for you to get onto the island. We had a rough idea where the island was, but needed all those involved to be together at one time. We needed hard evidence; which you gave us, for the court martial and imprisonment of Hines"

The next day after the usual official debriefing and celebrations, they flew back to London. Maria had been highly praised for a quick and positive operation and a satisfactory conclusion. But she knew that it could have easily been a far different story.

CHAPTER 19

Maria was extremely tired when she arrived back to England and a lot quieter than usual. Tom didn't ask too many questions, he knew she would tell him when she was ready, but he did get a feeling that it had been a hard assignment. He had told her that he was also called away the same day just after she left, but they had made a pact not to ask too many questions about their separate assignments. This time however, he was worried. He had tried to get her to talk; by telling her how bad he felt about loosing Max, but she never responded other than to sympathise, so all he could do was wait.

One morning a couple of weeks later, he was sitting in the garden reading the local newspaper; when Maria wandered out to join him. She sat down on the grass at his feet looking thoughtful.

"Tom" she said, "I have made a decision"

He put down the paper and waited. She looked up at him putting her

hand on his knee,

"I have decided that I don't want to work out in the 'Field' anymore. That last assignment required more than I was prepared to give, and I don't ever want to be involved with such, such," she struggled to find the right word, "depraved people again"

Tom thought something like this was on the cards. He had already put two and two together from a brief telephone conversation he had had with her colleague Terry. Maria locked her hands around her knees and leaned back staring up at the sky as she continued,

"I am prepared to help out with any training they require, but no more field work, I don't think there will be a problem with headquarters, but we will see what they have to say"

"You must do whatever feels right for you" Tom replied gently. "If ever you want to talk, you know I'm always ready to listen" Smiling she stood up, relieved to have made the decision. Leaning down she kissed him lightly on his forehead,

"I know darling. One day I will tell you the full story, but not yet."

A few weeks later Maria received the 'Ok' from MI6 London HQ, which was just as well, because she was now two months pregnant, due to be born sometime towards the end of May. Tom was thrilled at the prospect of becoming a father again; he rather hoped it would be a girl for Maria's sake, he knew she had always wanted a daughter of her own.

The next few months passed by very quickly; there was so much to do. She was very glad hat her mother was still with her to help with Tom's girls. But most of all; it was wonderful to share all the pleasure of preparing for the new baby.

At the beginning of March, Maria decided they should take the opportunity to visit Lebanon again, she felt that this might be her last chance before she had the baby, and of course all the family wanted to see her now she was pregnant.

"Maria, do you think you should be travelling in your condition, especially so near?" Tom protested, even her mother was worried.

"Don't fuss," she laughed, "I feel fine, and I have checked with the doctor."

He knew there was no point in arguing, but he did ask her mother to watch her carefully, and if she was worried about Maria in any way she was to let him know immediately.

During their visit they went to see Maria's aunt who was still living in the Muslims, Palestinian and Islamic fundamentalists controlled area of West Beirut. She greeted them with tears in her eyes; she had thought she would never see Maria again after she went to England.

But before they had time to enjoy their visit fierce fighting erupted once again between the warring factions. Shells started raining down all around them hitting nearby buildings. They huddled together in the corner of her aunt's small bedroom; this room being central was the safest part of the apartment. Maria gripped hold of her mother's arm shouting over the noise of the bombardment.

"I am so worried about Tom, he will get all this on TV, and he will be frantic wondering if we are alright"

She knew that he would hear the news from the BBC, and although foreign reports were often exaggerated, now; with the massive American support on behalf of the Israeli forces, any exaggeration would not be necessary.

Then later that afternoon came a major assault from an American destroyer anchored of the West Beirut coast, massive shells thudded all around them. They looked at each other worriedly. *'It's one thing to be killed by the enemy, but by friendly fire!'* It was a frightening thought. Maria wrapped her hands over her stomach in an unconscious move to protect the baby. Her mother watched her. *'I should never have agreed for her to come here'* she thought guiltily, but in her heart; she knew she would never have been able to stop her. They were hopelessly trapped in the small one bedroom apartment unable to get any message in or out. Luckily there was enough food in the apartment to go round; so they were not hungry, although sleep was impossible.

"Listen Maria, I am sure you can get out now" her aunt exclaimed turning the radio volume up. She had it tuned to the LF radio station; and the news reporter was saying that any British citizen who wanted to leave Lebanon could be airlifted by means of a helicopter to Cyprus.

Her mother looked relieved; but Maria as stubborn as ever told her,

"No way am I leaving without you"

On the morning of the third day, there was a slight lull in the bombardment, so she was able to go outside briefly to see the aftermath of the last two days. Maria covered her mouth with her hands as the stench of burnt flesh and rubber, wafted around her, she felt her stomach heave and ran to throw up in the corner of one of the scorched buildings. Taking a deep breath and wiping the sweat from her ashen face, she looked around and spotted one of her LF colleagues picking his way through the piles of brick and rubble, quickly she made her way towards him thankful that now she would be able to relay a message back to the LF to get them out.

. Later that afternoon, after three days trapped in the tiny apartment; the LF managed to transport them both through all the horror and destruction; back to the East; and relevant safety.

They tried to persuade Maria's aunt to come with them but she had refused, it was her home and there was no way she would leave it.

As soon as they could they returned to England. Tom met them at the airport, and without saying a word he put his arms around her and held her tight, no words were necessary, the most important thing was; they were all safe.

Maria spent the next few weeks resting, until as predicted at the end of May, she produced a beautiful daughter who they named Natalie. Tom was away in London on a business trip at the time, but when he heard the news he was over the moon, he was pleased her mother was with her, and that she could stay with them for a while longer to help until Maria was back on her feet.

Almost a year passed, not long after Natalie's first birthday that Maria confirmed to Tom that she was expecting her second child; Her mother arrived once more to help out and be with her daughter for the birth due at the end of November.

It was late one cold wintry evening when Maria felt the pains starting, so she rang the maternity hospital; who advised her to come in immediately. Once again Tom was away on a business meeting, so Maria phoned to tell him she was going to the hospital,

"Oh God not again" he replied "I'm coming home now"

"Tom its ok, you don't need to come," she knew he had a lot on his mind at that moment,

"Anyway, it's no place for a man, in my country it is the mother who goes with the daughter"

For a moment he hesitated, torn between the worry of work and his loyalty to Maria,

"Ok if that's what you want" he said unhappily, but let me phone for a Taxi. But once again she protested.

"No it's Ok, I have plenty of time, I can take your car it has a phone and I will phone you the minute I get to the hospital." He knew from the tone of her voice, that there was no point in arguing. About twenty anxious minutes later he got the call.

"Hi Tom, no need to worry we are here" Then she rang off. He stared at the receiver; she had given him no chance to ask if she was ok, he slowly replaced the phone on its stand and tried to concentrate on finishing his work so he could get back home as soon as possible.

The baby was born very early the next morning. They had another beautiful daughter.

When Tom arrived at the hospital the next day, he noticed that the door of his car was still wide open; Maria had obviously parked in a hurry in the grounds of the hospital. *'Oh god. How could she be so stubborn to have left it this late'* He thought as he ran up the steps into the hospital only to be stopped by one of the nursing staff,

"Sorry sir, you must remove this car before you come in, it's blocking the ambulance area"

He swore under his breath, and rushed back down the steps and dutifully re-parked the car, and then he took a deep breath and went to find Maria and the baby. Maria smiled up at him as he entered the room,

"Hi Tom, come and meet Francesca," He gazed down at the tiny bundle in Maria's arms,

"No man deserves four daughters," he said, and then added with a teasing grin to Maria,

"I even changed wives, but still I get girls, must have been something in my genes"

Maria retorted trying not to laugh,

"If you had kept it in your jeans, she wouldn't be here"

Tom looked surprised and burst out laughing

"Very good, I think I've turned you into a right smart ass"

Life settled into a harmonious domestic routine, with Maria and her mother sharing the chores between them.

She was a little concerned about the amount of time Tom was spending at work, and although she knew there were problems, she never interfered in his business life, and anyway she had her hands full looking after two babies and two teenagers, even with help it was a full time job.

It was about this time that a heavy recession hit in the UK, and Companies were going out of business very quickly. Some of the Companies that the Forsters dealt with; owed them serious amounts of money, which was even putting them into dangerous territory, giving them no option; other than to make heavy Company cutbacks.

After some serious thinking about the trouble the Company now found itself in, Tom knew that he had to make a life changing decision. He got to thinking that now the Cold War between the two major Superpowers had ceased, and the civil war in Lebanon had also finished, that perhaps they should return as a family to live there and make a new start. It wasn't an easy decision to make, especially leaving his family. So before he said anything to Maria, he talked it over with his father; who although reluctant; could see his son's point of view, he too was feeling that he had had enough.

Finally they agreed that they would down size the company; leaving just the one small business that they had had the foresight to place in Maria's name. But apart from the worry of the business, although he hadn't said anything to anyone, Tom had been feeling a bit unwell lately; and had to admit to himself that he didn't need such high stress levels.

One morning shortly after the discussion with his father, they were having coffee with Maria's mother, when Tom dropped the bombshell.

"How would you like to return to Lebanon for good" He announced quietly looking at Maria. He waited for the reaction from her, but she never said a word, she just reached out and took his hand. His mother-in-law looked bewildered, she couldn't believe what she had heard; she spoke to Maria in Arabic for clarification.

"When did you come up with this idea, Tom?" Maria asked quietly.

"Well actually I've only just discussed it with dad. But what is to keep us here now?"

"Nothing I suppose, except your family" She answered hesitantly,

"And I am not sure if you would be happy living there"

He looked deep into her eyes

"I have thought about it, and I'm sure we could make a go of it, the only problem is; I will still have to travel back and forth while I can still afford it. And when I can't," he grinned, "well; we will cross that bridge when we come to it. Hopefully what's left of the business will have picked up by then."

He squeezed her hand gently,

"We still have our apartment there in Almaya, which has everything we need"

Again Maria's mother asked her daughter for clarification still not completely understanding.

Maria sat down beside her and tried to explain all that Tom had said.

When at last his mother-in-law understood his full intentions, she never said a word; she just stood up and kissed Tom on both cheeks with tears in her eyes.

Later as they sat discussing their plans Tom put his ideas to Maria,

"I think it might be a good idea if you go over first with the girls, while I stay here until we have sold the house"

Maria looked a bit doubtful, but he continued,

"I know, I want to come too, but I have a lot to sort out here with mum and dad, and of course my girls, it will be hard on them." He sighed, "But thank God they are getting old enough now to look after themselves a bit more."

Maria agreed although she was a bit concerned it was all happening so fast.

"Tom you are sure about this? Have you really thought it all through?"

He smiled at her reassuringly,

"Of course, don't worry"

By the beginning of spring Maria had completed all the packing ready to move back to Lebanon, so he arranged their flight and took them to the airport. Maria was the type of person never to look back, but now she had mixed feelings. She was very sad to leave Tom's parents in England and all the friends she had made, but like her mother she was very happy to be going home.

One day in the office a few weeks later completely out of the blue, the Libyan Government contacted Tom again. They wanted him to continue with the survey of their Naval Fleet. *'Oh Christ, that's all I need at the moment'* He thought wearily. He thought about his previous experience with the Libyans, and reached for his phone to notify M16.

When HQ heard this they were extremely interested; and suggested to Tom that he should go ahead, but they would put two of their own people in with him posing as engineers. M16 were still very active in that area, and they knew that this was a great opportunity to get photographs of the condition of the vessels, and any evidence of naval activity at the various ports in that area.

It was not considered to be a dangerous operation since the Libyan Government had officially invited them, but at the same time they had to be very careful. The Libyans were no fools, they were aware that the West; and in particular the United States needed to monitor their movements.

The Hotel they were booked into was extremely run down, although it had been recommended as one of the best. On the first day they were out working; they arrived back to find that the Hotel had had a massive flood on the ground floor, Tom was lucky as he had left his suitcase propped up on a chair, but both his M16 colleagues were not so fortunate, and found their suitcases complete with all their contents; partly submerged under water.

"Bloody country" One of the men cursed, "They want to put a bit of maintenance in theirhotels, not their bloody boats"

"Perhaps you could sue for compensation" Tom joked,

The other man picked up his bedraggled clothes and tried to squeeze out the dirty water,

"Fat bloody chance of that"

But apart from that relatively minor incident they managed to get their photographs without attracting any attention; under pretence of doing Tom's survey, and got out as quickly as they could.

Once back home in the UK things were quiet as Tom continued to sort out the business, reluctantly he had to let Sally go, and then to top it all; his father was taken seriously ill, and urgently required a triple heart bypass. As soon as Maria heard she flew back to the UK, leaving the two babies with her mother. She stayed for ten days doing what ever she could to help before returning home.

Thankfully Tom's father made a good recovery, but it also made sorting out their lives a priority. Now that the down sizing of the business was complete, they took stock.

Tom still needed the small business he was left with to be able to support his family. The down side was that due to the expense he would be unable to continue his travelling to Lebanon as often as before. But all things considered there was no choice but to manage as best as they could. Tom ever the optimist counted his blessings, *'At least I still have a lovely caring wife and four healthy daughters. And thank God; father's on the mend'*

CHAPTER 20

Unfortunately things didn't work out for them quite as planned, the recession affected house sales to the point of almost bringing the market to a standstill, and unforeseen circumstances with the business meant that Tom was spending far more time in England than he had expected. He tried to get over to Lebanon at least once a month, not an ideal situation but there was not a thing they could do about it.

It was during one of these short visits to Lebanon, that he discovered a lump under Maria's arm very close to her left breast. A wave of fear washed over him.

"What the bloody hell is this?"

"What is what?"

Maria was clearly unaware of anything wrong, she felt under her arm and found the lump,

"I'll get it checked. Its most likely nothing, don't worry"

"Make sure you do. I know what you're like, you say you will; and then you'll ignore it."

She looked a bit surprised at his sharp tone,

"Not on something like this, do you think I am mad?"

Although he would rather have stayed in Lebanon until she had the lump checked, he had to return to the UK the next day, leaving Maria to check it out with her doctor. The day after he got back he phoned her,

"Well what did the doctor say?"

And just as he suspected, she hadn't made the appointment.

"I have been so busy what with Christmas and everything, I haven't had time to go, anyway, don't worry Tom, it's almost gone"

But he was adamant,

"Maria, lumps don't just go. Get it checked,"

She laughed.

"Ok, ok, I will phone the doctor tomorrow,"

But when he phoned again a couple of days later she had still not done it. This carried on for another week, until he got really angry with her.

"Maria, you said you're not mad, but you are being very, very stupid. Make that bloodyappointment now, I'm really worried."

It shocked her to hear Tom's reaction, and the following morning she made her appointment with the local doctor, who after checking her over stated that he thought it was most likely to be a 'calcified gland' but he would refer her to a specialist to be sure. Luckily the specialist was on duty in the same hospital so she could see him later that afternoon, and he assumed the same diagnoses; but still recommended that she should have it removed.

The operation was scheduled for the next day; it was quite a minor operation so they were not too worried. But the next morning the surgeon came to see Maria whilst she was alone waiting to go to theatre, he was now having second thoughts,

"I am sorry Mrs Forster, but this may be more serious than we thought"

She saw his worried expression,

"You mean cancer? Well if it is, then please don't tell the rest of my family yet." She looked him straight in the eyes, "And what ever you find, you have my permission to do what ever is needed"

The surgeon was a bit taken back by at her strong positive reaction, but then he realised; she had already considered cancer as being a real possibility and he knew that she meant what she said. He sat on the edge of the bed and took hold of her hand,

"Are you quite sure? Because it doesn't look good at all"

"Quite sure" she answered firmly.

As soon as the doctor left the room, she phoned Tom.

"Tom I am having an operation to remove the lump today, but you must not worry, Ok? Oh and Tom, I love you"

Tom was relieved,

"Ok, but phone me as soon as you can after it's done. Take care, Love you too."

The operation proved the surgeon correct; it was cancer, and it was very serious.

The Khoury family were utterly devastated, when they eventually heard the news from the surgeon. No one knew what to do. Maria's brother George took charge,

"The first thing we must do is get Tom over here as soon as possible. You sit with Maria and I will phone him" He almost ran down the corridor to find a telephone.

"Tom, how quickly can you come ---?"

Tom interrupted him anxiously,

"What's happened, is it Maria?"

"Yes Tom, she has cancer, breast cancer. It's very serious"

"I am on my way"

Tom went cold; he put the phone down, his heart thumping; he could hardly get his breath.

At that moment his daughter Charlie came into the office and found her father white faced and very distressed.

"Dad, what is it?"

He managed to tell her briefly what George had said, and she responded immediately,

"You must go at once dad. We can cope here for a while"

Tom nodded; his head was spinning in all directions. He sat down heavily at his desk and picked up the phone to call the airport reservation desk. He was very fortunate he got a flight the next day, which was not easy this near Christmas.

He tried to think clearly, his mind in a whirl, constantly thinking the worst. He gave Charlie an agonising look,

"After all we have been through, am I going to lose her now?"

"She will be alright dad, don't worry." She was stricken to see her father upset; she had never seen him like this and didn't know what to say to comfort him.

The next day after an agonising five-hour journey he finally arrived at Beirut airport. On their way to the hospital George told him as much as he could about what was happening with Maria.

"Things are not good, although the doctor thinks he got everything. Maria doesn't know yet how bad it is, so don't mention it to her" Tom did not believe that for one minute, he knew his wife too well.

When he finally arrived at the hospital most of the family were there. Celine had also managed to get a last minute flight from Canada, and had arrived just before him. He was delighted to see her, although he wished it were under different circumstances.

Tom approached Maria's bed, trying not to show his feelings,

"Hi sweetie, what have you been up to now?"

She smiled faintly, beckoned him to kiss her

"I am fine, nothing to worry about, why did they call you?"

He tried to smile, but it came over more as a grimace,

"Are you totally bloody nuts? If you had told me how serious this was, I would have been here with you from the start"

Still fencing with the idea that she may not know all the facts, he questioned carefully,

"What do you think you had done?"

She gave a weak smile

"It's Ok, I know I have cancer, and had a huge lump removed from my left breast, the family think I don't know. I told the surgeon to take it off if necessary, but thank God it wasn't so bad"

Trying to lighten the situation, but mainly because he was struggling for the right words he smiled saying in a whisper,

"Why did you tell him that? It is mine as well you know"

She winced in pain trying not to laugh,

"Can we see the surgeon yet?"

She shook her head,

"Not until tomorrow"

She looked around at her family still gathered around the end of the bed, a few understood English but not many, so she spoke in Arabic

"I will be alright now, Tom will stay with me. Go home now and get some rest, the girls will be worried with you all here"

When they were alone he sat down beside her and held her hand smiling cheerfully. He was feeling absolutely devastated inside, but managed to control his emotions in front of her although he was close to breaking point. Maria wasn't fooled, she knew him too well.

The next day the surgeon came to explain the situation. They had been very fortunate that the lump had been discovered in time, but only just. If it had been left much longer Maria's chance of survival would have been very slight, the tumour had been quite an aggressive one, and she was not totally out of the woods yet, she was going to need a lot more treatment. Only time would tell. Tom knew he was going to have to be positive and strong for Maria's sake and for the girls. Although; the doctor was certain that she stood every chance of recovery because of her positive attitude.

To everyone's delight, after four days she was well enough to go home, but as they left the hospital Maria laid her hand on Tom's arm,

"Tom before we go home I want to go to St Charbels to pray"

St Charbels was a beautiful church high in the mountains where they all worshipped most Fridays; it was a very special place for all Christians and very important to Maria and her family.

And for the first time in years, Tom also prayed.

After their prayers they left the church; Maria linked her arm through his, she could see how he was fighting to come to terms with all that had happened.

"Tom, I know this is hard for you, but nothing is going to happen to me, please believe me. It's not my time yet"

Tom looked down at her in anguish

"What would we do without you? I need you, the girls need you"

She squeezed his arm, smiling gently.

"Please don't think about those things. I love you and the girls too much to leave you now." He couldn't speak; his throat was so constricted.

"Have faith please Tom"

Swallowing hard, he cleared his throat, and asked curiously,

"How come you are so calm about the cancer? I don't think I would be if it had happened to me."

Maria stopped walking, and turned to face him. Although she was very tired and the pain was beginning to nag, a warm smile crept across her face; it was as if she had the answer to the turmoil going on inside him.

"The difference between you and me darling is that I always have peace in my soul, it's one of the things I learnt in the convent. And I have never questioned life or death. You see we are on this earth for such a short time; so we should take whatever life gives us. One day you will understand that it's my faith that carries me through difficult times." She reached up and touched his face gently,

"Also my darling, death itself holds no fear for me, and never has."

Tom was amazed, he has always known that she had a very strong religious faith, and how mentally strong she was, but he couldn't help but be moved by this latest revelation. He bent down and kissed her saying wistfully,

"I hope the girls have your faith, I only wish I had"

When they arrived home, everyone fussed around her, the family couldn't do enough they were so happy to have her back with them once more. Natalie and Francesca although they had missed their mother, they were far too young to understand what had happened, but they seemed to pick up on the atmosphere and wouldn't leave her side.

Christmas that year was going to be very quiet, but they were very happy just to be together.

Soon after Christmas Tom asked the surgeon to prepare a report so that Maria could travel with him back to the UK, they wanted to get another opinion concerning her course of treatment. He took Natalie with him to pick up the notes, and on the way home the little girl asked him,

"Is mummy going to get better daddy?"

Tom looked down at his daughter's worried face.

"I hope so sweetheart, I really hope so" He hesitated before continuing, "Do you know what was wrong with her?"

"Yes" She replied in a small voice, "She had an operation, and she might die"

Tom was rather concerned at how she had heard it; after all she was only two and a half. He asked gently.

"Where did you hear that from?"

"I heard people say" Natalie answered,

He crouched down and looked into her worried little face as he replied firmly,

"Well, mummy says she is not going to die, and we believe her don't we?"

She smiled confidently at him,

"Yes, and God will look after her; Teta (*grandmother*) said so"

Tom was pleased that she had talked to him about it, and answered as cheerfully as he could.

"Then there is your answer, so no more worrying sweetheart, Ok?"

Soon it was time to prepare for the flight home; they said their goodbyes to the family reassuring everyone they would keep in constant touch letting them know Maria's progress. They all tried to keep a cheerful face, but it was very difficult for everyone; to be parting at a time like this.

Not long after they arrived back in England Tom had to fly to Bangkok for three days, giving Maria the chance to catch up with her friends. One she was particularly close too, was a doctor married to a Lebanese woman; who had become a good friend, and he was able to talk with her about her problems. He recommended that she see another specialist for a second opinion, who; although agreeing with the treatment advised by the surgeon in Lebanon, also told her that in England her treatment would have been a little different. He would have recommended further surgery.

When Tom returned from Bangkok they discussed the results, Maria as usual was very upbeat and confidant reassuring him that all was ok. But later that evening Maria's doctor friend quietly took him to one side and told him that he was not very optimistic for a full recovery. This shocked Tom to the core, and once again he found himself praying for help to get them through this terrifying time.

Maria could see the next morning; that he was very upset; his face was pale and haggard,

"What is it Tom? Please tell me, we agreed would always be honest with each other"

He hesitated; it didn't seem fair to put his fears onto her,

"Please Tom"

He rubbed his hands across his tired eyes; and told her what had been said.

"And last night I prayed so long and hard for you I offered my own health in place of yours. Was that wrong?"

She shook her head but said nothing; allowing him to continue

"I cannot imagine life without you, it would be unbearable".

Tom was so choked with emotion; he could find no more words. She kissed him tenderly, trying to comfort him in some way, wishing she could help him feel her faith.

"God will not answer prayers like that darling; he would never inflict illness on any man by request. Sickness on earth is man made, and can only be cured by man"

Not long after that they returned to Lebanon so she could start the treatment they knew was going to be very severe. The first treatment of chemotherapy was given to her in a West Beirut private clinic. And Maria being Maria insisted that she do the driving,

"I don't think I could cope with chemotherapy and your driving all in one day." She laughed.

"Are you saying you don't trust my driving?"

"In England yes, but here no"

She still insisted on driving after the session, but when they got to near halfway home she had to stop urgently in the middle of heavy traffic and was violently sick. Tom felt useless, but he knew she was right about his driving in Lebanon.

"Oh darling; I am so sorry, I wish I could drive here. Next time we will get a driver"

He had no idea it was going to be as bad as this.

Maria remained in this condition for many days and she could see that Tom was suffering almost as much as she was. In a way she was rather glad when word came from England that there were business problems and he was urgently needed.

"You must go Tom, it is important, and there is nothing you can do here"

Reluctantly he agreed,

"I feel as though I am deserting you again. I never seem to be here when you really need me. But I promise I will be back just as soon as I can".

She was pleased that he had agreed, because this way she would have had most of her six sessions of treatment before he actually returned.

Although she had been warned after sixteen days she might loose her hair, Maria was still deeply shocked when it fell out in the shower, almost all in one go.

'Oh my God, I am so glad Tom is not here, he loves my hair' she thought choking back the tears.

After the chemotherapy Maria had to suffer thirty daily sessions of radiotherapy. And at seven o'clock every morning for five weeks, six days a week, she insisted on driving herself to the hospital. And although he phoned her every night, not one word of complaint did he hear from her.

When Tom eventually got back to Lebanon Maria's hair was just starting to grow again, and it took a lot of persuasion to convince her that it didn't matter. The only thing that mattered to him was that she was there, but there was no way she was going to allow Tom to see her bald.

But the events of the last few months took their toll on Tom. The stress of the business and Maria's illness eventually compounded and affected his health; he soon developed full blown Multiple Sclerosis and now required surgery himself. Although Maria was still a bit weak, her health had improved quite considerably since the treatment had finished, so she left the girls with her mother and flew over to England to be with him.

Tom had been transferred to a hospital in London, and she was able to stay in the hospital relative's apartment so she could be with him at all times. They tried to keep their spirits up making silly jokes the way they always had in the past. And they laughed when the head nurse came into his room every morning and saying in a strong Welsh accent,

"How is my lovely bunny today then?"

Maria had never heard such an expression before, and the thought of Tom being a 'lovely bunny' was hilarious.

Unfortunately the operation was not considered to have been very successful. And when the time came for Tom to leave the hospital, their house had been sold; so he went to stay with his parents and Maria returned to the girls in Lebanon.

After a couple of weeks rest, he returned to work; and started planning his first visit back to Lebanon since the operation. It was not going to be quite so easy to travel because now he had to use crutches. It was easy for him to adapt to his disability, mentally or physically. But he had a shining example in Maria on how to handle trauma, and he was determined to try to adopt the same positive attitude and faith.

He gazed out of the window at the clear blue summer sky; and a slight smile crossed his face as a thought struck him. *'Perhaps Maria was wrong, and God did answer my prayer. After all, she is making very good progress; I know she is not cured, but she is still alive'*

He picked up the phone to call the airport reservation desk, feeling a strong sense of peace and consolation, that in some way his prayers had been

answered.

CHAPTER 21

Over the coming months they reluctantly became used to their unorthodox way of life, Maria took up her work as an instructor working for the L.F Intelligence department in Lebanon, and Tom stayed in England to manage what was left of the business. Until the time came when he could join his family in Beirut, he had to content himself with visiting them once every couple of months. It was extremely hard and lonely for them both, and for the children, but for the moment there was no other option.

Early one morning Tom lay in bed thinking about his life and the way things had evolved over the past few months, and he felt the urge to give MI6 HQ a call. Feeling the old rush of excitement he immediately got up; washed and dressed and then dialled the number. Upon giving his code to the switchboard operator he was put directly through to Lane.

"Hi Lane, it's me, 101,"

"Tom, how are you," She sounded delighted to hear his voice, "I tried to get over to see you in hospital, but it was impossible. How are you doing? Can you get up to London? It would be great to see you"

He laughed at her enthusiasm

"Hold on a minute, that's why I am phoning. How are you fixed tomorrow? I could get to you around eleven."

"Brilliant" Came the excited answer, "I will inform the team. Take care and big kiss"

"You too love, bye now" He replaced the phone, smiling to himself at Lane's reaction.

When he arrived at Liverpool Street Station, the same driver that had taken him to Kings Cross a few years back greeted him again with a smile and a salute.

"How are you sir? Have you injured your leg?" he enquired as he noticed the walking stick.

"Yes in a way" Tom smiled back at the man. "M.S. or so they say"

"Oh, I am sorry to hear that, Major" He replied with sincerity as he opened the car door for him. Tom was little surprised at the title that the driver had just given him, but never questioned it thinking the man had just made a mistake.

When he arrived at the office, Lane couldn't hide the fact that she was overjoyed to see him again.

"Come here I want a kiss" She said holding out her arms to him.

He kissed her on both cheeks, almost losing his balance with her enthusiastic welcome.

"Mmm, that's a nice welcome, I must come more often" he laughed. "Now I want to hear all your news young lady"

Lane stepped away to look at him, tossing her head in her customary fashion; to shake her blond hair back off her face.

"Well, first I am no longer a young lady, although I thank you for that, and secondly I couldn't wait any longer for you; so," she stood back looking pleased with herself. "I am getting married"

"Lane that's great news. Not an operative, I hope," He said teasing her.

She laughed,

"I can't tell you that. But let's put it this way, not from MI6,"

"You don't mean MI5 or C.I.A."He asked in mock horror.

"Bingo" she grinned.

He shook his head sorrowfully,

"Oh dear, which is it? Is it someone I know?"

Lane laughed a little self-consciously,

"Well yes, actually it's C.I.A. your old friend, Clive"

That was the last name Tom had expected to hear. A little shocked; he replied carefully,

"Well that's a surprise, when did you two get together?" he smiled and gave her a hug, "I really hope it works out for you both."

"Yes I am sure it will, but we are still waiting for official clearance. Let's go and eat, and talk about you not me." She said changing the subject. Tom got the impression she didn't want to talk about it anymore.

Lane slipped her arm through his and they walked the few hundred yards to the little Italian restaurant he remembered so well. After they ordered their meal and wine Lane leaned back in her seat smiling,

"God it's good to see you Tom"

"You too love" he replied gently. "How long is it?"

She sipped her wine thoughtfully,

"I haven't heard from you since the island affair with Matheson Jnr. She shuddered, "I can't comprehend what Maria had to go through, she was so brave. I don't know who was worse, the father or the son, they were both completely obsessed with her" She lowered the glass slowly to the table and grinned at him,

"And I fancied you. Now isn't that strange?"

Tom laughed at the comparison,

"Very strange. But I don't believe you fancied me for one minute, because you made the rules, and all I did was obey them if you recall"

She laughed ruefully

"I threw that rule book away after I met you, but it was too late. Although I did hear some while back that you did love me" she paused looking woefully at him, … "Like a bloody sister"

Then she burst out laughing, seeing Tom's surprised expression,

"My god, does everything get reported back?" He asked.

"Everything, Major" She replied still laughing.

"And while we are on the subject of work" Tom continued, "Where did this 'Major' business come from, that's the second time today"

Lane smiled mischievously,

"Wait and you will find out, after lunch" She refused to be drawn any more on that subject, and was thankfully rescued by the arrival of the meal.

It was now almost two o'clock as they walked arm in arm back to the office. Lane glanced up at Tom

"How is Maria now, I mean after the cancer?"

"She is remarkable, not a word of despair. It really is incredible how she handled it" she noticed the pride in his voice as he spoke of his wife.

Lane gave a little sigh,

"I just hope Clive loves me half as much as you love Maria, I know he has been a devil in the past; but hopefully he will have sown all his wild oats and can settle down now"

Tom stopped walking and looked down at her saying very seriously,

"If not he will have me to deal with"

"Still my knight in shining armour, Tom, that's why I love you so much, as a sister ofcourse"

Tom laughed, although he had a feeling that there was more to that remark than she made out.

When they reached HQ they went straight into the boardroom, where other members of Lane's team joined them. Some Tom knew, most he didn't, but they seemed delighted to see him, and shook his hand vigorously, and then Lane announced,

"Ladies and gentlemen. Quiet please. Now Tom, I have to tell you in front of the team, you have been promoted to the rank of Major as from the first of this month. Congratulations."

Tom was silent for a moment as he reflected upon his personal situation; and then he spoke quietly.

"Thank you for this great honour fellow spooks, but I'm sorry, I have to tell you that I must refuse. What you may not know is I have M.S. and sooner rather than later I will be at least eighty percent disabled" He paused and looked at his colleagues with troubled eyes. "What use will I be to you and your people?"

One of the team interrupted him

"We already know about the MS Major, and everyone was in agreement, it's your brain and experience that is needed, not your physical attributes"

"Hear, hear," the chorus echoed around the room.

Tom was moved by their sincerity, and struggled to keep the emotion out of his voice as he accepted their offer,

"Then if you're really sure, thank you, I will do my best"

Lane then took over the meeting; saying with a knowing smile,

"Anyway Tom, it has been noted, you are married to one of the best foreign operatives we ever had the privilege to work with. I am sure you won't take offence at that train of thinkingby the men in suits"

Tom smiled proudly,

"Not at all, because it's a fact. But don't forget she has retired more or less"

"Well that's another discussion we need to have sometime…Do you have any questions Tom?"

"Only one, Can you enlighten me? I never did hear what happened in Libya"

Colin Prescott, Lanes second in command answered for her,

"Thanks to you major nothing, absolutely nothing. All the vessels rotted on the quayside.The survey was such that no company could act on it and make a profit, not even the Germans, and that was exactly what we wanted. We appreciated the fact you lost the business because of this, but it was in the national interest believe me"

Tom acknowledged this with a nod in his direction it was still a bit of a sore point with him even though he had known it could happen.

There was an awkward silence and Lane intervened quickly to change the subject,

"Oh and Tom, you must not forget, your wife can still pull rank on you, because even though she is semi retired, her rank stays with her"

Tom laughed,

"That's nothing new; she often does. And she's never needed a title to do it"

That caused a laugh all round. Then as the meeting started to break up Lane collected up her paperwork from the desk,

"Tell me Tom, did Maria ever tell you the identity of 'The Phoenician?'"

Tom shook his head,

"No never. Is he still active?"

Lane realized Tom knew no more than she did,

"Oh yes very much so, we still receive top classified information. He is very active and very, very clever. The flow has never stopped, even though Maria has semi-retired,"

Tom shrugged,

"Why worry then, as long as you are getting the information"

She nodded her head in full agreement

"Exactly, but we would like to thank him in person, a lot of our people's lives have beensaved due to information received from him"

Lane waited for the rest of the team to leave the boardroom, and then she continued with her personal news,

"Clive wants you to be best man if you feel you can. And I would like Maria to be my Matron of honour, and your beautiful little girls as my wee bridesmaids. Please say yes"

Tom beamed with delight,

"Of course, and I know Maria will agree. Where is the wedding being held, and when?"

"Twenty Eighth of next month, in Limassol" Lane smiled.

"That's quick, but it should be Ok" He replied, "And I am sure you will be very happy"

"Are you?" Lane looked up at him with an anxious expression.

"You have doubts?" He asked,

She avoided answering his question, but went on quickly to ask,

"Tom, please stay over tonight, I need to talk to someone"

He was a bit surprised at her request and not sure quite how she meant it, so he joked,

"Will your door be locked?"

"I will let you into a little secret" Lane gave a wry smile,

"It was never locked, not even on the last night. In fact I left my door open. Does that shock you Tom?"

He was a bit confused at the way this conversation was heading, and tried to be diplomatic,

"If I say 'No', you'll think I'm big headed," he grinned. "If I say 'Yes' I would be a liar"

She laughed, seeing the funny side of his careful reasoning. Picking up her car keys she took hold of Tom's arm in order to help him down the stairs to the garage at the back of the building.

"By the way, I already called Maria, and asked her if it was Ok if you stayed over"

This made Tom laugh out loud.

"You don't have to tell me the reply, she said 'No problem' I know my wife"

Lane shook her head,

"You two are amazing, is there never any jealousy between you?" She asked.

"No, and there never has been" Tom replied firmly.

The weather was glorious; it was coming to the end of a beautiful English autumn. Lane was still able to leave the roof down on her little MG sports car as she drove to her Chelsea apartment.

She made a striking picture with her blond hair blowing in the wind and her sunglasses perched on top of her head to keep the hair out of her face. Tom noticed that she was attracting more than just a few admiring glances from passers by.

It was only a short distance, but it took almost an hour through the heavy evening rush hour traffic, but he was feeling completely relaxed and happy in Lane's company.

As they drew up at the apartment she switched off the engine,

"Let's get cleaned up and we can have a wee meal just around the corner from my place. My treat. Or I can cook for us if you prefer"

She added as it suddenly occurred to her that he might be tired after his busy day.

"Let's eat out," He answered lazily, "I can manage a few steps around the corner, and it will save you cooking"

The apartment was just as Tom imagined it would be, very clean and everything in its place. The white carpet throughout was immaculate, as if it had just been laid. The room reminded Tom of a show house, beautiful, but not very homely. Lane poured herself a neat scotch, and waved the bottle in his direction,

"I'll do it, you go get your shower," he said reaching out for the bottle, adding as an afterthought, "Are you sure Clive doesn't mind me staying over"

"We are not married yet" She grinned

Tom smiled to himself, thinking 'Clive's not going to have such an easy time as he thinks, not with this independent Scot.'

Lane disappeared into her bedroom. He called out to her from the lounge as he poured himself a small glass of vodka.

"Lane, do you have any ice in the freezer"

"Hold on," she said "I'll get it"

Tom couldn't believe his eyes as she came from the bedroom barefooted wearing just the skimpiest lime green silk slip.

"Wow" was all he could say.

She casually walked through to the kitchen and returned with a bowl of ice,

"Will this do?" she asked with a twinkle in her eyes. She then disappeared back into her bedroom choking back her laughter at the expression on Tom's face.

Tom swallowed hard and took a large mouthful of his drink *'I hope Clive appreciates what he is getting'* he thought grinning.

After ten to fifteen minutes she re-appeared wrapped in a large pink bath towel clutching her empty whisky glass, and said with a cheeky grin,

"I have another bathroom but I think you will find my shower easier. And I will just outside in case you need a hand"

"I am not even going to answer that" He retorted.

Lane appeared to have no inhibitions in front of him and he tried to act the same. She sat at her dressing table and crossed her long bare legs watching him. He tried to joke in order to cover his uncharacteristic embarrassment as he stripped down to his under shorts,

"You really take your sisterly duties serious don't you?"

"I promised Maria I would look after you whilst you were in my care" she grinned, totally aware of the effect she was having on him

He retreated into the little shower room, feeling slightly unnerved by Lanes behaviour, he was really not quite sure if she was joking or not. Lane grinned to herself as he closed the door, *'Now the boots on the other foot, lets see how he likes it'*

When he came out of the shower; to his relief there was no sign of Lane so he dressed and walked back into the lounge. He had a feeling that there was a lot that she needed to talk about, especially over her forthcoming wedding plans to his dubious CIA friend.

"Lane, you said you wanted to talk"

"Let's eat and discuss everything later," She suggested, she wanted to enjoy her meal before getting into any discussions about her husband to be.

"Suits me" He replied adding

"You look lovely in that dress, red really suits you"

"Really Tom, you don't think it's too much? " She inquired twirling around to show him.

He looked at the revealing red silk dress with its low daringly low plunging back,

"Nothing is too much for me, but there, I'm a man. But it's just as well you didn't put it on back to front" He teased"

"Ah, but you're a gentleman" Lane retorted with an exaggerated sigh.

"Hey take it easy" He laughed, "You will ruin my reputation."

She joined in with his laughter as she picked up her short white fur jacket and door keys and handed him his walking stick. They left the apartment and strolled the short distance around the corner to the restaurant, where they spent the next couple of hours enjoying their meal and each other's company. Business was barely discussed neither was friends, family or weddings.

They left the restaurant around mid-night and walked slowly back at her apartment. Lane could see that Tom was becoming very tired and she was rather concerned,

"I will sleep in the lounge, you take my bed. It will be more comfortable for you."

"I will not hear of it." He protested, "You sleep in your bed; I will sleep on top of the duvet if it's ok with you. It wouldn't be the first time I have had to do that, ask Maria." He smiled to himself thinking back to Paris.

"No problem, it's ok by me," Lane agreed although a little surprised,

He left her alone and went back into the lounge so she could get changed. About five minutes later she called out to him, teasingly.

"You can come back now. I don't usually wear anything in bed, but for you I may have made an exception"

By the time she had completed her sentence, Tom was leaning against the doorframe watching her,

"Don't mind me, I have a broad mind"

"How broad?" She teased, pretending she was about to reveal whether she had or not.

He didn't move; his eyes dancing as he called her bluff, he had at last caught on to what she was up too. Lane laughed and shook her head.

"Sorry but I couldn't resist teasing you, I would never jeopardise our friendship, and besides; I really would have to be the biggest bitch of all time to take advantage of this situation. But you really thought I was going too earlier didn't you?" She patted the bed for him to sit down,

"Tom, I really don't know if I am doing right by marrying Clive. He has been around so much and I am not sure if I am marrying him for the right reasons"

"Who said he has been around that much?"

"He does," She grimaced.

Tom laughed

"Don't believe all Clive tells you, he is typical CIA, they love to dream, too many Hollywood movies"

Lane nodded her head slowly,

"He likes you a lot Tom. He said he would trust you with his life, and as far as Maria is concerned, I think he would rather marry her than me"

"I am sure that's not true. He admires her tremendously I know, but doesn't love her in that way. Besides he must love you very much, otherwise there is no way he would have asked you to marry him." Tom said trying to reassure her. "Anyway what are the right reasons? You love him don't you?"

Lane looked thoughtful for a moment, and then she slowly smiled,

"Yes, I really think I do. Thank you Tom"

"That's Ok." He wasn't quite sure what she was thanking him for, but he was pleased that's she looked happier.

"Do you plan to live in Cyprus?" he asked

"That's the plan providing we both get clearance," she answered giving a big yawn.

He put his arm around her shoulder, and she cuddled up to him, and within minutes she fell into a deep sleep. He rose carefully from the bed and adjusted the duvet around her, *'You're not as tough as you try to make out young lady'* he thought looking down at her. Then he took the other pillow and laid it at the bottom of the bed; switched off the bedroom light, and soon he too was sound asleep.

In the morning the postman rattled the letterbox noisily and woke Lane. She slipped silently out of bed to retrieve two letters, but both were bills, and for a moment she looked disappointed. Glancing at Tom she saw he was still asleep, so she threw the letters onto the dressing table and went into the shower room.

When she emerged from her quick shower, Lane smiled to herself, noticing Tom had turned his head away from the shower door. She bent over him and whispered in his ear,

"Should I leave it running, or do you want to have breakfast first"

Tom slowly opened his eyes but still kept his head turned.

"Let's have breakfast first, unless you have anything else to do today"

"No, that's fine with me," She agreed, as she quickly dressed and made her way to the kitchen.

At last he could turn his head *'Phew, I don't think I could have stayed like that much longer'* he thought rubbing the back of his neck. He went into the shower room and found a bathrobe, which he assumed was Clives; and put it on and went to join Lane in the kitchen

Soon they were sitting at the small kitchen table having coffee and toast; and looking out of the open doors across the Thames. Suddenly she turned to Tom with a wry smile.

"Why are you such a perfect gentleman?"

Tom looked a bit surprised; but he kept it light,

"Look here young lady, my reputation will be shattered if anyone knows I was with such agorgeous woman all night and didn't make a pass at her. In fact I may lose my new promotion if M16 hear about this"

She burst out laughing, somehow this night together had cleared the air between them; any misconception or awkwardness seemed to drop away, leaving them with a much stronger open friendship. Lane felt as though a great weight had been lifted from her, and now at last she was really looking forward to her wedding.

"Right Tom" she stood up and started to clear the breakfast things. "You go have your shower, and I will tidy up here"

After she had washed the dishes Lane went back into the bedroom and sat at her dressing table brushing her hair with her back to the shower cubicle, she heard Tom turn off the water and called out to him.

"Tell Maria that Terry was asking after her. He was so impressed with her work in Cyprus. Did you know that it was my operation; I was so proud of its success,"

"Yes," He shouted back, "it sounds as though she gave them something to remember. It would appear as if she spent most of the time in, and in some cases out of her undies"

Lane laughed,

"Yes, so I heard, we miss her a lot since she quit. Can't you persuade her to come back? She is wasted in that training department"

Tom emerged from the shower still wrapped in Clive's bath towel,

"I think she may do, once the girls are a bit older. She really loved her work but after that last assignment she doesn't want to use her looks and body anymore to trap the likes of the Mathesons in this world."

"I can understand that, but they still want her back Tom, do what you can"

Lane stood up and walked to the door,

"By the way "she grinned "That bathrobe suits you better than Clive, but don't tell him I said so will you?"

Tom finished dressing, and was ready to go; he went out into the lounge.

"I think I had better get moving. I hope you don't mind but I used your phone to call the taxi. We will see you in Cyprus next month for the big day, hopefully"

"I wish you had let me drive you" Lane said as the taxi arrived to take him to the station.

"It's ok, I'm happy with the cab, you would have been caught for hours in the rush hour coming back, and there was no point in that" he smiled.

She reached up gave him a kiss,

"One more thing, I wanted you to give me away. But Clive insisted on you as his best man, so I now have Terry to do that honour."

She smiled that funny little half smile he had seen before when she felt emotional,

"It's just that I wanted you to know you were my first choice since my dad died"

Always prepared to have the last word, Tom replied

"Funny I didn't think you looked on me as a father figure. Anyway I think you are far too precious to just be given away; I wouldn't have been able to do that"

She laughed although she had tears in her eyes, and kissed him again before he climbed awkwardly into the waiting taxi.

CHAPTER 22

They arrived in Limassol two days before the wedding, and booked into the Londa Beach Hotel with Maria's mother two very excited little girls. All of their bridesmaids' dresses had been made in Lebanon to co-ordinate with Lane's dress and design, and the little girls were finding it extremely hard to wait for the big day to come so that they could wear them

The evening before the wedding Tom and Maria had dinner with Lane in the hotel restaurant.

They were just finishing their meal; when they heard a voice that Maria would have recognise anywhere hailing them from across the room.

"If you don't move your hand you won't be able to walk back to the table"

Maria laughed; she didn't need to turn around, as it could only be one person, Terry. When he reached the table she stood up to greet him; kissing him on both cheeks still laughing,

"And before you ask, no I haven't gone commando tonight"

Everyone laughed, they had all heard about the incident in London. Tom leaned over and offered his hand.

"Hello there, I'm Tom; we have spoken on the phone, nice to meet you at last. Won't you join us?"

"Thank you," he pulled up a seat "But I can't stay long as I am still on duty"

Terry, as well as having the honour of giving Lane away, was also responsible for directing operations during the wedding. It was causing a bit of a headache for the security team, considering that there was now going to be a high contingent of C.I.A. members, and Her Majesty's Intelligence Service; all in one place at a given time. And so on Terry's instructions, security at Akrotiri Airbase had been stepped up to code red. He explained to the party,

"We will have armed police covering the rooftops of all the surrounding buildings to and from the church. Although we will be contained within the Airbase, I know there have been infiltrations in the past, so you just can't be too careful"

"Yes better to be safe than sorry" Maria nodded

A note of concern entered Terry's voice,

"Also, I have heard that since Matheson Jnr' was released from prison, intelligence have lost track of him. His last location was Jordan a month ago, but since then nothing"

Maria and Terry exchanged a meaningful look; this was an added worry, considering their run in with him on the island. There could be no doubt that revenge would be on junior's mind.

Then he changed the tone and turned to Tom

"You know, your wife is an extraordinary woman. It really is such a waste that she decided to pack it in"

"Don't talk about me as if I am not here" Maria jokingly interrupted.

"I apologise madam," he said giving her a mock bow.

"Anyway", Maria retorted. "I haven't 'packed it up' as you put it, I am very much involved with female training.

"Yes I heard, are you here in Cyprus; or Lebanon?" Terry asked

"Both, but as you may know within a couple of months Lane will be running Cyprus"

Then she smiled at Lane,

And, Clive will be on loan from our American brothers to assist Lane in monitoring Cyprus and Middle East as one entity"

"Yes" Tom joined in "Wonders never cease, London is getting it together at last"

Terry looked at his watch,

"I certainly agree there. I'm sorry, but I must be off, lots to do"

He went around the table and kissed the women, and slapped Tom on the back,

"It's a pleasure to meet such a lucky man"

Lane grinned at Tom.

"Don't mind him Tom, he never stood a chance. Isn't that right Maria?"

Maria just squeezed Tom's hand smiling, then said,

"It's time we all turned in, we have a long day ahead of us tomorrow"

As they all stood up to leave, Lane asked a little self-consciously,

"Maria, can I come to your room for a wee chat"

"Anytime Lane, anytime. Come up now if you want to"

"Yes if it's Ok with you both, I will be there in about ten minutes" Lane gave her a grateful smile

They all had rooms on the same corridor, the children and their grandmother were on one side, and Lane's room joined Maria's and Toms on the other.

Lane changed out of her evening clothes and came into their room in a pair of short pyjamas and a loose robe. She had a whisky glass in her hand and Maria noticed her hand was trembling, she patted the bed for Lane to sit down, it was obvious that she was having last minute nerves and needed reassurance from someone. She curled up on Maria's bed and sipped at her drink,

"I know it's silly but I still keep getting doubts as to whether I'm doing the right thing or not"

"But why Lane, you love him and he loves you. What else matters?" Maria asked as she poured herself a drink and joined her on the bed.

"If it's the reputation you told Tom about, even if it was true; it is all in the past, If I have listened to any the rumours or accusations in England about Tom, then maybe we would not have married."

Lane sighed,

"Yes I know you're right, I guess its just nerves; it's a big decision isn't it? I mean, committing to one person. " At that moment Tom came out of the bathroom.

"Hmm you look cosy, can anyone join in? Or is it a girl thing?"

"No it's ok" Maria laughed. "Its only Lane getting wedding jitters, you tell her how good married life is, and she will listen to you"

Their discussions went well into the night until they all fell asleep; not waking until the two excited children came knocking on the door. Hurriedly they all dressed and made their way down to the dining room for breakfast, and as soon as they had finished Lane got up from the table,

"I must be off for my hair appointment. Clive will be here in a moment and its bad luck if I bump in to him on my wedding day. Tell him I will see him at the Altar... If I turn up." She added with a giggle as she left them sipping their coffee. Maria was pleased that her nerves seem to have left her this morning.

When Clive arrived; Tom could not resist having a teasing dig at him.

"It's not often one gets the opportunity to sleep with two women, one your wife and the other the bride. Especially the night before she is going to get married to your best mate"

Clive knew of Lane's feeling for Tom, but he was not the jealous type,

"See how much I trust you old buddy"

"Like hell you do. Well I am not returning the complement" Tom retorted grinning.

Clive put his arm around Maria, and kissed her on her forehead,

"Now that's not fair, is it honey?"

They laughed and relaxed together over a second cup of coffee, until the time came to get ready.

Two hours later, Tom as best man checked once again that they had got all they needed, and then they were ready to go. Maria went in one car with her mother and the little bridesmaids, leaving Tom to organise Clive.

So far all had gone to plan other than Clive arriving late as usual; in spite of Tom's best effort, mainly due to the extensive security checks by the guards at the entrance to the Base. But at least it proved to them that Terry's orders were being carried out to the letter. During the ceremony Maria glanced at Tom's face; she could see he was in pain as he struggled with his crutches to stand beside Clive. But she knew he would never agree to use the wheelchair; because he was adamant he would not be in the wheelchair for the photographs.

The ceremony went off without any hitches, and later during the evening reception; Lane went to find Maria to ask her for a special favour,

"Anything, Lane what is it?" Maria smiled at her friend

"Will you please dance for us Maria, just one dance, please? I have heard so much about it, I want to see for myself"

Clive came over to the group; he already knew what Lane was requesting from Maria.

"Please honey, it would mean a lot to Lane," He said slipping his arm round her shoulder to encourage her.

Maria was a little reluctant; it was some time since she had performed publicly. But after a moment's hesitation, she agreed to dance for them. She had a word with the musicians and then persuaded two of the Lebanese bodyguards to accompany her on the dance floor. The music started, all eyes were upon her as she felt the throb of the drums seep into her body. It felt good to be dancing again. Maria swayed sensually completely absorbed by the music oblivious to the audience surrounding her. Lane was spell bound; she had never seen such hypnotic sensual dancing in her life. It was a memory of her wedding day she would never forget. The spell was broken when after a few minutes one or two other guests joined them on the dance floor, which caused plenty of laughter all round.

Tom sat happily watching from his wheelchair; he had at last given in. Although he couldn't join in, he really enjoyed the music, and of course; Maria's dancing.

As he watched Maria and, his mind wandered back over the last couple of years, he would never cease to admire her ability to carry on as normal whatever life threw at her.

He also knew very well that his condition would only get worse over the coming months and years, and he was very thankful that now he had adopted a similar faith as portrayed to him by his wife during her long life threatening illness. And he was just as determined that this attitude would help him overcome the major disabilities that were obviously lying ahead.

Maria came back to him smiling, and sat down beside him taking hold of his hand, she didn't need to be told what he was thinking. She knew.

CHAPTER 23

Later that evening back at the hotel Maria sat at the dressing table brushing her hair, she looked across at Tom, who was propped up in bed with a far away look on his face.

"What are you thinking about?"

"Top secret, only employees of MI6 allowed to know," He laughed,

"You know very well that I am fully associated with your lot" Maria retorted indignantly,

"So what is it?"

Tom pulled back the covers for her to get in beside him,

"It's about this Phoenician, and how does this man get information that our boys can't?"

"Why do you all assume it's a man?"

He looked surprised

"Because it has to be, no woman could do what he does"

"How very chauvinistic!" she swiped at him with her pillow. But I agree; he is good"

"See, even you say he and not she." He laughed.

But Maria wasn't listening. Tom looked at her concerned; her face had turned quite pale.

"Maria, what is it?"

"Oh my God!" she gasped, "Matheson,"

Tom was confused,

"What? Where? Which one; the father or the son?

"The father," Maria sat bolt up in bed grasping Tom's arm excitedly "He is not dead. I remember now, when the helicopter came onto the island the son intimated that we all believed we had killed him, sort of suggesting that we hadn't. I didn't think much of it at the time due to the mayhem going on," her grip tightened on Tom's arm as she continued breathlessly. "But when I was talking to Clive tonight; he said that the father and son must have compared notes about my dancing performance."

She looked at Tom with worried eyes,

"How could that be if the old man went overboard?"

Tom thought for a while, trying to remember the circumstances on that night,

"No actual body was found" he said slowly.

But Maria's mind was running way ahead, she was becoming very agitated

"But it goes deeper than that. Think Tom, think about it"

It hit him like a bombshell.

"Clive!"

"Exactly, If he didn't waste him on that night, then why not?"

Tom was racking his brain trying to find a solid reason or excuse for his friend.

"Perhaps by some miracle he survived"

She shook her head

"Impossible,"

They both fell silent as the enormity of the situation hit them. Maria shook her head slowly looking very distressed,

"We have to turn him in Tom, you know that, but what do we tell Lane?"

She thought for a moment, before saying miserably.

"I am sorry darling, but you have to be the one that who tells her, she will believe you"

"Thanks a lot!" he felt sick at the thought. "Christ, what a mess."

"Even worse" Maria continued,

"If both of the Matheson's are still operating, then none of us are safe until they are either dead; or securely locked away. And that also includes Lane."

She looked at Tom anxiously,

"We should tell her now, not let her believe her marriage is for real"

He looked horrified

"How can we interrupt their wedding night?"

Both fell silent once more wandering how on earth they would be able to do this to their friend. And then Tom's face cleared,

"Wait a minute. I have an idea, but we are going to have to play this one by ear." With that he got up and left the room.

Within minutes the fire alarm sounded, Maria still in her sleeping shorts and top cursed, but she realized instantly that it was Tom who had raised the alarm. She guessed that it was his way of distracting the honeymooners without drawing to much attention, and wondered what else he had planned. She knew it would wake the children, so she threw on her robe and quickly went to their room to find her mother already awake with her girls.

"It's ok" she said quickly to her mother "It's only an exercise, but we must still follow the safety rules"

Hurriedly they put the children's robes on; and went swiftly down the back stairs and out to the rear of the building near the pool area. The little girls didn't seem at all worried; to them it was just another big adventure. When they reached the designated point most of the other guests were gathered around in their dressing gowns and other various states of dress. There was a buzz of excitement in the air with people asking each other if it was a real fire, or complaining about being woken up.

Maria could see Clive and Lane talking together some distance away, and watched as Tom made his way through the throng of people towards them. Just as he got to them she managed to catch Clive's eye and beckoned him over.

Lane started to follow him and jumped as Tom caught hold of her arm.

"Oh Tom it's you. Come on Maria's over there. Would you believe this? My wedding night!" She laughed, then stopped short at the look on his face.

"What is it Tom? What's the matter?"

"Lane, it's up to you how you handle this, but Clive is now under suspicion concerning old man Matheson, who we have good reason to believe is still alive."

Tom was talking fast and looking across to make sure Maria was still managing to keep Clive occupied.

"He originally reported that he dumped him overboard, but it looks as if we were all given deliberate false information. Until we know the facts of what happened Clive must be considered to be hostile towards British Intelligence"

Lane went pale; she was completely shocked by Tom's revelations.

"So what do I do, kick him out of my bed" She looked wildly about her, "This is what all this is about isn't it? A bloody diversion so you could tell me about Clive. Well thanks very much!"

He gazed down at her sympathetically; the look on her face was heartbreaking.

"I am so sorry Lane, but we didn't want you having regrets, and if he is working for the other side then you could also be at risk"

"Oh hell Tom, I'm sorry, I know you have my best interests at heart"

At that moment the 'all clear' was given. Lane looked over Tom's shoulder and noticed Clive was on his way back to her, she fought back the tears as she whispered to Tom,

"Damn the bloody service, Ok, so I have a headache coming on in ten minutes. But you had better double check this information by tomorrow night. I won't be able to pull the samestroke twice, especially being on honeymoon."

"Maria said she would contact the Phoenician and start the investigation straight away," he whispered kissing her on the cheek.

"Maria wants you back Tom" Clive said with a curious look at Lane's face. "Are you ok honey?"

"Right I'm off" Tom replied with a slight nod to Lane. "I'll let you two get on with your honeymoon; you don't need any more interruptions"

Then he quickly made his way back to Maria, leaving Lane to sort out her headache problem.

The next day, Maria was due to return to Lebanon with her mother and the children; but decided she would stay on a couple of days extra with Tom She knew that this next few days would be rather like walking on eggshells considering their close friendship with Clive and Lane.

Maria had already called for an armed back-up team. She had received information from one of her sources that they had sighted Matheson Junior, on the border of the Cypriot Turkish sector forty-eight hours ago.

The four friends had arranged a late lunch together at the Hotel restaurant, and it was a very difficult lunch under the circumstances. Their opening conversation was a little strained, and although Clive picked up on this, he put it down to Tom's irritation at having to use the wheelchair more.

He leaned across to Tom speaking quietly.

"You Ok old buddy?"

But before Tom had chance to answer, Maria decided to meet Clive head on.

"Did you know Matheson Senior is still alive?"

She watched him closely to see his reaction. Then Lane joined in,

"I thought you had orders to terminate him"

Clive looked at them slowly one by one his face expressionless, but they knew he was searching for an answer. After some considerable time he gave his carefully worded reply.

"I received last minute orders to spare him."

"Why and from whom?" Tom interrupted rather sharply.

"What are you suggesting? " Clive responded quietly looking keenly at Tom.

"I am suggesting" Tom's replied in the same quiet tone. "That you may have been acting without official authority my friend."

"No" He got up to leave the table, but Lane restrained him with a hand on his arm,

"Clive, it looks bad for you. If you're innocent then work with us to understand what the hell is going on here. Was the CIA working alone on this one? If they were, then we need to know the reasons" By now there were tears in Lane's eyes. "Walk away and you're as guilty as sin in everyone's eyes, including mine"

He was torn apart by the look of anguish on his wife's face, and he knew that he had a lot of explaining to do. Sitting down heavily he started his story.

"Well as you now know I didn't dump Matheson off the ferry, I had him locked up out of sight and sound until I could hand him over to our boys in CIA. And then I threw a weighted box overboard close to your cabin to convince you that it was him"

He paused for a moment and took a sip of his drink before continuing,

"Matheson and his son are vicious rapists and killers, make no mistake about that. He wouldhave definitely killed Maria on the ferryboat. But the CIA needed him to do one more job forthem before they could send him to hell. He knew the likely outcome and refused. That's whywe arranged the whole operation in Cyprus with Matt Grainger. We thought we could kill three birds with one stone, smash the sex racket, capture the son; and have control over the old man." He looked at their faces trying to read their thoughts,

"It was well known that he idolized his son, and the idea was; that we could use him as a bargaining chip."

Although Maria knew from what Terry had told her of Grainger's input in the affair, she pretended innocence,

"You mean Matt Grainger was undercover?"

A slight smile crept into Clive's eyes,

"That's right, although he is a total womaniser just like his so called mate Hines. The bigdifference being, Hines was running the sex racket with Matheson and the Russians, and Grainger was working with us and MI6."

He waited for some reaction; but nobody said a word, so he continued,

"Once we got Matheson junior, we knew the father would do what we wanted, and then wecould hang him out to dry, afterwards"

"In typical C.I.A fashion you mean" Tom chipped in sarcastically.

Clive ignored the remark.

"We held Matheson senior in custody for a very long time, until, thanks to Maria we had the son in our care. We were then able to release him for the job we needed him to do."

For once Maria said nothing, but a lot of other things were now slowly falling into place in her mind.

"Ok, then what" Lane asked

"Well unfortunately after the CIA released the father to do the hit, they lost contact with himand he disappeared"

Tom interrupted him at this point

"Unfortunate? That's a joke. Another cock up by the CIA! Why am I not surprised?"

Clive shifted nervously in his seat; he was beginning to feel uncomfortable with this direct line of questioning.

"Well yes it was unfortunate, because the job was never completed"

"Who was the hit?" Maria asked.

"That's not important"

"It is; if you expect us to believe you." Tom replied sharply

"It is; if you need me in your life" Lane added

Clive pondered over their joint ultimatums; it was a difficult position he now found himself in with his two best friends and his new wife. He made his decision.

"Your second in command, Colin Prescott"

"Why for God's sake" Lane burst out in shock, it was the last person she expected.

"Because he is closely linked to Matheson Senior, and we have proof that he authorised a hit on the 'Phoenician.' This alone proves he was a traitor"

Clive continued with his explanation`

"At this precise moment Prescott is in Cyprus, supposedly on holiday, and Matheson we believe is in the Turkish sector of the island. And as you know in our business, there is no such thing as coincidence."

"Why not simply have Prescott arrested?" Maria queried.

Clive nodded in partial acceptance of the idea, but argued,

"Too much security would have to be disclosed if there was a court case of any kind. The CIAcould not take that risk. Prescott knows too much, and once we had proof of his guilt we found evidence of his involvement in at least eight of our agents disappearing."

Lane ran her fingers through her hair in despair,

"You do know; he has a wife and children"

"So did most of the missing eight." Clive retorted quietly. "Anyway it is far better if he is killed in the line of fire, than his kids growing up knowing their father was a traitor" then he offered a shocking revelation turning to Tom. "Why, do you think you had problems in Libya? It was all down to Prescott, he tipped them off, and you were very lucky"

Tom wheeling his chair backward and forward from the table in frustration, chipped in,

"Ok, that's true, and if you are very smart maybe you can still get Matheson to take the blame"

"Yes I think that was the general idea" Clive nodded in agreement and relief that Tom was beginning to understand; especially now he knew how much of a traitor Prescott was.

"That's been the reason for the delay; we needed them both in the same country at the sametime, so we let them think the 'Phoenician' was here in Cyprus" He leant forward saying quietly, "However, you should also be aware that the armed backup team here at the base are under Prescott's control, if it comes to a shoot out"

Maria caught her breath as she remembered it was she who had alerted them.

"Will you all excuse me for a minute there is something I must do"

She quickly left the room. A few minutes later she was on her way back to the table, hoping that the call she had just made requesting the armed back up unit be stood down; was in time.

"Our problem now is who the hell can we trust?" Tom questioned, looking around the group for an answer.

"Simple answer, no one" Maria replied overhearing her husband as she joined them again.

There was not much else they could say on the subject, but a lot to think about, so they arranged to meet up again later that afternoon to discuss a strategy to resolve their dilemma. The two couples then left the table each to ponder their own position. Lane and Clive decided a long walk was necessary to clear the air, and they were soon deep in discussion.

In the lift on the way up to their room Tom and Maria analysed the confusing and delicate situation.

"Well that appears to be an acceptable explanation, I suppose" Tom said. "What do you think?"

"Questionable. I am not really one hundred percent sure" Maria replied thoughtfully. He looked surprised,

"Why?"

"I believe if I were writing a novel, I could have dreamt up a far better story than the one he just gave," She replied.

"Well, he didn't exactly have much time to cook up a better one did he?"

A broad smile spread across her face,

"Tom darling, you are brilliant, that makes me think it just may be true. Anyway; I will get it checked out" The lift door opened and Maria pushed Tom's wheelchair out and along the corridor to their room.

As soon they were behind closed doors she picked up the phone, dialled a number and left message for a call back.

Tom moved his wheelchair onto the balcony overlooking the sea, while Maria went to freshen up.

About twenty minutes later the phone rang. Out on the balcony Tom heard her pick it up and answer, he sat quietly listening to Maria's side of the conversation.

"Where is he now?"

"Are you sure?"

"Here in the Greek side or Turkish side?"

"Do you know if he is armed?"

"I see. No problem; we will take the required precautions where and when.

"Ok in one hour. Bye"

Tom wheeled his chair back into the room.

"What's the verdict?"

Maria looked thoughtful

"Clive is being led up the garden path over Prescott, or so it appears. He may or may not be a traitor, but somebody wants him terminated. Apparently it was someone in the CIA that supplied the false information that led to Prescott issuing the order to terminate the Phoenician."

Tom looked up sharply at this point,

"Then that could mean Clive is in danger, too."

"That's my reading of the situation, and of course that could also include Lane,"

Maria stood up removed her robe, and put on a deep red half-length slip. Tom sat and watched her get ready, after all these years he still appreciated his young wife's slim suntanned body as she sat down at the dressing table combing her now shortened hair and applying her makeup.

"Will you be Ok for an hour or so darling? I need to see someone"

Having learnt over the years never to ask too many questions, he agreed, but he insisted on going down stairs into the hotel lounge in case Lane and

Clive came back. Tom saw his wife off the premises and watched as she got into a waiting military vehicle that she had obviously arranged. He assumed correctly; that she was going the short distance to the air base at Akrotiri. Then he wheeled himself back into the lounge and ordered a cup of tea

"Hi sweetie how was your afternoon. I hope you and Maria behaved yourselves"

"Fat chance in this bloody contraption, but I am willing to try anything once" He retorted.

She laughed, but the comment didn't go unnoticed, she was still finding it hard to come to terms with Tom's progressive illness.

"Do you fancy something?

Then knowing Tom's way of thinking, she added with a grin,

"From the bar I mean"

"It's a bit early isn't it?" Tom replied smiling.

"Ok daddy, how about tea for two" She said in a little girl's voice as she beckoned over the young waiter.

He was pleased to see Lane happy again.

"A Scot with a sense of humour, that's very unique," he replied sarcastically "Unless they are football supporters, then they must have one".

"You cheeky bugger" She grinned.

"You seem happier now, did you sort it out with Clive"

"Yes, I told him until I know the truth; he doesn't sleep in my bed"

Tom burst out laughing at her ultimatum,

"Second night of your honeymoon; what a thing to tell the groom. I thought the weddingnight was a disaster, and now you follow it up with that. I guess he was not too happy"

"Tom, seriously, what does Maria think? Does she think he is telling the truth?"

He hesitated for a second, enough time to show her there were doubts,

"Well, she has certainly given him the benefit of the doubt so far" He reached out and caught hold of her hand. "But do you want to know what I really think?"

To Lane it was very important what Tom thought.

"Yes, darling tell me"

"Right" He said, gesturing her to sit in the chair beside him,

"First of all, apart from the fact I don't think 'them upstairs' like the idea of the CIA and MI6 getting married. I think the CIA is using Clive as a pawn. I also believe he is being set up. I think they want him to arrange the demise of Prescott, and then they plan to............

"But why" Lane interrupted horrified as the true picture began dawn on her.

"Well by then he will know too much. And while they have a rogue assassin like Matheson available who they thought they could control, they didn't think they would get their own hands dirty. He will be blamed for any assassination that they want to arrange, while he is running free, and ultimately Clive will come under suspicion for releasing him."

Lane face turned pale as she realized what this could mean for her husband.

"Where is Clive, right now?" Tom questioned.

"No idea, she looked around the room, "I thought that he had walked back here, you didn't see him?"

"No. But he could have come through before I came down."

The conversation was interrupted when the waiter brought their tea, and they waited until he had left before continuing.

"Where is Maria?" Lane queried.

"I suspect at the base," Tom answered cagily, he was not quite sure how much Maria wanted that known. He winced with pain as he tried to adjust his sitting position.

"Tom, are you in permanent pain with this M.S?"

He hadn't realized she had noticed, and replied with a grim smile,

"Not at first, but now yes I suppose I am, when I have to stand or walk"

Lane reached out to take his hand,

"Tell me about it, is it bad?"

He paused for a while, thinking of how he to explain what he felt, before answering.

"It's hard to explain, but years ago we used to live very near to a railway line, and trains passed our garden every ten minutes or so. People that visited us would jump every time a train passed. But after a few weeks we were so used to them we never heard them." He gave a rueful smile. "Do you understand? Lane looked a little puzzled, so he continued, "What I'm trying to say is, that's how it is now with the pain, you get used to it, and it becomes part of your life. I suppose you forget what life was like before it happened" he gave a little laugh, "But I do swear a lot more now"

She tried to smile although she felt a bit choked up inside.

"Is it life threatening, long term?"

"Well, it's not necessarily life threatening on its own, but with time the muscles get weaker and everything else in your body gets weaker, including I suspect your heart." He gave a twisted grin, "And when that happens, puff your gone", and then his smile broadened, "to a far better place; so Maria tells me"

Lane could think of nothing to say, but she suddenly realized she was still gripping his hand rather tightly. She released his hand and smiled at him with tears not far from her eyes.

He noticed and lightened the atmosphere as usual with a joke.

"But she has always said that she has to go first, otherwise St Peter won't let me through thePearly Gates."

"Oh Tom, I really admire the way you think so positive; and manage to keep your sense of humour" she exclaimed.

His smile faded briefly,

"Well, don't, because what you see is not what is going on inside, he said gruffly, "I try to keep it from Maria and the kids of course, but most of the time I am very uptight and veryfrustrated having to depend on everyone else."

Lane interrupted him,

"Of course you feel like that, you wouldn't be human otherwise, and I am sure Maria knowsanyway. I know how I feel just seeing you like this"

Tom laughed gently at her,

"You're far too sensitive to be a director of spooks"

She wiped a tear from her eye laughing at his job description of her, and leant forward again to squeeze his hand.

"I do so love you both, don't ever forget that, will you?"

She rose from her chair and kissed him tenderly on the forehead and left the room without saying another word.

Tom sat there for a while after she had gone thinking, *'I hope to hell this situation works out for her, she doesn't deserve this'* He manoeuvred his wheelchair out into the hotel terrace to wait for Maria.

When Maria arrived at the base, Terry met her at the gate and they walked back to his office together. He was staying on the base for a few days; and had already been notified briefly of the situation, so she quickly filled him in with the rest of the details. Without hesitation he picked up the phone and ordered four armed officers to escort Prescott and his family from their beach hotel back to the base. As he replaced the receiver he gave Maria a searching look.

"You know, you are still the best bait to catch Matheson"

"Oh no, she protested, "I am a mother now and far too old for that game"

Terry shook his head in disagreement and laughed,

"Never. Anyway this time you get to keep your clothes on, you know he is obsessed with youwith or without."

She pulled a face,

"I keep meaning to ask, what happened to Matt?"

"He left the force, a year or two back, set up his own photographic business, mostly glamour as you might suspect, of course he had a good start with some pictures he had taken in Cyprus" He kept his face serious, waiting for Maria to respond, but she ignored him. Still trying to tease some response from her he pressed on.

"Matt Grainger is a bit like me, I suspect obsessed by you."

Maria shook her head in mock exasperation,

"I would have thought you would both have set your sights on a younger model by now,

Having said that she knew exactly what he was going to say before he had even opened his mouth.

"I know, women are like a fine wine" she grinned.

Terry laughed, she knew him only too well.

"By the way;" he said, reverting back to the more serious problem confronting them "Prescott will be interrogated and undoubtedly charged"

"That's good news I suppose, but I feel sorry for his family. It's always the families that bearthe brunt in these situations"

"You're right"

Just then there was a knock on the door. "Come in" he called.

A young soldier came in and handed him an envelope, Terry signed for it,

"Excuse me Maria, but this is marked priority and secret"

"Carry on, please" She watched as he read the contents. His face tensed,

"You have some news?"

He looked up with a frown,

"They shot Matheson Junior; but the father got away, both trying to get into the base. The son is in a bad way they don't think he will make it. But at least we have one of them,"

"If the father is on the loose, I better get back to the hotel and warn them"

"Yes good idea, you never know what information Prescott has passed on to the old man"

"Oh shit," Maria swore. "He will know where we are staying because I asked them to cancel the armed back up unit at our hotel, and Prescott would have seen the request."

Terry picked up the internal phone, barked out an order for back up. He picked up his keys,

"Quick the car is outside, let's go"

They jumped in the car and headed for the Londa Beach Hotel with four-armed officers following at high speed.

When they arrived they couldn't see Tom, Lane or Clive in the lounge, they checked the pool, nothing. She headed for the hotel lobby,

"You check the gardens; I'm going up to find Tom"

She went up in the lift her heart pounding, and was relieved to find him sitting in his wheelchair relaxing on the balcony reading. "Hi Darling, what's up you look flushed"

"Can't explain now, have you seen Clive or Lane?"

"Yes, I was with Lane half an hour ago, but Clive wasn't about; Lane went to her room as far as I know. Why what's going on?"

"Tell you later, keep this door locked Tom, and don't answer it too anyone"

Tom didn't argue, but he was worried, he thumped the side of his wheelchair,

"Christ I feel so bloody useless" he cursed bitterly.

Maria knocked on Lanes door there was no reply so she banged harder. The door opened slightly, it was Lane.

"It's not a good time right now, later"

Maria was surprised at her friend's cold tone,

"I just came to warn you old man Matheson, is on the loose in the Limassol area, so be very careful"

Instantly the door swung open to reveal Matheson holding a gun at Lanes head.

"Come in my dear, you are most welcome"

Maria went cold,

"Let her go first," she replied in a controlled voice.

He redirected the gun away from Lane and pointed it at Maria.

"Ok, a fair exchange." He jerked his head at Lane. "You, in the bathroom, now"

Reluctantly Lane went into the bathroom; she didn't dare try anything while he had the gun at Maria's head. He locked the door without taking his eyes off of Maria. She knew she had to stay calm, although every nerve in her body was alert.

"You know your son is on life support, don't you?" She said casually. Matheson showed no emotion to her comment, he knew that she was trying to de-stabilise the situation to gain advantage.

"You still look good after all this time" he observed greedily running his eyes over her body.

"That was a long time ago, we are all older and in some cases wiser" she replied calmly.

"Maybe. But some things don't change, and now is the time to catch up where we left off. You remember that don't you?" he leered taking a step towards her. "I have nothing to loose now. Don't forget I am already dead as far as you lot are concerned, and with my boy dying, I have no wish to live. This way I can die a happy man"

Maria prayed that Terry had worked out what was happening. He knew she had gone up to her room to find Tom, and Tom would know she had gone to look for Lane. '*Oh Christ*' A thought struck her. '*I told Tom not to answer the door to anyone*' her attention was drawn back to Matheson as he pulled up a chair and straddled it resting his arms on the back. He waved the gun at her,

"Ok, now where did we leave things on the boat, you know what to do, so do it"

Maria slowly started to unbutton her dress thankful for the full-length slip underneath; she had her back to the balcony window, her shape silhouetted by the glare of the late afternoon sun.

She knew that the only way for her to survive this ordeal was to put on a performance; and hope that Terry would make it in time, but after two children and the cancer, it was going to be difficult. Time seemed to stand still as she tried to remember her routine and dance to the silent rhythm in her head all the time aware of the gun pointing at her.

"Stop" Matheson stood up pushing the chair away. Once more Maria froze, *'What now'* she thought

"I can't see with that bloody sun in my eyes" He dragged the chair around so he had his back to the open window; now the sun was behind him.

"That's better" This time he sat on the chair leaning forward lustfully.

"Now take that thing off, we got past that stage didn't we my dear?" Maria could see the lust in his eyes and the sweat breaking out on his forehead.

She slid the straps of her skimpy red slip off of her shoulders, but even before it hit the floor, a single shot shattered the silence. Matheson gave a grunt and slumped forward in his chair. A blood spattered Maria swiftly pulled up her slip and bent down to check for a pulse although she knew from experience he was already dead.

Very carefully she stepped onto the balcony and looked over to the sniper in the room directly opposite, she drew a line across her throat with one finger, 'he is dead' Turning back to look at Matheson's body she gave an ironic smile, *'At least he almost died a happy man'*

She unlocked the bathroom door and Lane fell into her arms.

"It's ok; he is dead".

"Thank God," Lane was as white as a sheet. "I thought when I heard the shot it was you"

They clung to each other in relief,

"I never want to go through that again," Lane laughed shakily.

"Me neither and I don't want to be stripping at my age" Maria joked

They heard banging on the door; and she went to open it,

"Maria, Thank God you're alright," it was Tom first through the door.

"I'm fine darling; Thank goodness you ignored my warning and let Terry in. I shudder to think of what would have happened otherwise.

"Cheated again" Terry came in behind them. "Every time it gets interesting around you; something happens to stop it" he laughed giving Maria a hug.

And then he turned to Clive,

"Looks like you're in the clear my friend, Matheson was actually looking for you, but got lucky"

Hearing this Maria breathed a sigh of relief. She looked across to where Clive and Lane stood with their arms around each other and grinned.

"Perhaps you can get down to some serious honeymooning now"

Terry put his arm round Maria's shoulder,

"Come on let's get out of here." He jerked his head towards Matheson's body, "I'll get someone to clear this up. And I expect you all for dinner at the Base tonight; we can at last celebrate the end of this saga"

"Fine" she agreed. "And I have something to announce, so it will be better if you are all together."

That evening the five friends dined at the officers club around nine o'clock. Dress was formal and as usual the two women looked stunning.

After they had eaten Maria leaned forward and tinkled her spoon on the edge of a glass to attract their attention.

"I would like to say something in confidence to you all, I am very pleased Clive has been exonerated of any wrong doing," she grinned mischievously at Clive, "but he has to admit, it was mainly of the CIA making"

"Hear, hear," they all laughed. Maria continued,

"I just want to tell you all that I am retiring from both services. I want to give more time to my children and my darling husband, even though circumstances dictate we are still living in two countries, we hope that it won't be for much longer. But tomorrow we are both returning to Lebanon for a long holiday. And, as the storybook goes, we hope to live happily ever after,"

Lane rose from her chair came around the table to Maria and hugged her with tears in her eyes,

"Oh I shall really miss you Maria" then as an afterthought she asked,

"But what about the 'Phoenician' who will liaise with him?"

Maria replied casually, looking straight at Tom.

"Well, that's simple; the Phoenician will retire also."

- - - - - - - - - - - - - - - - - -

The afternoon had now turned into early evening as Tom tuned his mind back to the present day; he found himself smiling happily at the vivid memories.

He focused on the lights that now flickered from a few fishing boats in the Blackwater estuary, and the redundant Power Station silhouetted against the dimming sky.

He decided to call Maria on her mobile.

"Hi Maria, can you open your MSN chat line I need to talk to you"

"Is there something wrong darling?"

"No, just I felt the need to hear your voice and to chat you up" he added.

Maria laughed

"That's nice after all these years, Ok I'll try, but you know it's not that easy"

She opened her laptop computer and it instantly connected, which was not always the case with the continued loss of electricity in Lebanon.

"Put your camera on" Tom insisted.

She did as requested; now he could type his message and see her at the same time.

"What's wrong Tom" I sense you're not feeling too good, do you want me to come over?"

"No it's ok, it's just I have been thinking about you and your work. I don't want you to stay in retirement, and I won't be around for ever, it is a waste, and the country needs you, now more than ever"

"What brought this on?"

"I feel you are missing it, as much as it misses you, am I right?

"Yes I suppose so; Lane has been on at me lately to come back. But are you sure darling"

"There is one condition," he grinned up at the camera,

"What's that?" she tapped into the keyboard; and then looked up enquiringly at the camera.

"I move to Lebanon, or you base yourself in UK"

"Deal" She blew him a kiss.

"But, my question is, do you still have what it takes?" he typed swiftly, smiling to himself.

She leaned back in her chair and slowly started to unbutton her shirt in front of the camera.

"What do you think?"

"I don't know, keep going I will let you know in a minute," he tapped back, calling her bluff.

Maria laughed and leaned forward, and then a message flashed up on his screen

"Sorry darling the electricity is going." She quickly blew him another kiss before the screen went blank.

Tom leaned back in his chair and laughed; he enjoyed these teasing conversations with his wife on the chat-line, but he just couldn't wait to be with her again. He knew she would love being back in action, even though she would have to be a lot more careful this time around than she had been in the past.

Printed in the United Kingdom
by Lightning Source UK Ltd.
119391UK00002B/97-105